LEGENDS OF THE WEST

VOLUME THREE

Hope Valley War

The Legend of Storey County

Cumberland Crossing

BROCK & BODIE THOENE

TYNDALE HOUSE PUBLISHERS, INC., CAROL STREAM, ILLINOIS

Visit Tyndale's exciting Web site at www.tyndale.com

For futher information on Thoene titles, visit www.thoenebooks.com and www.familyaudiolibrary.com

TYNDALE and Tyndale's quill logo are registered trademarks of Tyndale House Publishers, Inc.

Legends of the West, Volume Three first printing by Tyndale House Publishers, Inc., in 2008.

Designed by Stephen Vosloo

Edited by Ramona Cramer Tucker

Unless otherwise indicated, Scripture quotations are taken from the Holy Bible, King James Version.

Scripture quotations marked NIV are taken from the HOLY BIBLE, NEW INTERNATIONAL VERSION®. NIV®. Copyright © 1973, 1978, 1984 by International Bible Society. Used by permission of Zondervan. All rights reserved.

This novel is a work of fiction. Names, characters, places, and incidents either are the product of the authors' imaginations or are used fictitiously. Any resemblance to actual events, locales, organizations, or persons living or dead is entirely coincidental and beyond the intent of either the authors or publisher.

Library of Congress Cataloging-in-Publication Data

Thoene, Brock, date.
   Legends of the West / Brock and Bodie Thoene.
     p. cm.
   ISBN-13: 978-1-4143-0362-8 (hc)
   ISBN-10: 1-4143-0362-9 (hc)
   I. Thoene, Bodie, date. II. Title.
   PS3570.H463L44 2007
   813'.54—dc22   2006039065

Printed in the United States of America

14   13   12   11   10   09   08
7   6   5   4   3   2   1

JOHN WAYNE, LEGEND OF THE WEST*

v

Our youngest son, Luke, was born in the summer of 1977, when I was still working on a book called *The Fall Guy*. It's the autobiography of Chuck Roberson, John Wayne's longtime stuntman. When Luke was born, Duke sent a tiny pair of cowboy boots and an autographed picture that says:

> Luke,
> *Welcome to our world! Be happy! You are loved. . . .*
> Duke
> 7-22-77

Duke was directly quoting Dr. Robert Schuller, a famous Southern California pastor whose teaching he admired greatly. Duke was letting our little guy know that he could be happy every day of his life, because God loved him!

Duke counted Chuck Roberson among his closest friends. It was my association as Chuck's ghostwriter that led to Brock's and my jobs

* For more "John Wayne, Legend of the West" stories, see Legends of the West series introductions for Volumes One, Two, and Four, by Brock and Bodie Thoene. For further information visit: www.thoenebooks.com and www.familyaudiolibrary.com.

working at John Wayne's Batjac Productions. Duke loved *The Fall Guy* and wrote the foreword for it, saying to me, "You've got all the good stuff in Chuck's book. There's nothing left for me!"

But as it turned out, there was a wealth of stories about John Wayne that Brock and I would hear and record over the next several years of our lives as researchers and writers on the Batjac Productions staff.

We were privileged to meet the greatest directors, movie stars, writers, and producers of that generation. We learned the craft of writing from the men and women who had multiple Oscars on their mantels.

All who knew Duke spoke of his integrity and loyalty. He was someone who could be counted on to come through, no matter what the challenge. Director Henry Hathaway spoke of Duke's battle with lung cancer in the early 1960s. The shooting location of the movie *The Sons of Katie Elder* was high in the Rocky Mountains, where the air was thin. Duke was living on three-quarters of one lung after his surgery, but he never complained. His courage set the tone for the entire crew.

I am often asked if John Wayne was a Christian . . . if he'll be in heaven. Each time I am surprised, because he was a man of such deep and authentic faith.

Early on Brock and I got to know Lowry McCaslin, one of Duke's fraternity brothers at USC in 1926. The two men remained close throughout their lives. Lowry was the son of a Methodist preacher. He and Duke attended several of the revivals that took place in Los Angeles, and both went forward during an altar call. After that they had a weekly Bible study and prayer time in the fraternity.

As Brock and I learned more and more about John Wayne's life, we saw that his early commitment to Christ remained at his core, no matter what challenge life brought his way.

Among the many personal insights we had were copies of letters Duke sent to literally thousands of fans battling cancer over the years. Every morning he sat out on his patio overlooking Newport Harbor and dictated letters offering hope to those who needed it most.

You're going to have to put your faith in God. That's the thing that will get you through. . . .

Duke often called Jesus "The Man Upstairs" or sometimes "My Boss"—out of respect for the authority of God over his life.

He had a Christian Zionist's love for the Jewish people and for Israel. This led him to produce *Cast a Giant Shadow,* the film about the rebirth of Israel as a nation.

Years later he asked me, "Bodie, what is your passion? What story do you most want to write?"

I replied, "Mr. Wayne, I would most love to write a novel about the struggle to establish a Jewish homeland in Israel."

He replied with a smile and a pat on my back. "Well, little lady, you gotta do it! It's the Jewish Alamo!"

And so our dream of writing the Zion Chronicles series and the Zion Covenant series began at that moment.

Duke went to heaven in June of 1979. We remained as regulars at Batjac Productions, interviewing everyone who had known and loved him.

Nearly ten years later, Duke's friend, Chuck Roberson, lay dying of cancer in a hospital in Bakersfield, California. Over the years Chuck had become like a member of our family. We loved him and he loved us. Long before this final terrible illness, Chuck had given his life to Christ. In our last moments together we prayed before I took my leave.

He clasped my hand. "Bo . . . I'll see you. . . ."

I answered, "Sure, Chuck. I'll be back tomorrow."

He searched my face. "Listen to me now. . . . I mean . . . I'll be seeing you. . . ."

"Sure . . ." I faltered, understanding that he meant this was good-bye.

He smiled. "I want you to know . . . Duke and I . . . we'll be there . . . holdin' the horses."

Chuck died the next morning. At Chuck's funeral his pastor, himself a former stuntman, shared the message of salvation. Nearly all those actors and stuntmen in attendance raised their hands to say they accepted Jesus as Savior and Lord! Brock and I knew that heaven was going to be filled with the familiar faces of many who had appeared in John Wayne movies!

I treasured Chuck's final words for many years, even though I didn't understand fully what he meant when he told me that he and Duke would be there "holdin' the horses."

Then Brock and I began to research the Civil War novel *Winds of the Cumberland*, contained in this volume as *Cumberland Crossing*. We came across a reference to cavalry troopers who had been wounded or who, for some reason, were unable to advance in a battle that was proceeding on foot. Those men, who had already fought their hardest and given their best, remained to hold the horses for their comrades who must continue the fight. When the battle was over, the cavalry-men would return to their mounts and their comrades.

When Brock shared that information with me, I suddenly under-stood what Chuck had meant.

Chuck and Duke had fought their battles here on earth. When the time came for them to stand down, they simply moved on. They would be watching our struggles and waiting in heaven, "holdin' the horses," while we continued to fight our battles here in this world.

The reality of Hebrews 12:1-2 overwhelmed me in that moment:

> Therefore, since we are surrounded by such a great cloud of witnesses, let us throw off everything that hinders and the sin that so easily entangles, and let us run with perseverance the race marked out for us. Let us fix our eyes on Jesus, the author and perfecter of our faith. (NIV)

Those men, and others like them, are true "Legends of the West." They were rough and not to be trifled with. But at their core was an abiding faith that carried them through even their last battles.

I have no doubt they are among the great cloud of witnesses who watch us now. I believe they will be among those who will be in heaven to greet us when we have fought our last battle here on earth.

They'll be there . . . holdin' the horses!

BODIE THOENE, 2008

Hope Valley War

John Thornton left Hope Valley nine
years ago, determined to forget the ranch,
the sawmill, and the only woman he ever
loved. But now his younger brother,
Lucky, has been lynched, and his
beautiful widow begs for John's help.
A conspiracy of silence descends on
Hope Valley as John rides back in, yet
he's convinced somebody has to
know the truth. Step into the wild Utah
territory of the 1850s—a time when
vigilante justice reigns. . . .

For our grandbabies . . .
Chance, Jessie, Ian, Titan,
Connor, Turner, and Wilke
. . . with love and hope!

✴ PROLOGUE ✴

The faint summer breeze that rustled the curtains smelled of the pines up Schoolhouse Canyon. It was a pleasant reminder of the nearness of the forested Sierras that reared their jagged peaks a scant quarter mile behind the town of Genoa, Carson County, Utah Territory. The year was 1858.

In the upstairs bedroom of the white-frame home, twenty-nine-year-old Maria Thornton awoke and inhaled the soft, scented air. Her husband, William "Lucky" Thornton, lay snoring beside her. Maria pinched Lucky's elbow, and without waking, he obligingly grunted and turned over. His snoring tapered off to a low rumble.

Maria shook her hair to untangle the mass of dark curls that tumbled around her head on the pillow. Settling back into the feather mattress, she was soon on the edge of sleep. Maria barely heard the owl's hoot from the snag of the locust tree, nor did she take note of an answering hoot from down the road that led toward Carson City.

What did rouse her again was the low growl that came from her dog resting on the coil rug at the foot of the bed.

"What is it, Samson?" she whispered. "Bobcat up in the arroyo? Go on back to sleep."

But Samson refused to be still. He stood up with a shake and paced stiff-legged toward the bedroom door, his nails clicking on the hardwood floor.

"Samson," Maria repeated with more authority, "lie down!"

The dog refused to obey and whined as he scratched at the panel.

Maria glanced at her husband. He was still sound asleep. Best to let him rest, she thought. There had been nothing but trying days of late. Whatever it was, she and Samson could handle it. She felt no fear of robbers, for the Thorntons had nothing of value to steal. Nor was she concerned about attack by Washoe Indians, with whom they were on friendly terms.

"A skunk after some eggs again," she muttered to Samson as she drew a robe on over her cotton nightgown. "You can chase him off, but you'll sleep outside after!"

Samson bustled past her down the steps toward the front door. The staircase was dark, but Maria lit no lamp as she descended. She guided herself by one hand on the oak banister. When she reached the bottom, she spared a quick look at the entrance to the bedroom where her husband's younger brother, nineteen-year-old Kit, was sleeping, along with her only child, George, age nine. Apparently they had not awakened either. Maria smiled at the uselessness of menfolk.

Beside the front door she paused, one hand on the brass knob. The dog was whining eagerly to get at whatever was out there. Was there any cause for alarm? In the deepest part of the previous winter, a mountain lion had been driven by the deep snows to seek easier prey in the valley below. The cougar had raided three ranches, killing calves and sheep, before being shot. This was June, but caution might still be wise.

Maria recrossed the front room and took down the loaded double-barrel shotgun from above the mantel. For a girl who had come of age in the mining camps of the California gold rush, grasping the stock of the weapon and checking to see that the percussion caps were in place came naturally.

"All right, Samson," she declared, "I'm ready." When Maria flung open the door, the dog dashed out, leaping off the porch and charging around the corner of the house. The barn! She had been right all along. Some nocturnal prowling critter was after the henhouse. Maria could hear Samson's growls and yelps as he traced the path toward the stable.

Cradling the shotgun across her chest, Maria turned in the doorway to reach for the lantern hanging there when the dog's barking ceased abruptly. "Samson?" she called. She fumbled in the pocket of her robe for the matches.

Suddenly a hand shot out of the darkness and grabbed the barrel of the shotgun, wrenching it from her. At the same instant, another hand clamped across her mouth, stifling the scream that jumped into her throat. Her eyes grew wide with terror at the apparition that confronted her. A figure dressed all in black with a grotesque scarecrow's face dragged her out of the doorway, flung her cheek-first against the living-room window, and held her there.

"Keep her here!" her assailant commanded. "Now move! Move!" the creature hissed. "Upstairs!"

A different set of rough hands pressed Maria against the window, but the exchange was not made without a squeak of warning escaping from her mouth.

Through the wavy pane of glass, Maria saw half a dozen similarly dressed forms hurry out of the night and into her home.

5

When three of the men had dashed up the stairs, the downstairs bedroom door was flung open and Kit appeared. "Maria?" he called. "Keep back, George!" he warned his nephew. "What's all the—?"

He never completed his question as two hooded forms jumped him. Kit fought back, landing a punch that staggered one of his attackers. Then a pistol barrel clapped him alongside his left ear, and he slid to the floor.

Maria could hear the upstairs bedroom door being kicked open, and there was a roar of gunfire. The scene on the landing was both illuminated and frozen in the muzzle blast. The foremost intruder fell backward, clutching his arm and swearing.

From a place of concealment beside the fireplace, the leader of the attackers ordered, "Lucky Thornton! Give yourself up!"

Another gunshot from Lucky's .44 replied to this decree, tearing a furrow in the oak planks.

"We've got your wife and brother," the hoarse voice of the commander asserted. "Throw your gun out and come peaceable, and they won't get hurt."

There was a moment's silence before the heavy-framed Colt bounced on the landing and thumped to the floor.

The ringleader of the mob struck a match and lit an oil lamp. By its smoky yellow glow, Maria saw her husband, closely guarded by two men with six-shooters, come slowly down the stairs. Lucky wore only a long, white nightshirt. The pale shroud of his dress matched the ashen hue of his face. The contrast between her husband's pallor and the evil black garb of the intruders was riveting.

Maria wanted to scream, wanted to demand, "What are you doing to him? What is this? Who are you?" but none of these outcries would pass her lips.

Instead she watched with paralyzed dread as her husband was escorted across the front room toward the door. As Lucky drew even with his son's room, George darted out of the shadows to grab his father around the waist. "Don't go!" he cried. "Don't go with them!"

One of the marauders seized the boy roughly by the shoulders and jerked him away, but the leader of the group intervened. "Leave 'em be a minute." Then to Lucky he added, "Tell him not to try and follow us."

6

Maria saw her husband stoop to the boy's height. "Be strong," he said. "Thorntons are tough. Stay with your mother and take care of her. Understand?"

George wiped away a tear with the back of one hand and nodded without speaking.

"Go to your mother," Lucky said, gesturing toward the window.

George ran to Maria's side.

"What about him?" one of the night riders growled, pointing toward Kit, who still lay unconscious on the floor. "He ain't tied up . . . or dead." The phrase ended on a suggestive note.

"Leave him alone," the commander ordered. "He won't be awake soon enough to bother us. Tell your wife not to follow or try to set anyone else on our track," he repeated to Lucky. "We don't want anyone else to get hurt. That's not our intent."

Maria's knees buckled at the import of the words *anyone else*. She sagged against the window and put her hand on the shoulder of her son to steady herself.

The band of raiders had reached the doorway with their prisoner. "Tie his hands behind him," the chief said.

"Wait—just a moment more," Lucky pleaded, showing the first sign of emotion.

The scarecrow's head nodded once. "Make it quick." The leader gave a shrill whistle into the night. Another whistle answered from the grove of scrub oak up in the draw.

Lucky went to Maria and folded her in his arms. George pressed close against them both. "Good-bye," Lucky said simply. "I love you. You are the best wife a man could ever want."

Maria watched from the front porch as the men tied Lucky's hands and hobbled his ankles so he could not run. Then they led him away—down the steps and toward the sound of approaching horses.

When they had gone, Maria stumbled back into the house and sat sobbing on the floor. She cradled the wounded head of her brother-in-law while George obeyed her gasped instructions to fetch water and bandages.

✳ ✳ ✳

Lucky Thornton lay in the wagon bed of his captors, trussed and gagged like a Christmas goose. The brown and white mules that drew the rig were alike in the way they rolled their eyes at the masked figures on horseback flanking them. They started and jerked at every bat and nightjar that flew, making the driver swear and saw at the leads to keep the mules from jumping the ditch beside the road.

The cavalcade headed north, away from Genoa and from any hope of rescue by Thornton's friends. There was no undue haste among the raiders. They were unafraid of any interruption of their work. The troop followed the northward bend of the Carson River till they reached the junction of Clear Creek, then turned aside.

Lucky Thornton knew exactly where he was and where they were taking him long before the troop pulled through the gates of Manny Penrod's ranch. The night riders had chosen well. The barn was in the center of flat acreage and pastureland that extended for miles in every direction. If anyone mounted a rescue attempt, they would be spotted a long ways off.

Two of the guards spurred ahead and opened the passage into the barn so the wagon could be driven directly inside. Only after all were in and the doors closed again were lanterns lit, and Thornton's abductors removed their masks.

He knew them all. Some were open enemies like Major Frey and the gambler Bernard King. Others were respectable townspeople captive in some way to Frey's power, like Curtis Raycraft, who owned the livery, and rancher Manny Penrod. There was even one whom Lucky had thought a friend: Lute Olds. Then there was Rough Elliott, a saloon tough hired to do an unpleasant job without any troubling pangs of conscience.

"Take off the gag," ordered the leader, "and untie his legs so he can stand. We need to proceed with the trial."

Thornton fixed his eyes on those of his chief opponent. As soon as he could speak he said, "Let it alone, Frey. What's the point of playing charades when everyone, including me, knows what's to be? The only thing you'll hear from me is that none of you will get away with this."

Frey ignored the gibe. "Lucky Thornton, you stand accused of conspiring with the criminal Amon Edwards to rob and murder the rancher Francois Gordier. How do you plead?"

Getting into an argument about this mockery of a trial was pointless. Thornton occupied his time looking from face to face among his captors, searching for any hint of mercy or weakness to which he could appeal. The lantern light within the dusty cavern of the barn exposed only the pitiless countenances of his enemies and the fixedly downcast stares of the others.

The major droned on about Edwards and Gordier, about Hope Valley, about cattle rustling and homicide, weaving a concocted tale of justification for what was to come. Frey sounded as though he had even convinced himself that this night's business was completely honorable and just.

Amongst all the bearded faces of the major's cronies and hired thugs, the pale glow from the single lamp fell on only one unshaven cheek. Thornton squinted and contorted his body, trying to peer around a post and into the gloom at the boyish features of one not much different in age from his own brother Kit.

The young man saw Thornton's gaze light on him and dropped

his own face to the straw-covered dirt floor. Thornton continued to stare at the boy, silently urging him to raise his eyes again. Unwilling, yet unable to resist, the young man did so, like a kangaroo rat transfixed by the stare of a sidewinder. Thornton recognized him then: Frey's own son, Lawrence, eighteen years old.

The major was getting his money's worth from the bought-and-paid-for witnesses. "You were seen in the company of Amon Edwards one day before Gordier was found brutally murdered with an ax. Your conversation was overheard as you conspired to cause Gordier's death," Frey summarized.

"Give it up!" Lucky interrupted at last. "On the day before Gordier was killed, I was on the other side of the mountains, clear up at Bone's Toll Station. Mister Thick, who runs the station, will verify this. A little more attention to detail, if you please."

"Sir," erupted Manny Penrod, "have you no sense of the seriousness of this occasion?"

"My sense," replied Thornton with a sneer, "is that you mean to hang me in cold blood for no proven wrongdoing whatsoever. My death, ordered by this caricature of a court, is to satisfy the greed of all of you and the ambition of the major at whose trough you all feed. Serious, sir? Deadly serious but ludicrous, for all that! Where is Edwards, who is accused with me? Where are the witnesses who can establish my innocence in this matter? What about Thick? He is my alibi, but will you be allowed to hear from him? No sir, you will not!"

Lucky's remarks were directed toward Penrod, the balding man with the graying beard and mustache, but he was intent on observing the reaction of young Frey. Suddenly Lucky spoke directly to the boy. "Run, Lawrence! Get Constable Denton! Don't have my blood on your conscience! Make them call Thick. He'll clear me!"

"Don't move, Lawrence!" Frey ordered. The major laid a restraining hand on his son's arm. The teenager grew even paler, but he raised no objection. "And pay no heed to his lies. Mister Thick is the very man who has testified that he saw Thornton with Edwards!"

The burlesque hearing wound to its conclusion. The major, in his best judicial manner, intoned to the group, "You have heard the evidence. What says the jury?"

9

"Guilty," snapped Rough Elliott before anyone else could speak.

A chorus of guilty verdicts concurred. Some were loud and firmly spoken, like Bernard King's and Major Frey's. Others were mumbled and doubtful, as uttered by Curtis Raycraft, Manny Penrod, and Lute Olds, but in the end, no one disagreed, though Lawrence Frey's voice could not be heard at all.

"Sentence to be carried out immediately," declared the major. "And we here, constituting this lawful court, all agree to the justice of the sentence and do hereby bind ourselves on pain of death to never reveal the identities of any of the members of this body nor speak of this night's particulars."

Thornton snorted again, wondering if he was the only person in the room who saw the irony behind secret justice and coerced silence.

Lawrence Frey was trembling, visibly shaking. He looked as though he might bolt out of the barn and into the sagebrush.

Rough Elliott, with his wire-brush beard and potato-shaped nose, noticed also. "What about him?" he growled, jerking a thumb at young Frey. "He don't look steady."

"He'll stick," said the major. "Won't you, Lawrence?"

The boy snapped his head downward to show his agreement.

There was a whispered conference between the major and Elliott; then Frey made an announcement. "We'll draw straws to see who drives the team. I'll draw first; then each man in the room until the short is drawn. Go on now—get it done."

Four men took their wisp of hay before it was young Frey's turn. He pulled out a twig half the length of the others and stepped back with a look of horror. "What? What's this mean?" he gasped.

"Means you're the executioner, sonny. Get up on that box."

Lawrence extended his hands in protest and tried to back away, but Elliott caught him by the arm and yanked him forward. "The duty's yourn. Get goin'."

A coil of hemp was flung over a beam, with a noose formed on the end to dangle in front of Thornton's face. He did not wait to be manhandled into position, so he thrust his head into the loop. "I'm better than any of you. And since you mean to hang me, I won't die like a hog!"

Lawrence Frey sat on the wagon with the reins dangling limply from his bloodless fingers. Tears gathered in his eyes.

"They didn't steal your humanity either, boy," Thornton said. "Don't be afraid. Whip 'em up sharp and get it done."

A moment later, Lucky Thornton's string of luck had all run out.

✳CHAPTER 1✳

It was near the end of the fall gather, and we were pushing cattle down from the high feed of Tobias meadows toward the lower Carver pastures. It was a sleepy afternoon, and my horse, Shad, was doing most of the work.

I was riding easy when Stoney Brooks came charging up the Frog Creek Trail like a whole tribe of Comanches was after him. His buckskin leggings were flapping, and his bay was lathered. Since there were no hostile Indians in nearly four hundred miles any direction, my first thought was that he was racing somebody, on a bet probably. Stoney had been below, to Glennville, to pick up some salt and coffee that Cookie wanted.

My next thought was that it was a good thing the ramrod, Abner Slater, was nowhere about to see Stoney's uphill gallop. You could break your own neck doing any fool thing you pleased, but damage Bar C stock to no purpose, and Slater would wrench your head off and hand it to you.

Stoney spotted me up in the rocks where I was hazing a cow and a late-born calf out of a gooseberry tangle. He gave a whoop and a holler and spurred straight across a shaley place that a sane man would not have walked his mount over.

"John," he yelled, reaching inside his leather jacket and waving a paper, "you got a letter! Look here! A letter!"

Such was life in the cow camps that a little thing like a letter could raise such a fuss. Still, I had to admit that my own heart jumped up a notch in rhythm. Who would be writing me, unless it was bad news? My own people were far away, back East for the most part. For anyone to bother writing must mean trouble.

"And lookee," Stoney cackled. "It's from a female, too!" He yanked his panting, jug-headed horse to a stop on the ledge, scaring the calf and its mama. They plunged back into the thickest part of the scrub.

"Give me that," I said, leaning across and snatching the letter out of his hand.

When Stoney perched there with a stupid grin on his freckled face, I knew he was not going anywhere until I had shared the news, good or bad. At least he had not been fooling me. The paper had my name, John Thornton, written plain as anything.

Despite Stoney's impatience, I sat for a spell holding the letter in my hand, studying the outside and thinking. From the date on the front it had taken nearly three months to get to me. The original address on the pale blue envelope was in my sister-in-law Maria's elegant hand. I knew it right off. I also recognized the faint lavender scent that still clung to the paper despite a number of greasy finger smudges and nose prints from appreciative letter carriers.

Maria had recalled that I once owned a share of a mine in Downieville in the new state of California and had sent the letter there first. It tickled me to think she remembered.

But I had long since moved on from Downieville. Drifting south in search of that elusive big strike and the even more elusive ease for my soul, I had gone on to Coarsegold. The letter had properly tried to follow me there. But after arriving sometime behind my departure, it had unaccountably gone off to the old Spanish mission town of San Luis Obispo, while I had actually crossed the Sierras to here near the upper Kern River.

After a time I opened the envelope as carefully as my big, callused hands would permit and unfolded the single sheet inside. I could feel my face get warm when I read her greeting, just as if she stood right in front of me.

Then, an instant later, I caught my breath, and my skin grew icy cold.

"What?" Stoney asked. "What is it? I ain't seen your map this set in granite since you caught them drunks roughin' up that Yokut squaw."

I read the first two lines again, just to make sure there was no mistake: *John, I need your help. Lucky has been lynched.* Maria went on to explain what had happened, but all that mattered to me was this: My brother was dead, and Maria had asked for me.

"Hey!" boomed the whiskey-roughened voice of Abner Slater from the next ridge over. "Mister Carver don't pay riders to have no tea parties. Light a shuck under you both and shift them cows."

Stoney pricked his nag so sharply with his spurs that it almost jumped sideways off the ledge. "Let's get goin'," he muttered in a guilty tone, "double-quick."

When I did not move fast enough to suit Slater, he yelled again. "You hear me, John Thornton? Shake it up or you're through."

I was thinking hard. Then I carefully folded the letter and tucked it into my shirt.

"Come on," Stoney urged. "He sounds mad enough to swallow a horned toad backwards." Then, in a syrupy voice, he said loud enough for Slater to hear, "Right away, Mister Slater."

Directly I nudged Shad into a lope away from the cows and toward the ramrod. I heard Stoney yell something to me, but I paid him no mind.

"What do you want, Thornton?" Slater grumbled. "Didn't I tell you to get back to work?"

"I'm leaving," I called, simple as that. Slater looked dumb-founded. "Today. You know this is my horse and my rig. Nothing I have here but what's my own. I'll leave an address with the home ranch where you can send my time."

And with that I was gone, heading north toward Utah Territory, Maria, and God only knew what kind of trouble.

✳ ✳ ✳

It took me the better part of a week to make the journey from the southern Sierras to the mother-lode country. They were my worst seven days in many a year, what with fretting about Maria. The

Pioneer stages covered the same distance in thirty-five hours, making my slow pace all the more painful. But having neither enough money for coach fare nor wanting to kill Shad, I had to take it slower.

We traveled the main highways as far as Placerville and then followed the stage route over the Carson Pass and down the eastern slope through Hope Valley in the Sierras. When I got even with Snowshoe Thompson's place in Diamond Springs, California, I reined Shad aside and reflected once more on what I was riding into.

I stood in need of more information than was contained in Maria's letter. Almost a hundred days had already gone by since she penned those lines. What direction was the wind blowing now?

Snowshoe was the man to ask for news right enough. The long-bearded Norwegian carried the mail across the mountains between the American River diggings and the Washoe mines. Being much in demand and genial with all, he heard everything within a fifty-mile radius and was free with what he heard. And if we had not been especially close in the old days, he bore me no ill will that I knew.

Unfortunately, there was no one about at the Thompson cabin, so I had to press on no wiser than before. It had been years since I was last in these parts, and it was unlikely that many folks thereabouts could call me to mind. Still, a man has to be a fool to walk into a rattlesnake's den in his bare feet. It seemed best to me to go quietly straight to my brother's ranch before anyone with unfriendly notions found out there was another Thornton about.

With that in mind, when we came to the fork, Shad and I followed the deserted path called the Old Emigrant Trail where it skirted the valley of the Carson until we reached a hillside above my brother's ranch. Or rather, his widow's place, I reminded myself.

It was just after dawn. I sat for a spell beneath a jack pine that stood sentinel on the knoll overlooking the spread called the Lucky T. A blue jay scolded me from the branches over my head, chattering about my being where I did not belong. I paid him no heed.

All was quiet below me. A lamp came to life in the downstairs sitting room, and a wisp of smoke curled lazily upward from the kitchen chimney. Peaceful enough it was, without a danger in sight.

When Shad and I eased into the yard by way of the back pasture,

15

it seemed to me that some things had changed after all. There was an air of disrepair about the place. The barn stood in need of a coat of whitewash, the garden was overgrown with weeds, and a buggy with a busted seat was hoisted off the ground on a pair of barrels. It was grit covered, as if it had been awaiting help a long while already. When Lucky was alive he would never have tolerated such shabbiness, meaning Maria would never have permitted it.

It would not do to present myself at the kitchen door like a saddle tramp hunting a meal, though that description fit me better than most. Still, I was family, so brushing the road dust off myself as best I could, I tied Shad to the rail beside the front porch and climbed the steps. Even before raising my knuckles to knock, I thought I caught a glimpse of a face sneaking a look at me through a window, but it darted back as I turned.

Knowing that folks were about made me bold to knock the third time when no one answered my first two raps. If I had been expecting a warm reception and an embrace of welcome, I had sure been singing from the wrong hymnal.

The door, when it finally opened, parted a crack barely wide enough to let a cat through. The dark eye that regarded me though the slit was unfriendly, suspicious, and fearful all at once. It also belonged to nobody I recognized.

"What do you want?" a reedy voice inquired in an anxious way that confirmed all I had guessed from appearances.

"'Scuse me," I said, polite enough. "Isn't this the Thornton place? I'm trying to find Maria Thornton."

"There's no one here by that name. This is our place. You just get on out of here!" The words of what I judged to be a late adolescent boy rose to an almost frantic pitch for no reason that I could see.

"Now look here, sonny, I don't mean to cause any trouble," I said, holding my hands up. But when he started to close the door in my face, I will admit to getting a touch riled. I shot my boot forward and wedged the toe between the panel and the frame. "No trouble," I said as the boy's face grew even more wild looking, "but I do need an answer to my question."

"She ain't here!" he repeated forcefully. "Now I told you to go! Get away!"

There was much more going on here than a lack of neighborliness. This green sprout seemed positively panicked at my inquiry, scared as if he'd seen a ghost.

Before I could even raise the issue of Maria's whereabouts again, a woman's voice, shrill and unpleasant as a crosscut saw hitting a rock, yelled from across the room, "Lawrence, who is that? What's he want?"

The door that had been held closed to the width of my foot was now flung widely open. It revealed a woman of about forty, lean and careworn, as if her twoscore years had cost her threescore in grief and toil.

"What do you want here? What's this all about?" She roughly shoved aside the youth I guessed to be her son and by sheer force of will backed me up a pace. She appeared to be of the belief that you can win any argument by never letting your opponent speak at all. "Whatever you're selling, we don't want any. Now go on before I sic the dogs on you."

It seemed that the quiet, easy approach was not producing helpful results. So just that quickly I threw away my resolve to keep my identity secret. I guess I hoped to startle them into some response. "I'm not selling anything," I remarked real fast in the split second when the woman paused to draw breath. "I'm John Thornton, brother of Lucky, who used to own this place. I'm searching for his widow."

The boy's face showed a strange mix of worry and relief, almost as if my words had lifted one burden and left another in its place.

His ma narrowed her eyes and gazed up toward her mousy brown hair like she was hunting cobwebs in the corner of the doorframe. I knew from her expression that she was searching for the right lie to tell me. "This is the Frey place now. We own it. My husband bought it. We don't know anything about any other owner nor this woman, whoever she is. Now get along. We don't want strangers here."

"Well, now, ma'am, maybe I could wait and speak with your husband when he gets home," I said reasonably.

"You will not!" she snapped, stamping her foot on the floor. "Lawrence, get the dogs! And call Rough Elliott to get up here . . . tell him to bring his gun."

"No need for that," I said, making gentling motions with my hands as I backed down the porch. "What's your husband's name so's I can ask for him in town?"

"Get the dogs!"

As the boy darted past me and around the corner, I tipped my hat politely and said I'd call again some other day. Then Shad and I trotted off toward Genoa.

✳ ✳ ✳

Genoa, pronounced for some unknown reason with the accent on the second syllable, had grown up since I saw it last. Back when I was prospecting in these parts, the community that nestled in a crook at the base of the Sierras had been called Mormon Station, on account of being the westward-most outpost of Brigham Young's empire. In fact, he had ordered families to move there in large numbers, so as to guarantee a faithful voting population when it came to selecting judges and so forth.

At first no more than a stockade and a trading post on the Emigrant Trail, the town had been renamed after it prospered enough to be selected the county seat of Carson County in the Utah Territory back in 1854.

Shad and I attracted no particular notice as we rode into town on Main Street. I reined in at Raycraft's Livery and flipped the stableboy a nickel to feed, water, and curry the bay. Then I sauntered down the boardwalk past the Masonic Lodge, the Gomez barbershop, and the smithy.

From the corner outside the blacksmith's, I could study a hotel with the name Frey displayed over the door and had a clear view of both directions up and down the street. I stood there wondering where to make my first call and waiting to see if something would happen to give me a clue. I did not have long to wait.

Before five minutes had passed, thundering into town came that same kid I had seen out at the ranch. He was accompanied by an evil-

18

looking cuss that I took to be Rough Elliott, the ranch hand the boy's mother had been hollering for.

I pulled the brim of my hat down over my eyes and leaned back in the corner where the brick front of the Mason's building stuck out past the barbershop. The man and the boy split up almost right in front of me, with the hard case trotting his wiry-looking buckskin toward the courthouse.

The boy, Lawrence, as I had heard him called, first went into the hotel, but came out a minute later and headed on a slant across the street as if coming right for me. He did not see me, though, and popped into the barbershop.

I leaned out from my spot and moved just enough to where I could hear what passed inside the tonsorial parlor. "Major," I heard him address a big fellow sitting in the chair while the barber stropped a straight razor. The man's neck below his coal black beard was already lathered.

"What's wrong, Lawrence? You look like you've seen a ghost, Son."

"Yessir," the boy stuttered. "That is, someone's been asking after Missus Thornton, and Ma told me to find you pronto."

What can be said about a man who made his own son call him Major?

"Why all the fuss? We bought the place fair and square. Why didn't you tell the party she sold the ranch and moved away?"

"I tried to, but he wouldn't leave," the kid protested.

"Pay it no mind," the burly man in the chair said. "It doesn't signify."

"But he said his name was Thornton, too . . . John Thornton!"

Peeking around the corner, I saw that distinguished-looking gentleman almost cut his own throat, so fast did he sit bolt upright under the razor. Pushing the barber's arm aside, he demanded, "What'd he look like, this Thornton? What'd you tell him? Where'd he go?"

Lawrence had certainly gotten his father's attention, and now he didn't look at all sure he wanted it. "I don't know where he went. He asked after Maria Thornton; then he rode off. He was a big man, better'n six feet and a couple hundred pounds, I guess. Older looking than . . . than . . . " Here the boy ran out of words, but I guessed he was comparing my looks to my younger brother's. His next words confirmed my thought. "When he first come up to the door, I thought it was Lucky alive again," Lawrence squeaked.

"That is not possible," asserted Major Frey with the confidence of one who knew something beyond a doubt. He scrubbed the lather from his neck and tossed the towel on the floor. "Come along, Lawrence," he ordered brusquely. "Let's go over to the courthouse."

"Yessir," Lawrence agreed. "Rough Elliott is already down there looking for you."

As he and the boy made for the door, I quickly sunk back into the shadows and bent over to straighten my chaps. Outside they turned away from me toward the brick building at the other end of town without so much as a glance my way.

I was filing away names and descriptions for later use. There was much unexplained here, but my first goal was still to locate Maria, so I made no move toward confrontation just then.

Directly across the street from me was J. R. Terwilliger's General Store. It looked like as good a spot as any to continue my research, even if I had no expectation of actually speaking with the proprietor. Terwilliger had been as old as the Sierras when I knew him back in the earlies, and I imagined that he had long since gone to his reward.

That just shows what jumping to conclusions can do. I opened the door to the center aisle of a store that smelled of oiled harness leather and roasting coffee beans. As soon as the bell jingled, Twilly poked his knot of frizzy white hair out from behind a stack of blankets on the counter, as he was too short to see over the top.

Scrawny and with a birdlike conversational habit of hopping from one topic to another, Twilly looked and sounded like a woodpecker. "'Lo, John," he said sprightly. "Been expecting you. I knew you'd be back when you heard the news. Ever strike the big bonanza? You've aged some . . . more'n some."

Twilly had always made more money in one day selling camp goods to me and other prospectors than I ever saw in a month of panning for flakes in icy streams. "No," I said with a grin. "But you, you old coot, don't look one day older than ever."

"Clean living," Twilly said, slapping together his bony hands in front of his fence post–sized chest. "It was a bad business, John, bad."

I gathered from this shift that he was referring to what happened to my brother. A fella had to be nimble minded to keep up with Twilly. "Tell me what happened."

His eyes widened, and he clapped a hand over his mouth like he'd said too much already. "I don't know anything. Best you ride on, John. You'll only get in trouble if you stay around here."

"What about the ranch? Where's Maria, Twilly? And the child?"

"You been down in Spanish Californy, John? What do they think of President Buchanan over there? Folks say he's too soft on the slavery question. Just wants to get along any old way."

"Maria," I said again. "At least tell me where she went."

But Twilly, contrary to a lifetime habit, refused to say more.

"What are you scared of, Twilly?"

"Not now, John, not now," he begged. "I—"

The door chime jingled again, and the big plug-ugly known as Rough Elliott walked in. When he saw me his chin went up, and his hand dropped toward the gun butt that protruded from his pants pocket. I could see from the look on his face that he figured me for the one he had been searching for, but he was not entirely certain.

"All right, Twilly," I said. "I'm going now. See you later." Elliott and I kept our eyes locked on each other, though neither of us spoke. Even after I passed him, I could feel his stare on the back of my head.

Not having any desire to cause Twilly any trouble, I walked in front of the shopwindow like I was heading for the hotel. But as quickly as I came to the alley between Terwilliger's and Olds' Meat Market, I ducked down it and circled to the back of the general store. I remembered the layout from the old days. Twilly lived in a pair of rooms at the rear. Then the stockroom was in the middle of the building with a curtained entrance into the store proper.

The back door opened with barely a squeak, and I tiptoed across his kitchen, through the stockroom, and put my ear up to the drape.

21

"Was that John Thornton?" I heard Elliott demand. "Answer me, you old sack of bones."

"I don't know any John Thornton," Twilly protested. His denial ended with a strangled croak, and there was the sound of leather scraping across something.

Peeking through the gap in the cloth partition, I saw Rough Elliott grab Twilly by the arms and hoist the little man up. The tips of Twilly's boots dragged on the counter, knocking the blankets every direction and busting a pair of stick candy on the floor.

"We'll see how much you remember when I poke your face in the lye pot." Elliott laughed. He spun Twilly around in his arms like a child and held him upside down. Twilly was shrieking, but he was squeezed so tight that only a frantic squeal like an injured rabbit makes came out. Elliott kicked the clay lid off the crock of lye, exposing the caustic chemical only a foot below Twilly's jaw. "Was that Thornton?" the cutthroat demanded. "What did you say to him? Tell me, or I'll burn your eyes out!"

I jumped through the curtain and grabbed the first thing that came to hand, which was a keg of nails. As I had guessed, the noise I made caused Elliott to spin around, still holding Terwilliger. I shouted, "Here, catch!" and flung the fifty-pound drum as hard as I could.

Rough Elliott did real well. He dropped Twilly like a flash and almost got his hands up to catch the keg. He managed to keep it from bashing him in the chest, but his sudden move deflected the barrel upward to strike him in the chin. The keg shattered in his face, and he stumbled backward over the lye crock. When he hit the floor, he was out cold.

"Thanks, John," Twilly managed, gingerly flapping his skinny arms around his ribs to see if any were busted.

"I'm not so different from him," I warned. "I want answers too."

Twilly looked Elliott over to see if the man was really unconscious, such was the terror this ape inspired in defenseless folks. Then Twilly said, "He works for the Freys. Maria lives in the old sawmill cookshack. I swear that's all I know, John."

"All right, Twilly," I said at last. "I'll drag this carcass out into the street, and you lock up."

"What are you gonna do with him?"

"Drop him beside the horse trough," I said. "He'll thank me when he comes to and feels the lye that splashed out of the crock eating through his britches."

☀CHAPTER 2☀

I felt the eyes of all of Genoa on me as I dragged Elliott to the horse trough. Then I mounted Shad and lit out toward the mountains and Lucky's sawmill.

It was plain from the condition of the road that it had been a long while since Lucky's lumber carts had passed this way. The deep ruts carved by the iron rims of the freight wagons were rounded from last season's rain. The packed earth bore the recent hoof marks of two shod horses and a clutter of smaller tracks made from half a dozen shoeless pack burros.

What had happened to Lucky's thriving sawmill business? It was clear that the town of Genoa was still growing. I recalled the sound of hammers and the frames of three new structures on Main Street. It had not occurred to me to ask where the stacks of fresh-cut lumber had come from. When Twilly explained that Maria and the boy were staying out at the sawmill, I figured she had taken over Lucky's business. But the derelict road told a different tale.

By the early afternoon, the sun had moved west of the craggy Sierras and my path was all in shadow. I reined up on a rise and turned to look down on the distant, sunlit buildings of Genoa. A quail called a warning to his fellows from a clump of manzanita. A gray-backed lizard skittered across a boulder on the slope beneath me. Wind rattled the dry autumn sagebrush, then rushed through the pine trees on the high slopes.

Peaceful, I thought. *Peaceful as death.* Gazing at the dusty trail,

I shuddered as Lucky's face came clear to my mind. It was in this very place that I had last seen him alive. He had been driving a six-up team pulling a wagonload of planks down to the valley. It had been my team. My wagon. My lumber. He was smiling because I had lost everything to him. Including Maria.

Strange how his grin was still branded on my memory. The image of him slapping the reins hard on the backs of the horses sent a wave of renewed anger through me.

He had bid me farewell with a light, laughing voice. "You always were a fool, John! But you were right from the start. We can't share everything," he'd called as the wagon rumbled past me. "The lumber mill? The ranch? Small potatoes. We might have stayed partners in all that except for Maria. Can't share her, can we, Brother? She loves me, you know. Winner takes all. That's what we agreed. Whilst I'm alive I won't have you looking at her like you do. Now gather your gear and clear out."

I could have killed my brother easily that day. Instead I had stopped at the sawmill long enough to pack, then rode up the spine of the mountain to where the waters of the great Tahoe sparkled. For a month I had camped beside the lake and considered committing the sin of Cain against my brother.

Then news from Genoa had come to me by way of an old placer miner named Spike who stopped at my camp near suppertime. Miss Maria Foquette had married Lucky Thornton only four days after I left Genoa. Over beans and bacon the grizzled relic told me about the wedding and the big feed that Lucky put on for the entire town. A right handsome couple were Maria and Lucky. The bride looked at the bridegroom with such adoration that it made even the toughest men in Genoa weep.

With Spike's recitation of the event, I knew it was Lucky she loved, not me. Lucky was right. A sawmill and a ranch were small potatoes compared to her.

I gave up my thoughts of vengeance that very night. Next morning I broke camp and rode on. For nine years I carried the bitterness of that day with me. Hatred was the only thing I kept from all my memories of Lucky. I held on to it when I had nothing else. I rehearsed it in my mind late nights at a campfire, substituted his form when I killed coyotes.

"Whilst I'm alive . . . ," Lucky had said to me at our parting.

How often in the long seasons that followed had I wished him dead?

Now it was done. Someone else's hand had shed his blood, but I had wished it so. It was true that Lucky had a way of making enemies out of the best of friends. I was not surprised that someone had murdered him. Nor was I surprised at the manner in which he had been killed.

What surprised me was that all my anger toward him suddenly turned to regret. The memories of happy times we had spent together flooded through me. I thought of the son he left behind. I thought of our mother and father and our boyhood in the hills of New York. For the first time since our harsh farewell nine years earlier I felt the loss of my brother. Good-bye was hard after all.

All this came to me clearly as I gazed down at the shifting shadows of Carson Valley.

✳   ✳   ✳

A steep, treacherous trail branched off from the broader path of Sawmill Road. It cut a swath straight up through the long switchbacks and would save a full hour on the journey.

But it was not the consideration of time that caused me to turn from the easier track. When I left Genoa, the feeling came strong upon me that I was being followed. The wagon road was wide open. A lone rider made a stark target against the backdrop of the hillside. A crack shot with a Sharps .52 rifle and a clear view could turn me to crow bait before I spotted him. Experience had taught me that only a fool would skyline himself. I did not intend to become anybody's fool. That afternoon I felt something like a deer must feel when a hungry mountain lion is on the prowl. I had yet to see the face of the lion who stalked me, but I knew he was lurking there just the same.

I glanced up at the narrow track and, trusting that Shad would find footing, gave the horse his head. Shad was a mountain-bred pony, and he took to the ledge with ease. Picking his way between

boulders and moving carefully over loose shale and crumbling granite, he seemed unperturbed as we rose a thousand feet and more
above the floor of the canyon. As for myself, I never much cared to be
any place higher than my own head. I simply leaned into his shoulders to make his burden lighter and tried not to look down. I fretted
and prayed in alternate breaths.

From the opposite cliff, a golden eagle leaped from the rim of
her large nest and glided downward to fly past me at eye level. With
a piercing cry, she circled once as a warning that I was an intruder
in her world. I heard the swish of her wings upon the updraft as she
soared effortlessly back to her chicks.

For thirty minutes the gelding climbed steadily, coming at last to
where Sawmill Road emptied onto a gently sloping meadow. Lucky
and I had carved out the track and built the sawmill ten years earlier. Half a mile wide and a mile deep, the bench of thin soil over
granite was overshadowed by a range of peaks at the westerly end. I
could clearly see the spindly frame of the old flume rising from the
red-painted shingles of the sawmill. Silhouetted against the boulder-
strewn hillside, a section of the flume was broken, and a steady
stream of water flowed from it.

My first thought was that I would have to mend the flume. Then
it came to me that, the last time I had been here, the place had been
alive with the earsplitting noise of the lumber business—the buzz
of saw against wood, the shouts of teamsters, and the clatter of iron
wheels.

Today the mill was silent. Stacks of weathered planks were in the
yard as if waiting for wagons that never came. Uncut logs lay rotting
beside the main building. More than the flume needed mending.

What had happened here? I wondered as I stared at the bullet-
ridden sign that still read Thornton Brothers. The only hint of life
was a crooked finger of woodsmoke pointing skyward from the
cookshack stovepipe. My heart beat a little faster then. Maria and
the boy were here, I reasoned as Shad crossed the distance in a
gentle lope.

I allowed emotion to let down my guard. That was a mistake.

When I was still a hundred yards from the cook's cabin, the sharp

27

crack of a rifle rang out. I felt the hum of the bullet as it whizzed close by my head. Shad spooked and crow-hopped ten feet sideways. I nearly lost my seat but managed to hold on awkwardly as yet another round exploded from behind the clump of brush and boulders to the right of the barn. Tearing my Volcanic rifle from its scabbard, I hurdled from my mount and scrambled to crouch behind a stack of uncut logs. A dog, more wolf than tame by his look, barked fiercely and dashed out from the same cover as the shots. Shad lunged and bolted toward the flume with the dog nipping at his heels as I levered in a .41-caliber reply to the unfriendly messages.

Long moments ticked past in silence until a child's voice called out, "Samson! Come here!" The dog left off harrying Shad to return obediently to the brush; then I heard, "Are you dead, mister?"

It came to me all of a sudden that this was Lucky's boy. "No, sir, I am not."

"I'll remedy that right soon." At that, the child let loose with another shot that hit a log just above my head and sent a shower of bark onto my hat.

"Whoa up there!" I cried.

"I got me a clear sight, mister. You move one inch, and you're a dead man."

I had no intention of moving even an eyebrow until we got this misunderstanding cleared up. My young nephew was a fine shot. His daddy had been, too. "Is that you, George?"

"Throw out your piece onto the ground so as I can see it."

I hollered, "You are a fine marksman, George. So was your daddy at your age."

Another bullet answered, gouging a second hole in the bark only a fraction of an inch from the first. The boy shouted, "What would you know about my daddy, you thievin' . . ." Three more shots followed in quick succession.

I tossed out my rifle and laid low. Where was Maria? I wondered. And just who did the boy imagine me to be?

"George!" I called. "There's my piece. I'm your uncle John Thornton, come at your mother's request."

There was a long silence.

I tried to communicate once more. "You hear me, boy? I'm your uncle John."

"Prove it."

How could I prove it? For the first time, I wondered if George had ever been told of my existence.

"Where is your mother?" I asked.

"Never you mind."

"She'll know me."

Silence followed. Then a challenge. "If you are my uncle, you will know where I come by the name George."

For an instant my mind drew a blank. Who in the Thornton family had been named George? The answer came to me in a flash. "You're named after a horse."

His reply was suspicious. "Maybe he told you or maybe not. There's more to it than that."

Just like Lucky to name his firstborn after a horse, I thought. "Fine animal, King George was. Your daddy won him off a former slaver in a game of chance. Handsome sorrel . . . Narragansett pacer. Stood sixteen-three hands high. He won the big race in Buffalo. After that we called your daddy Lucky. He vowed he would name his firstborn child George, be it a son or daughter. You would have been Georgia, I reckon, if you'd been a female."

Evidently he did not like my speculating, because he squeezed off another round to focus me.

"What'd you do that for, boy?" I was getting angry now.

"Stick to the facts," he barked.

Wiping the perspiration from my brow, I continued. "With the cash we two got enough to buy fare to California on a packet ship. Crossed the Isthmus and came to San Francisco in '49. Left the horse, though. Your daddy was sad to leave that horse behind." I paused at this point. Certainly I had told enough to satisfy him. "Well, boy? Can I come out now?"

After a long consideration, he consented. "Real slow and easy though." He qualified his permission and instructed me to put my hands high into the air. I was more than a little uneasy as I stepped into the sunlight.

29

George stayed behind his cover eyeing me.

"As you can see," I said in a syrupy voice, "I am unarmed."

"Take off your hat," he said, "and hold it over your head."

I obeyed. It was clear to me that the cub was badly spooked by something.

A couple more minutes passed with the wind stirring the aspens. I was about to speak again when I caught sight of movement in the brush. The dog Samson charged out once more to circle me from a dozen feet away, growling with his fangs bared.

"Call off your dog, George," I suggested. "Call him off, I say, and come out here."

His gun barrel pointed toward my midsection, my nephew stepped out from behind the boulder. He was smallish and scrawny. His dark brown hair was parted down the center and lacquered with pomade to keep it in place. This was proof positive that his mother was somewhere around. Maria was always one for straight parts and pomade. George's two front permanent teeth had come in, giving him a muley, toothy look when he squinted up at me. And he was dressed like he was going to church—woolen knickers and jacket.

George walked slowly toward me. "Samson," he said finally. "Down, boy."

The wolf critter lay down, but his eyes never left me, and he did not put his teeth away neither.

"I am putting my arms down," I warned. "Keep your dog back."

"Samson, get on the porch."

Samson obeyed, but he seemed reluctant to leave off guarding me. I purely did admire that dog, but I will say distance improved my esteem some.

"You look like my daddy." George eyed me warily as if he were seeing some image of Lucky returned from the grave.

"Folks have remarked on the resemblance," I said, replacing my hat.

"Except you don't dress like him. And you need a bath."

He was right, but I ignored the gibe. "I admire your choice of weapons. Except a Volcanic repeater is a man's gun. And point that thing somewheres else." He carried a New Haven–made lever-action, identical to mine. Resting with its butt on the ground, that firearm would have been taller than him.

"At least I still got mine. More than you can say." He glanced at my discarded rifle.

"You're no bigger than a corn nubbin." As he complied with my demand that he aim the .41 elsewhere, I leaned forward and wrenched the rifle from his hands. He gave a growl and charged me. I picked him up by the seat of his knickers and held him at arm's length.

"Lemme down! You're not my pa!"

"Well, howdo, nephew George! I'm your uncle John. Not a rabbit or a squirrel for you to hunt for your supper! Not a bobcat or a rattlesnake or any other sort of varmint neither! Uncle John! That's who you was shooting at! I ought to tan your hide!" I gave him a swat on the rump, and the boy squalled.

Samson shot off the porch like a Roman candle aimed straight at my knees.

"George," I warned tersely, "call off your dog or I'll shoot him." I would not really kill such a fine loyal beast . . . I hoped. George kicked and swung at me but yelled for the dog to go away, which Samson did. "What's the idea drawing a bead on me, boy?"

"I didn't know . . . who you was! Lemme down!" He was a scrapper, this youngster. I appreciated his spunk but held on to him just the same.

"I'll let you go when you take me to your mother."

"She's . . . in the cookshack! I didn't know who you was! She's . . . she's . . . I got to look after her!"

"Hold still or I'll . . ." I did not finish the threat, but images of a willow switch and George's bare behind came to my mind. Scooping up my gun, I carried my nephew toward the shack. Samson growled at me as we passed by.

✳ CHAPTER 3 ✳

Ishould have known there was some good reason for young George to be so protective. If I had thought about it, I would have realized that no child raised by Lucky Thornton would so much as point a loaded weapon at another human unless circumstance compelled him to do so.

The instant I walked through the door of that dim little cabin I knew something was powerfully wrong. There were dishes piled in the dry sink and a heap of laundry in a wicker wash basket. Pine needles and a few dry leaves had snuck over the threshold and lay scattered on the floor. The small cot, where I figured George spent his nights, was made up in a childish way, the red woolen blanket all askew.

I heard a soft cooing from behind a red-and-green curtain that concealed an alcove where the cook used to sleep. It came to me that Maria was sick. I knew she would have to be near dying before she would let so much as one plate sit unwashed. Maria was the daughter of a Texican army officer who had fought beside Sam Houston. She had been raised with a passion for square corners on the mattress, a floor so clean a man could eat supper off it, and a rule that anyone who passed through her door must take off his spurs and muddy boots or else.

"What's wrong with your mama, boy?" I whispered as I placed my nephew on the floor.

"I tried to tell you . . ." His lower lip went out. He cast a sullen look toward the alcove.

"Is she . . ." I took a step forward.

The smallpox epidemic in Kansas Territory came to mind. I imagined the marring of that beautiful complexion. Then images of typhus and cholera leaped into my fearful consciousness.

George straightened his shirt and smoothed his lacquered hair, then stepped out smartly to rap on the wall beside the cloth partition. "Mama? You awake, Mama?"

I heard an exhausted sigh and then her voice. It was feeble but still the song of a lark to my ears. "Hunting, George?" she managed.

"Yes, ma'am." He threw a black look at me.

"Get a squirrel?" How desperately weary she sounded.

"You could say so." George cocked an eyebrow in a superior gesture that reminded me ever so much of Maria at her most haughty. "I have brought back Uncle John Thornton to see you."

Maria gave a little cry. "My dear boy! George, have you brought John?"

I blurted, "That he has, Maria. Caught himself a big squirrel."

"John Thornton? You've come then?"

I doffed my hat and looked guiltily down at my muddy boots. I needed a bath indeed. "Yes, ma'am. I have been a'horseback practically ever since your letter caught up with me."

"Oh! Oh, John!"

I was tempted to throw back the curtain and kneel beside her bed, but I did not stir.

"Shall I fetch a doctor?" I ventured.

Her reply was weak. "No need for that now."

What did she mean? Was she dying? Had I come too late?

She began to weep. Womany little sniffles issued from behind the calico curtain.

Wringing my hat in my hands, I took one step toward the recess.

George, as ever the protective wolf cub, thrust out his chest and held up his arms to bar my way. "You can't go in there! You stink, and she ain't done feedin' it yet!"

There was the rustle of bedclothes; then Maria whispered, "A moment, John, please."

I was befuddled. "Feeding . . . it?"

"The baby. What do you think?" George spat. "Go wash or you don't get near neither of them."

I called gingerly, "Maria? You got a baby in there?"

She answered me softly. "A baby girl."

George was defensive. "Yesterday night it come. I tried to tell you!" He snatched a bar of lye soap from the bucket and thrust it into my hands. "Now get out and go wash b'fore you come near my baby sister!"

Humbled, I obeyed, backing out of the cabin and walking a wide circle around the snarling Samson. Fact was, I had not had a bath for three months, not since the stray Mexican steer had pulled me out of the saddle into Tobias Creek last summer. And that had not really been a bath since I had kept all my clothes on.

George was right about one thing. I reckon I smelled like a polecat. Fortunately, I had been carrying one clean pair of breeches and a shirt rolled up in my saddlebag that I had meant to wear to Harry Dourty's wedding at Tailholt. I missed the wedding when a heifer delivered her first calf breech and needed my help to pull it out with a loop of rawhide riata around its little hind hoof.

Working around critters, I knew something about birthing. It was never easy. I thought about Maria . . . in labor alone with no one but a child to give her comfort! I stared with awe through the doorway and called out to George, "Did your mama bring that child into the world all on her own last night, boy?"

Now he replied in a small, tired-sounding voice. "I helped her some. There wasn't much I could do. It was . . . she told me what to do. But . . . there wasn't nobody else if that's what you mean." It was plain from his tone that it had been a long, terrifying night.

With this, his behavior at our first meeting was explained to my satisfaction. Considering the ordeal, it was a pure wonder George had not blown my head clean off. It was no surprise at all that he wanted to protect his mama and baby sister from a dirty, mean-looking stray who had come riding up the canyon unannounced. I thought better of the boy after that.

I carried my clean clothes up the path toward the sheer rock face at the head of the little valley. Standing beneath the broken flume, I scrubbed all over with lye soap and melted snow water, then walked back, shivering and barefoot, to the cabin.

As I returned to the cookshack, I surveyed the ground carefully. I expected an ambush by Samson, but as I drew closer, I saw that he was tied to the corral railing.

Rapping gingerly on the doorpost, I was surprised when Maria said in a strong and amused voice, "Who could that be, George?"

"It's John Thornton," I replied, knowing that she was fully aware of who was knocking.

"All washed and curried and presentable, are you?"

"Yes, ma'am. Only I am barefooted, I fear."

"You are forgiven. Come in and welcome," she answered.

I mumbled, "Yes, ma'am." But in a sudden attack of bashfulness I stared down at my toes and hung back long enough that she called to me.

"Are you coming in, John? Or shall I come out?"

I lifted the latch and stepped into the warmth of the room. What I saw surprised me.

In the time I had been washing up, the room had been swept and George stood wiping clean dishes at the sink. The gingham curtain was pulled back to reveal Maria sitting up in bed, holding the little baby in her arms. She looked almost holy to me, like the image of the Madonna and child I had seen once in the mission of the Spanish fathers in Monterey.

My heart jumped at the sight of her, so beautiful she was. She was weary looking, sure, but she had color in her cheeks, and her luminous dark eyes were filled with the serenity of a woman who had weathered hard times and come out the other side into daylight. Her long black curls cascaded over the shoulders of her white nightgown. The newborn babe of my dead brother rested peacefully in her arms.

I stood rooted and gawking, shifting nervously from one foot to another.

"Howdo, John." Maria seemed pleased that I had come.

"A-are you well?" I stammered.

"George is taking fine care of me." She inclined her head toward my nephew and the dishes and the broom propped in the corner.

There was a long, awkward silence as George stacked the last plate. "I'll go chop the kindling now, Mother," he said, not acknowledging my presence.

"That will be fine, George." When she dismissed him, he brushed past me without looking at my face.

It took me some time to gather my thoughts and make myself speak. I heard the steady crack of the ax against the wood outside. It came to me that George was a boy any man could be proud of. He was more like Maria than any part of Lucky, I thought.

Maria cleared her throat. "You have come a long way, John. Have you nothing to say now that you are here?"

There was plenty I had wanted to say over the years, but every phrase eluded me. "I went to the ranch looking for you."

"The ranch was sold to pay Lucky's gambling debts."

"I went to Genoa after. Old Twilly said you and the boy were up here at the sawmill. Didn't mention anything about a baby, though."

Her shoulder rose in a barely perceptible shrug. "I had not spoken to anyone in Genoa about my condition. That is not the sort of matter one talks about."

There was something momentarily hard in her expression as she said this to me. What was beneath the words?

"You are a courageous woman."

"The Lord helps us bear what we must."

"But why didn't you and the boy stay closer to town . . . to a doctor?"

"After the funeral, Kit was arrested and . . ."

"Kit?" The reference to my baby brother confused me. Last I had seen him he had been younger than George and still with Ma and Pa on the farm back East.

"Didn't I mention Kit in the letter?"

"No."

"Kit had been living with us most of the year when Lucky was murdered. The shock of it made him wild. He is incarcerated in Genoa for making threats and disturbing the peace. The sheriff may have locked him up to keep him from getting killed, but I felt quite unprotected after that."

This news added another dimension to my understanding of why folks were so eager to see me leave Genoa. "How long is he in for?" I pictured Kit as a nine-year-old kid locked up in a sunless cell, but of course he was full growed now.

"Three months was the sentence. He will be out soon."

"I'll see to it." I sensed that there was still more unhappy news for her to tell me. I waited silently while she sorted her words from emotions.

Touching the cheek of the infant, she raised her eyes to meet mine. "After Lucky was . . . after he . . ." She stared out the small square window set in the flimsy plank wall. "A woman all dressed in black came to his funeral. She works at Frey's saloon. A dance-hall girl, I heard from Kit. Her name is Nell. Beautiful, too, though I could not see her face clearly through the veil. Lucky met her at Frey's, you see? Lucky had another woman, and I never knew it until after he was gone. The shame of it was too much to bear. I could not stay in Genoa with George." She cast a furtive glance toward where George chopped the wood. "You understand, John. George idolized his father. He must never know of Lucky's faithlessness. This place is the only refuge left to me."

The news of Lucky's philandering ways filled me with such anger that it came to me I would have killed him myself if he was not already dead. Could Maria see the emotion in my face?

"I came soon as I could." My words sounded empty to me.

"I am glad for it." She held out her hand, and for the first time I saw how fragile and wounded she was behind this show of grit. I grasped her fingers. The skin was callused where once it had been soft as silk. I did not let myself gaze on her face but instead focused on the tiny head of the babe. The sight of such a perfect and inno-cent being sleeping through such heartache turned my heart to putty. I purely thought I might shed a tear, but I did not. I consoled myself with the thought that you can never trust a man who can look a pretty woman in the eyes, so I reckoned I was as reliable as they come.

37

"She has black hair like you," I remarked after a time. "A pretty little thing."

Maria smiled. "I have not thought what name to give her. Have you any ideas, John? She should be named after someone good and strong hearted. Is there . . . a good woman you are fond of?"

"I am partial to only one who would be worthy of the honor. Her name is Maria, and I have been faithful only to her all these long years since I parted from her."

She bowed her head as if my clumsy declaration had shamed her. "Please, John . . ." She implored me to be silent.

"All right, then. I will not open my mouth on the matter again. But . . . what is your full Christian name?"

She became cheerful once more. "Maria Madison Foquette. My father once shook the hand of President James Madison, and the experience never left his mind."

"You were well named. And this baby could not do better than to be called after her mother." At that, I picked up the baby and held her carefully as if she might break. I whispered in her little ear, "Madison Thornton we will call you, after a great lady. You will be Maddy for short."

✻ ✻ ✻

Every good thing I had missed hit me with full force as I laid that baby back in Maria's arms. All those wasted years looking for my fortune had brought me back empty-handed to the place where I had begun. I still had strong feelings for my brother's widow, and this disturbed my peace of mind considerably. The thought lit up my brain that maybe I could just forget the fact that Lucky had been murdered. Maybe I could take up where he left off.

Guilt immediately slammed into my head like a two-by-four.

"I'll need to be on the road again by morning," I said abruptly. "There are questions to be asked about Lucky. I aim to get to the bottom of it."

"The bottom will still be there in a week or so. Won't you stay awhile, John?" Maria asked in a dreamy voice.

"George might not like it much."

"I could use the help."

"Then I will stay. A week anyway."

She needed sleep, yet would have forced herself to stay awake to keep me company. Under the pretext of needing to hunt fresh meat for supper, I loaded the old shotgun and left the cabin. Without a word to George I took to the hills to think and pray awhile about what would be best to do. There was an old stump half a mile up the patch beyond where the flume jutted out into the void. I sat there as the shadows lengthened, listening to the pop of George's ax echoing from below.

A covey of four dozen quail scurried onto a fallen tree, then down the other side. They paid me no mind. With a single shot I might have brought a dozen home for supper, but I did not raise the muzzle.

Perched on the cedar stub, I set to work considering the dangerous situation in which I found myself. It was not Lucky's murderers I was worried about at the moment. It was my own unsteady heart.

It had been only a little more than a week since I got word that my brother was killed. Now here I was, riding in like a knight to the rescue. However, I was not anything like the hero in a Walter Scott story. Instead, after five minutes in Maria's presence, I had found myself thinking how nice it might be to marry Lucky's widow and raise his children! All these things I freely confessed.

The high esteem in which I had held myself sunk to zero.

Maria and her young'uns needed more than a scruffy saddle tramp like me to look after them. It occurred to me that if I settled in with the intention of lending a hand for a week or so I might never want to leave. All those numb places in my soul might awaken permanently. If I spent much time rocking Maddy, I would be a goner.

I have found that there are times in life when examining motives and too much soul-searching does not ease a troubled mind. Then a man just has to leave it in the hands of the Lord and do his level best to do what is right no matter how hard it is. No matter whether someone else has done wrong or not. As the Book says, there will come the day the Lord will pass all deeds and motives through the fire and burn up the bad but keep the good. And I knew I was only responsible for my own.

But Maria needed my help, and I couldn't let her down. Nor could I let down my brother . . . even a brother I'd hated for nine years.

The tangle became too much to unravel. "Lucky is lynched," I told myself. "You will find who done it and why, and justice will be served. That is the right thing for you to do."

Having set my priorities straight, I determined that I would sort out the question of comforting the widow and orphans at a later time. Feeling much relieved, I shot two rabbits and took them to the cookshack.

It was near dark when I got back. Holding the game for Maria to see, I said, "Does fried rabbit sound good to you?"

"I was just dreaming of it."

George, who was reading his McGuffey in the lamplight, commented that he would rather have had quail.

I set to work. "These skins will make a warm blanket for your baby sister. Come here, George, and I'll show you how it's done."

"I got to do my lesson," George replied, sullenly pulling the lamp closer to the book.

The boy would be a hard case to win over, I figured. But as I fried up our meal, I could hear Maria singing to Maddy:

"Bye baby bunting,
Daddy's gone a'hunting
To get a little rabbit skin
To wrap the baby bunting in."

⋆CHAPTER 4⋆

I stayed on at the sawmill for nigh onto a week to see after the mother and the child. I believe at first that George resented me as much as if I had been among the men who had lynched his father. He did not speak more than two words to me and cast dark looks at me when I conversed with Maria or tended his baby sister. I let him do all the regular chores, chopping wood, and keeping the fire burning.

It was clear from the wild geese flying overhead in perfect V formations that winter was coming soon and hard. I repaired the roof and rechinked the logs of the cookhouse. I also inspected the flume on the high bluff, though the view from the edge gave me the fantods. I concluded that the mill could be put in order again, then set that thought aside. It would mean a much longer stay than I was planning. While Maria was still in bed, I also managed the womany stuff, doing laundry and cooking and such as that.

The third day it came to me that I might make friends with my nephew if we were to share some sport. With Maria's permission I took him hunting, leaving Samson tied up and whining at home. We hiked up the high meadow, then worked our way downslope with the breeze in our faces, as the Indians will do. In this way the deer would not catch our human scent.

Removing a small glass bottle from my ammunition pouch, I anointed George and myself with a few drops of the strong-smelling contents.

George balked. "This stinks worse than you did the first day you rode up."

"A dab of this, and a deer will think you're his grandpa come a'calling." I held up the vial. "Musk. A Cheyenne showed me the trick. Pure ambrosia to a deer. Regular perfume of lilac to a doe. Taken from the scent glands of a killed buck. The glands are little sacks, just under the hide on the belly side of the hind legs and right below the knee. I'll show you how to cut them out when we've got our deer."

After this, George perked up a bit. He studied my bottle of scent and listened while I showed him the tricks of hunting like an Indian. I showed him how to camouflage himself and explained that a Washoe brave hunted with a bow and arrow and was required to use stealth and brains. This was unlike the white man, who generally blasted away with big guns and killed more than he needed to.

Two quiet hours passed with us well hid behind a stand of trees on the slope above the pasture. Along about sundown I spotted a movement of the manzanita brush on the far side. I nudged the boy.

First one doe emerged from the shadowed forest and then a second. They lifted their heads to sniff the wind. The breeze had changed, pushing our musky aroma into the clearing. The deer were unconcerned. A fawn scampered out and then another. Three more does followed and at last a small fork-horned buck.

George made as if to take aim on the largest doe. I stopped him, indicating that females were not to be taken. This was more than chivalry. There was a reason for this rule in the Indian camps. Female critters were the promise of the future. Bucks, on the other hand, were always too many. It took only one buck to populate an entire herd. The indiscriminate killing of does and fawns by the white immigrants was only one reason the native population had grown to dislike and mistrust the white man.

These were important matters that I would explain to George later. For the moment, however, we turned our attention to the enormous rack of antlers that crowned the head of the largest buck I had ever laid eyes on.

I resisted the temptation to give a whistle of astonishment as the eight-point critter strutted into the broad grassy space and snorted into the breeze. Like a wise general or a completely immoral bounder, the old stag had sent his harem out first before exposing himself to danger.

I nudged George, indicating that meat for the winter had arrived. The boy raised his weapon, took aim, hesitated, and looked at me. He spoke in a barely audible whisper. "I can't."

I did not comprehend his meaning right then. My blood was up with the excitement of seeing such a magnificent animal. I drew a bead on the buck. I had a clear shot at its heart. But before I could squeeze off my round, the air erupted with the explosion from George's rifle. In a flash the field was a confusion of white tails waving good-bye, all except for the deer George had made his target.

The small fork-horned buck reared up before dropping to his knees. One convulsive twitch and he was dead.

"What'd you do that for?" I asked in astonishment. "I had the big one right in my sights."

George lowered his gun and stood up with a sigh. "He's lived a long time. We didn't need so much meat. Leave it at that."

My appreciation of George deepened after that. He was right, of course. I consoled myself that the old buck would have been tough to chew on anyway, but I have never again had such an animal in my sights.

We hung the buck from a tree, bled him, and cleaned him. I showed George how to take the scent glands. We hoisted the carcass up to the top of the tree and left it there overnight to chill when the temperature dropped to thirty-eight degrees while we camped all night on the mountain. The next day we went back to the cabin and returned to the mountain with Shad so we could tote the deer back to the sawmill.

In the butchering room in the barn I taught George the proper way to skin and quarter the autumn-cooled meat. It surprised him that butchering a deer was not much more complicated than cutting up a chicken for frying—only bigger. Soon enough George was hard at work sawing the front quarters into blade roasts, arm roasts, and steaks. He sectioned the ribs for spare ribs and stew meat, which we canned. There was quite a collection of soup bones in the bone box, besides the ones I used to finally win over Samson.

I was satisfied that George could repeat the process on his own if he had to. This was a relief to me. Not one particle of the deer was wasted, and when it came time for me to leave, he would be more capable of caring for his mother should I not return.

George admired the antler handle of my skinning knife. "Would you make me one like yours?" he asked.

I promised him I would do so and sawed off the largest piece of tine from our buck's antlers.

I showed George how to preserve the hide. We scraped it clean and rubbed it with pickling salt. I explained that he must tan and keep the buckskin as a remembrance, because this was his first buck and he had hunted in a manly and respectable way. I was proud of him and said as much. It came to me that Lucky would have been proud too. My approval pleased George, I think, and we became friends.

That night I fried up fresh liver and onions. As we ate, I sat quietly while he told his mother all about the musk scent and the Indian way of hunting and the old buck who we named Old Man of the Mountain.

As young George rattled on in the soft firelight, I thought I saw Maria study me in a kindly, almost loving, manner. When I turned to look at her, she glanced away, and the spell was broken. Perhaps it was only my hopeful imagination.

As I held little Maddy in my arms I realized that I had not felt such warmth in many lonely years.

That night, as Maria prayed at the bedside of George, she thanked God for answering her prayer and sending me to them. The last thing I would ever call myself was an answer to a prayer. Could she mean it? I wondered. Trying to put thoughts of her from my mind, I headed out to bunk in the stall next to Shad.

Over the next several days George and I jerked the toughest cuts of venison, smoking it slowly over a mesquite fire. I did not forget to toss some scraps to Samson along the way.

When Maria was well enough, I saddled up to head back to Genoa to get some information about my brother's murderers.

I do believe that both Maria and George were sorry to see me go.

✳ ✳ ✳

If I had known what danger awaited Maria, George, and little Maddy, I would never have ridden out that morning. I had no reason to suspect any harm would come to them, however, so the last word I'd said to my nephew was this: "I'll be coming back soon enough with Kit in tow, I reckon. This time I expect that you will keep your rifle hanging on the pegs instead of trying to blow our heads off."

My admonition must have come back to George the first time he laid eyes on the two riders who approached from the ridge above the sawmill. Because he was gathering dry bark for kindling, he did not pay the strangers any mind as their mounts carried them down the steep slope of the upper trail. He left the rifle on the wall just like I had told him to do.

I'd been a full hour's travel toward Genoa when Rough Elliott and a slimy Mississippi gambler by the name of Bernard King stopped to water their horses in the trough beside the sawmill's barn. George had eyed them from the woodpile and thought about the rifle, but the memory of my words kept him from doing what instinct told him he ought to do to protect his mother and baby sister.

Samson was tied up near the front door, but his alarmed barking penetrated the walls of the cookshack.

Maria, her hands covered in flour from the kneading trough, stepped outside to join her boy. "Who is it, George?" The afternoon sun was bright behind the intruders, making it hard to see their faces.

Had she been able to quickly identify King, she would have gone inside and thrown the bolt across the door. But it was too late by the time she recognized the man standing near the corral. King was the same fellow Lucky had once called "the most crooked, no-good, thimble-rigging, cardsharp anywhere west of the Mississippi."

Bernard King was a cheat and a bully. He was skilled at his deception and because of this was a wealthy man. Lucky had discovered it too late to save his fortunes. He had lost his ranch to King in a game of five-card draw in the back room of Frey's some six months earlier. But even the ranch had not paid all that Lucky owed to King. Lucky was murdered while still in debt to this little weasel.

So King had come to pay a call on Lucky Thornton's widow in order to collect the balance of what was due him. Maria had a reputation as a woman not to be trifled with. For that reason, cowardly as he was, King had brought Rough Elliott along to back him up in his claims.

Maria tried to withdraw when she saw who the callers were. "George," she said quietly, "come inside."

George had no knowledge of all the misery his father had brought upon the family. The boy did not know the coarse characters with whom Lucky had consorted. Worst of all, the boy did not move fast enough to avoid the grasp of Elliott.

As George turned to obey his mother, Elliott lit out after him, grabbing him by the scruff of his neck and holding him up at eye level. "Well, look what I done cotched myself, King. A leetle pup."

Samson snarled, and his barking took on a frenzied tone. He flung himself at the leash time after time, attempting to break free of the restraint.

If Maria had fired a cannon, I would not have heard her. I was already too far away. And she knew too well that I would not be back until a full day and night had passed. A woman alone, still weak from childbirth . . . there was no one to whom Maria could turn for protection but the Lord. So at that moment, as she watched her boy struggle against Rough Elliott, she resolved that she would trust God, as she always did, but also do her best to defend herself and her children against those who threatened them. Instantly the words of the psalmist leaped to her mind: *"He teacheth my hands to war, so that a bow of steel is broken by mine arms."*

In that same moment Maria knew she was not alone. Someone unseen—yet mighty—stood beside her on the porch. She felt the presence and was no longer afraid. Courage filled her, and she hollered out in a voice so fierce that it startled the attackers. "Put him down, sir!"

King spit into the watering trough to show that he did not pay Maria's protest any mind. He delicately stroked his waxed mustache with the back of his hand and swaggered over to where Elliott held George.

Laughing, King patted the struggling boy on the cheek and

remarked, "This pup is like to need drowning, Rough. What you think? Should we cull the thing or just keep him for ransom till his mama pays what I am owed?"

Jerking his chin downward, King gave the signal for Elliott to plunge George into the trough. The boy came up sputtering and coughing but no less feisty than before. The two men laughed at the boy's ineffectual kicks and punches . . . until one of George's little pointy-toed boots connected with Elliott's chin. Elliott stopped laughing and angrily dashed the boy into the tub again.

At that moment Samson surged against the rope that held him, and this time the cord snapped. He took off at full speed, like a runaway buzz saw, straight toward Rough Elliott.

Bernard King backed away from the onslaught, but with a flick of his wrist, a hide-out gun appeared in his palm. As Samson charged, King fired the derringer. His first shot hit the dog in the side and spun him around. The second bullet killed him.

George yelled, "Samson! Samson!" He continued to wail and kick furiously.

Maria did not speak another word. She turned on her heel and went in to fetch the lever-action rifle. Snatching it from the wall, she emerged with it at the ready. "Put him down!" she demanded as Elliott was again about to treat George like a load of Saturday wash. Her voice was strong and sure.

Both men glanced up from their sport, and their grins melted. "Well, now, missus . . ." King spread his hands out to show that he was only joking. "We can talk this over quietly."

"Put down my son."

George continued to struggle, managing to sink his teeth into Elliott's black and filthy thumb. Elliott yelped and booted the boy hard on the behind. George's fight was to no avail. Elliott gave him a shake and cursed him.

King replied, "Where is your hospitality, Missus Thornton? I figgered we might discuss our problem over a meal. Do I smell venison stew?"

"I am serving .41-caliber Volcanic repeater pudding, if you have an appetite for it, Mister King. And I am a crack shot."

47

King let out a nervous laugh, as if he did not believe her. "Come now, Missus Thornton. We know your brother-in-law is no longer here to take your part in this quarrel."

At that, Maria gave him fair warning. "First shot will be three inches to the right of your boot, Mister King."

The cartridge exploded, the bullet tearing the ground right where she predicted.

King jumped back, his tall stovepipe hat falling to the ground.

Maria drilled the top hat with a second shot, sending the thing rolling toward the rail fence of the corral.

"Next shot will be clean through your kneecap, Mister King."

"That hat came from St. Louis!" he cried.

"You'll be showing it off for Saint Peter if you press me further, Mister King."

King's face was white with a combination of humiliation and rage. "I don't take kindly to a woman who tries to best me."

"Then you should not trifle with a woman who is your better."

"I heard you were a religious person," King scolded, pretending shock and outrage. "Never heard of a true Christian woman to shoot a man."

She pivoted to direct her aim at Rough Elliott's shinbone. "Mister Elliott, what Mister King says is true. I do not hold with killing. But I can blow your leg off without feeling a twinge if you threaten my boy with harm anymore."

Elliott blurted, "She means it."

"Right," Maria confirmed. "And my second shot will be you, Mister King. At least there will still be two good legs left between you."

George still dangled from the end of Elliott's meaty paw.

King said, "I can see you are not going to be sensible nor reasonable."

Maria was smiling from behind the sights. "That is correct. You have shot my dog, and now I am inclined to make a gelding out of you, unless you do exactly as I command. Now . . . let go of George. Then reach high in the air."

Rough Elliott lowered George gently to the ground; then both men stood with their hands up, waiting for instruction.

Maria continued in a sweet, motherly voice, "George, step away from the gentlemen, if you please."

"Yes, ma'am." The boy obeyed, giving his mother a clear field of fire.

Elliott muttered to King, "You ain't gonna tell no one about what she done, are you?"

King's eyes narrowed as he threatened her. "We'll be back. I got the law on my side."

Maria replied, "I know your sort of law. The same law that lynched my husband!" She fairly spat out the words. "Now back up. Get on your horses and ride out of here! And know this! From the time you saddle up until you are out of my sight there's a .41 caliber aimed at your backside. Turn around, and I'll serve you up a dish you'll not soon forget!"

The duo obeyed her, riding without looking back until they were certain they were out of range.

For the moment, she and the young'uns were safe.

∗CHAPTER 5∗

When I had last seen Kit he was only nine years old. Mostly my mind still saw him as a boy in knee britches. But when I gave him serious consideration, I imagined him going to some eastern school, becoming a teacher or a lawyer, perhaps.

His given name was Christopher. He was named partly in honor of the famous scout Kit Carson, whose given name was also Christopher. And our Kit had been born small, just like the illustrious mountain man. My brother Lucky and I had held out for calling him Runt, but Mama seemed not to care for that idea.

And now here he was, not only out West but in Genoa and in jail. I did not know if Lucky had enticed him to come to the territory with strike-it-rich tales, or if he had come of age with the same wanderlust that afflicted his elder kin, but he was in deep now—no mistake about that.

Maria had told me that Kit was being held for threatening folks with a pistol and for being drunk and disorderly. None of those were hanging offenses, it seemed to me, but given the state of things in Carson Valley, I was not too sure.

I was thankful that Si Denton was still town constable. He was a good man and a fair one, and I could not believe that he had been involved in Lucky's death. The manner of it was not Si's style. He would have held Lucky for the territorial marshal even if he had been convinced of Lucky's guilt.

The Carson County courthouse was a two-story brick structure at the east end of town. The front was all offices and courtroom and such. At the back on the ground floor was the jail. Shad and I circled to the rear of the building and approached the steel door that was the only outside entrance to the prison.

When I hammered on the metal with my fist, a small spy panel opened. I thought I recognized Si's pale blue eyes, but he seemed unable to place me. "What d'ya want?"

"Don't you know me, sir?" I asked. "John Thornton. I hear tell my brother is a guest of yours."

Si gave the same wheezy chuckle that had always passed for his laugh. Then I heard the sound of bolts being thrown back, and the door opened. "Well, John, after three months had gone by, I had hopes that you weren't coming."

"Why say it like that, Si?"

He shook his thinning crop of gray strands, and his dark-complected face looked sorrowful to me. "No good will come of it. Let the dead bury the dead. Take your brother and Maria, too, if she'll go, and get out of here. We don't want trouble in this town."

"Si," I protested, "I'm not looking for trouble, but I do want some answers. Now if you don't mind, I'd like to see my brother and then talk to you some more."

"Fine," he agreed, leading me to the rear of the dark room and pointing me toward where a steel wall rose from floor to ceiling. The Genoa jail consisted of two side-by-side metal cubes. The one against the outside wall was empty; the other held my brother.

I peered in through the barred window in the otherwise solid door. Sitting on the cot that was the only piece of furniture, I saw a thin young man with his head in his hands. He was pale compared to me and Lucky, and slighter of build. If I had gotten the height and Lucky the bulk, Kit seemed to have neither.

"Kit," I called to him.

"Go away," he said without looking up. "I'm not hungry, and I don't feel like eating."

"Kit," I said again. "I'm your brother."

He looked up sharp at that. "My . . ."

"I'm John," I explained. "I came when I got Maria's letter. I saw her already, and she told me about you."

He stood up and regarded me through the bars. "Is she all right? I mean, the baby and all?"

"She's fine," I assured him. It pleased me in some deep way that even locked up as he was, Kit had asked after Maria's welfare.

"Can you get me out of here?" he continued.

I turned to look at Si, who pursed his lips and frowned. "Sentence is almost up. I suppose I could release him into your custody," he said doubtfully. "But I think he's safer here."

"Safer!" Kit shouted, flinging himself against the door of the cell. "Safer for the murderers who killed Lucky. You're protecting them! Letting them cover their tracks. Let me out so I can get after them again!"

Si said, "You see what a temper he's got? He was waving a six-shooter around on Main Street, yelling that he was gonna make somebody talk. He threatened the major and some others. I don't know how much of it he meant—"

"Just give me a gun, and I'll show you how much!" Kit interrupted angrily. "I'll show all those butchers when I catch up with them."

Si raised his eyebrows as if to say, "See what I mean?"

I shrugged and turned away from the door. "You're right, Si. He's safer in here. Leave him be for now."

"Hey! What kind of brother are you? Are you on their side?"

"Simmer down," I suggested. "I'll be back later. Come on, Si. I'd still like to talk with you."

We went into the front half of the courthouse, then into Si's office. We had to close two doors on the way, just to shut out the noise of Kit's yelling.

After we had shut Si's office door behind us, Si sank into the rolling oak chair behind his desk and waved me toward a bench.

"What happened here, Si?" I questioned as I sat down. "Maria could only tell me what the result was, not the why of it . . . or the who."

Si steepled his fingers together and frowned. "You know your brother was a gambler. And sometimes he ran with a pretty seedy bunch like Lute Olds and Sam McWade."

"Yes, and he also owned two houses, a sawmill, and a ranch," I retorted. "He was friends with Judge Hyde, Elwood Knott, and Justice Van Sickle. I even seem to recall that he elk hunted with a certain town constable, Si!"

Si turned his head to look at a rack of elk antlers that stretched from halfway up the wall clear to the eight-foot-high ceiling.

"You telling me Lucky was hanged for who he played cards with?"

"No, no!" Si protested. "Look, I'll tell you what I heard, not what I know for a fact, all right?"

"Fair enough."

"Your brother was accused of being involved in the murder of a rancher named Gordier up in Hope Valley . . . of having plotted the man's death so as to steal his cattle."

"Was there any proof?"

Si thumped his meaty palm flat down on the desktop. "Of course not! If there had been anything more to it than gossip, I would have seen to it personal. The fact is, the rancher was killed, and your brother had been to see him a week before he was bushwhacked."

"What's that prove?"

"Not a thing. Then Lucky brought me this." Si pulled open the center desk drawer and drew out a paper. He hesitated over showing it to me, then finally turned it around so I could see it.

It read: *Lucky Thornton, you are a thief and a murderer, but justice will overtake you in the end if you don't clear out at once.* It was signed *The Committee.*

"What'd you do?"

Si made a face as if he had bitten into a sour apple. "Lucky showed it to me, but he was laughing about it. Said he didn't scare easy and for certain not by midnight callers who hid their real names behind fancy titles. I told him he ought to go away for a time till things settled down some, but he never heeded me."

"Maria never saw this."

"No. Lucky said he didn't want to frighten her or the boy. Asked me not to say anything about it where she would hear it either. 'Course that tied my hands pretty fair."

I thought about what Si had said. It was just like my headstrong and proud brother to want to face up to things without any help. "Did he try to find out who had sent it?"

"If he did, he didn't tell me."

Now here was the main matter. I stared at the toes of my boots for a minute before I quietly asked, "And what have you done about his lynching?"

I studied Si's face. His eyes showed real pain. "I can't find anything. Nobody saw anything, or if they did, they are scared to talk about it. I wasn't even in the county that night—"

"Why not?"

Si worked his jaw like he was chewing his words instead of a plug of tobacco. "I got a line on a border ruffian name of Edwards. The word was that he was in the Honey Lake country, so me and Paul and Knott and some others rode up there. But it was a cold trail."

"Who's this Edwards?"

"He's wanted for a killing over in Placerville." There was a long pause before Si continued. "And he's the one said to have dropped the hammer on Gordier."

"That's mighty convenient, don't you think?" I exploded. "You and Lucky's friends sent off on a wild-goose chase the same night this committee lynches Lucky!" Then another thought struck me. "Who told you about Edwards?"

Si shook his head. "If you think you can connect that information to the night riders, you're mistaken. It came by Snowshoe Thompson."

Just then the door to Si's office burst open and in rushed a lean, young man, aged twenty-five or so, with a pair of pistols on his hips and a flush on his face. "Si!" he shouted, right up against Si's desk and in front of me. "John Thornton's in town, looking for trouble. A week ago he busted up Twilly's store and scared Missus Frey half to death. We've got to bring him in pronto!"

I smiled and looked to see what Si was going to say now. He was grinning too. "Did you bust up Twilly's?" he asked me.

"Not by a jugful! Some character name of Rough Elliott was leaning on Twilly to find out about me. I just cooled him off some."

"You!" the young fella said, stabbing at me with his index finger.

"You're Thornton!" He went to slap leather, but I saw it coming. By leaning forward in my chair I grabbed both his wrists and held his hands at his sides.

"Who is this temperamental character?" I asked as the blond-haired man struggled to draw his pistols and got even more flushed in the process.

"Paul!" Si snapped. "Settle down and leave your Colts holstered or you're through working for me!" To me he said, "John, meet my deputy, Paul Hawkins . . . who, if he is going to remain my deputy," he added pointedly, "had better not be so quick to be on the shoot!"

As I felt Hawkins' muscles relax, I let go of his wrists and turned him loose.

"But he's a killer, same as his brother!" Paul argued.

Si looked disgusted. In a no-nonsense tone he ordered, "Wait outside, Paul. Better yet, go over to the hotel and get my supper."

"But—"

"Git!" Si concluded.

Hawkins went but with bad grace, slamming the door behind him.

"Seems he must think my brother got what he deserved," I remarked.

"Don't be too rough on Paul," Si cautioned. "He's hotheaded, but he's a straight arrow when it comes to the law, and he was with me the night of the hanging."

I still had my doubts about Hawkins, but I kept silent. "And what about this Elliott?"

"He's a bad'un. Drifted into town six months back. Caught a job with Major Frey. I hear he's foreman now. Watch out for him. He came with a bad reputation."

"Like me, Si?" I asked with a grin. "I guess that's all for now. If you'll let me, I'll take responsibility for Kit."

"He's likely to be a handful. You sure you can manage him?"

I nodded.

"I'll have to keep his pistol." Si paused. "And yours, if you're pack-ing." Then a look of remembrance passed over his face. "You still handy with a rifle?"

Shrugging, I agreed. "Need to be, up in the high lonely."

Si set his jaw. "Then I want you to fetch in your piece for as long as you're staying in town."

"That isn't friendly, Si," I complained, but he did not rise to the humor. "It's outside with Shad. You take good care of it."

"There's one more thing," Si said. "Don't spread this around, but we've got Indian trouble. Six times in the past few months tenderfeet coming over the trail have had their stock run off in the night. The seventh was last week, and three men got wounded."

"Why tell me this?"

Si shook his head. "There's present trouble enough in the world. Let the past alone. Let the dead stay dead."

I stood and said stiffly, "I need to get back to Maria."

At the mention of Maria's name, Si's face clouded, and he stared at the torn and faded blotter on his desktop. "John," he said quietly as I turned to leave, "you won't tell Maria that I knew before the hanging . . . about the warning, I mean?"

"No, Si," I said. "She doesn't need to know."

✸ CHAPTER 6 ✸

K it groused more than a little about not getting his weapon back.
"Whose gun?" I said, teasing him. "Si remarked that when
you were waving it around, it looked a mite . . . heavy for you."
My little brother seemed a touch embarrassed but just as
hostile as ever. "So it was Lucky's . . . but it's mine now! And I aim to
use it to catch the dirty snakes who killed him."

"Easy," I said, shushing him as Si closed the steel door of the
jail behind us. "Don't give the constable a reason to throw you back
in the hoosegow. Come with me over to the hotel. You could use a
decent meal, couldn't you?"

Though disposed to stay on the prod, Kit's stomach betrayed him
by growling. "All right. And . . . thanks for getting me out." Then he
froze in his tracks as if he'd just spotted a sidewinder at his feet. "To
the hotel . . . you mean Frey's place?"

"You think he was involved in Lucky's murder, right? Well, if
you're gonna beard the lion," I said, "you gotta do it in his den."

The clink of my spurs sang a soft tune to the evening as we
walked to the hotel with my leading Shad. The horse's head bobbed
in time to the music.

"You know that's where the gal . . ." Kit's words trailed off.
Perhaps he thought he was speaking ill of the dead to mention
Lucky's infidelity.

"I heard about Nell," I pointed out. "Maria has had a load to
carry, but she is tougher than you think. Now I have the same

intentions as you: to see justice done and Lucky's killers brought in. But we need to go about it smarter. You get further by listening than by shooting off your mouth. Savvy?"

On the way down Main Street we passed Terwilliger's. The shutters were closed over the windows, and the front entry was double-locked and barred.

"Looks like Twilly figgers on an early winter," I observed.

"How do you mean?"

I thumbed at the sign that read Gone Away on Bizzness tacked to a doorpost. "The bird has flown south till the storm blows over."

The Frey Hotel was a two-story affair with saloon and dining room on the ground floor. A hall separated the saloon to the left from the eatery to the right. I guessed that upstairs there had to be a dozen rooms for travelers' lodgings. Major Frey's office was likely to be there too.

As we entered I spared a glance for occupants of the bar. There was the usual assortment of hangers-on: two cowhands leaning over the counter like they were in dire need of its support, two gals bent on relieving those cowpokes of their pay, a barkeep with an elegant curled mustache, and a table of poker players in the far corner.

I wanted to see if anyone took note of us. None did, except one of the cardplayers. He was a weaselly-looking feller with a waxed mustache and imperial beard that matched his slicked-down hair. He looked up at me, then ducked his head as if afraid I might recognize him, but I did not.

I pushed into the saloon and said loudly to the barkeep, "My name's John Thornton. Is the major about?"

"Gone home for the evening," the barman said in a friendly tone. My name seemed not to mean anything to him, but I noticed that the slick-looking gambler stiffened in his chair and so did one of the saloon gals.

"That's her!" Kit hissed in my ear. Then louder he complained, "Are we drinking or eating? What are you looking at, anyhow? Come on, John. I'm hungry."

I turned and gave him a good-natured shove across the hall into the restaurant. "For a man who might still be eating cold beans and drinking springwater inside a steel cage, you're awful free with your complaints."

Just behind me in the bar I heard the slick fella say, "Cash me in."

Someone else retorted, "Where do you get off quitting now, King? Sit down and play cards."

The dining room was empty except for us. Kit pulled a chair out from a table in the middle of the room. I shook my head and moved him over to a corner out of view from the corridor. Nobody could get behind me there, and I could watch all the windows. I could also get the first look at whoever came in before they spotted me.

The floor squeaked under our chairs when we sat down, and a pretty red-haired gal poked her head in from the kitchen. "Be right with you, gents," she said.

"So what can you tell me about Lucky's business dealings?" I asked Kit.

He shook his head and frowned with frustration. "Not enough, I reckon. I hadn't been out here that long. I know the mill had gone bust, and Lucky lost the ranch gambling."

"Why? Why put up the ranch?"

"Said he needed the money for something really big, a cattle deal. He told Maria and me not to worry, that he'd be back on top again soon. 'Course he was still saying that right up until . . . you know."

The red-haired gal, youngish and cute, approached our table. I judged her to be about Kit's age or maybe a year younger. My brother, I noticed, was right taken with her smile. "What'll you have?" she wanted to know.

"Beefsteak for me," I allowed. "And potatoes if you got 'em."

"We do," she agreed, "and pumpkin pie for dessert."

"You're reading my mind," I said.

"How about you?" she asked Kit.

"Perfect," he mumbled like a moonstruck calf, staring at her green-and-gold-flecked eyes.

I kicked his shin under the table. "The lady didn't ask what you thought of the weather. She wants to take your order."

Kit jumped like I remembered he always did when caught with his hand in the cookie jar. "Uh," he stammered.

"He'll have the same as me," I said. "And, miss, if it isn't too forward, would you mind telling me your name? My brother here won't be able to carry on any kind of conversation until he knows."

She laughed. "I'm Angela Frey. Angie to my friends. My uncle is Major Frey. And you are?"

"John Thornton," I said without blinking. "The mute here is my brother Christopher . . . Kit."

"Pleased to meet you both," she concluded before bustling off to the kitchen.

I turned to reproach Kit for being so tongue-tied, only to find him wiping his face with both hands. "What ails you?" I demanded.

"She's the most beautiful girl I've ever seen," he moaned.

"Is that cause for lament?"

"Don't you see? She's the major's niece . . . and he is the one behind Lucky's lynching!"

I reflected on the fact that young Lawrence Frey had gone straight to the major with news of my visit to the ranch and that Rough Elliott was sure enough nerved up about my presence in town.

Still, none of this was proof.

"Slow down," I cautioned. "You don't know for certain. Anyway, she doesn't recognize the Thornton name, so don't get crushed so easy. What do you know about this man Gordier and the cattle?"

Kit studied the oil lamps hanging from the wagon-wheel chandelier. "Lucky planned to get his business going again by selling cattle to the immigrants coming through. Gordier had a herd up in Hope Valley that Lucky understood was for sale."

"Why?" I wanted to know. "Why would Gordier not sell the cow critters to the immigrants himself?"

Kit shrugged. "Lucky heard the man was in a big hurry to get back East and needed the cash, but when we rode up there we couldn't agree on a price."

"And after?"

"We came straight back here, and then a week later we heard that Gordier had been killed."

"And what do you know about Edwards?"

Kit frowned and said he was not sure. He knew that Edwards was the man accused of murdering Gordier, but he was not certain whether Lucky had ever mentioned Edwards before the shooting.

Nell, the dance-hall gal, entered the dining room. She looked both ways, as if to make certain there was nobody hiding under the tables, then came straight to my side. "You know who I am?" she asked.

"I do," I agreed.

"Then believe me when I tell you that your life is in danger if you stay here in Genoa."

"You don't say," I said with a smile. "Why don't you sit and explain why that should be." I stood and offered her a chair.

She backed away suddenly with an angry look. "It's not funny. Nobody put me up to this to try and scare you. Talking to you could get me fired . . . or worse, only I'm leaving town tomorrow myself on the early stage."

I tried to match the earnest quality of her message. "We could really use your help. Finding out who killed our brother."

"Don't be stupid," she said. "Get out of the territory, and take anyone else named Thornton with you."

Another man came into the dining room about then. It was King, the little, oily-looking gambler I had seen in the saloon.

Nell caught one glimpse of his entrance and swirled away toward the kitchen as if she had passed our table without stopping.

King sat down across the room from us. Every time I looked up I caught him staring at me. The dapper-dressed fella seemed pretty harmless right then, so I chose to ignore him and said nothing about him to Kit.

I resumed my conversation with my brother. "Anybody ever catch Edwards or know if he really even exists?"

Kit shook his head, but I'm not sure if he even heard the question, because Angie came across the plank floor with a big camp kettle of coffee and a pair of mugs. "You two care to have coffee?"

"Please," Kit said, jumping up. "Let me tote that for you. It looks real heavy."

"Oh no," Angie protested. "You don't need to do that."

But Kit had already swept the handle of the enameled pot out of her grip. He poured me a cup and one for himself, then gestured for her to lead the way back to the kitchen.

Even while observing my love-struck brother, I had been keeping an eye on the other table. I saw King hitch his chair around a bit. Kit's path following Angie took him right beside where the gambler was sitting. I toyed with my coffee cup and watched.

Just after the girl passed by, the toe of the gambler's boot snaked out and hooked Kit's ankle. My brother shouted and pitched forward. Being young and limber, he swung around real sharp and managed to set that coffeepot down without sluicing it all over the floor, before he fell down there himself.

No more than a few drops splashed on the cardsharp, but he reared back as if he'd been scalded. "You clumsy oaf! Why don't you watch what you're doing?"

"You tripped me on purpose," Kit retorted, jumping up, all pepper and vinegar.

The gambler did not respond by leaping to his feet at the challenge. Instead he leaned back in his chair and hooked his thumbs in his waistcoat at chest height. "You're the same Thornton kid who was waving a gun around town. You're as crazy as your brother was crooked."

Kit started forward with his fists clenched, but I saw the outward flick of the gambler's wrist. It's a good thing I have always had a fair throwing arm, because I whipped my coffee mug around and hit the cardplayer in the forehead just as he was sliding the hide-out gun out of his sleeve. His arm flew up toward his face and the little two-barreled pistol arced in the air and clattered across two tabletops. Angie snatched it up.

Kit jumped in the middle of the man then, knocking him over backward in the chair and falling on top of him. I could not be sure that the gambler did not have another gun somewhere or a knife in his boot, but I had evened things up for the moment.

My brother and the cardplayer were much of the same build, but Kit's blood was up and his fists were flying around the man's ears and nose. King clutched Kit around the neck, and the two of them rolled over, scattering chairs.

There was the rush of boot steps from the saloon, and half a dozen faces poked into the restaurant to watch the fun.

I shoved a table across the floor to block the doorway and keep the fight from escalating into a brawl. "Private affair," I said, folding my arms across my chest.

Kit came up on top again, looking even angrier than before. "You low-down snake. I oughta tear your head off." He looked like he might do it too. How he could talk and fight at the same time, I'll never know. It made me think that maybe he was tougher than he appeared after all.

"Hold it, Kit," I warned. "Before you strangle him, let's find out who this skunk is and why he went to pick a fight with you."

"His name is Bernard King," Angie spoke up.

King looked at her as if she were a traitor. "Miss Angie, your uncle won't like you taking up for any of the Thorntons."

Keeping a wary eye on King, Kit got to his feet. King may have gotten in a lucky punch, because Kit's nose was bloodied some, but then he might have done it when he first hit the floor.

Si Denton's voice bellowed in the hallway. "Break it up! Get out of my way! Let me by here!"

"Howdy, Si." I welcomed him, moving the table aside.

"John!" he said with amazement. "Can't you keep this young hoodlum out of trouble for even one hour?"

"Just hold on there, Si," I advised. "The other fella started it—"

"That's a lie!" King interrupted.

"—and," I continued, "he drew a gun besides." I gestured toward the pistol that Angie was still holding.

"Self-defense!" the gambler claimed.

"Have you eaten yet?" Si asked me, taking his read of the situation.

"Nope," I allowed.

"Neither have I," King protested.

"He hasn't even ordered yet, Mister Denton," Angie pointed out.

King gave her a withering look.

"King, you go eat somewheres else," Si concluded. "And, John, I told you I don't want any trouble in my town."

"No trouble," I agreed. "We're just in town to have a meal and do some business, that's all."

"Keep it that way."

✻ ✻ ✻

Kit thought we'd be leaving for the sawmill right after dinner, but two things kept us in town. First, it was a lonely road and worse at night. Why make things easy for a bushwhacker intent on mischief? Second, it came to me that Miss Nell had laid uncommon stress on the word *early* when she announced her travel plans. I intended to see if I might catch a word with her before she left.

I let it be known that we were staying the night in the livery stable, but of course we did not. Kit and I slept out under the stars at the opposite end of town.

✴CHAPTER 7✴

The stage was late, and I found Miss Nell sitting atop her trunk some distance apart from the more respectable passengers. I caught her eye upon me as I emerged from the livery stable across the street. Remembering how skittish she had been about speaking to me in public, I strode first to the ticket window, where I asked what the fare to Sacramento was.

The clerk named a price, and I told him I would be back when my plans were firmed up. Was it my imagination or did he seem relieved that I might be leaving town soon? He smiled and told me there would be a place reserved for me on the outbound stage any-time I wished to go.

Thanking him, I turned and caught a glimpse of Miss Nell's kelly green, satin hoopskirt as she scooted down the alleyway between the freight office and the meat market of Lute Olds. She cast a backward glance my way. This informed me that Miss Nell would be waiting to have a word with me out back.

I did not follow her directly but entered the meat market and engaged in conversation with Lute about the going price of beef on the hoof in California. The cattle business was of interest to me, I explained. My statement sent a flash of some unexplained alarm across the features of the butcher.

Without preamble he said, "If Lucky was here, he would want me to tell you that you're makin' some people nervous by poking your nose where it don't belong."

"I hear you were a friend of my brother's."

"As much a friend as Lucky ever had." His face screwed up with some terrible thought. He swallowed hard and said, "I got a beef to cut. So long."

I thanked Lute Olds for his indulgence and left his establishment the back way.

Miss Nell was waiting for me by the rear entrance of the freight company. I walked toward her as though I meant to go past. Tipping my hat, I greeted her politely.

She gave her head a slight shake. "You do look like Lucky."

"Enough so as some gentlemen hereabouts get nervous when they lay eyes on me."

"I don't wonder." That painted mouth of hers turned up in a wide grin. "Order a side of beef from Lute, did you?"

"Small talk is all. Wanted to come out this way so as not to draw attention."

She laughed. "I'll bet Lute is all in a sweat."

"He's in on it?"

"It?" She was playing coy.

"Whatever it was that got Lucky killed."

"I'll tell you what got him killed." Miss Nell tossed her head and gazed thoughtfully toward the weather vane atop the livery barn. "He wanted to know which way the wind blew. He asked too many questions."

"Never hurts to ask."

She shrugged. "Curiosity killed the cat."

"Some cats have nine lives, I hear."

"Lucky used his all up. And you can take this little word of advice along with you: Do what I'm doing. Leave the territory before you use up your lives too."

"I want answers."

"Then ask Lucky. You'll be meeting up with him soon enough."

"Why was he hanged?" I grasped her arm and held tight.

"Let go of my arm."

I said, "Lucky was no murderer."

"I told you. He knew too much."

"That's no crime."

"Depends on what you know about whom and what you intend to do with the information."

"Blackmail? You're saying Lucky was a blackmailer?"

"And, thanks to me, someone was blackmailing Lucky right back. The problem is, I came to be fond of your brother. Furthermore, I came to pity that wife of his."

"Then help me. What did Lucky know?"

"Those details I was not privy to, else I might be strumming a harp on some cloud myself. I don't want to know more than I know."

Sensing she was telling the truth, I stepped away from her.

She smoothed the satin of her sleeve where my hand had been, then straightened her hat. "I was paid a'plenty to lure your brother away. It was not a difficult task, which leads me to believe he was no stranger to living a secret life."

"Who paid you?"

"Come now, Mister Thornton. You're not altogether a fool."

I was certain she was speaking of Major Frey, but I did not say it, lest Miss Nell bolt. I could not comprehend what Lucky had held over the major's head that led to such desperate measures.

I stuck my hands in my pockets in a gesture of resignation. "So, Lucky had something on the major, and you made sure the major had something on Lucky."

"Something like that."

"I believe you are an honest woman."

The smile crept back, only this time there was a tinge of sadness when she spoke. "Honest enough to know what I am." She lowered her eyes. "I am sorry for what happened to Lucky. I do not wish to see the same thing happen to you." She patted me on the cheek. "Leave Carson Valley, John Thornton. And when you've cooled out a bit, come look me up in San Francisco, will you? I'm opening a swank little house on the Barbary Coast. I intend to name it after myself, so you will have no trouble knowing where I am. You look enough like Lucky that I am certain you must share other fine qualities." With a tilt of her head, she kissed me on the mouth, then swished back down the alleyway, leaving me to ponder the things she had said.

✷ ✷ ✷

After Miss Nell's departure on the early stage, I had two more pieces of business. The first was to retrieve my rifle from Si Denton. His deputy, Paul Hawkins, was rummaging through a file of Wanted posters when I came in. He studied me real hard. When he looked again at the sketches of the criminals, he seemed disappointed that he could not make me match any of the descriptions.

Si gave the lever-action and Lucky's pistol to me willingly enough, but he could not let the opportunity pass without telling me once more that I'd be better off leaving town forever—preferably the whole territory.

Hawkins looked as mean as the night before and ready to shoot me, poster or no.

I said thanks for the hospitality and went on to my other transaction. With my last double-eagle gold piece I purchased a U.S. Army mule for Kit to ride back to the sawmill, while I rode Shad.

Kit considered his long-eared mule an insult to his dignity. "Why'd you have to buy an army-surplus mule?" he complained as we took off up Sawmill Road.

"All I could afford."

"That's because no fool in his right mind will own one of these beasts. You know what the U.S. brand means?" He gestured grandly at the big letters burned into the hide of the critter.

"I reckon it stands for the United States."

"Wrong!" Kit barked, shifting his seat uneasily off the creature's backbone. "Them letters mean Un-Safe at both ends!" Then he exploded, "What kinda horse trader are you, anyhow? You shoulda bought me a saddle and made old Paco throw in the mule for free."

I defended myself. "I tried that. Didn't have cash enough to buy the saddle. You don't need a saddle anyhow, Kit. Didn't Mama name you after Kit Carson? Carson rode all over the West a'bareback, Indian-style, with nothing but a blanket to sit on. Follow his example and quit grumbling."

"I'll lay odds Carson never had children," Kit muttered.

I did not let him see my amusement at his discomfort. At least his aching backside kept his mind off the Frey girl and Bernard King and the original reason he had ended up in Si's jailhouse.

In the short time since I had reacquainted myself with my youngest sibling, I had come to the conclusion that he had a lot in common with the animal he was astride. Like every mule west of the Mississippi, Kit Thornton believed he had horse sense. Truth to tell, all he had was the inclination to kick first and ask questions later.

With Kit at my side I was confident that any attempt to get to the bottom of Lucky's murder would fail. The boy was a lit firecracker waiting to explode.

I had spent a lot of time alone over the years and did my best thinking when there was no one around for miles. This morning I needed a while to study on the situation without having to listen to Kit's complaints.

Pointing straight ahead to the narrow switchback trail, I said, "I'd wrap my fingers in that pup's mane if I was you. It's a steep climb. I'd hate to see you slide off his rump."

"What! I ain't going on that trail. I would not ride up that ledge with a good horse and saddle under me! I surely will not balance my life on the knife-edge spine of a four-legged troll walking a high wire."

This was exactly what I had hoped for. Kit's contrary personality made things easy for me. I had learned to treat a muleheaded man the same as I'd corral a mule: Don't try to drive him in; just leave the gate open a crack and let him bust in. Kit was a mule who usually did the opposite of what he was told.

"Little brother, it will take you two hours longer riding if you stick to the wagon road. Don't be so fool stubborn. That mule is sure-footed as a mountain goat. Ride the shortcut with me."

"On old U.S.? He'll slide and fall for certain."

"Suit yourself, little brother," I remarked, reining Shad off the main road and letting him have his head up the steep climb.

"Don't call me little brother!" Kit bellowed.

69

I did not look back to see if Kit had followed until Shad had carried me most of the way up the pass. Gazing downward, I saw my brother plain as a fly on a white-linen tablecloth as the mule plodded along Sawmill Road. I figured Kit would have difficulty walking without aid by the time he reached home. I paused long enough to unsheathe my repeater and scan the surrounding boulders and ledges in the canyon for any sign of ambush.

The hair on the back of my neck prickled as I spotted a wisp of dust rising from a ledge on the far side of the canyon wall. There are times when a man can unwind a mile of thread from what seems like a mighty small spool. A little dust might not seem like much, but it crossed my mind that a keen marksman could be the cause of it. In this case, however, the dust was nothing more than a bobcat scrambling after a varmint.

I rested Shad on that overlook for ten minutes more just to be certain that Kit was not riding into trouble. I had a clear view all the way back to Genoa. If anyone had been trailing the pair of us I would have spotted him. Confident that the way was safe for Kit, unless he got thrown from the mule, I lit out toward the sawmill.

The sky got bluer the higher I rode. As the autumn mist cleared, so did some of the fog in my brain. I still had more questions than answers, but I began to see clearly what I would have to do in order to find the men who killed Lucky.

First off, there was the little matter of Major Frey. It seemed plain that he was connected with Lucky somehow. And what about the bandit named Edwards? He was supposedly Lucky's accomplice. If I could find him, perhaps I could get the truth out of him.

Lastly, there was the matter of how I could manage to leave Kit behind when I rode out again tomorrow morning. Bloodthirsty and vengeful, Kit desired nothing in the world so much as pumping lead into the heads of the night riders who had struck him down, then hanged Lucky.

"'An eye for an eye, and a tooth for a tooth,'" Kit had quoted when he spoke to me of that terrible night. I figured that what Kit had in mind was to make most of the men in Carson Valley toothless and blind to avenge Lucky's death.

* * *

Sawmill meadow was quiet as I rode Shad to the corral. Smoke rose from the stovepipe. I smelled the rich aroma of venison and fresh-baked bread wafting from the cabin.

I loosened Shad's cinch, hefted the saddle onto the top rail of the corral fence, then cooled out the bay before letting him drink from the trough. About a quarter of an hour had passed, and still no one had come out of the cabin to say howdy and welcome back.

Perhaps they had not heard me, although that was doubtful. I called for George. My voice echoed down the draw. After a few moments the cookshack door groaned on its hinges and Maria stepped out.

Shading her eyes against the sun, she waved broadly but not at me. I followed the line of her gaze to where George and the Volcanic rifle were perched high in a nest of boulders that he called the Rock Fort.

"Come in, George," Maria called. "It's John."

The reply echoed back, "Can't come. I can see there's a bad'n coming on a mule! Gotta keep my eye on him!"

I stepped out of the corral, cupped my hands around my mouth, and hollered, "Don't shoot him, George! That's your uncle Kit riding on that mule!"

As George skittered down the slope, I joined Maria on the porch. "I came the shortcut," I said to her gruffly. "Kit is on an old swaybacked mule. I thought I told you not to put the repeater back in George's grip where he might bag himself some two-legged critter by accident."

Hands on her hips, Maria cocked an eyebrow at me and let fly with one of her mind-your-own business looks. Not moving a step, she set me straight about the cause of George's return to sentry duty. I got the entire tale about Bernard King and Rough Elliott nearly drowning George in the water trough and killing the dog and the fact that King would surely be returning. It was Maria's intention to send the man to his eternal judgment if he ever laid a hand on her child again. The shotgun was inside where it would be handy to her if George raised a warning that danger was approaching.

When George rushed across the field to where we stood, Maria gestured triumphantly to her son. "You see he knows his duty."

"I am justly chastised, ma'am." I doffed my hat.

"So you should be, John Thornton," she said.

George piped up, "Is that Uncle Kit on that mule? Looks like that army-surplus critter Paco was trying to get rid of down at the livery. He said the old thing was costing him too much to feed. Tried to give it away, but nobody'd have it. Said if anybody had a toothache the sure cure was to stand behind that mule, and he'd get his dental work free. Paco said he'd shoot it, only he thought maybe somebody in a wagon train might be fool enough to buy it for ten dollars or so."

Maria's eyes narrowed with amusement at the blush I felt rising behind my whiskers. She said, "Paco gave you the mule, did he?"

"Practically."

She took my arm and leaned her head against it. "I know of no one more deserving to ride that mule than dear Kit."

A considerable length of time passed before the mule arrived without Kit. It waltzed up to the water trough just as pretty as you please, like as if it had lived there always.

An hour after that Kit staggered into the cabin. He was walking with his legs all a-spraddle. From the look of the ground-in clay on the seat of his trousers, he had landed on a soft spot. "Gimme a gun!" he shouted. "I'm gonna shoot it! And after that I'm gonna cut John down to a stump!"

I slipped out the back window and waited behind the outhouse. I was too full of Maria's good cooking to fight Kit. Not that I could not take him down any day of the week, but I did not fancy being punched in a full gut and losing all that good food.

Maria forbade Kit to say another word. There would be no shooting the mule or fisticuffs in her house or else. She snatched him by the ear and told him he smelled like a hog wallow. Then when his energy was squashed, she comforted my brother with the best meal he had eaten since he got himself arrested.

I waited outside long enough for Kit to finish his second plateful. If he started anything with me now, I knew just where to strike in order to put him out of commission.

Not pausing for him to speak first, I reentered the place and gave Kit a big hello. "Well, little brother, I see you made it."

"No thanks to you. And don't call me little brother."

"Did you hear your old friend Bernard King was here to pay a call yesterday?"

This made Kit sit up in his chair and leave off sopping his bread in the gravy. "Here?"

George took up the recitation from here, leaving Kit blustering and full of fight. The mule was all but forgotten.

"Let him show his face around here and I'll make him sorry for it!" Kit exclaimed.

Mindful of my need to travel fast and alone, I once more enacted my strategy for muleheaded men. "He'll be back all right." I sat down opposite Kit. "But we won't be here when he comes . . . worse luck. We're pulling out tomorrow morning."

Maria gave me a sharp look. Was that disappointment in her eyes?

Kit scoffed. "What is this *we*, amigo? I'm staying right here where I can meet that polecat."

The bait was taken. Now I set the hook. "You are coming with me, Kit. You think I would leave you here where you might get mixed up with King and Elliott?"

Maria blinked at me in disbelief. Did I intend to leave her and George to fend for themselves?

Kit said hotly, "You don't have anything to say about it now, do you? I ain't going with you, and that's the end of it!"

In this manner I managed to make the mule want to do what I wanted. "All right, then," I said grudgingly. "But you'll have to do some work around here, then."

"Name it."

"Before I can rebuild the flume, the flow of water will have to be shut off. Climb up to the head gate on top of the cliff and plug the outlet with rocks." I figured the heavy labor would serve to reduce Kit's restless spirit . . . and for a time, I was right.

Early the next morning, as I set out to find Major Frey and the highwayman Edwards, it was Kit who sat perched and watching from the Rock Fort. Maria and George and the baby had protection, and I had my way. I was alone.

✦CHAPTER 8✦

Way before sunup I was off and riding back into Genoa. It was my plan not only to slip past any watchers but to turn the tables on them by showing up where least expected. Besides that, I figured Major Frey was a methodical man—a creature of habit—and I meant to turn his habits to my advantage.

Behind the barbershop was a bathhouse. In point of fact, it was a lean-to shed stuck on the back of the one-room frame building, but it had an outside door that could be bolted from the inside.

I hammered on the front door of the tonsorial establishment and roused the little Mexican fella who operated the place. I could hear him grumping in Spanish as he arose from his cot in the corner of the room and shuffled across the floor.

"*Bueños dias, amigo,*" I greeted his sleepy face, "I am in need of a hot bath and a shave and a haircut."

"Come back later, señor," was the reply. "The shop, she is closed."

"It's worth *ocho reales* if I can get cleaned up right away," I offered. "I need to look sharp to meet my gal."

I calculated this to be an irresistible combination. The Spanishers are incurable romantics, so that was one appeal. The other ingredient in my persuasion was that I had offered him eight Mexican coins that were the equivalent of a dollar for services that usually traded for two bits.

"Come in. Come in, señor," he agreed, bowing and smiling. He put a white smock on over his undershirt and bustled around setting a tub of water to boil on the bathhouse woodstove.

"One more thing," I added, heading toward the back room. "I like a good, long wash to soak off all the real estate I'm wearing, *sabe*? Don't be trying to sell my bathwater before I'm finished with it."

"Oh no, señor," the short shear master agreed. "It is yours for as long as you wish."

I poured a bucketful of hot water into the tin washtub and mixed it with cool rainwater from a barrel mounted on the wall. I swirled it around from time to time so Señor Gomez would know that I had not drowned, but mostly I sat and waited.

Another customer showed up while I studied the shop through a knothole. I thought about striking up a conversation about Frey and King and Rough Elliott to see if he knew anything, but when you go out to hunt grizzlies, you should not waste time chasing rabbits. The man, who must have been a banker by his clothing, got his shave and his hair dressed with lime water and then took his leave.

The next two men who came along looked and smelled like they needed bathing, but that was not what they were after. Seems they had spent too much time in the company of tarantula juice the night previous. Señor Gomez had a renowned spider-bite cure for just such a need. The boys must have had heads in terrible need of shrinking back to their hat sizes, on account of they watched the barber mix raw eggs, cayenne pepper, vinegar, and bicarbonate of soda into a frothy, slimy mess, and they each took a slug anyhow. They even muttered thanks before staggering back outside.

This sideshow was all very amusing but not profitable for me until the fourth patron arrived. It was the major, come at last. I held back until he had his beard all wrapped in a hot towel; then I called out to Gomez, "Hey, señor, you got any seegars? I want a smoke with my soak."

When the barber replied that he had no cigars, I told him I'd give him another fifty cents to fetch me some. I heard him ask permission from the major, who grunted his consent. Then the door opened and closed, and the major and I were alone.

Through the knothole I saw that Frey's tan, knee-length frock coat hung on a brass hook near the door. He wore a gray plaid waist-coat and gray-checked trousers. An oval of the major's face could be glimpsed in the center of the swathing.

I came out of the back room scrubbing my hair as if it were wet. "Howdy," I said.

"How do," he acknowledged without seeming to know who I was. "What brand do you smoke? I have a couple here in my pocket if you'd like one."

"No, thanks," I said. "I don't believe in taking things under false pretenses."

At that, the major's eyes widened from their drowsy, relaxed condition. "What do you mean by that?" he inquired, starting to sit upright.

I put my palm in the center of his chest and pushed him back down. "I'm John Thornton, and I mean to ask you some questions."

"I do not conduct business from a barber's chair," he said bluntly. "You may come to my office."

"This suits me fine," I said, leaning on the buttons of his waist-coat with the heel of my hand. "We won't get interrupted here."

"Are you threatening me?" he demanded. "If so, I'll have you arrested."

I shook my head and laughed. "Are you hiding something, Major? I don't have to threaten, and you have nothing to fret about if you can tell me truthfully what you know."

That settled him some. He could tell that bluster would not make me leave, and he could read in my eyes that I was deadly serious. "All right," he agreed. "Ask."

"What do you know about my brother's death?"

Shrugging, Major Frey answered, "No more than anyone else. Your brother met his death at the hands of men who believed him to be guilty of murder and other crimes. He had been accused of thieving as well as harboring criminals. Most folks say he got what was coming to him."

"Is that what you say?"

Weighing his words carefully, the major replied, "I won't deny that we had our differences when it came to business. He never forgave me for besting him at the sawmill business or for winning large sums from him at cards."

"You beat Lucky?" I said, sounding amazed. "I never knew him to lose unless he meant to."

"Maybe the game was not to his liking."

This was a thinly veiled way to accuse Lucky of being a cheat without really using those words. I don't know if the major said it to get a rise out of me, but I made no response, and he continued. "You know he threatened my life?"

"What was that?"

The major nodded vigorously as if he was anxious to convince me that he had been wronged. "I heard from Lute Olds that Lucky said he'd pay cash money if someone would kill me."

Señor Gomez returned right then with a fistful of cigars that he extended to me.

I flipped him the quarters. "Give the cigars to the major. I owe him something for the conversation. By the way, Major," I concluded, "there is just one more thing. I intend to keep looking till I find out the truth, and then heaven help you if you lied to me."

"Is that a threat?" he asked.

"Nope. No matter what some other black-hearted scoundrels may think, it's high time that the rule of law really came to this territory. I'll see that the proper authorities take care of it, and you'll get the fair trial that Lucky never saw."

☀ ☀ ☀

Si gave me a description of the man named Edwards. The paper on him from the Placerville killing described him as thin, two inches below six feet in height, with light brown hair and a beard. Most importantly, he was said to have a notch in one ear from an old gunshot wound.

"But even if you catch up with him, what will it prove?" Si asked me. "Do you think he'll confess to murdering Gordier and put his own neck in a noose?"

"No," I said slowly, "but I have to start somewhere if I'm ever going to untangle this knot. Somebody tried to connect my brother with a man wanted for murder. He may know why. Besides, Si, you wouldn't object if I brought in a wanted man, would you?"

Shaking his head to show he thought I was crazy, Si wished me luck and slapped Shad on the rump to speed me out of town.

From the steps of the Frey Hotel, Bernard King watched me as I passed that way. It was clear that a lot of folks were very interested in my comings and goings.

I had given out to Si and others that I was headed to the Honey Lake country, the same region as the last reported whereabouts of Edwards. But that was just to put any followers off my trail.

In actual fact, my plan was to ride out north, then double back through a canyon till I could circle around to Hope Valley to the south and west of Genoa. I was minded again to see if I could locate Snowshoe Thompson. He knew all the gossip in those parts, and if anyone matching Edwards' looks was anywhere around, he would know of it. More than that, if one of the vigilantes had let slip a single word of their participation in my brother's hanging, Snowshoe would know.

My scheme evidently worked. A plume of dust behind me on the road north showed at least one pursuer, but my swerve behind a barn-sized boulder went unremarked. Shad and I made our way out of Carson Valley, looped behind the Old Emigrant Trail, and soon found ourselves again at Snowshoe's place.

This time I was in luck. A trickle of smoke rising from the stove-pipe of his cabin and a shirt and two pairs of unmentionables drying on a rock were evidence that the letter carrier was at home.

The tall, lean frame of the man straightened from bending over a washtub when he heard the hoofbeats of my approach. He shielded his eyes for a minute and then waved me to come up to his home. "John Thornton!" the long-bearded Thompson exclaimed. His accent made my first name sound like Yon, and I was pleased that he recognized me.

The inside of Snowshoe's home was just as I remembered it, but then it looked like hundreds of other log cabins, including one I had built myself once. It was a single room with a door that faced south and a fireplace built against the solid rock face that formed the north wall. On the hearth were a coffeepot, a fry pan, and a Dutch oven. Leaning in a nearby corner were the eight-foot-long, flat, wooden snowshoes that gave Thompson his nickname. Since winter can arrive in the Sierras as early as October, it would not be long before he pressed them into service again.

A table occupied the center of the room. Its top was embellished with fanciful curlicues by Showshoe's jackknife, the result of many a lonely night's carving. On the table rested most of his worldly goods: tin plates and cups, bottles of molasses and vinegar, boxes of salt and sugar, and a well-thumbed Bible, recovered in buckskin. Dried strips of meat hanging from the rafters completed the domestic arrangements.

"A bad business 'bout your brotter," Snowshoe began. "Very bad indeed. You vill find who done it, yah?"

"Why I'm here," I agreed. "Hoping you could point me in the right direction."

Snowshoe stroked his chest-length beard and pondered. "It is strange. I don't hear notting. Oh, sure, I hear vat day say your brother did, but no von brags about his killing."

I was disappointed, but a cold trail could warm up suddenly with the right turning. "What about Edwards? Who told you he was in the Honey Lake country?"

Snowshoe thought a moment. "It vas a gambler fellow. King, I tink his name is."

I nodded. Snowshoe had deliberately been fed the wrong information. King had known that Thompson's report would send Si Denton on a wild-goose chase. "Lucky was supposed to have this Edwards as an accomplice. Have you seen anyone matching his description?"

The mail carrier looked puzzled. "Why you tink he be around here?"

"Just a hunch," I said. "I think Si Denton and the posse were deliberately sent away from Genoa in the wrong direction. Since I don't think Edwards would go back toward Placerville, the only direction left is this way, toward Border Ruffian Pass."

Showshoe said nothing as he stood and went to his cot. Reaching beneath it, he produced a leather pouch and a pair of clay pipes. "It makes sense, vat you say. I need to smoke and tink on it some. You vant to join me?"

I shook my head. "I passed a covey of quail in a draw a ways back. The least I can do is get us fresh meat for supper." I wondered if Snowshoe had guessed that his unknowing role in the deception had led, in part, to my brother's capture and hanging.

His head already wreathed in a blue haze of smoke, Snowshoe waved me toward the door. It was plain from the faraway expression on his face that he was casting up Edwards' portrait alongside men he had met in his travels.

✳ ✳ ✳

After a supper of fried quail, Snowshoe reared back on his bench and screwed up one eye. This was a sure sign that he was about to deliver either information, innuendo, or advice; Snowshoe dispensed all three with equal enthusiasm.

"I gif your man Edwards some tought," he said, scratching a match on the plank floor and lighting an after-dinner pipe. "And dere is someone who could be him. Mind you, I do not say he is de one, only he could be."

"Whereabouts?"

"As you say, it vas down in Border Ruffian country across de pass at Bone's Toll Station. Man named Tick runs it now. Anyvay, a feller who looks like your man sat in a corner by himself."

"Did he act suspicious or nervous?"

"No, but he kept playing with his hair, like a girl with pigtails, pulling on it so." Snowshoe demonstrated what he meant by yanking on his own graying locks.

It was a far piece to Bone's Toll Station—a good two-day ride and a chilly one at eight thousand feet above sea level and the turn of the season past. It was not a journey to make lightly, especially to leave Maria and the others alone to no purpose. Snowshoe was waiting for my response. "Lot of brown-haired, medium-sized men grow their hair long," I said. "Anything more?"

"Yah," Snowshoe agreed. "I hear a stage driver ask dis feller's name just as Tick trow down a bowl of beans. Dis man jump vhen de bowl tump on de table." Showshoe's eyes were sparkling. He was plainly spinning out his news for all he was worth and enjoying the suspense. "Den he sputters like Tick's coffee vas choking him, vich I do not say is not possible."

"Snowshoe," I warned, "get on with it."

"Dat is all," he concluded, looking offended at my lack of enthusiasm. "He says his name is Ed . . . Ed Coombs, but I swear he start to say someting else. And, Yon—" now Snowshoe's kindly eyes showed concern—"I hear someting else at Bone's. I hear dat Indians been raiding and stealing cattle down dat vay. You vatch yourself."

✳ CHAPTER 9 ✳

bove Snowshoe's cabin at Diamond Springs the road forked into a choice between west and south. West lay the route through the Carson Pass toward Placerville, over which I had lately come. South continued the Old Emigrant Trail through Hope, Faith, and Charity Valleys, past Blue Lake, and over Border Ruffian Pass.

Bidding Snowshoe good-bye with thanks, I directed my course southward, up from the country of sagebrush and rocky gullies into God's own landscape. Reading the signs, I could tell that someone driving a small herd of cattle had passed that same way not long before.

There surely was some beautiful scenery that direction. Just beyond Charity Valley I came across a long slope covered in lodge-pole pines and red cedars. Shad and I rode upon a promontory to survey a big meadow, fully two hundred acres in space, spread below us. The stream through its middle was winding and bubbled over ripples that begged a man to hunt him up a cane pole and some worms. The course of the creek was bordered with quaking aspens, their fluttering leaves turning golden yellow. From my point of rock the aspen trees looked like thirty-foot-tall flames in both shape and color.

The road ahead was plain enough, but I took advantage of the high ground to survey the distance. Though I could see no fumes, I caught a whiff of campfire smoke. Shad must have noticed it too, because I saw an interested set to his head. When I followed his gaze,

I spotted it at last—a covered wagon mostly sheltered by the over-hanging boughs of a cedar on the far side of the meadow.

Back in the days of the great westering of the '40s and the gold rush stampede in '49 and '50, this had been a well-known route into El Dorado and points south. There were stretches where the trail crossed hard-pan rock that was worn into ruts by the passage of the wheels. Scarified trees sported bark calluses that would forever show the rubbing of countless hubs. But what with regular stage service by way of the Carson Pass now, few new arrivals ventured down this way anymore. Mostly the Old Emigrant Trail was traveled by folks who already had some reason to be heading down to Calaveras Country.

Whoever this party was, they had made a precious late start of it. Camping this time of year was an invitation to wintering over with-out planning to do so. Those left from the Donner folks could tell of such an experience. Still, there was no sign of snow in the sky yet, and these travelers should be all right.

I shaped my course toward their layout, hoping for a cup of cof-fee and a friendly word.

Viewed from a couple hundred yards distant, there seemed to be no one about the immigrant camp. What with all the possibilities for rustling up mule deer and brook trout, that was not too surprising. Something bothered me about the setup, though, even if I could not put my finger on it. The rig looked well-cared for, its canvas cover made of whole cloth and not patchwork. Just beyond it, even further hidden by the shadows of the trees, were the remains of the campfire I had smelled.

"Hello, the camp!" I hollered as I drew nearer. Politeness called for such an announcement, but personal safety was another factor. Newcomers to the West tended to be nerved up when it came to Indians and outlaws. After George had come near to parting my hair with a bullet, I really did not care to give anyone else a turn.

In reality there was precious little for travelers to fret about. Cholera, accidents from tomfoolery with firearms, and drownings had far and away accounted for more deaths on the trail in one year than all the hostile attacks put together. Add in the tenderfeet who had gone to glory by arguing with long-haired whiskey drinkers and Indians as a threat were downright overrated.

The local tribes, mostly Washoes, Paiutes, and a sprinkling of Miwoks, had never done more than drive off herd beasts and such. The last Indian raid on a mining camp had been clear back in 1853 and had brought fearful reprisals on innocent and guilty alike.

Coming upon a newcomer encampment churned all these thoughts in my mind. I wondered if they had also heard tell of new Indian troubles and if they were lying low and spying on me because of it. "Hello, the camp," I called again, though I was naught but a hundred yards away now and they must certainly have heard my arrival. "I'm friendly."

It was then that what had bothered me became plain: Not only were there no people about, neither were there animals. Where were the oxen or mules that had pulled these wagons to this lonely spot? Even if their human masters were out foraging, the critters should have been grazing in the nearby grassland. That was precisely the reason why a traveling party would stop in that place. For that matter, where were the rest of the cow critters whose fresh tracks I had seen earlier? I should have caught up with them by now.

Shad snorted and drew up sharp. His ears were pricked forward, but they flicked toward the rear, and the skin of his neck twitched. I have never been the easily agitated sort myself, but I had learned from long experience that paying attention to animal signals can save your hide. Long ago, Shad's timely warning of a nearby grizzly mama and cub had convinced me that he was trustworthy.

With the ring of trees around me and the open meadow behind, I was too easy a target for an unseen watcher. Without giving any notice of my intentions, I swung Shad's head toward a big pine tree and put in the spurs.

The bay covered the distance in a pair of bounds, one of which took him over a four-foot-high fallen log. I slipped off his back and shucked my repeater from its scabbard in the same motion.

From behind that tree trunk I surveyed the encampment with a different eye. Too silent and too still could mean a trap, but for who? No one knew I was coming this way—or so I hoped.

A flash of crimson from a spot beyond the wagon caught my attention. Something was nearly hidden in a clump of dark red manzanita, but whatever this was had a brighter color than the bark of the shrub.

Leaving Shad ground-tied back of the log, I circled to the left, ducking from tree to tree and looking over my shoulder real regular. No sounds came to me, and no gunshot rang out when I took my slouch hat off my head and raised it on a branch. The back of my neck prickled, and I shivered once, but I continued on toward that clump of manzanita just the same.

There I saw a man lying in the brush. He was dead. What I had spotted as a gleam of scarlet was his blood-covered shirt. A pair of arrows pierced his back between the suspender cords holding his striped britches. He would never see his twenty-fifth birthday.

I found his partner in a gully about twenty yards away. Much the same age, he also was shot with an arrow in the back. When I turned him over, his chest had another wound just over his heart.

These were Paiute arrows by the look of them. My read on what happened was that the two men had been sitting peaceable, drinking coffee around their campfire, when a party of savages jumped them. The fact that neither man had a weapon to hand suggested that the Indians had approached and pretended to be friendly before bushwhacking and slaughtering the pair. The second feller must have been a regular bull for strength, I guessed. His chest wound had bled considerable, but he had been able to run off a ways before his attacker put an arrow in his back to finish him. There was not even much blood on the man's back, him having almost bled to death before.

It took me the rest of the afternoon to bury the pair there under the big cedar. I committed their souls to God, hoping that the two had been square with the Almighty before their deaths. I couldn't help but reflect all the while on the timing of my arrival. If I had come along sooner, could the Volcanic lever-action and I have prevented this? Of, if I had gotten my wish to share their coffee and fire, might I have shared in their death as well?

The thought made me shiver. I knew that someday I would meet my Maker—that everyone would—but I wasn't ready to do that any-time too soon. Just being near Maria again, after all these years, gave me a reason to live on.

I found papers that told me their names and a small Bible given to one of them with the inscription *Good luck out West, but come back to me soon.* It was signed *Sally.*

The documents and the Bible I tucked in my saddlebag. I would try to see that they got sent back to Sally. It was as far back to Genoa as it was on to Bone's and either would do to report the deaths, so I decided to press ahead. When the spoor of the stolen cattle turned aside from the Emigrant Road and into a side canyon, I marked the turning to show a posse later but made no move to follow.

❉ ❉ ❉

I met no other travelers between the site of the killings and Bone's Toll Station. Whether this was because of an already spreading fear of Indian attacks or not, I could not know.

Bone's was an unappealing wide spot in the road, to say the least. Established at the height of the gold-fever immigration to collect fees for road maintenance, it also served as a meal stop for man and beast. But nothing better described its character than its nickname: Old Dry Bones. The roof was swaybacked like a broken-down horse, and the three remaining props holding up the porch were trying to run away south. The interior smelled as if all the chinks in the log walls had been stuffed with rancid bear fat, which they probably had.

The current proprietor was called Mr. Thick, and this was equally as good a description as it was a name. He was almost as big around as he was tall, and he wore a floor-length apron that came up under his armpits. It seemed to me that the apron was the same as I had noted on a previous owner some years earlier, but then one streak of axle grease looks much like another.

Mister Thick invited me to turn Shad into the corral with two other horses and a brace of mules. One of those horses, a palomino, had the look of a champion about him: long, ground-covering legs and big hocks for drive.

"Fine-looking animal," I commented. "Yours?"

Thick muttered something in reply and suggested that we join the guests inside.

I grabbed his elbow outside the door to have a word before entering. "You know about the Indian trouble?"

"Know about it?" he sputtered. "If I had that Snowshoe Thompson here I'd wring his scrawny neck! His wild stories have got everybody panicked clean back to Salt Lake! Ain't nobody crossing this trail no more, and what he says is all tall tales!"

"Lower your voice," I muttered. "It's real. I just buried two men on the other side of Border Ruffian Pass. They were shot full of Paiute arrows and their stock run off."

I looked to see if Thick would turn pale at the news, but beneath three days' beard and a layer of other substances, it was impossible to tell. "You figger they'll come this way?"

"I doubt it," I said. "They got what they were after. But somebody needs to know and get up a posse."

Thick nodded. "I'll get word to the sheriff, but I don't know how many volunteers he'll find."

"One more thing. Is there a man name of Coombs hereabouts?"

Thick's eyes narrowed, and he studied some high mare's tail clouds before he replied. "Nope, don't ring no bells."

"Brown-haired man, about your height, with a notch missing out of one ear."

"That don't bring nobody to mind neither. Why? What's he done?"

"Did I say he had done something?"

That ended the conference. I took my gear off the fence rail and entered the station.

If I had thought to find Coombs—or rather, Edwards—waiting for me inside, I was mistaken. Instead there was a troupe of actors and actresses from a traveling company. They were on their way from the mining towns of Calaveras County to winter quarters in Carson Valley when their wagon had chosen this spot to bust a wheel. Three men and three ladies comprised the company, and none could possibly have been Edwards.

They were yammering something fierce, picking on their leader mostly, as if he had personally caused their misfortune. That tall, white-haired man with the aristocratic nose was trying to soothe them, saying that it would only mean a delay of a day or so, but they seemed to be as unimpressed with the comforts offered by Bone's Station as I was.

I settled myself in a corner of the room and pulled my hat brim down a bit. I watched Thick shuffle around the room, ladling plates of beans out of a cauldron. When one of the ladies complained that her dish was none too clean, Thick graciously took it, wiped it on his apron, and set it back down in front of her. I noted that she seemed to lose her appetite after that.

After getting everyone served, Thick said he would go see to the horses, and out he went.

I counted to ten, picked up my repeater, and slipped out the back door.

As I had guessed, after tossing a few bundles of grass into the corral, Thick headed into the woods, away from the station. He kept looking back over his shoulder, but I had enough woodcraft in me to always be behind cover when he did so.

About a hundred yards across a clearing there was a lean-to built against a rock. Thick looked around once more, then slipped inside. A minute later he emerged and retraced his steps, with me watching all the while from behind a screen of willows.

After he passed by me, I levered a shell into the repeater and cocked the hammer back. The lean-to had no windows and only one door, which I approached as soft as a whisper. From inside I could hear rustling and clattering . . . the sounds made by someone in a hurry to pack up.

I kicked open the door with the Volcanic held waist high.

A medium-sized man dropped the satchel into which he was stuffing his shirts and stooped toward a Colt Baby Dragoon that was lying on the floor.

"I wouldn't touch that pistol just now if I was you," I warned.

"Who are you, and what do you want?" the man asked in a squeaky voice.

"I'm the federal ear inspector on my rounds," I said. "And I'm here to see yours. Now flip that hair back."

Reluctantly, but complying in the face of my rifle's persuasion, he did so. The top of his left ear was shy about half an inch of its circumference.

"Coombs," I confirmed, "or Edwards. Which is it?"

"It was self-defense," he argued. "It was him or me. What else was I supposed to do? Let him kill me?"

"Pipe down," I ordered. "My name is Thornton, and I'm taking you back to Genoa."

"Genoa?" he asked with a puzzled look. "Don't you mean Placerville?"

"I know that you're wanted in Placerville, but this matter concerns my brother's lynching over in Carson Valley."

"You're gonna shoot me in the woods!"

I shook my head. "Not if you don't try to run. I want the truth out of you, and then you'll be turned over to the authorities, but I have no plan to act like them who executed my brother. Now get your things."

CHAPTER 10

ow that I had located Edwards, it was in my mind to take him back to Genoa for Si Denton to hold. Then I would send word for the territorial marshal to come, even if I had to go to Salt Lake City to fetch him myself.

I had Edwards back away from the pistol while I stooped and picked it up. Stuffing the Colt in my waistband, I motioned with the rifle for him to get on with his packing.

Edwards stuffed the satchel with his belongings, including a tintype of a gray-haired woman in an all-black dress with a high collar. Her expression would have clabbered milk, but Edwards was blubbering when he gazed at it. "My own dear mother," he whimpered. "She warned me not to come out West. She said I'd fall into evil companions and dire trials, and she was right. Oh, how I hate to bring this shame on her when she finds out."

This was not at all what I had expected. The man I thought I was trailing was supposed to be a hardened criminal who had killed at least twice and had no feelings of remorse. What was the game here?

"A little late for regrets now," I retorted. "I don't know about the Placerville shooting, but killing Gordier in cold blood to steal his cattle—"

"But I didn't kill Gordier!" Edwards protested. He threw up his hands in a gesture of appeal and stepped toward me. I waved him back with a warning wag of the Volcanic. "I wouldn't harm that old Frenchman. He did me nothing but good!"

Seeing as how he was disposed to talk, I was inclined to let him.

Even if I had to sort the truth from the fiction later, I might learn something. Edwards struck me as the breed of man who would do anything to save his own skin. He might even spill what he knew about someone else.

"All right," I said. "I'm listening."

Edwards sat on top of the single threadbare blanket that covered his cot. He gazed at me with a pitiful, pleading stare. "It was in a saloon in Placerville. There was a girl and a man name of Snelling—"

"I don't care about Placerville," I reminded him. "What happened after?"

It was getting dark outside, and the inside of the shack was steeping in gloom.

"I got away by stealing a horse," he admitted. "I thought they were gonna lynch me without a trial!"

"It's been known to happen," I said dryly. "Go on."

"This was a racehorse, see? Bald Hornet. Ever hear of him? Fastest horse I ever seen, I—"

"Friend," I said abruptly, "you are sorely trying my patience, which is already in short supply. Now either get to the point or I might change my mind and haul you back to them Placervillians."

Swallowing hard, Edwards wiped his stubble-covered face. "I distanced the posse, and when I come to Hope Valley, I hid out with Gordier. He took me in, see, on account of I knew him when I first come West. Said he'd hide me till the trouble blew over. I didn't kill him! He was my friend!"

"So what happened?"

Edwards cast a look toward the door.

A glance told me he was ready to bolt. "Don't even think it," I cautioned. "You can't outrun a lead slug."

That settled his hash a mite, and he continued. "One day late last spring, the old man sent me out to check on a calf. Said he thought a lion had got it. When I come back, he was dead!"

"How do you mean?"

Edwards shouted, "Dead, I tell you! There was blood all over and the ax that killed him still lying on the floor. I picked it up. . . ." He shuddered all over, like a man with a fatal chill. No matter what else

91

he might be concocting, this emotion was genuine. "That's when they showed up."

"Who's they?"

"I don't know their names! A gent, a big man, and another smaller feller. Got the drop on me. Said I'd hang for certain. I tried to reason with them. Told them what happened, same as I'm telling you. They said it wouldn't wash, that I was good as hanged unless . . ."

"Unless what?"

But the discharge of words had halted as quickly as it started. Edwards had gone from being unable to control the gush of his tale to a stony silence.

"Unless what?" I repeated.

"I'm not saying any more," he vowed.

"Why not?"

"Not till you get the marshal and the judge. I don't want to die. Not by lynch mob and not by those men neither!"

"Just tell me what you know about them."

Edwards shook his head.

I was sorely tempted to crack him across the teeth with the barrel of the repeater, but I refrained. "Then get up!" I said roughly. "We're going back to Genoa now, tonight."

Edwards marched out the door ahead of me like a man resigned to his fate, like a man in control of himself. Like a man who had an ace up his sleeve.

The chunk of stove wood that hit me in the back of the head might have been a whole giant redwood falling out of the forest for the effect it had on me. The rifle flew out of my hands, and I pitched forward. Just before I hit the ground I had time to call myself a few choice names for being so stupid. Edwards had been playing for time until his accomplice arrived. And I had fallen for it.

✳ ✳ ✳

A woman's heart-shaped face, framed by cascades of dark ringlets, was hovering over my head when I came to my senses again. "Maria?" I murmured hopefully, rubbing my hand across my eyes in a futile effort to brush the fog away.

"No, more's the pity," the lady answered. "From the tone of your voice I'd say you must care for her a whole lot."

I struggled to sit upright and made it about halfway before a lightning bolt ripped through my skull and I sank back with a moan.

"Easy," the woman cautioned. "Don't get in a hurry. You've had a blow that should have cracked your head like an egg. Tess has gone to fetch the men to help you into the station. I'm Lavinia."

"Coombs . . . I mean, Edwards . . . where did he go?"

My vision clearing at last, I could see that my words made no sense to Lavinia. "I don't know who you mean, unless it's the fella who took out of here with Thick."

"They're both gone?"

Lavinia nodded. "We were just beginning to wonder where our portly host had gotten off to when he and the other man came tearing out of the woods. They wouldn't stop to answer any questions, just saddled up and took off. Knocked Tyrone down—that's our manager—when he tried to find out what was up."

So that was who had clobbered me. Edwards had played me like a hooked fish until Thick returned to the cabin. That explained why Edwards had talked so loud at times—to let his accomplice know how to get ready. I struggled to my feet, with no more than a few Independence Day fireworks going off in my head. I needed to get on their trail and fast.

A white-haired man came puffing up the path about then. With him was a blonde gal and another man. "What is it, Lavinia? Bandits? Did that cursed proprietor flee and leave us to our fate?"

Lavinia, who seemed calmer and more sensible than the rest, answered by pointing to the knot on the back of my head. "It seems that Mister Thick and another man have waylaid Mister . . . Mister?"

"Thornton," I supplied.

"Thornton," she repeated. "And then they decamped."

"Leaving us undefended?" squeaked the blonde, much to the evident embarrassment of the two men.

"There's nothing much to be afraid of now," I said. "Thick has just helped a man wanted for murder, so I'd say the danger is gone. Just show that you are wary, and the Indians won't bother you."

"Indians!" all of them exclaimed.

I had forgotten that they did not know about the killings, so I had to explain. This undid all the reassuring I had tried to do. "Where's your broken wheel?" I asked, trying to get back to practical considerations.

"Thick sent it to a blacksmith in Tamarack," one of the men answered. "He promised to have it back tomorrow."

I nodded. Tamarack was a village several miles down the road. "You'll be safe here tonight. Tell the blacksmith what I said. Then you can either wait here for the posse to escort you through or turn back the way you came."

"What about you?" Lavinia wanted to know.

"I'm going after Thick and the other man."

There was some argument about my condition and the sense of riding at night, but I was determined not to give them too long a head start. With luck, Shad and I might catch up to them by sunup.

"I'm afraid," Lavinia said, "that they've stolen your horse."

* * *

Shad was gone and so was the palomino. Thick had opened the corral gate and turned out the last horse and the mules. His intent was to prevent any possibility of my following, but he had been in too big a hurry to do the job right. The critters had only run off as far as the meadow behind the station.

I found a sack of grain and rattled some in a tin cup. Soon enough I had a bridle on the remaining horse. He was old enough to vote, by the look of him, and not built for speed, but he was sound. Fortunately for me, the fugitives had not thought to take my saddle or rifle with them, so I rigged up my gear and headed out into the night.

Lavinia had told me that the pair of renegades had galloped east, back toward Border Ruffian Pass. There was a full moon rising over the crest of the Sierras, and I was soon making good time.

Some might question my decision to follow at night, but I knew the country roundabout. There were precious few places where a man could break new trail through the brush without leaving a sign that stood out like an old man with a young wife.

What's more, I had a secret weapon. This unexpected advantage was actually because they had stolen Shad. The wind was coming from the southwest, directly behind me. That circumstance meant that whenever I drew close to them Shad would smell me coming, and when he did he would try to get back to me or give me a call of welcome.

All in all, I felt pretty sanguine about my chances of overtaking them, despite the lump on my head. What would take place when we met up was something else again. That they would fight was a certainty, but it was equally clear that I needed Edwards alive. Who were the men who had confronted him at Gordier's? Had he really been framed for the killing, or had that all been part of the ruse? What did he know about my brother?

After a couple hours of steady riding I was crossing the boulder-strewn reaches of Petrified Valley. Here I was near the headwaters of rivers that flowed down into Calaveras County. In the glow of the moon's orb sailing high, the shadows on the land were sharp as daytime. Every ancient petrified tree stump had skull-like features and deep-set eye sockets. It reminded me that the old Spaniards had named the region Calaveras—"Calvary"—for the bones of all the dead Indians they had discovered there, unburied a century after some forgotten quarrel.

The landscape around me was littered with fallen trees and antique stumps long since more rock than timber and eerily frozen between life and death. It had an evil, unnatural feel, as if under some long-abiding judgment of the Lord. Pretty soon some of the ossified spars of the vanished forest began to resemble what I imagined Lot's wife and all her kin came to look like after they were turned to salt pillars for looking back at the destruction of the evil town of Sodom.

I spurred the old horse and jogged on. His hooves clattered over some loose stones. Then, amid the sharp rattle of the rocks, I thought I heard Shad whinny. It was a soft sound, still a ways off, but unmistakably his call.

Throwing a loop of lead rope around Lot's dearly departed, I shook myself out of spooky tales and back to practical concerns. Ahead of me was a brace of men with at least a pistol and maybe more weaponry. If I did not want to become part of this eternal graveyard, I needed to use caution.

From stub to boulder to heap of stones I dashed, always trying to look more like part of the shadowy countryside than a living intruder. Popping out from behind a granite-hard tree and flinging myself into a gully, I made unintentional acquaintance with a skunk. Luckily for me I made my exit before he could load and fire.

There was a broad expanse of open ground just ahead of me. For a good thirty yards there would be no cover unless I backtracked and circled around, but that would cost precious time. Time was not something I was willing to waste. If I was concerned about walking into their fire, I was also worried they would hear my approach and decide to flee instead of fight. I did not want this chase to go on much longer.

While I was still debating what to do, Shad whinnied again. Silently I urged him to be quiet and not give the game away. In the meantime I had reached my decision. I slithered forward on my belly, thankful that the nights were now chilly enough to have driven the rattlers underground—or so I hoped.

I had crossed perhaps half of the exposed area when I heard a footfall and then another, coming directly toward me. I froze, sliding the repeater forward an inch at a time.

The rifle was still not where I wanted it when the noise of someone treading on the rocks came again, almost close enough to touch. A long shadow stretched out across the stone table and reached for me as if seeking to grab me.

I rolled over to free the lever-action and snapped to my knees. "Freeze. I've got you dead to rights!" I was hoping a little bluff would make up for my bad position. It would scarcely make it worse.

Without a reply the shadow and the footsteps came forward, falling across me there as if the weight of the darkness could pin me to the moonlight-drenched scene.

It was Shad. Obedient to my unspoken request, he had stopped calling for me but had still ambled forward to locate me.

I stood up slowly, aware of the fact that a cunning enemy might play just such a trick—send my horse out to find me and turn the tables on my scheme. I had not thought either Thick or Edwards to be that clever.

I rose and slid my hand up the stirrup leather, using the horse's bulk to shield my movements. I had just reached full upright with my hand on the cantle of the saddle when my fingers encountered something wet and sticky. Even by moonlight it was not difficult to interpret—it was blood.

Shad and I traveled together across the mesa. I retraced his route as best I was able, judging by the direction from which he had appeared and the compass point from which I first heard him call. It took no great trail craft to know that foul play was afoot. But whose blood was it? Did it belong to Edwards or to Thick or to an unknown? And who had spilled the blood? Was it the Paiutes again, an accident, treachery, or something else altogether?

These thoughts were a mental exercise that did nothing to relieve the tension of the hour. Any combination of them might still spell trouble for me. If it was possible, I slunk forward even more cautiously than before.

Shad stopped for no reason I could see or hear. He seemed reluctant to go forward, and a ripple of nervousness passed over his hide. He was once again giving me plenty of warning . . . but about what?

A low groan came from the darkness ahead of me. Almost a sigh, it was a sound of such weariness and misery that I was half inclined to credit the Indian tales of what baneful spirits inhabited that ridge. But not many ghosts call for water, and if it was a Paiute spook being canny, well, it also spoke English.

"Water," the weak voice croaked again, and in that moment I recognized the pitch as Edwards'.

It still might be a trap, so I dropped into a crouch and surveyed the surroundings. Even in the dark some things look natural and proper. What I was scanning for was something out of place—a shape that did not fit.

Just ahead of me a pair of petrified logs lay tumbled together. The moon illuminated the space between their trunks, right up to the point where they crossed. Exposed to view ahead of that shade was a tree limb . . . except that it looked wrong. It was bent funny, and it did not sparkle like the mineral-laden surface of the fossilized timber.

And then it moved.

Edwards was gut shot when I found him and nearing the end of his string. I fetched my canteen, knowing that nothing I could do would postpone his death. At best I could ease his passing.

After he had taken a gulp of water, he moaned, "Thick did this to me! I told him I wouldn't talk . . . don't shoot! I'll keep still! Don't!"

He was raving in his agony, but when he quieted, I urged him to make his peace with his Maker.

"I can't pray!" he cried. "Help me, stranger! Help me pray! I betrayed a man to his death, and I'm lost . . . lost!"

What a dilemma was here before me. The one source of information about my brother's fate was in my hands, and the man was dying, one ragged breath at a time. How I wanted to wring what he knew from him . . . to threaten him with hell's fire if he did not instantly confess all he knew!

98

But I did not. It was not because of some innate goodness of my own but purely because I knew that we all have to face the terrors of the dark hour. To see Edwards gripped with horror for the way he had lived his life was to look down the road at my own mortality. When it came my time to bid the world good-bye, how would I do it? What regrets would I have? I wondered.

And so compassion stirred within me. I spoke to Edwards of the thief on the cross—a murderer and a thief justly condemned and punished. That man, brought to the very edge of the abyss, was accepted as forgiven at the moment he asked it. I urged Edwards to consider his eternal destiny. It was not too late.

And so with trembling lips and gasping breaths Edwards did ask forgiveness, and I trust that God will pardon me for eavesdropping on his confession.

"I repent of my wickedness. They told me I'd hang if I did not lie for them," he groaned. "They told me what to say, and I did it."

"Who?" I urged gently.

"Thornton. I lied about Thornton. I said he put me up to killing Gordier. Then they let me escape."

"Who?" I goaded him. "Who put you up to it?"

Edwards lurched against the tree trunk, and bloody foam appeared on his lips. When he spoke again it was with great difficulty. "Penrod . . . and Olds," he said at last.

This was not at all what I was expecting. "Who?" I asked again, dumbfounded.

"Said I had to convince Penrod . . . Olds . . . others . . ." he mumbled, his voice trailing off to a faint whisper.

"Who made you do it?"

"Frey . . ." He sighed, the feeble word trailing downward like a thread of spider silk drifting on the breeze.

"Why?" I demanded. "What was the cause?"

But in the fragment of time between his last reply and my question, Edwards was already in another place, before another questioner.

There was no point in following Thick any farther that night. I had found what I had sought. I would lay the evidence before Si Denton and have him send for the territorial marshal and the judge. I had no doubt that Thick would also implicate Frey when he was caught and tried for murdering Edwards.

✶ CHAPTER 11 ✶

Edwards proved to be as much trouble dead as he was breathing. I remembered a printed poster on the wall of the jail that offered a reward for the villain, dead or alive. It seemed to me that the cash offered for his capture had not been significant enough for a man to risk his life to obtain it. However, since Edwards was already dead and my pockets were altogether empty, I determined that I would bring in the corpse and trade him for bacon and beans.

The problem was, that antique relic of a horse that left me back at Bone's had turned up lame. Not just a mite lame, neither, but full-blown stove-up lame. I turned him out, knowing his instincts would drive him toward lower altitude, pasture, and water.

It was forty-five miles back to Genoa. I now had but one horse with which to haul my grisly freight. This meant I had to walk the entire distance and lead Shad. It would be slow going. Such an enterprise would take several days at a quick march. After that length of time with Edwards slung over the saddle, I figured the boy would be as ripe as old sauerkraut, stiff as a post, and bent into the permanent shape of a horseshoe. The undertaker would have to stuff him, rear-end side up, into a rain barrel in order to bury him.

I apologized to Shad as I rolled Edwards up in a length of canvas tent, bound him like a hog, and hefted him across my saddle. Expressing the sincere hope that I could find a shorter route back to Genoa, we set out at the break of day.

The first several miles of our trek lay over the well-beaten Emigrant Trail back across Border Ruffian Pass. After six hours I came to the place where the familiar road branched left through Faith, Charity, and Hope Valleys. On my right, the unnamed Indian track taken by the cattle-thieving savages snaked down a steep canyon. It seemed to me that it might cut a shorter route to the floor of Carson Valley.

I took the less-traveled route, moving at a good clip down the mountain. After an hour, we came to a clearing. I unloaded Edwards beside a heap of household goods that had been discarded by immigrants years before as they had faced the towering mountains. A rusting cookstove kept mournful company beside a mahogany picture frame and a milking stool. I took the saddle off Shad and rested him for thirty minutes, allowing him to graze where the bones of oxen bleached in the sun.

The edge of the clearing was thick with a tangle of wild rosebushes. Were these left behind by some pioneer? Had they been planted on the grave of a wife or child and then multiplied into a thicket? For a moment I considered scooping out a shallow grave for Edwards in this place, but common sense got the better of me.

I resaddled Shad and hefted Edwards onto my horse's back. Gathering rose haw, or seed pods, from the tangle of wild rosebushes at the edge of the field, I popped them into my mouth, then pocketed another handful for the journey. I had learned of this source of nourishment from the Indians, who ate the wild-rose haw like candy. It helped to stave off sickness, the Shoshone claimed, and made teeth strong. I had simply developed a taste for them.

From the meadow, we traveled down the narrow path through a succession of clearings much like the first. We entered a dense forest that rose in solemn stillness around me and cast shadows that seemed to me an almost tangible omen of approaching evil.

I told myself the uneasiness I felt was spurred on by the fact that I had none for company save a dead man, but even Shad seemed skittish about something. I began to sing hymns in order to comfort myself, but as the shadows deepened, so did my foreboding.

The sun set early. I had made only little more than half the distance

101

I intended. Still, I pushed on through the forest shadows. The moon rose full and bright in the east, lighting the mountains in a mono-chrome glow. Now I walked in silence, listening to the creeping night sounds all around me. An owl hooted as we passed below him. The rush of bat wings swept close past my head. From the canyon beyond, brush wolves began to howl with screams that resembled those of humans in torment.

I considered all the fragments of the puzzle surrounding Lucky's death—the part that Edwards and Thick had played. It was a picture somewhat like the moonlit landscape surrounding me. Gray and shadowy and full of unseen threats. I now knew more of the who but still did not have the key as to why.

I had spent nights riding herd when a newborn calf was lost in a thicket. Its mama would bawl and fret until I lit out and brought it back. In such times it came to me that the Lord knew the answer to where that baby was. Only the Lord could help me find it before some mountain lion took it home for supper. I had often found the remains of a calf, but my search had not ended there. I had then gone on to hunt the lion.

The predator who had killed Lucky was still on the loose; now he was stalking me. I felt this as I walked through the deepening shad-ows that night. I needed help that was beyond my own power, and I called upon the Lord to show me which way to walk next.

The wind rose. Clouds from the northeast passed across the moon and gave the scene an even more weird and somber character.

I said to Shad, "As long as the moon gives us light, we'll get on with it." Then I explained to my horse that if we did not press on, it would likely take three days to get Edwards back to Genoa, off the saddle, and into the barrel. Shad seemed willing to go ahead as long as I did.

The hour was late when the moon finally slipped below the west-ern peaks. Stars frosted the sky above us, but on the ground, utter blackness descended, making further progress impossible.

I unceremoniously dumped Edwards at the base of a tree some distance away. Shad was hobbled with rawhide loops around his fore-legs that enabled him to graze on the thin grass. Sensing that a campfire might draw unwanted guests, I made cold camp and fed myself dry crackers, jerked venison, and wild-rose haw.

❋ ❋ ❋

Sometimes the most confusing, tangled circumstances have the easiest solutions. Unfortunately, it is also true that just when things appear straightforward, they are most likely to get complicated or take an unexpected turn.

Such was the case with my plans.

While I was still traversing Border Ruffian Pass, keeping a sharp lookout for Indian raiders or an ambush by Thick, the real trouble was unfolding down in Genoa. And I wouldn't know it until later.

❋ ❋ ❋

Thick had ridden hard all night and made good time. And why not? He was mounted on the stolen racehorse, Bald Hornet.

He changed mounts at Frey's ranch, so as not to be too conspicuous, then went into town and tied up behind Frey's hotel. He went up the back stairs to the second floor and Major Frey's private office, where he burst in.

The major was none too pleased at the interruption either, since he had a saloon gal sitting on his lap. He jumped up abruptly, dumping the girl on the floor, where she landed with a squawk. "Get out, Phoebe," he hissed at her. "And close the door."

She got up, rubbing her backside where she had bounced off a spittoon, and left as ordered.

"What is this?" Frey demanded as soon as the door was shut. "I told you never to come here! There must not be any connection between us! Now get out, Thick! Come to the ranch tonight after dark."

"No," Thick disagreed, shaking his ponderous jowls. "You need to hear this, and it won't keep."

Something in the bearlike man's serious tone convinced Frey of urgency. He waved Thick into a chair and reseated himself. "All right, spill it."

"There's another Thornton, Lucky's brother, nosing around."

"Old news." Frey discarded the information with a wave of his hand. He extracted a cigar from a brass-bound walnut case and examined it, leaning toward a copper-and-glass smoking lamp.

"Then hear this: Thornton found Edwards. Caught him in the lean-to."

"What?" Frey said, biting the end off the cigar with more force than strictly necessary. "What did Edwards tell him, and where are they now?"

"I don't know what all Thornton knows. Edwards swore he said nothing, but I wasn't there when they were alone. I helped Edwards escape."

Frey rose from his chair and drew a Colt pocket revolver out of the cigar box. "You did what?" he shouted, waving the pistol in one hand and the stub of his cigar in the other. "You idiot! How could you let him get away?"

"Calm down, boss," Thick pleaded, spreading his mittlike palms. "I didn't say he was alive."

The major subsided, settling back in his leather chair. "Go on."

"I clobbered Thornton over the head, and Edwards and me took off. When we got clean up to Petrified Valley, I killed him."

"And Thornton?" Frey asked eagerly. "Did you finish him too?"

Thick shook his head. "I dunno. He's got an awful hard head. I could hear someone calling for me from the station, so I grabbed Edwards, and we lit out. Even if Thornton follows, he's way behind. Edwards took his horse, and I rode Bald Hornet. The palomino is at your place now."

Furrows creased the major's forehead.

Thick waited a respectful time, then carefully ventured, "There's more. Thornton found the bodies of the immigrants. He's spreading the word about the Indian raids."

The major said nothing, but gradually a smile crept across his face. "It's perfect. Two birds with one stone . . . or maybe three? Thick, you are more valuable than I thought. You've done well. Now here's what I want you to do. Go to Constable Denton. Tell him that you were on the way here to pass along information about the wanted man, Edwards, when you found the bodies of the immigrants. Tell him there needs to be a posse formed at once; then you lead them. Only don't take Bald Hornet. Leave him in my barn. I'll handle the rest. . . ."

✳ ✳ ✳

What was it that roused me from sleep? The morning air was bitter cold, as it often is in the high mountains just before sunrise. I tucked my face deeper beneath the rough wool of my bedroll and began to drift off again.

There was a moment between waking and slumber when the sound of Shad's abrupt snort jerked me back to consciousness. Right after that I heard leaves rustling beneath a shuffling footfall. Sitting bolt upright in the blue light of predawn, I strained to see who or what approached my camp.

Shad called and strained against the rawhide hobble that held him. A dark shape emerged from the thicket of manzanita and lumbered toward the canvas-wrapped corpse of Edwards. It was a young bear—a grizzly, I reckoned, by the shape of the hump on its back. It had caught a whiff of Edwards and had come for breakfast.

With a squall, it swiped at the body with its claws, rolling Edwards against the tree with no more effort than a child tossing a toy.

"Four-legged vulture," I said as the beast tore at the canvas.

Shad screamed and tried to rear. I rushed to grasp his halter and hold him steady against his terror. Tossing his head, he connected hard with my chin and sent me sprawling. I jumped to my feet and talked softly to calm my horse. Shad fought against the hobbles, lunging and stumbling as he attempted to put some distance between himself and the grizzly.

Leaving Edwards to the bear, I plunged after Shad. "Whoa up, boy," I called gently. "It's just a young'un."

It was no use. Shad had smelled the bear and would not be hindered. I let him go, figuring he could not get far with the hobbles. Better to scare the cub away from Edwards first and then catch up with my horse.

Even a young grizzly in search of food can be deadly when challenged, so I paused long enough to grab my repeater from its scabbard.

My thinking was to scare the critter off, rather than taking a chance on wounding it. Grizzlies are notoriously hard to kill. I fired a shot into the air, and the cub let out a long, mournful growl. It hesitated, then proceeded to rip at the tent fabric again.

Fumbling for my tin plate, I banged it against the rifle stock and whooped a few times as I advanced up the slope against the young marauder. Had I known what waited at the head of the trail, I would have turned and run for my life with Shad. I should have abandoned Edwards, who was past caring anyway, but it went against my grain to leave him as a meal for a bear.

Any experienced mountain man knows that where there is a young grizzly, there is likely to be an old one close at hand. Owing to the late season, I had assumed this critter had been abandoned and left to make his own way in the wild. That assumption proved to be dead wrong. I was about to meet Mama grizzly.

Three steps nearer, I gave a Paiute war cry, yelping like a brush wolf.

Baby bear gave me a worried glance over his shoulder and retreated from Edwards.

"Git!" I cried bravely, hurling a stone at him.

He bawled unhappily and scooted away a few more yards.

I was feeling something like David must have felt when he ran the lions away from his herds of sheep. Then, suddenly, as the small bear charged along the trail, an enormous black boulder came to life one hundred feet from where I stood. It was not a boulder but a mountain of Mama grizzly that reared up on her haunches and fractured the Sierras with her roar. Upright, she towered a full nine feet. A thousand pounds of fury advanced toward me. Saliva dripped from her bared fangs as she pictured me as the main course in her last supper before hibernation.

All the nearby trees had their bottom-most limbs too high for me to reach. There was no retreating that way or I would have taken it.

Dropping my dinner plate, I raised the Volcanic to my shoulder and fired at her chest, which was some ways over my head. The shot was received with yet another roar! She brushed at the wound as if it were of no more significance than a fly and continued her advance.

Malice flared in her eyes. I backed up a step and fired again. The second bullet did not stop her, nor did the third or the fourth.

Levering and firing as I continued to retreat, I knew better than to turn and run. Grizzlies can move downhill like freight trains . . . like avalanches!

All too soon the hammer fell on an empty chamber. There was no time to reload the tube magazine. You cannot call for time out when facing half a ton of buzz saw. I was a goner. Soon enough the pair of grizzlies would have two carcasses to feast on. The sow slashed at the empty air, dropped to all fours, and moved down the slope, shaking her head from side to side. She was intent on ripping me to shreds.

I stumbled backward, falling over my saddle. The rifle flew from my hands. I scrambled to open my saddlebag and groped for Edwards's pocket revolver. Thirty-one caliber was not much more than a peashooter against a beast the size of an ox and with the disposition of an alligator, but it was not in my nature to go down without a fight.

Since the bear was rumbling toward me like a wave about to dash a rowboat against a reef, I did the only thing I could think of to gain time: I started backing uphill as fast as I could, praying that the manzanita and chaparral underfoot would not trip me and become my final resting place.

The nearsighted silvertip got distracted for a moment by the saddle, which she almost knocked into the next county. Edwards received another blow that would have killed him had he not already been defunct. Then Mama grizzly caught my scent again, and her head swung back toward me.

Grizzlies are slower moving uphill than down, and the change in her onslaught made her rear up to get her bearings. It may also have been that my earlier shots were finally having an effect. When she opened her mouth to let out another bellow, I put a shot between her gaping jaws.

The bullet struck her in the back of the throat, but even before I knew this, I thumbed back the hammer and fired two more rounds in the same spot. The sow toppled over backward like a falling tree, and the cub bolted for the tall timber.

After making sure the grizzly was dead, I set about retrieving the remains of my gear and catching Shad, whose timely alert had once more spared my life. It took me some time to piece together the shreds of canvas to reload Edwards for travel.

⋆CHAPTER 12⋆

Later I found out that Si Denton was not slack about gathering a posse when he heard Thick's description of slaughtered immigrants stuck full of Paiute arrows. Deputy Hawkins rounded up Manny Penrod, Lute Olds, Curtis Raycraft, among others, and assembled them in front of the courthouse. Even Bernard King showed up.

"Men," Constable Denton said, "these murders are the worst threat to the safety of this region in ten years. We have had a season of stampeded stock and wounded drovers, but now there's been killings, and the raids must stop. Now, who'll ride with me?"

"We all will!" Raycraft asserted. "And we won't waste time about it either! Let's ride straight to Winnemucca's camp and wipe them out!"

Growls of agreement were accompanied by the brandishing of weapons.

"Now that's exactly what I will not have," Si ordered sternly. "We are after the braves who killed the two men and no others! Is that clear? I am out to bring the guilty to justice and to prevent a war, not start one. Anyone who doesn't see it my way will not be coming along, even if I end up going by myself!"

There was a great deal of grumbling at this declaration. Paul Hawkins, who was standing next to Si, murmured, "All we want to do is make good Indians out of them."

Si rounded on him fiercely. "That'll be all of that from you too, Paul! Either back my play or hand over your star!" The deputy ducked his head and said nothing further, but Si was not done lecturing the others. "This isn't about vengeance. It's about justice. That's the difference between law and mob rule! Now I say again, if you don't agree, I don't want you."

The grousing did not completely subside, but a dozen riders were mounted up and ready to head out in less time than it takes to spit. Thick led the troop into the Sierras, past Waterfords Station, and down the road into Hope Valley.

The trail narrowed in a rock gorge to where they had to walk their horses, and single file at that. Thick was riding point, followed by Hawkins on a roan, and then came Si Denton on his big, easily recognizable paint named Cimarron.

Si, old Indian fighter that he was, glanced at the walls of the ravine towering over both sides of the track. It was a perfect spot for an ambush. But such an attack was unlikely, given the strength of the posse and their obvious firepower. Any Paiutes who were this close to Carson Valley would undoubtedly have gotten wind of the pursuit and fled. Si and his posse did not expect to locate the killers until tracking them back to their encampment, and that could take days.

A flash of tawny hide appeared briefly between the gnarled trunks of a pair of wind-twisted, bristlecone pines.

"Cougar?" Paul Hawkins guessed, bending around in his saddle to ask Si if he had also seen the animal.

Si Denton opened his mouth to reply, but the response was never completed. The boom of a big-bore rifle, like a Sharps or a Springfield, split the afternoon's tranquility.

As if Si had been riding full tilt and reached the end of a tether, he snapped backward off his horse and flew through the air. In mid-flight, the constable's chest bloomed with a bright red flower.

Cimarron spooked and galloped forward, jostling Hawkins' horse as it tried to get by the confined space. Both mounts reared and plunged while Hawkins drew his pistol and scanned the ledges.

Behind him Lute Olds fired both barrels of his shotgun into the canyon wall. Bernard King drew his pocket revolver and fired straight into the air.

"Ride!" Thick yelled. "It's death to stay in here!" The big man clapped the spurs to his mount and galloped ahead.

No more shots came. Though the riders had been as much in a box trap as rats caught pilfering grain, they rode forward unchallenged. How could that be? Hawkins wondered.

"There he goes," Thick shouted, pointing ahead.

"Olds," Hawkins ordered, "you and Penrod take care of Si. The rest of you, follow me!"

The chase led up out of the canyon along a narrow ledge that opened on top of the mesa. The sniper was too far away for his features to be recognizable, but his honey-colored palomino was easy to follow. It was also plain that this was no Indian.

At first the assassin appeared headed for Border Ruffian Pass. He skirted Little Blue Lake, and that was where Hawkins and the other pursuers made a mistake. Instead of splitting both sides of the small body of water, trapping the assassin in the middle, the posse all followed the palomino along the west shore. When the fugitive reached the head of the pool, he doubled back, turning so the lake lay between him and the posse. Then the rider on the tawny horse charged up the top of the ridge and took off northward.

111

Hawkins urged his horse to its greatest effort and, after several minutes, succeeded in gaining on the escaping sharpshooter. But all the others in the posse were winded, blown, and dropping back. In his anger and frustration, Hawkins drew his Colt again, even though he knew it was long odds against hitting anything at the two-hundred-yard distance that separated the two riders. Hawkins fired, thumbed back the hammer, fired again, and was rewarded by seeing the palomino stumble.

Hawkins gave a shout of triumph, but his cry of success died in his throat. It had been only a loose rock and not a wound that made the yellow racer falter. The palomino spurted ahead, pulling away and foiling any additional shots by darting into the trees.

The deputy spurred and kicked, but his roan was spent. In a matter of minutes, the yellow horse and the shooter were completely out of sight, still heading north, back toward Carson Valley.

Hawkins reined in and waited for Thick and the others to join him. He put Thick on the track of the sniper while he himself retraced his path back toward the canyon where the constable had been shot.

He caught up with Penrod and Olds, who were headed to Genoa but not far from the place of the attack. They were pulling Si on a willow-frame travois.

"Why aren't you farther along?" Hawkins demanded. "Si's hurt bad. Why don't you hustle?"

Even as he asked the question Hawkins knew the reason. It was too late for Si Denton, and no amount of rushing would make a difference now.

"What about the killer?" Penrod wanted to know. "Did you get him?"

Hawkins shook his head grimly. "No, but if we catch him before he has a chance to change mounts, we'll know him by that palomino."

✳ ✳ ✳

It took me some time to get ready to leave the scene of the combat with the bears, but my legs were still trembling. They say that some folks feel weak in the knees when facing danger, but with me, I have always found that the shakes come afterward. Perhaps if I had better sense, I would know enough to be frightened beforehand.

Shad snorted so at the aroma of dead grizzly that I had to lead him off a ways before he would let me saddle him. Even then he whuffed and stamped at the smell of the bears on the canvas shroud. It was just as well that I would be walking and leading because he seemed uncommonly fractious.

Half a mile down the trail toward Carson Valley, Shad suddenly threw up his head and whinnied in that deep-voiced way of his that sounds almost like an elk bugling. I grabbed the Volcanic double-quick. It was not likely that another bear would be so close to the territory patrolled by the sow and her cub, but given my recent escape, I would take no chances.

Whatever was disturbing Shad lay across the trail just ahead, because he shied and began to prance sideways. The canyon was too narrow to go around whatever it was, and we had come too far to retrace our steps. I tied Shad to a tree and went forward to reconnoiter.

The breeze that swirled up from the valley brought me the answer. There was the smell of death on the wind, the metallic scent of old blood and decay.

On this occasion I marked the location of a handy-limbed climbing tree before proceeding farther, but my caution was unfounded. All that disturbed the morning was the savaged remains of a steer. The bears had plainly been at the carrion and had scattered bones and hide about a small clearing in which was set a crude corral. Someone had used a small box canyon as a temporary pen for cow critters by driving them into the stone-walled draw and blocking the entrance with a brush arbor.

From the tracks I guessed that the Paiutes had driven their stolen property to this spot. While holding the herd here, they had butchered one of the steers to feed their band. Mama grizzly had come upon the offal after the Indians and their plundered stock had moved on.

All this information was told to me by the ground—by the tracks of moccasins, horses, cattle, and bears. But something was wrong, disturbing the satisfaction of my conclusion. It was not a worry or a threat exactly, at least not a present danger. The nagging concern was more a notion that I was missing something important.

Idly kicking at a palm-sized piece of dark red hide, I reflected how the bears had left virtually nothing of use to their survival. As the bit of cowhide flipped into the air, I found myself staring at the print of a booted foot. Paiutes did not often wear boots in those days. Could the track be my own? I wondered. A quick comparison showed the step to be too small to be me. Of course, the boots could have been stolen from a settler. Maybe some brave had taken a fancy to a white man's footgear.

Then the full truth struck me with a rush, and I saw clearly what had been right in front of me all along. Indians, like bears, waste nothing. Even if they had felt secure enough in this canyon to kill and cook a beef, they would have packed out the hide. No Indian, unless in a terrible hurry, would butcher a steer and leave the hide for scavengers.

Leather was clothing and shelter and trade goods—far too valuable to be left behind.

That was the answer, plain as the big nose on Rough Elliott's face. The raids on cattle had not been the work of Indians but of whites masquerading as Indians. The reason the one dead man I found had bled so on his front but not from the arrow in his back was because the arrow had been plunged in after his death. A fistful of Paiute arrows and the finger of accusation pointed square at the Indians. The rustlers had even worn moccasins for the attack to hide their identities, but down here in the corral, one had gotten careless.

Now I felt like I knew it all. This was the secret my brother Lucky had held over the major. This was the information that had gotten him killed. Frey and his gang had been driving off the herds of the immigrant parties, and somehow Lucky had stumbled onto that fact. Major Frey had then manufactured a way of seeing that Lucky could not tell anyone—ever.

Days and nights at the sawmill were mighty peaceful after I left. Hard labor and the expectation of the return of King and Elliott kept the restless mind of Kit entertained for a short time. When the dam was completed and it became apparent that there was nothing to protect Maria and the children from, Kit became rapidly bored.

As I was struggling to get Edwards back to Genoa and safely deposited with the undertaker, Kit was playing mumblety-peg with George and losing.

Kit said to George as they sat on the top step and tossed the knife at the target, "I reckon you surely do regret that you cannot go to school with the other boys and girls."

"Not so much." George hit the circle dead center. "You're almost as much fun."

Kit got up, plucked the blade from the ground, and sat back down. He took aim, threw, and missed. "What about girls?"

"What about them?"

"Aren't you old enough to be noticing females?"

"Sure. Notice what?"

"Aren't there some pretty ones at school in Genoa?"

George scratched his pomaded head with one finger and peered at the sky as if he could not recollect seeing any. He replied with a negative shake of his head. "All the ones my age are taller than me. The younger ones are missin' teeth. They all hate boys, and we hate them."

"That makes you fortunate." Kit threw the knife and lost to George again. "You seen Angie Frey?"

"Yeah. Major Frey's niece. Works at the café."

"Think she's pretty?"

"I never thought about it," George answered truthfully.

"I can't stop thinking about her. Here I am at the sawmill. Stuck here. Day after day. I would go down to Genoa and pay her a call if it wasn't for that mule. I won't go riding into Genoa on that army mule."

"Uncle John said you ought to stay here all the same."

Kit's eyes narrowed. "John just didn't want me going anywhere at all. He wants me to stay here and . . ."

". . . stay out of trouble," George finished.

Kit sighed. "I wouldn't go pay Angie a call riding on that old mule anyway. I would be a laughingstock."

The two sat in silence, staring at the broken flume. Then George said, "My dad thought a lady at Frey's saloon was pretty. Miss Nell. She is a . . . a harlot."

Kit gawked at him. "Who told you that?"

"Billy Teckler at school. What is a harlot?"

"Never you mind."

George cocked his head. "Was he lyin'?"

"Never you mind." Kit tried to dodge the subject.

"Must be somethin' awful if you won't tell me. I seen the word in the Bible. In daily devotions Mother won't so much as read the word aloud, so I sneaked back and looked, but it don't explain nothin'."

George's talk made Kit nervous. After all, Maria had made Kit swear he would not talk with George about all the wrong that Lucky had done.

"Well," Kit said as he got up, "I guess I'm going to ride up to the ridge and have a look."

"What for?" George asked.

"In case someone is coming," Kit answered him gruffly.

George grinned. "You just want to go away and think about Angie some place where I won't see you moonin'."

George was partly right, but Kit did not let the boy know it. He snatched up the repeater, saddled the mule, and rode out for the ridge, where he could look down over the valley and think about Angie Frey without the boy asking any more questions about Lucky and the harlot named Miss Nell.

An autumn haze concealed the valley floor below him, but Kit could not get it out of his mind that Angie was down there wishing for him to come pay a call. He closed his eyes and imagined her face. He pictured her serving the rowdy types who came into town to eat at Frey's. This made his blood boil. It came to him that he ought to be in Genoa protecting her from the likes of King, instead of sitting on a mule way out here waiting for King to arrive.

Using the mule's ears like a gun sight, Kit peered down Sawmill Road.

It was then that he noticed something moving at a fast jog toward the sawmill. First he thought it was a deer. Then, as the animal emerged from the haze, Kit made out that the critter was a horse— a riderless palomino.

※ ※ ※

My brother was a hot-blooded fool, but I cannot blame him for what he did next. How could he have known that the palomino figured so prominently in a murder?

But the instant Kit laid eyes on Bald Hornet, the palomino, and set out to catch him and ride him into Genoa, the prospect of a disaster and total ruin multiplied for our family.

After all, Kit had heard of Bald Hornet. The horse was a legend in gold country. Kit knew, like every other man on both sides of the Sierras, that the racehorse had been stolen from its rightful owner in Placerville and used in a number of escapes from the law.

The sensible thing for Kit to do would have been to ride his own mule and lead that stolen horse west over the toll road that led to

Placerville. Once there, he could have returned the animal and maybe even collected a reward. But Kit was not sensible. He was smitten to imbecility by Angie Frey. She just happened to be one hundred and eighty degrees in the opposite direction from where Bald Hornet belonged. For this reason alone, Kit planned to ride Bald Hornet eastward to Genoa.

So Kit led the palomino back to the sawmill, where George helped him uncover an old bronc saddle in the tack room. Too prideful to ride into town on his mule, Kit threw the saddle onto the back of Bald Hornet instead. It did not occur to him that a man caught riding a stolen horse might well be accused of being a thief. Many an innocent man had gotten his neck stretched from the stout limb of an oak tree for being intercepted with another man's horse or herding another man's steer. Hang first, ask questions later, had become the policy when dealing with missing livestock.

No doubt it was Kit's intent to turn the stolen animal over to Si Denton after he visited his lady love. He ponied the mule behind him so he would have a mount to ride back up to the sawmill after dark. But it was foolhardy for him to ride the stolen horse.

He did not meet a soul on the way to Genoa. Outside of town he tied his mule to a tree lest Angie see it. Kit rode the last half mile into Genoa on Bald Hornet, arriving at the rear entrance of Frey's establishment. Leaving the horse at the hitching rail among half a dozen other mounts, Kit went in under the pretext that he wanted a meal.

Angie was clearing tables in the restaurant, which was empty after the noon seating. In the adjacent saloon, the remnant of the posse were drowning their misery at the death of Si Denton. Frey and Rough Elliott were at the center of the group. Frey had provided drinks on the house. The rage of the men seemed to increase as they consumed more whiskey.

Kit, knowing nothing of these terrible events, entered the café with a grin on his face. He doffed his hat when Angie Frey looked at him, and he stammered that he wished a pitcher of cow's milk and a bowl of corn bread.

Angie, blushing at the sight of him, seated Kit at the table in the back corner of the room. "There is also one fine piece of roast beef left in the warmer. The posse fairly cleaned us out of every other morsel."

"Posse?" Kit asked.

"You haven't heard?" Angie fetched the milk and brought corn bread in a bowl. Pouring the milk over the corn bread, she told Kit the news about the ambush and the murder of Si Denton. What she failed to mention was the fact that the murderer had been seen making his escape on a palomino horse thought to be Bald Hornet. If only Kit had known that one small piece of information, everything might have turned out differently for him.

"Si Denton killed?" This was a blow to Kit. Si had been kind to him while Kit had been in jail. Kit had become attached to the constable, as a man will do when kept in such close quarters for three months.

"Those fellows in there with my uncle—" Angie lowered her voice—"they say when they catch up with who did it—"

118

She did not finish the sentiment. Paul Hawkins, his badge gleaming on his vest and fury in his eye, burst through the front door, a loaded double-barreled shotgun cradled in his arms.

Kit had just taken a bite of corn bread. He raised his hand to greet Hawkins.

Hawkins asked, "You ride into town on the yeller horse, Kit Thornton?"

"Sorry to hear the news about Si."

"Lawrence Frey says he seen you ride into town on that yeller horse tied out back."

"I reckon that was me."

"Bald Hornet, ain't it?" The buzz of angry conversation hushed in the saloon as Paul Hawkins stepped nearer Kit.

"I intended to bring him round to Si after I ate. . . ." Kit faltered when he saw the look of pure hatred that filled Hawkins' face.

Hawkins spoke in a low, menacing voice. "Move away from the table, Miss Angie. There's a rattlesnake coiled up behind you, and I intend to see it don't strike nobody else."

Angie grew pale. She looked at Kit, then backed away.

Hawkins swung the barrel of his shotgun and pointed it full at Kit's head.

The spoon dropped from Kit's hand. "What . . . what . . . is this?"

Hawkins glared at him. "We all seen Bald Hornet runnin' away full gallop after Si was killed."

From the saloon an angry voice repeated that Kit Thornton had ridden Bald Hornet into town. Other voices joined in. Before long, a crowd of enraged faces appeared at the doorway.

Kit spread his hands in a gesture of innocence. "I only just found the horse wandering loose on Sawmill Road, Hawkins! I swear I . . . I was bringing the horse back here to—"

"Save it! Hands over your head!"

"I tell you I was only—"

"Hands up, I said! You are under arrest for the murder of Si Denton, and I, for one, intend to be there when you hang!"

✳ CHAPTER 13 ✳

Without any warning about what had happened during my absence, Shad and I, together with the aging corpse, arrived back in Genoa. I will admit that we were a spectacle as we headed along Main Street toward the courthouse.

I spared a glance for Frey's place but fended off the temptation to confront him at once with his crimes. Cornering something low-down and sneaky like a badger is liable to have unpleasant consequences. My plan was to lay my evidence, so to speak, directly before Si Denton, tell him all I knew, then let the law take its course.

The gaping eyes and wagging tongues that followed my progress I attributed to the obvious. It never occurred to me that the whispers and pointing had more to do with me than with Edwards.

Shad was standing patiently at the rail, and I was untying the rawhide thongs with which the corpse was bound to the saddle. "Hey, sonny," I called to a dirty-faced street rat loafing nearby, "get Constable Denton. Tell him John Thornton wants to see him *muy pronto.*"

Instead of running into the courthouse like I figured, this kid stared till I thought his eyes would pop.

Then a female—his mama, I reckoned—dashed out of a dry-goods store across the street. She grabbed that youngster by his shoulder, whirled him around, and marched him straight off. But the strangest thing of all was the look she gave me—like I was the worst desperado to hit these parts since Joaquin Murrieta. I mean, she looked scared.

While I was still undoing the bands, the scene with the kid just about replayed itself. A hand was laid roughly on my shoulder, and I was jerked around. That is where the similarity ended, because Paul Hawkins' fist landed right on the point of my jaw.

I jostled Shad, who jumped sideways, and the canvas containing Edwards shucked his remains right into the middle of the street while I sprawled on the ground beside it.

"What did you do that for?" I demanded. I made a move to jump up, but I was suddenly nose to nose with a .44.

"Get up slow and easy," Hawkins ordered. "Keep your hands where I can see 'em all the time or you won't live to figure out what you did wrong." He jerked my rifle out of the scabbard.

"What is all this?" I asked, all the while taking him at his word and rising slowly to my feet. Now my chin hurt, and the back of my head started aching all over again.

"I'll say this for you, Thornton," Hawkins said, waving me toward the courthouse with his pistol. "You've got some kind of sand to come waltzin' in here."

"What nonsense is this? This hunk of earth is Edwards," I said, touching the body with the toe of my boot, "but I didn't kill him. I followed him from Bone's, but somebody else shot him and left him for dead. Get Si, and I'll explain everything."

Hawkins swung his pistol barrel toward my head like he was going to clock me with it. I ducked, and he stopped just short of taking out my teeth. "You are a cold character," he concluded, much to my confusion, "but it don't matter none. I figure you're a party to the killin', and you'll hang same as Kit."

"Kit?" I said, stunned into using real short words. "What now?"

"It won't do you any good to pretend you don't know," Hawkins said. "We caught Kit dead to rights after he bushwhacked Si. I just didn't think it would be so easy to take you."

* * *

There are times when a man can do a heap of thinking in a mighty brief spell of time, and right then was one of those times. It came to me like a flash of lightning that Kit was in terrible danger. If Si was really dead, what if Paul Hawkins was part of the vigilantes? It would mean that Kit—and me, too, for that matter—could be blamed and hanged before anyone gave it a second thought.

If Kit was to be saved, there was no other course but for me to remain free. As I say, all this stampeded through my mind in less time than it takes to tell.

Hawkins had unknowingly done me a favor by laying hold of my repeater the way he had. Every man alive has one hand that works better than the other, and encumbering the one hand always seems to interfere with the use of both.

As we started up the plank steps of the courthouse, I knew in that instant what I was going to do. I let Hawkins crowd me a bit, getting closer behind me. As I stepped with my right foot and the weight came off my left leg, I drew it back sharp and gave a low kick that hit him on the right knee. At the same second, I pivoted my body around and clamped both my hands around his right wrist—the hand holding the pistol. With his body being knocked one direction and me pulling the other, I almost broke his hold on the gun.

The Colt exploded with a roar, the slug tearing a half-inch-deep furrow in the oak planks of the county treasurer's floor after busting through his window. Folks dived for cover, but there was really no more danger to them. There was no way I was going to let Hawkins cock the hammer back for another shot.

Exactly as I figured, Hawkins knew that I would win the battle for the pistol if we continued my two hands against his one. He did the only thing he could do, which was to let go of my rifle. He flung the Volcanic as hard as he could, and it slithered across the ground like a thing alive. Worse luck, it was out of reach.

Shad, who had never been hard-tied to the rail, jerked away from it and backed up a few steps as if giving us room to wrestle. The gunshot had sent all the onlookers off the street, so our only company in the struggle was the body of Edwards, which was mostly clothespin shaped.

Now we were more evenly matched, with Hawkins' Colt stuck between us both. I could hear voices shouting all up and down Main Street and knew that my time was fast running out.

Hawkins and I rolled over in the dirt of the courthouse yard. We were both head-butting and kicking our knees up, but neither of us was willing to let go of the pistol to throw a punch.

Then I spotted the stone mounting step a few feet away and knew what I had to do. Rolling furiously, I got up a good bit of speed across the ground. Keeping to a straight course in such a melee was like lassoing a grizzly. It's almost impossible, and you get only one chance to do it right. By sheer providence, I completed the third rotation when our movement was stopped abruptly by the contact between Hawkins' head and the granite block.

His eyes crossed and his grip on the Colt slackened. In that moment I wrenched the pistol free, jumped up from across him, and bolted for Shad. The bay skittered away from me, trailing the reins, so I ran alongside, reaching for the horn.

It is surely true that to have one hand encumbered when you need both for a piece of business means that no good will result. I planted both feet and sprang for the saddle in a running mount, using Shad's momentum to propel me into the seat. But I lost my grip on the revolver even as I got aboard Shad's back. The last I saw of the weapon, it was flying through the air, heading toward Lute Olds' feed lot.

123

Even weaponless, I counted myself successful as Shad sprinted out of town. I had no thought for the moment other than escape. I would fill in the details later. But I had reckoned without Lawrence Frey, who despite his youth, showed more presence of mind than all the grown men of Genoa.

Lawrence had been approaching Main Street from the north when he heard the shot and saw the struggle going on in front of the courthouse. Instead of riding into a shooting war, he tossed a loop of his riata around a branch of the giant water oak that marked the northern boundary of town. Then he rode across the road and dismounted.

Taking a turn of the hemp rope around a fence post, he dropped the slack in the dirt and waited. When Shad and I thundered toward freedom, Lawrence yanked the line taut, blocking the road.

Shad tucked his head when he saw the barrier rise in front of him, but I had used up all my quick thinking for the day: I forgot to duck. The trap set by Lawrence Frey clotheslined me, and I have counted myself fortunate ever since that it did not break my neck.

As it was, the line caught me across the midsection and cleaned me out of the saddle while my horse ran on without me. I landed flat on my back. I was not knocked out, though winded a mite. Aside from my disappointment at not making good on my escape, my first thought was how tired I was of being beat up and abused by men, grizzly bears, and hard, hard ground.

When Hawkins marched me up the courthouse steps the second time, he did so from behind the triggers of a double-barreled scattergun. He stayed a respectful distance behind me, too, ordering me to march ahead or he would blow me in half. I obliged him because I was feeling pretty used by then, and for another reason as well: I believed him.

He stuck me into the same iron cage with Kit, who, I must say, was not pleased to see me, at least not under these circumstances. He looked some the worse for wear too. His eyes were puffy and the color of ripe plums, and his lips were split. Hawkins slammed the door on the two of us and left us to get reacquainted.

Between holding my ribs and rubbing my head and jaw, I managed to ask Kit for his story. He told me about the palomino horse and his capture and what he had heard about Si Denton's murder. It seems that Bernard King had been real pleased to share the word that the whole valley was up in arms that Si had been ambushed and that hanging was the certain outcome.

I brought my brother up to date on my whereabouts and what I now knew to be true about Major Frey and company. "Much good it may do us," I said, "until we get an impartial hearing."

"We don't need a hearing," Kit announced. "I ain't staying to get lynched." He peered through the grate on the door to see if anyone was about, then dropped to one knee. From his boot top he pulled a knife. "We'll grab whoever brings our supper and cut their throat if they don't get out of the way."

"That's real fine," I said in an offhanded way, leaning forward as if to see the blade. Then I lunged at him, caught the knife handle in both fists, and cracked his wrist down on my knee.

Kit squalled and dropped the weapon, which I retrieved and thrust into my own boot.

"Yow!" he complained, shaking the injured arm. "What'd you do that for?"

"Do you want to give them any more reason to shoot or hang us?" I demanded. "Are you trying to prove us guilty? We need a lawman or a judge, not a hostage. You stay cool, and we'll beat this thing yet."

Kit retreated to the corner of the cell, putting us all of ten feet apart. Once there, he sank down to sulk.

Later, when we saw who brought our supper, I wondered if Kit recalled what he had said. I doubted it, because when the tap on the door came and Paul Hawkins demanded to know the caller's identity, it was Angie Frey's voice that answered.

Kit sat up and brushed his hand through his hair when he heard her. I swear he was thinking of how to make himself presentable when he was in the hoosegow facing a murder charge! Such is youth.

The door swung open, revealing Hawkins armed as before with the shotgun. When Angie was admitted to the cell, she was carrying a pan. Its fragrance announced the contents to be fresh-baked corn bread. In her other hand she carried a clay jug of milk.

"You didn't get to eat your corn bread," she said, then stopped at the sight of Kit's ravaged face. Stepping close despite Hawkins' warning to keep clear, she stretched out her slender hand and tenderly touched Kit's battered eyes. If he had been butter, he would have turned into a little yellow puddle on the floor.

"Now, Miss Angie," Hawkins scolded, "your uncle wouldn't like you . . ."

She rounded on him suddenly, and there was flame in her countenance. "Did you do this, Paul Hawkins, or did you just let it happen?"

Hawkins bristled right back. "Si Denton was shot from ambush, and—"

125

"And you've already decided who did it!"

"Miss Frey," I said softly, "would you like to help us?"

Before Hawkins could voice a word of protest, Angie stared him into silence. "Certainly," she said. "How?"

"Send for Snowshoe Thompson. He'll know who to bring here who will listen to our side. Then please fetch Maria. She will testify that Kit stole no horse."

"I'll get Snowshoe myself," Angie vowed, "and Maria."

"Your uncle won't—," Hawkins tried again.

"Don't you dare say one word to my uncle!" Angie flared. "I am of age and able to make up my own mind!"

With that she marched out, leaving Hawkins dumbfounded, Kit starry-eyed, and me hopeful.

My state of mind did not stay positive for long. Before the sun had dropped behind Monument Peak, the loudmouthed soaks, brimful of tanglefoot, gathered on the corner opposite the jail. We could not see them, but their boozy voices carried clear to our cell at the back of the building.

"Hang 'em, I say," demanded the growling voice of Rough Elliott.

A chorus of agreement responded to his suggestion.

"That's right!"

"String 'em up and be done with it!"

"Stretch their necks 'til their eyes pop for what they did to old Si!"

"The Thornton gang should have been run out of these parts long ago!"

I knew that there was not enough liquor in them yet to make them challenge Hawkins and a double load of buckshot. But he was only one man . . . and what if he stepped aside and let them come?

CHAPTER 14

It seemed right that Snowshoe Thompson lived at the head of Hope Valley because he was our only hope. It had come to me clearly that the fate of Kit and me would be the same as Lucky's unless we had someone to speak up for us.

In all the Sierras there was no one man as well trusted and liked as Snowshoe Thompson. His vocation was delivering the mail to the remote mining camps tucked away in the Sierras. It was his avocation to deliver the souls of men from despair by sharing the hope of the gospel wherever he went.

In 1853 I had seen him disperse an angry lynch mob on the rampage in the early days of Hangtown by preaching on the gallows steps from midnight until dawn. The three men he had saved were proved to be innocent later on. Once, in Downieville, I had watched him talk sense to a drunken young miner in a saloon who proposed to end his own life by blowing his head off with a scattergun. As Snowshoe counseled the desperate fellow, he leaned so close that the blast would have killed him as well.

Snowshoe was a man with a keen sense of justice and no fear whatsoever of death. This enabled him to do the right thing in the midst of terrible danger when weaker men stayed out of the line of fire.

Kit and I needed just such a man as this to stand in the gap for us. I knew that if Snowshoe Thompson were able, he would come to our aid in Genoa. If Angie Frey did not find him in time, then he would be the only one to pray over our graves.

✳ ✳ ✳

Angie, heedless of the disapproval of the Genoa townsfolk, whipped the team up smartly and raced the buckboard through the gathering gloom to Snowshoe's log cabin. The horses were lathered and spent by the time she turned onto the property. They pulled up short at the door as Snowshoe Thompson stepped out of his house.

He helped Angie from the wagon and said in his singsong voice, "Velcome, young lady. Dese here horses is nearly kilt. Nobody drive horses that vey 'less somebody dying and need help."

She collapsed into his arms and managed to gasp out the story of our predicament as Snowshoe calmly looked after the horses, leading them to his barn.

Angie followed him, talking all the while and finishing with these words, "John Thornton says if you can't help him and Kit tonight, then they will be hanged before morning."

He turned from the hayracks. "Yon Thornton is right, for sure. I better git."

With the long, swift strides of a man who routinely covered hundreds of miles of snowy terrain with slender planks strapped to his feet, Snowshoe hurried back to the cabin, where a kettle of stew simmered over the fire. He jerked his thumb at the tin plate waiting on the table. "Eat something, miss. Sleep a vile. Come morning, you git up to de sawmill and stay dere with Vidow Thornton and her orphan babies till your horses get rested, den get her to Genoa fast as you can. I'm going to Genoa now." With that pronouncement, he threw another log on the fire, put on his mackinaw, and gathered his Bible, which was open on the table.

At the door he remarked quietly over his shoulder, "Ain't no accident you find me here. I vas supposed to be long gone to Placerville. Only two days ago I'm prayin', and I git a feeling I'm supposed to stay here and vait."

"But what can I do tonight?"

"You know how to pray, young voman?"

Angie nodded.

He said, "Den you pray I ain't vaited too long."

✳ ✳ ✳

It was a sleepless night for me, expecting to be dragged from the cell at any moment and hanged from a limb of the same water oak that had arrested my escape. I don't believe Kit slept a wink either, despite the fact that we were both beat to thunder.

Earlier than I ever thought possible, I heard Snowshoe Thompson's particular accent and believed again that we might escape with our lives. It was just after midnight when a new ruckus competed with the drunken, angry harangue still going on outside.

"You bet you gonna let me in to see dem," Snowshoe argued. "I don't care vat you tink he did. Yon Thornton is a friend of mine, and I vant to speak wit him!"

The cell door creaked open, and Snowshoe was permitted to enter.

The bearded beanpole of a man was the most beautiful sight yet to my blurry eyes. "Thanks for coming, Snowshoe," I said warmly. Then I explained why we were being held and what I knew was behind it all.

Snowshoe had no liking for Major Frey, and he was incensed that we had been arrested on such a flimsy pretext. "But, Yon, to stay here vhile I go fetch Justice Van Sickle or the marshal is not so good. There is armed men at de hangin' tree. Rough Elliott is bellowin' to everybody who comes how dey don't vant de Thornton gang to break in and set you loose."

I snorted. "The Thornton gang, eh?"

"Dere is no cause of laughin', Yon," Snowshoe said seriously. "If dey play like dere's a gang, dey could also play at shooting you to keep you from escaping, you betcha. And de talk is to hang you now and not vait."

Snowshoe was right. Stone and steel could not keep a determined mob from dragging us out to meet our doom if such was determined beforehand. "Hawkins," I called to the deputy, "what do you mean to do to keep us from getting lynched?"

Hawkins came to the grate with a sneer on his face. "I sent for the marshal already. You'll get a fair trial before we hang you. It won't take more'n a couple days."

"Days, he says!" clamored Snowshoe. "You tink dat mob is gonna vait for days? If dey know dat you sent for de marshal, you haf already signed de death varrants for dese two men."

Hawkins looked surprised at the vehemence of the normally peaceful letter carrier. "I told Major Frey to quit settin' up free drinks till after the marshal got here."

Snowshoe spat angrily. "You told de biggest volf to keep de udder volfs under control? You gotta do better dan dat, Paul Hawkins! Si Denton wouldn't let no mob kill his prisoners nor see 'em lynched, nor turn over his job to no snake like de major! Vat you do vhen you gotta sleep, hah?"

I wisely kept my mouth shut and motioned for Kit to do the same. Snowshoe was arguing all the identical points that were in my mind, and Hawkins was listening.

"But what else can I do?" Hawkins demanded.

"Get dese two out of here! Take men you trust and get 'em over de mountain to Placerville! And don't vait. Do it tonight!"

"But how?" Hawkins mused. "You saw for yourself the mob that's already out there. If we get caught, there'll be shootin' for sure."

I spoke up for the first time. "What we need is a diversion."

There was a period of silent thought while we all turned this over in our minds. Then Snowshoe said, "Yah. It vill vork. I am this diversion."

"Not good, Snowshoe," I argued. "Even if we get clear away, they'll know who to blame."

Snowshoe shrugged as if the matter was of complete indifference to him. "All of dem is in dere cups tonight. Tomorrow, vhen their heads is aching, dey forget it all already."

"What do you say, Hawkins?" I asked.

The deputy nodded grimly. "If we don't go, I'll end up havin' to shoot some of the crowd, and I don't want to do that to protect the likes of murderers like you. We'll go."

I did not much like his reasoning, but I was not about to dispute the conclusion.

✳ ✳ ✳

Thirty minutes later three mounts were tied to the brush in back of the courthouse. Hawkins bound our hands together with leather thongs, but he left our feet unshackled. I suppose he thought he was giving Kit and me a chance to make it if we had to run for it.

Above Rough Elliott's gravelly voice came a new sound. A higher-pitched, piercing speech penetrated the air. "You men stop and tink vat you are about! Do you want innocent blood on your hands?"

Snowshoe's argument may not have been convincing to the alcohol-addled brains itching for a hanging, but more to the point, it was something different and therefore attention getting. Snowshoe took up his lecture on the stump of a tree even farther out of town to the north, drawing the crowd away from the jail.

To give Hawkins his due, he elected not to trust anyone else with the secret move. That did not mean that he was any more friendly toward us, though. "This coach gun is loaded with double-ought," he said, "and buckshot means buryin'. Dark or not, don't try anythin' funny or they'll pick up your brains over in Sacramento."

With that he poked his head out the rear door of the jail and looked around. Then he unlocked the cell and motioned with the shotgun for us to precede him to the brush. He did not need to tell us to keep perfectly quiet, and I had already warned Kit not to attempt an escape. Even if we somehow avoided being blown to kingdom come, a single shot would bring the mob howling down on us.

We made it across an open space of gravel without incident, but when we entered a draw on the far side Kit stumbled over a tree root. He caught himself from falling with a quick step to the side but landed squarely on a branch that cracked loudly in the frosty air.

The three of us froze low in the shadows to see if a cry of pursuit was raised, but all we heard was, "Vhen you stand before de great Judge, vat will you say to Him? How vill you plead your case?" Snowshoe, not one to waste an opportunity, be it diversionary or no, was conducting a revival meeting.

Right after that we slipped into the depths of a ravine, out of sight and earshot of the road. I heard Kit mumble, "Oh no."

"What?" I hissed back.

"It's worse than mules!"

It was true. The transport provided for us was a pair of scrawny Washoe canaries, otherwise known as donkeys. Hawkins, on the

131

other hand, was mounted on his own horse. He did not need to explain his thinking. Between our knotted wrists and the deliberate pace of the critters, we would not be racing away.

We hoisted ourselves onto the bare backs of our mounts with our feet almost dragging the ground. Up the ravine and out on a ledge Hawkins directed us, then a swing west to bypass Genoa, and we were on our way.

Given a peculiarity of the cold, dry air, Snowshoe's sermon still drifted up to us from time to time. I had no doubt that he would keep the gathering occupied until dawn, at which time we would be well out of harm's way.

I felt good about our departure and relaxed enough to be amused at Kit's complaints.

This was only possible, however, because none of us had spotted the figure lurking in the trees, watching our exit.

✳ ✳ ✳

There was no alarm when we circled through the foothills of the Sierras and rejoined the Old Emigrant Road. Once again I found myself headed away from Carson Valley toward Hope Valley.

The weather was gathering cold, and the scent of the wind swirling down from the high country had more than a hint of snow to come. I hoped that our passage would get over before the storm arrived, as I did not have my heavy coat and did not relish camping on the mountainside. Sierra storms can last for days before blowing themselves out and even early in the season can be dangerous to the unprepared.

Westward and up we went, climbing past five thousand feet of elevation on our way toward a pass that would top eight thousand feet. A coyote was the only traveler who challenged our right-of-way. Gray and bushy furred, he darted into the road ahead at first light. In the middle of the road he turned and faced us, as if startled to see us there. Then he plunged into the mesquite on the other side and disappeared.

The west fork of the Carson River tumbled beside us at this stretch of the track. Though it was the time of low water, it was still musical, dancing across the rocks and pattering over four-foot water-falls. The melody of the river was loud enough to cover our passage and make it difficult to talk.

"That old brush wolf must not have known we were coming. He should be too canny to run out like that," I observed to Kit, raising my voice so he could hear. Then an unpleasant thought struck me. "Or else he was already running from something when he met up with us."

I turned on the donkey's back to pass this worry on to Hawkins. He ignored me.

"That place ahead, beside the big redwood cedar," I said, "where the trail narrows . . . it would be a great spot for an ambush."

"Turn around," Hawkins growled, turning up his collar and hunching inside his wool jacket. "Don't bother playing games with me, Thornton. Nobody is out here but us."

I shrugged and swung back around, but I also kicked the donkey in the flanks and nudged him closer to Kit. "The leaves look deep on the downhill side. Nice and soft."

"Get back there," Hawkins scolded. "Quit talking."

The next bend in the trail was around a boulder the size and shape of a wagon. When the turn was passed, the road was directly in line with the shoulder of mountain guarded by the cedar.

As soon as Kit turned the corner there was a flash from the hill-side near the big tree, and then the boom of a rifle reached us. Kit's donkey reared and screamed, toppling over on the trail. My brother had not needed my advice because the plunge of his mount had tossed him into the heap of alder leaves. I joined him there myself a second later. My own animal clattered off down the trail.

Another shot boomed, striking the boulder and sending a cascade of sparks and rock slivers into the night. Kit and I were not in a good spot, with the lip of the trail barely high enough to cover our heads. Hawkins was in a better position, having the bulk of the stone slab to hide behind. He had his shotgun out, but it was of little use at such a distance.

"This is Deputy Hawkins," he yelled. I guessed he was trying to impress our attackers with his authority. "Stop shootin' at once."

133

The words of reply were surprising. "You are surrounded by the Thornton gang. Let our chief and his brother go!"

Hawkins swung that cannon to cover us! There is nothing that looks any bigger than the business end of a twelve-gauge from half a dozen feet away!

"Don't believe it," I urged. "Whoever is out there wants us dead and maybe you too."

It was all completely clear to me what was up. If Hawkins got away alive, then he would spread the word that he had been jumped by the Thornton gang. After that, no one would care if Kit and I were ever seen again. And if Hawkins was slaughtered too, well, someone would let it be known that the Thorntons had done it, and the result would be the same.

"Give me your Colt," I said.

"Not a chance," Hawkins snarled. "Don't move an inch, or by heaven I'll kill you where you lay and take my chances with your gang."

It came to me that there could not be many men on the ridge. If they really had us surrounded we would have been cut to pieces already. There could not be more than one or two gunmen.

Another probing round was fired, parting the grass near Kit's head.

"You see that?" I spat. "He's aiming for us."

Hawkins ignored me. "If you want 'em," he yelled, "come and get 'em!"

I bunched up in the leaves like I was trying to make myself as small as possible, which was actually a good idea. But my other thought was to reach my boot top and catch the butt end of Kit's knife. My fingers inched downward slowly. All the while I was praying that Hawkins would stay focused on the rifleman. In the increasing predawn light, even a quick look my direction would give my labor away.

Hawkins decided he might as well make the other party keep his head down, so he blazed away with the coach gun. At such extreme range the shot only rattled in the branches and knocked down some needles, but it would put the gunman on notice.

Unfortunately, the unknown out on the hill was really after us. The next two shots thumped into the body of the donkey where it lay in the road. Any minute now there would be enough light for the shooter to pick out the outlines of our heads from the brush covering, and then we would be up the flume.

Firing again, Hawkins let fly with both barrels, then jumped up and ran around the side of the boulder. I do not know if he was beginning to believe me or not, but he quit watching us so closely. He was trying to outflank the man on the ridge.

As quick as Hawkins moved, I pulled the knife, jammed it handle-first in between two rocks, and started sawing away at my prisoner bracelets. The leather straps parted in a wink, and I hollered to Kit, "Here, catch." I tossed the knife in a gentle arc to land close beside him.

The morning sun beaming into the east-facing canyon caught on the blade. It sparkled in the light, and the flash of movement drew a shot from the hillside.

"I'm hit!" Kit yelled. "John, I'm hit!"

I belly-crawled over to him, which caused a bullet to come my way, smacking into a pinecone bare inches from where my head had been. Ripping off his jacket, I found that Kit was struck in the arm. The bullet had gone clear through but did not seem to have busted the bone. He was losing blood, so I yanked off the bandanna from around my neck. I tied it in place over the wound, using the rawhide strings that had lately bound my hands. I also retrieved the knife.

"Thornton," Hawkins yelled from the other side of the boulder, "take my horse and ride. Get out of here."

So he was a believer at last. It did not set well with me to leave him so, shotgun against rifle, but I had no gun at all, and Kit needed help. If we got away clean, I did not think that Hawkins would still be a target for no reason. Right or wrong, I made up my mind to go.

I waited till Hawkins had reloaded both barrels. The bushwhacker must have known something was up because his next shot came from a different angle and went square through Kit's coat where it lay on the pile of leaves.

135

While Hawkins hammered away, I grabbed Kit and tossed him over my shoulder. My heave on his injured arm must have pained him considerable, because he groaned and went limp. Then I was running for the horse that was back in the brush beside the stream.

✴ CHAPTER 15 ✴

That roan of Hawkins' was not big, but he was young and sturdy. He set off down the trail at a fair pace, despite the double load he carried. He drew another shot as we passed the boulder. The rock slivers that peppered the flank of the horse pushed him to greater speed to escape the terrible biting critters.

As fast as we rounded the first bend in the trail, I drew rein and cut the roan sharp toward the creek. Just because only one man had been shooting at us did not mean that he did not have confederates waiting below to cut off our escape. Returning on the road was almost certain to lead us into more gunplay.

I was perplexed about where to go. Genoa was not an option. Snowshoe's cabin was not far but not defensible and would not serve Kit's need.

The only choice remaining seemed to be the sawmill. I knew that Major Frey would locate us there. My only hope was that the news of our deliverance would be slow in reaching him. If I had time to get back to the mill and fort up with a repeating rifle, perhaps there was still a chance. Maybe we could hold out till Hawkins and a marshal showed up. Didn't the attempted ambush prove our innocence? At least partly?

So putting all this together in my mind, we forded the Carson, and I put the roan at the bank on the far side. It was a steep place and precious little footing. The horse stumbled when his foot slipped on some moss, and Kit and I almost ended up in the river.

We climbed out of the canyon on a zigzag path, taking advantage of every little bit of deer trail. The rifle fire continued from behind us, answered by the roar of Hawkins' shotgun. The higher we rose on that incline, the more sheer it became. I forced myself to think that it was only five feet to the ground from the horse's back; otherwise I would have felt every inch of the two hundred feet down to the stream.

Just above us was a place where the grade leveled out. I was concerned that we might expose ourselves to gunshots when we popped out high on the ridge like that, so I looked around for a solution. The lip of the precipice was thick with elderberry brush. I gave the roan his head, praying that he would be sensible about finding a way through the tangle. He put his ears back and plowed straight forward into the densest part of the thicket.

Inside, it was like being in a cave of brush. I could not see out, but then neither could anyone see us. Then, near at hand, I heard another horse whinny. It could be where the sharpshooter had tied his mount, or it could be an accomplice waiting to catch us unawares.

I had to scout ahead on foot to see what we were riding into. I slipped off the roan and fastened it in the elderberry scrub. I looped Kit's still-bound hands over the horn and once more pulled the knife from my boot. I bent low to the ground. Parting the undergrowth with the tip of the blade, I peeked out.

Twenty-five feet away was a saddled horse, and he was looking right at me. Luckily for me, his rider was not so canny. A dozen feet beyond the animal, a man stood with his back to me. He was staring up the canyon toward the gun shots. He was armed but held the rifle with its butt resting on the ground as if he were only a spectator.

Using the bulk of the horse as a cover, I slipped out of the brush and rushed him. He turned at the sound of my running steps, but long before he could raise the weapon, I was on him. The next second, I tossed the rifle away from him and knelt on his chest with the knife pressed against his throat.

It was young Lawrence Frey. "Don't kill me, Mister Thornton," he blurted.

"What are you up here to do to us?" I snarled.

"Honest, I didn't want anybody to get shot," he pleaded. "It was just to recapture you."

"Who's with you?" I demanded.

"Only Mister Thick."

"Who else?" I snapped, leaning down on the knife a fraction.

Young Frey's eyes bulged. "No one else, I swear it. The major and King . . ." He stopped, obviously afraid of me, yet fearful of his father's wrath at the same time.

"What about them?" I growled, giving him no pity. Was there another ambush? Were they on the way to join the trap even as I delayed?

"They're going to the sawmill."

My blood chilled in that instant. Maria, George, and the baby at the mercy of those two. "What do they want there?" I asked, shaking the boy's shoulder. "What are they going to do?"

"Nothing," he said, clasping his hands together to beg me not to cut his throat. "Nothing! They just want to keep Missus Thornton from going to town to tell what she knows . . ."

"About the horse," I concluded for him. "Kit was framed."

He nodded miserably.

"Get up," I ordered, yanking him to his feet.

"What are you gonna do to me?"

"Nothing unless you give me any trouble," I warned. "I just figure you may come in handy, so I'm taking you with me."

Lawrence was so frightened that I did not even need to encourage him with the knife. He acted more than willing to be obedient and was soon bound by the arms and tied to the saddle horn of his horse.

※ ※ ※

It was just after sunup, while Kit, Lawrence Frey, and I were hightailing it toward the sawmill, when Maria was awakened by the clanking of trace chains and the groan of wagon wheels. Wrapping a blanket around her, she peered out the window into the early, pale yellow light to see Angie Frey climb down from the wagon while two lathered horses stood with heads bowed at the rail.

No need for Angie to tie them off. The worn-out animals would not move a step unless urged by the whip. It seemed that Angie Frey had disregarded Snowshoe's orders to stay put on the Thompson ranch until morning. Instead, the young lady had finished her supper, allowed the team of horses only three hours in the stall, then had hitched them to the wagon and driven all night over perilous roads to reach the sawmill.

"Missus Thornton!" Angie clambered up the steps and pounded on the door. "Wake up, ma'am! There is trouble in Genoa. You are needed in town."

Knowing that the girl was a close relative of Major Frey caused Maria to hesitate before she opened the door. It came to her mind that those men who wanted to take over the sawmill might well use another female to make Maria lower her guard.

Angie rapped hard on the door. "Missus Thornton! Kit and John are in difficulty! Ma'am? Please open the door! I must have a word with you!"

From his cot, George whispered, "Could be a trick, Mother. Shall I get the gun?"

Maria hushed him with a wave of her hand.

Angie tried once more. "They say Kit shot Si Denton, then rode away on a stolen horse. A big yellow horse, it was. They mean to hang him and John Thornton, too. Kit says you'll know he didn't steal it. He says you and George can testify that he found the horse."

Believing the girl at last, Maria hurried to throw open the door and let her in. "Si Denton has been shot?"

"Yes, ma'am." The girl was trembling all over. "Killed stone dead he is! And everything has gone sour."

"Well, girl, you look all together done up."

"I am."

"Come in then and have a cup of tea. Tell me the news."

Pale, cold to the bone, and exhausted, Angie crumpled into a chair. Near hysterical from weariness and terror, she prattled on about Snowshoe Thompson taking off for Genoa to save Kit and John from a lynching. Then she went on awhile about the terrible crowd that had gathered outside the jailhouse. She finished her tale with the story of the trip over the mountain with nothing but starlight to light her way.

Maria stoked the fire in the stove and made the girl sit near it. She set a kettle of water on to boil and made blackberry tea. The girl's hands were so cold she could not take the cup when Maria gave it to her. Clearly Angie was not a shill sent to lead Maria astray.

"Why, Miss Frey, your hands are ice." Maria rubbed the girl's red, swollen fingers between her own.

With this simple act of kindness Angie began to weep and laid her head against Maria's shoulder. "Oh, Missus Thornton! If we're not on our way again soon, they'll hang Kit and John for certain!"

Maria instructed George to go see to the livestock. The boy obeyed, reluctant to miss the rest of the story.

Stroking Angie's head, Maria proclaimed, "Mister Thompson will not allow Kit and John to be lynched. Even the worst of the bad men respect him. They will not cross Snowshoe Thompson. You need to rest awhile. Your team is spent."

"You don't understand, Missus Thorton! They believe Kit shot Si Denton! You and your son are the only ones who can testify about the getaway horse!"

Maria looked out the window at the horses. White flecks of lather covered them, and foam dripped from their tongues. They were over-heated even in the bitter cold of the morning. Steam rose from their hides. It was plain that it would be hours before they could leave for Genoa.

George glanced up from the horses and caught his mother's concerned look as he unhooked the harness. Giving his head a broad shake, he indicated that he had never seen animals so near collapse as these.

Maria opened the door a crack and called to him, "Don't let them near water until they're cooled down. A drink will kill them."

With a curt nod of agreement, George led the animals from the traces and began to walk them slowly. "They're near to dead, Mother. This bay is lame in the right foreleg. He had a stone wedged between the shoe and the frog. I got it out, but his hoof is bruised. The mare is in better shape. She could take us down the mountain. But there's not much left in either of them."

"Keep them on their feet if you can, Son."

From the crib, Maddy whimpered and began to awaken. Maria closed the door, gathered up the baby, then turned to ask Angie, "Miss Frey, how long has it been since you . . . ?"

But Angie was asleep sitting upright in the chair. Her head nodded forward. Strands of damp hair fell around her face. The half-empty teacup balanced precariously on her lap.

"Poor little thing. You've nearly killed yourself as well as your horses getting here." Maria, holding Maddy to her shoulder, took the cup, roused Angie, and guided her to the bed.

The girl tried to protest that time was too short for rest, but she lapsed into a deep sleep even before Maria covered her with a quilt.

✳ ✳ ✳

Maria knew the bay gelding was a goner from the first moment she laid eyes on it. There was nothing George could do to stop it. The animal dropped into the dust, rolled, twisted a gut, and was dead within an hour.

Angie Frey slept without stirring even after George entered the house with a slam of the door.

"Well, that's that," George said grimly, sitting down to eat a bowl of grits. "I think the mare will live, but she ain't pullin' any wagon down to Genoa." He jerked his thumb at Angie on the bed. "She might as well stayed at Snowshoe Thompson's and slept for all the good her night ride has done. One horse is dead, the other useless. . . . And look at her. Is she still breathin'?"

"Snowshoe will send someone to see to us when we don't show up in Genoa." Maria took a seat across from her son.

"Uncle John and Kit will be killed by then."

Maria did not reply for a time. She had no way of knowing that Kit and I were riding for our lives at that very moment, but she sensed that we were in a bad way. "George, we're stuck in this cabin, and there's no resurrection for that horse out there. The Lord will fight for Kit and John if we cannot."

"If I was in Genoa I'd fight the whole territory."

Maria inclined her head toward Angie and said solemnly, "The Almighty never wears out. That being the case . . . since we have a dead horse in the yard and we're stuck right where we are . . . I shall pray on the matter and leave it where I must!"

This seemed to satisfy her own mind that Kit and I were in good hands. (I was having grave doubts at that moment.)

George clenched his fist and gazed at the muscle on his toothpick arm. "I'm gonna pray I meet up with some of those . . . like Bernard King and Rough Elliott! For what they done to Pa and Samson! When I'm grown . . ."

Maria rose suddenly, signaling the end of the discussion. "Have you chores to do? Have you chopped your kindling?"

"No, ma'am. You know I haven't because of the horses . . ."

"Get to it."

George did not have time to throw his coat on before one portion of his wish was answered. The clatter of hooves put a light in Maria's eyes. "There! You see, George? Mister Thompson has sent someone to fetch us back to Genoa."

Rushing to the door, she threw it open just as Bernard King leaped from his saddle and bounded onto the porch. Maria hollered at the sight of the villain. With a rough shove, he pushed Maria into the cabin and followed, snatching the shotgun from its place beside the door and seizing the Volcanic repeater from the wall.

George charged him.

King grabbed him by his trousers and hung him on the gun rack by his belt. "Well, well, well!" King strutted over to the bed. "Lookie who is here! Indeed! Will you look at this!" He was grinning as he turned to the open doorway.

Major Frey strode in.

George called him for the skunk he was and struggled to free himself from the gun peg.

"Let him down," Maria demanded as Frey patted George too hard on the cheek.

George spat on the major and received a blow in return.

Maria attempted to help her son and was pushed hard onto the floor.

"Mother!" George cried and got slapped again, a ringing blow that bloodied his nose and left him limp and stupefied.

When Maria attempted to defend him she was shoved to the floor again and commanded to stay where she was or George would pay for it.

King waved the rifle over the sleeping form of Angie. "Look here, Major! It's your niece!"

The major cussed the girl and said he would send her back to the orphan home for what she had done.

King shook Angie, but Angie could not awaken.

Major Frey towered over her. "My dear niece repays my kindness by stealing my wagon and driving one of my best horses to death. I'll have to take her transgressions out of her hide."

"What do you want with us, Major?" Maria attempted to push herself upright.

King kicked her arm out from under her, then stepped on her wrist, pinning her to the floor. "What will we do with this lady?" He had not forgotten his humiliation at Maria's hands.

"Why, Mister King, we will just keep her company for a while. It would be no good at all if she were to show up in Genoa as Snowshoe said she would. She might well rouse the good citizens to pity—"

"Pity!" Maria gasped. "Only the truth will serve justice! You know Kit did not steal that horse or shoot Constable Denton."

King stepped harder with his boot against her forearm until she cried out with pain. "Somebody's got to die for bushwhacking Si Denton. It don't matter to the law-abiding citizens who gets hung as long as their appetite for justice is satisfied."

Frey rubbed his whiskers thoughtfully. "You see, Missus Thornton, we cannot have you keep the vigilance committee from doing its duty!" He pantomimed the hangman's noose around his neck and gave a strangled cry. "Kit and John will soon be on their way to the hereafter, and then Missus Thornton may go free. She may go wherever she likes as long as it is nowhere in my territory."

✳ ✳ ✳

When a couple of hours had passed, Angie was awake but still groggy and frightened besides. The three hostages formed a row of downcast figures seated on the cot. George was still spoiling for a fight, but his mother convinced him that he would endanger the baby if he acted up.

When hoofbeats were heard coming up the road, Frey motioned for King to stand guard over the prisoners. "Keep 'em quiet," he ordered the gambler. The major opened the door a crack and held the repeating rifle at his side. An instant later he announced, "It's Rough."

Elliott reported how Hawkins had succeeded in getting Kit and me out from under the noses of the lynch mob. Rough weathered the major's temper tantrum by explaining how Thick had left in plenty of time to set up an ambush in the Hope Valley narrows. "It'll be the Thornton gang that did it," he said. "However it turns out, they are done for now."

Maria gasped, and King made an elaborate shushing motion as if her dismay was a great and humorous occurrence. Then he asked a question. "I thought we had a guard back of the jail?"

"That's right," the major agreed. "That crazy Norwegian preacher might gull the crowd, but what happened to Lawrence? Did he fall asleep?"

Elliott grimaced before he replied, "Lawrence came and told me about the escape . . . but he acted like he wanted them to get away."

The major harrumphed and pondered aloud what the younger generation was coming to. "Unreliable," he concluded. "I'll settle with him . . . and you—" he looked at Angie—"later." Then to Elliott he said, "I want you out in the sawmill. Get up on the roof where you can keep an eye on things."

CHAPTER 16

Many and troubled were the thoughts in my head. I had planned to seek help for Kit at the sawmill. Now it seemed I was riding straight into a bigger problem than before. At least Kit's wound had stopped bleeding. He did not appear as bad off as I had first imagined, only hurting and weak from the blood loss.

My brother was half awake, at least enough to sit on a horse and hang on, and I figured to make better time by having him ride behind Lawrence Frey. The two of them together just barely weighed as much as me, and we rode toward the sawmill.

It felt good to have a rifle in my hands again. Though I would have preferred my own repeater, Lawrence's .52-caliber Sharps was a solid weapon. There was a pouch of powder and shot and a tine of primers as well.

"Why didn't you shoot?" I asked Lawrence. "From your angle you could have nailed all three of us."

The young man shook his head. It was plain he had no interest in gunplay or killings.

"Who killed Si?" I asked.

"Rough Elliott," was the not-unexpected reply.

It was a concern to me to know Elliott's whereabouts. Of all those who ranged on the side of the major, Elliott was the most hardened case and the most adept killer. Leaving him unaccounted for made me want to look over my shoulder regular.

I was still searching all around when we finally arrived at the bluff overlooking the sawmill. Since I was expecting to find Frey and some of his men in the front yard, I intended to get in by way of the back. My one advantage was that they were not expecting me. The major probably figured to hold Maria until he got word that Thick had succeeded in killing Kit and Hawkins and me. Then he would let Maria go . . . I hoped.

The question was, since I did not intend to die to oblige the major's plans, how could I get Maria and the children free without harm coming to them? Maybe a trade could be arranged?

When I took stock of the situation, it did not look too good for our side. I had a single-shot rifle—accurate, to be sure, with plenty of ammunition—but still only one gun. Kit, though in no immediate danger, was still a worry, since he could not defend himself. Holding Lawrence Frey was a definite ace for this high-stakes game, but how to play him was the question.

On the other side were three big strikes against me, and they were named Maria, George, and Maddy. If any threat was leveled against them, I doubted if I could go through with my plan. If that was not enough, ranged against me were the major and King. Rough Elliott was out there somewhere and maybe Thick as well. For all I knew, Elliott might be on his way right now with a lynch mob, unconvinced by Snowshoe's preaching.

As the saying goes, when the music starts, it's time to dance.

I propped Kit in the shade beside the sizable lake behind the dam above the flume. Grasping Lawrence by the rope tied to his wrists, I went to the edge of the drop and hollered down, "Major Frey! It's John Thornton. I've got your son!"

There was no sound and no movement for a time. Then the door of the cookshack creaked open, and the major yelled back, "Let him go, Thornton. I don't want to hurt Maria or the children."

"Let me see her, Frey," I called. "Let me see that they are all right now."

"Not yet," he countered. "Let me see my son first."

I pulled on Lawrence's leash like dragging an unwilling puppy. He approached the cliff silent and with his head hanging down. I could not read whether he was abashed about being captured or ashamed at his father's business.

"There he is, Frey. Let me have a look at Maria."

"You know, Thornton," the major countered, "the smartest thing you could do right now would be to hightail it out of here. There'll be a posse arriving before long, anxious to hang the killer of Si Denton. And Hawkins too? Did you dry-gulch him?"

"Give it a rest, Major! Thick failed. And Hawkins knows the truth. There'll be a posse along all right, but they'll be after you, not me."

Frey seemed to study on this awhile, and he still did not bring out Maria. A new thought struck me: Was it possible that he did not have them after all? Could she be safe already?

A movement on the roof of the sawmill was all that saved my life. I flung myself onto the ground and dragged Lawrence with me. I got a mouthful of sand for my trouble, but I missed catching a slug with my teeth. When Rough Elliott fired, a rifle bullet slammed into the post in back of where my head had been. The major's speechifying had just been a play for time to let Elliott get in position. I guess I'm a slow learner.

From my prone position, I took a steady rest for my weapon and squeezed off a shot of my own. That Sharps bucked and kicked like Kit's mule. The shell tore through the shingles at Elliott's feet, making him dive for the cover of a gable. "Watch it! He's got a gun!" he yelled, somewhat unnecessarily to my way of thinking.

The Sharps was shooting a touch low, so I adjusted the sights accordingly.

The battle was on. Major Frey triggered off a couple of rounds as he ducked back inside the cookshack, but they were both wide and high.

Lawrence seized the opportunity to try and crawl away, but I caught the trailing end of the rope and whipped it a couple of turns around the flume post. "Where you bound to?" I asked. "You don't want to miss this party."

Elliott had moved to the other side of the gable to change his angle on me. When he fired this time, the bullet hit in front of my face. I scooted back quick, digging in the pouch for the bullet and powder flask. The Sharps loaded a single round at the breech when you cranked down on a lever, dropping the block and exposing the chamber. I shoved in another .52-caliber lead slug, wadding, and powder and clamped it shut. Applying a new percussion cap made the weapon ready to fire again.

I waited till Rough Elliott leaned out from behind the gable before I let fly. This bullet must have creased his cheek, because I heard him yell and saw his hand fly to his face before he ducked. "Major," he yelled, "this ain't workin'. Let's rush him."

This was bad for me if they carried it out. I could not hope to reload fast enough to hold them both off. What I had going for me was the fact that nobody wants to die, and what they both realized was that if I could not get both of them, I could surely get one.

"I've got a better idea, Major," I hollered as I reloaded. "Let's work on that trade again—Lawrence for Maria, George, and Maddy, and you can ride out of here."

There was silence for a time. I had another worry still: Where was Bernard King? I knew he was no kind of hand with a long gun. Sneaking close for a back shot was more his style.

"All right, Thornton," Major Frey finally replied through the barely cracked door, "you win. I'm bringing Maria out now."

"Call off your dog, Elliott," I countered. "Get him down off the roof and keep him where I can see him."

With Elliott beside the mill building, the major brought Maria outside. She had a bandanna tied over her mouth as a gag.

"Let me talk to her," I said, making Lawrence Frey stand in front of me.

The major untied the cloth.

"Are you all right?" I asked.

She gave a terse nod.

Behind the major I saw Angie Frey emerge from the cookshack window. She had a bundle in her arms that could only be Maddy. With the attention of both Elliott and the major fixed on me, they did not see her disappear into the side door of the mill building.

"What do you say, Thornton? Is it a deal?"

From behind me I heard Kit yell, "John! Look out for King!"

There was no time to think. Once more I flung myself to the ground, just as my prophecy came true: Bernard King fired both barrels of his palm gun from a distance of twenty feet away at what would have been my spine.

But what he hit instead was Lawrence Frey. The boy took two bullets in his midsection. He grabbed his belly with his bound hands and doubled over, then slumped to his knees.

I gave King the benefit of a reply from the Sharps, and no farther apart than we were, the slug did not just hit him in the stomach, it tore his middle clear out. King was flung backward, but he was dead long before he ever hit the ground.

"Lawrence!" the major shrieked, having seen his son go down. "Lawrence!"

The boy struggled to reply. "I didn't tell, Dad," he pleaded in a barely audible voice. "I didn't tell." Then he fell facedown on the ground.

Rough Elliott had not waited to see how the little scene would play out. He was already running for the base of the hill, trying to outflank me. Firing his rifle from the hip as he ran, he forced me to stay low.

I barely had time to spare a glance for Maria. What I saw was the major shoving her roughly back inside the cookshack. I guessed he would tie her up again, but with him crazed with grief, I was more frightened for her now than before.

I slithered over to the drop-off and fired downward at Elliott as he approached the base of the flume. My shot missed, and he fired back at the same instant. By the worst of unlucky breaks, his bullet hit the muzzle of the Sharps, knocking it out of my hands. Worse still, the barrel shattered. I was weaponless again.

Although he could not see the result of the volley from where he was, it would be only an instant before Elliott figured out what had happened. When I did not return his fire, he would be all over me.

I looked around for something with which to fight back. A rock, a shovel, anything. Then it struck me—a shovel *and* a rock! I grabbed a nearby shovel and tried to dig into the dam holding back the water from the flume. Three sharp, clanging blows had no effect against the wall of rock. I stuck the blade of the shovel under the boulder at the base of the pile and heaved on my makeshift lever with all my weight. Still nothing. Elliott would be gathering himself for a rush soon.

I threw myself onto the shovel's handle again, and the old wood snapped with the force, throwing me to the ground.

But the boulder at the base of the dam moved. A fine spray haloed the rock and pushed it ahead a little, then a little more. The pressure of the water rushing from the dam increased as it found the weak spot and forced the gap even wider. Then suddenly, with the impetus of a fire hose, a gush of unleashed power not only jetted through the opening but rolled the boulder in front of it as well.

A rumble and a roar erupted, as if the mountain was suddenly seized in the throes of an avalanche. I took cover behind a support pillar to see if I had been in time.

Elliott was climbing the hillside cautiously, running from boulder to tree stump, fearful that I was laying a trap. How right he was!

He had just arrived at the gap in the wooden conduit when the first of the water reached him. I saw him look up as a couple of drops fell on his head from what had been a dry channel before.

His countenance showed amazement as the noise reached him. He looked so startled you could have knocked his eyes out of his head without touching the rest of his face! The next second that boulder, propelled by tons of water dropping eighty feet, hit him in the chest and bowled him over. He disappeared from view.

Things had evened up some. King was dead and so was Elliott— or at least incapacitated for the time. Now it was me against Frey, and I was ready.

The major had to be holed up inside the cookshack still. At least he had not rejoined the fight. I scampered down the hillside, slipping and sliding. At the bottom lay Rough Elliott. He was clutching that rock to his chest as if it were a pillow. I spared him little regard, apart from picking up the rifle he had been carrying. It was my own Volcanic, and the magazine was fully loaded.

"Frey," I yelled from the cover of the millrace, "King is dead. So is your son. So is Elliott. It's all over, Major. Give yourself up."

The door opened and Frey emerged, but he was holding his pistol against Maria's head. "Come out, Thornton, unless you want her to die. You are not going to outlive my son, except at the expense of her life."

"You can't mean it, Major," I responded. "You know you can't hurt a woman and rest easy. There'll be no place in the world that will shelter you if you harm her." Now it was my turn to play for time.

Major Frey pressed the muzzle of the revolver into Maria's ear. "I mean it, Thornton. Get out here and take what's coming to you, or I swear I'll kill her."

"Don't come out, John!" Maria called. "Save yourself."

"Shut up!" The major ordered, and he swiped Maria across the back of the head with the pistol.

It made me so mad I stood straight up.

It was then that George came dashing out from under the porch. He had an ax handle in his paws, and he swung it with all the force his young body cold muster, right at the back of the major's knees. "Don't hurt my mother!" George screamed.

Major Frey's aim was caught in an arc between me, Maria, and the boy and pointing at nothing when the club knocked the props out from under him. The gun went off, shooting into the ground at his feet.

Maria broke free of his grip, and George raised his sights a touch and clobbered the major's gun hand, knocking the pistol spinning away.

After one futile grab for the boy's hair, the major ducked behind the cookshack and out of sight before I could fire another shot.

Maria and George ran into my arms. I held them for only a moment. Though I wanted the moment to last forever, right then was not the time. "He's still a rattler," I warned. "As long as he's loose, nobody is safe."

Maria was already past thinking about Major Frey. She bent down and cuddled George, who struggled and made protesting sounds. Then a new worry came to her. "Maddy! She's with Angie, John. Where can they have gone?"

"It's all right, Maria," I said. "I saw her sneak out and run to the mill." The mill! My words trailed away with the recognition that the mill was the direction the major had taken. "Go in the cabin and bar the door," I said, hurrying them along. "Don't open it unless it's me or someone you trust. And don't worry. I'll get 'em."

I heard Angie screaming before I ever got inside the mill. "Keep back, Uncle," she was yelling. "Keep away from us."

Levering in another shell, I called out, "Give up, Frey!"

A sawhorse tumbled down from the floor above, barely missing my head. I was afraid to shoot, because in the dusty and dim interior of the building, I could not be certain I would not hit Angie or Maddy.

I believe that Major Frey was genuinely crazy by then. He could not be reasoned with. He was out for revenge, and nothing, not even my rifle, would easily deter him.

The sawdust on the floor stilled my footsteps, but then it did the same for the major's. By passing the main stairs, I crept to one end of the building and climbed a ladder to the second floor. The sound of running feet came to me from high above. I could make out Angie, still carrying the baby, running along a catwalk. Reasoning that Major Frey was chasing her, I started onto the catwalk to cut him off.

A sixty-pound block and tackle swung out of the gloom and smashed into my side. I barely had time to drop my shoulder and meet the blow or it would have busted my ribs. As it was, the impact numbed my right arm. I switched the Volcanic to the other side, but I was awkward at best shooting left-handed.

Knowing that Angie was safely up another level, I triggered off a shot in the direction of the pulley's travel but hit nothing. Worse, the muzzle flash blinded me. As I groped along the catwalk, holding the rifle before me as if it were a sightless man's cane, I almost walked right into my death.

Frey waited until I was directly under the giant saw blade suspended from the works overhead before he threw the lever of the jacking gear. I had only a flash of movement to warn me as the blade descended. Even unpowered as it was, its weight alone and the dagger-like teeth would have cut me in two if it had connected. The cutting edge hit the gun barrel of the repeater instead of my flesh, sending it spinning to the bottom of the mill. The saw blade hung in the void, swaying back and forth and leering like a hideously fanged mouth.

Then he was on me. Major Frey jumped at me out of the darkness. His hands closed around my neck, and I was little able to fight back after the blow to my shoulder. We rolled over and over on the catwalk. He was snarling and biting, no longer even human in his actions.

He put his forearm across my throat, leaning down and pummeling me about the face with his fists. Feeling my consciousness slipping away, I fumbled with my boot top, feeling for the hilt of the knife.

I had only gotten it half drawn when Frey realized what I was about. With a shout of triumph, he released his grip with one hand and seized the knife, flourishing it near my face.

But the change in position was all I needed to give me some leverage. I kicked up hard with both legs, catching Frey off balance. His body lurched toward the edge of the sawpit below, his hands scrambling frantically for purchase on the planks. His fingers twined in my hair as he tried to stop himself from flying forward, but his momentum was too great.

Hurtling through the air, a handful of my hair clutched between his hands, Major Frey shot over the edge of the walkway. A moment later there was a terrible scream, then silence.

I looked over the edge of the catwalk. Frey hung in midair, swinging back and forth on the great circular cutter. He was impaled on its teeth and quite dead before I got to him.

✶ ✶ ✶

When I shepherded Angie and the baby past the gruesome sight and out into daylight, the yard was filled with people. Snowshoe Thompson had arrived, and with him were Paul Hawkins and Curtis Raycraft and others from town.

"Where's Frey?" Hawkins asked.

"Dead," I said quietly. "King and Elliott too. Also young Lawrence, shot by King when he was aiming for me."

Hawkins shook his head sadly. "What a terrible price the major paid for his greed."

"Do you know it all now?" I asked.

Hawkins nodded. "Snowshoe and I pieced it together. We confronted Lute Olds, who was selling meat from the stolen cattle. He's in jail now. Thick got away, but I've already sent word to Placerville. We'll get him."

Maria, holding Maddy in her arms and clasped around the waist by her son, joined us. "Did King really own the sawmill?"

Snowshoe Thompson shook his bearded visage. "He chust thought he could scare you off."

"Then perhaps we can restore it and put it back to work?"

"You don't know the half of it," Hawkins added. "There was reward money up for Edwards that belongs to you, John. And an even bigger sum was offered by Gordier's relatives for his killer . . . who was Rough Elliott. That money rightly belongs to you too. You and Kit."

"Kit!" I said, slapping myself on the forehead. "I clean forgot him. I left him lying wounded at the head of the flume."

"I'll go get him," Hawkins volunteered. "It's the least I can do after almost gettin' him hanged."

"It's all right," I said. "You better see to Frey's body. I'll take care of Kit."

Struggling with stiffness that seemed to be settling in over my whole body, I labored back up the precipice to where my brother still sat with his back against a tree.

"'Bout time," he scolded. "I was beginning to think you got yourself killed."

"Not me," I disagreed. "But you look enough like death that I'll bet Angie Frey will need a month to nurse you back to health."

But Kit wasn't listening. He was staring over my shoulder as if he saw the grim reaper approaching. Then he yelled, "Look out!"

A battered and bloodstained Rough Elliott rose behind me. Over his head he held a large rock with which he intended to bash out my brains.

I caught his arms just before he could throw it. The two of us, both abused almost to the point of collapse, struggled to keep the boulder aloft.

We staggered toward the brink of the cliff. I made the mistake of looking down and felt the world spin beneath me, all eighty feet of drop.

"If I go, I'm taking you with me," Elliott growled.

I believed him.

There was just one chance. If I could use the momentum in the weight of the stone . . .

We danced a drunken waltz of death there on the brink, and then, just as Elliott felt me sway and gave a yelp of victory, I sprang for the flume. The overbalanced motion pushed me into the V-shaped channel. With the water now flowing, I shot like a log toward the bottom, fetching up through the gap in the structure and landing hard on my injured shoulder. But the water and the mud cushioned my descent, leaving me only stunned.

Elliott was not so lucky. Without me to support his weight, he also fell toward the flume, but he did not make it. He tumbled over the edge of the bluff and bounced once more on the rocks at the bottom. This time he was well and truly dead.

✻ EPILOGUE ✻

Wise way beyond his years, George asked me why his daddy had not yelled out the name of his abductor, since he must have recognized the major's voice. I replied that no matter his faults, my brother Lucky had cared for his family and knew such knowledge would endanger their lives. Thinking on that fact helped George some. Maria, too.

Kit and Angie got hitched on the same spring day as Maria and me.

In a year's time Genoa doubled in size. Travel from the East grew more and more regular, and Carson Valley attracted folks eager to ranch and lead civilized lives. The business of the sawmill boomed, and no more was heard of The Committee.

Then silver was discovered in the mines of Virginia City— creating hundreds of miles of tunnels and shafts, all needing to be propped up with square-set timbers, of which Thornton Lumber was the proud supplier.

We debated long and hard about the company name. Kit was square in favor of Thornton Brothers, but that name would not have told the whole story for long. Soon enough it should have been Thornton Brothers, Sons, and Nephew, and even George allowed that was way too cumbersome.

157

✳AUTHORS' NOTE✳

The late 1850s were a time of tremendous upheaval across North America. Bloody struggles in Kansas and Missouri spelled out the confrontation that would set the United States on the inescapable path toward civil war.

The far West was in turmoil. By 1858, the early-placer deposits that had sparked the gold rush of '49 had long since given out. The time when a lone man could make a fortune from the streams of the Sierras was gone. Many who could not find the expected easy pickings in a gold pan refused to go back to dreary occupations in the East. Some settled down to ranching and raising families . . . some took up revolvers and masks.

When arson and looting in San Francisco were ignored by corrupt officials, it led to the organization of vigilante groups. But all too often, vigilantism produced "lynch law" and private vendettas in the name of justice.

Genoa's brush with The Committee is only a small reflection of what happened throughout the West in the middle decade of the nineteenth century. Snowshoe Thompson saw it all and became a sort of one-man CNN of his day.

The Legend of Storey County

Jim Canfield and his friend Sam
Clemens flee the troubles of Missouri
to stake their claim to the richest vein
of silver in the 1860s West, in Nevada.
But are their troubles really over
. . . or just beginning?

This story is for Mom,
Hazel Elizabeth Thoene,
with love.

✶PROLOGUE✶

The Last Run of the V&T Railroad
Carson City to Virginia City, Nevada
September 27, 1938

The chuffing steam engine of the Silver Short Line was decked out in red, white, and blue bunting borrowed from the Virginia City Masonic Lodge's Fourth of July decorations box.

"Don't know why they've dressed the old girl up like she's goin' to a party." The ancient conductor's voice quaked. He squinted out the window at the volunteer firemen's brass band as it played an off-key medley of Sousa marches. His pale blue eyes were nearly hidden beneath folds of skin and grizzled eyebrows, and his leathery face seemed like a topographical map of the desert. "Ain't no celebration. It's a funeral, that's what. Should've dressed her in mournin'. All in black. In black, I say!" He jerked his gnarled thumb at the black armband on his sleeve. "They oughta be playin' 'Death's Harvest Time'! That's what."

Eyes heavenward, the conductor hummed a refrain of the morbid hymn. With tremulous flourish, he punched the ticket of the sandy-haired, studious young man in the rumpled brown suit who sat in the back of the train car with half a dozen other passengers.

Seth Townsend, reporter for the *San Francisco Examiner*, had been sent to write the obituary of the Virginia and Truckee Silver Short Line as she made her final run from Carson City to Virginia City, Nevada.

From the sparse company of travelers, Townsend surmised that there was not much interest in the event. But somebody at the *Examiner* thought it was historical, human-interest type material, and who was Townsend to argue with a three-day journey and an expense account?

Never mind that the trip was plagued by the searing temperatures of the hottest summer and early fall in Nevada history. Never mind that his expense account was barely enough to pay for a sagging bed in a squalid brick rooming house with a window opening onto the belching smoke of the train yard. This was Townsend's first assignment out of the Bay Area. He was determined that he would bring back a story even if he had to make one up.

Careful to maintain a respectful expression, Townsend flipped open his notebook, wagged his head in mock sorrow at the demise of the steam train, and wrote *"Death's Harvest Time"*?

Townsend's gray eyes followed the conductor's gaze to the water-stained passenger-car ceiling as though he were trying to recall the lyrics of the song. He sighed heavily as if struck through with the tragedy of the occasion. It was best not to mention that he was being paid five cents per column inch for the article. Bad poetry could certainly take up at least an inch and a half in an *Examiner* column. Quoting a hymn was easy money.

"'Death's Harvest Time.'" This time Townsend said it aloud as he tapped his forehead. "It's right here. . . . Lemme see . . . something, *something*, something . . . 'Death's Harvest' . . . something?"

The conductor, who smelled of stale whiskey and old tobacco smoke, blinked suspiciously down at the shorthand scribbles in Townsend's notebook and then fixed his eyes on the bulky Speed Graphic news camera on the seat beside Townsend. "You some kind of newspaper wag or somethin'? Newspapers down here in Carson have been all for progress. All for shuttin' down the V&T—"

"Not a bit of it. San Francisco boy. Come to pay my respects—that's all," Townsend said, adopting a mixture of sincerity and innocence in his tone. "Take a picture to hand down to my kids . . . if I ever have kids. Historic day. Last run and all. The V&T Railroad and Virginia City mines together is what built San Francisco, they say. I wanted to have a look."

The old conductor peered at Townsend intensely again . . . wondering, perhaps, if he'd found a kindred spirit in the youth from San Francisco. Was he thinking, *Maybe young people aren't going to the dogs after all?*

"True enough!" He roared his approval and added instruction. "Take a good long look. The end of the V&T means the end of Virginia City! The end of the city that built San Francisco. All those Nob Hill millionaires? They got their start grubbin' in the dust of Mount Davidson! Up there through Six Mile Canyon. All of 'em. Name any of the big-society fellas in San Francisco! No better than you or me. Just lucky, that's all! Don't forget it either. They struck it rich at the end of the line! The Comstock. No place like it in the world. Never was before. Never will be again! Like mines of King Solomon—only richer. And my! How they lived like kings. Forgot where they come from. Forgot you and me and the V&T, too."

The conductor's eyes clouded. He hovered over Townsend in silence and smiled wistfully as if he could see some pleasant image in the distance.

163

Then the shrill wail of the train whistle pulled the conductor's thoughts back to the present. "Well. They ain't worth anythin' now! Bones and dust. Worth less than those heaps of yellow mine tailin's they left all over them hills. All that fuss. Now they ain't anythin' but slag heaps with fancy headstones. And what's it for in the end?"

"Guess you saw it all. The silver boom. Mother-lode tycoons." Townsend touched the pencil lead to his tongue, ready for the story.

"I'm only seventy-seven, a sprout." The conductor dismissed Townsend's flattery, which implied he was the best choice to deliver the eulogy for so venerable a pair of corpses as the V&T and Virginia City.

"Lots of memories?" Townsend's pencil poised over the paper.

"Only enough for my life. You're a few years late, young fella. There's only one left who saw it from the beginning. Old Jim. Oldest man in Storey County. But he don't like strangers much. The real boom was over when I come along." He shrugged and changed the subject. "But you've got the words to 'Death's Harvest Time' all wrong."

"My mother's favorite hymn," Townsend threw in.

The band bleated Sousa's "Stars and Stripes Forever" as the conductor carefully dictated the lyrics to the funeral dirge for the Virginia and Truckee Silver Short Line Railroad.

> *I saw Death come in the springtime*
> *And enter a lovelit bower,*
> *Where from the breast of a mother,*
> *He gathered a fair young flower.*
> *I said to him, "Death, what doest thou here?"*
> *"My harvest," said he, "lasteth all the year."*

Mentally calculating seven and a half cents for verse one, Townsend wiped a feigned tear from his eye, murmured his thanks, and said something about the true heartfelt beauty of great old songs as the conductor shuffled away through the car.

The hike up to Virginia City's C Street from the V&T train station was tiring enough. It was more like mountain climbing than walking. Townsend stopped on the uneven planks of the boardwalk, pulled a white handkerchief from his pocket, and mopped his forehead and his neck. Below his chin, his throat prickled along the line where his scraggly beard ended.

Ducking under an awning, Townsend paused in the shade. Maybe chasing after some old coot was a bad idea. Hiking around the windblown remains of a semianimated ghost town in 110 degrees was seeming less and less like a good plan.

The reporter wiped the cloth across his face once more and noted that it came away stained with pale red dust. He snorted as the pun crossed his mind that maybe this was what his editor had meant about "soaking up the local color." Maybe he could just load up his story with phrases like *once glorious past* and *proud achievements of the pioneers*. That should do the trick. Then add a few photos of the ancient relic of a train and that would be that.

Almost against his will, he thought that the story would be

improved if he could find some old photos of the town in its heyday—steam engine and cars shiny and new, a company of volunteer firemen marching to the train platform before a Fourth of July picnic—something that suggested a present, instead of merely a long-forgotten past.

The sign over the door of the redbrick building against which Townsend leaned proclaimed that the premises were occupied by the *Territorial Enterprise.* A newspaper office! Some vague memory stirred in the newsman's head, a single answer on a USC multiple-choice exam in the history of journalism. But what had been the question?

The place looked deserted. A window shade, broken loose from its mooring, slanted limply across cracked panes. The faded and warped wooden panels testified that the building was not in use, yet the door was ajar.

Townsend poked his head into the dusty interior but heard nothing. He rapped on the door with his knuckles and called out, then succumbed to a fit of sneezing brought on by the dust dislodged by his knock.

"Yeah? Wha'da you want?" growled a voice. A short, bald man emerged from the gloom. From his round face protruded an unlit cigar stub.

"Is this the office of the *Territorial Enterprise*?" Townsend inquired.

"Used to be," the stubby figure affirmed. "Been out of business ten years already."

The reporter was disappointed. "Sorry I bothered you then. I'm with the *Examiner,* covering the last run of the V&T. Thought maybe I could find some old photos to go with my story."

"Yeah?" The cigar stayed firmly clenched between the pudgy lips, but the growl took on a note of interest. "Good idea but too late. Most of the files burned up years ago. The rest . . . I dunno. Blake's my name. I used to work here in the twenties."

Townsend was still trying to recall why this flyspeck of a paper would have been on a college exam. "Did anybody famous ever work here?"

"Plenty!" was the emphatic reply. "Did you ever hear of Joe Goodman?"

Townsend shook his head.

"Dan DeQuille? Rollin Daggett? Real, rip-sawing newspapermen. Not like today's sniveling pen pushers."

Townsend shook his head again and received a heavy sigh in return.

"I suppose it was too much to hope for. All right . . . you have heard of Mark Twain, I hope."

The reporter from the *Examiner* snapped his fingers. "That's it! Twain—Samuel Clemens—was here."

"Got his start here!" Blake roared. "Never was a good newspaperman. Too busy making up lies to bother with digging for the truth!"

The connection pleased Townsend. He would figure out some way to work Mark Twain into his tribute, give the piece a literary bent. "Well, thanks for the information," he said, turning to leave.

"S'pose you'll be writing about Twain now," Blake grumbled. "Well, at least you can still get the truth about that!"

Townsend stopped in his tracks. "What do you mean?"

"Old Jim Canfield, who lives on the corner of Howard and King. He can tell you stories about Twain."

This had to be the same man the conductor had mentioned. "He was here? With Mark Twain? This man knew Twain personally?"

"What have I been talkin' here, Swahili? 'Course he knew Twain. Are you a reporter or not? Go see the man! Ask him."

* * *

The hill from the center of town up to Howard Street was every bit as steep as the climb from the train station to the *Territorial Enterprise.* Puffing and panting, Townsend composed a sentence about how Virginia City perched on the shoulder of Mount Davidson like a . . . like a what? A fly? A crow? What would Twain have said?

The little house located at the end of Blake's directions was faded blue, much the same color as the pale sky overhead. It was tired looking and in need of paint. The tin roof was dull and streaked down from the rusting stovepipes that protruded through the steep pitched metal.

The back porch leaned out over a yard that dropped away beneath it in miniature imitation of the way the whole town clung to the hillside. The structure sagged in the middle.

In the corner between the porch and the house sat an occupied rocking chair. Each creak of the chair was replied to by a squawk from the floorboards. Townsend peered into the shade, but the contrast between the glare of the sun and the shadow prevented him from being able to make out the features of the occupant, except for a glimpse of white hair.

As the reporter leaned over the short picket fence and shielded his eyes from the sun, a voice called out to him from the porch. "You looking for me?" It was a deep tone, husky with age. A dignified rumble to clear the throat followed his question.

"Excuse me," Townsend said. "Are you old Jim—I mean, Mister Jim Canfield?"

"Reckon so. Been that for most of a hundred years. You came to talk to me, right?"

"Yessir. How did you know?"

"Ain't nobody gonna climb this hill in the midday heat 'less they're coming on purpose to see somebody. Everybody else is down to the train station doings, 'cept me. So you must be coming to see me. Come on in."

Townsend swung open the gate into the garden, then ascended a narrow flight of wooden steps to the porch. Once on the planks, his eyes adjusted to the light, and he studied the man seated in the rocking chair.

The face that regarded him from below white hair slightly yellowed with age was a deep tan. Down the dark face coursed creases and wrinkles, like those found across the toe of a well-broken-in leather shoe. The hands that gripped the knobby ends of the rocker arms were themselves knobby with age, knuckles protruding as if the muscles of once-powerful hands had shrunk away from the bone.

Everything about Jim Canfield spoke of immense age, and Townsend began to believe that the stooped figure really was that of a man one hundred years old. But could the memory of one so ancient be relied on?

The issue was settled when the reporter looked into Canfield's eyes and found a steady gaze studying him with amusement. Embarrassed, Townsend peered through the back window of the cabin, pretending to examine a row of photographs lined up on a shelf inside the small parlor.

"Know what you're thinking," Canfield said. "Still got all my marbles. Now have a seat and ask your question."

Townsend sat down in a nearby rocker. "Were you . . . did you . . ." He was baffled. Where to begin? What was the proper first question for someone who had seen a whole century pass? "Were you here the first year that the V&T operated?" he said at last.

Canfield chuckled. "Long before that. I seen this town when the ore wagons went whooping down through Devil's Gate loaded with ten tons of rock. Dug some of that rock my own self, a thousand feet and more under where you're sitting right now."

Townsend looked down at his feet, concerned that the porch might give way and drop him all of that thousand feet. "But you weren't born here? I mean, you're even older than Virginia City, right?"

The deep chuckle came again. "I'm most as old as the Comstock Lode itself, or so everybody round here thinks."

It seemed to Townsend that it was like climbing into a time machine. Not an old newspaper, not an ancient dusty book, but a real, human memory that reached back a hundred years. "Maybe you should just start wherever you like."

"Have a glass of tea," Jim Canfield said, indicating a pitcher and tumbler beside his elbow. "This may take a while."

⁕CHAPTER 1⁕

It weren't the best way to begin life, I suppose. My mama was a slave on the MacBride cotton plantation just outside of Memphis. Her name was Ophilia, and she was a house slave, which is different from a field slave . . . better than a field hand. She was young and pretty. Miz MacBride was a good woman, Mama said. Treated all the workers fair and taught the young'uns their ABCs and how to cipher some.

169

Mostly it weren't a bad life, 'til one morning when Ophilia was hanging out the washing and she caught the eye of the young master. She was in her eighteenth year, and like I say, she was a pretty woman. The young Master MacBride was twenty. He come home from the college down in Memphis and took a fancy to Ophilia, sweet-talked her, and took her to his bed. Such things happened quite a lot back in them days.

She loved him all right, but no good ever come of it. All the long summer he'd take her by the river or meet her in the woods. Then summer come to an end, and he went on back to Memphis while Ophilia stayed on the plantation.

Long about November there weren't no hiding the fact that Ophilia's belly was all swelling up, and no field hand on the whole plantation would claim the child.

Old man MacBride, he figured out that whenever Ophilia had been off somewheres doing something, the young Mister always found some reason why he ought to leave the house, and the two of them always come back looking weary and kinda sly. So old man MacBride, he cornered Ophilia, and she admitted what went on all summer.

The end of all that was when the old Mister took Ophilia on down to New Orleans and put her on the auction block. She fetched a high price because it was clear that buying her was like buying a mare in foal: two for the price of one.

I was born in New Orleans in February of 1838. There I was, the color of coffee splashed with cream, but still as much a slave as any in the South. I don't remember nothing about them first years. Mama worked in the kitchen, so the two of us was never hungry.

Long about the time I was weaned, the master lost Mama and me in a game of chance played with Colonel Georges, who was famous for fighting with Jackson in the War of 1812. He later made his fortune by running some of the finest bawdy houses in New Orleans.

That's where my first memories begin. He put my mama to work in the kitchen of a place called Madame Nellie's. Mama was a good cook, and she had lost her figure by then or it might not have turned out so good for her. The cookhouse was in back of the main building, and Mama and I slept in a little lean-to behind it. I hardly ever went into the main house. It was like some kind of palace to me—all shimmering lights and music drifting out in the nights.

Anyway, I spent my first years turning the spit in the kitchen. Colonel Georges always had fresh-cooked beef or a suckling pig over the fire. Only the best food for his customers, he said. I had me a good strong pair of arms at an early age.

Later on, when I was about six, Madame Nellie took a look at me and said how I ought to be dressed up in a turban and silk knickers and pointy Persian slippers. Said I could walk around the parlor with a tray of champagne and serve it to the menfolk who come to relax at the house.

So they decked me in that rig and made out I was a little prince come from some faraway place—India, I think it was. In the daytime I still turned the spit and chopped the kindling, but come evening I carried a silver tray with crystal glasses to the fancy ladies and their old gentlemen callers.

To this day I close my eyes and hear the piany music. I can see them women in their feathers and satin gowns. The reception room was red-silk walls and potted palms and mahogany woodwork.

For all that, life weren't easy for them girls, and girls they was, too. I know that now. But they was good to me and Mama. They're long gone, but I can still call them all by name these ninety years later.

I don't remember much about the menfolk who come calling. Their brocade vests were stretched across big bellies hung with gold watch chains, and their top hats were a'hanging on the coatrack.

All of us in that house was property of one sort or another. Colonel Georges owned us all. We was put on this earth to serve the gentlemen who come to Madame Nellie's. Long as we did that, we was all right. Madame Nellie took a strop to me on occasion if I didn't move fast enough, but I seldom got in real trouble, except for one time.

I was forbid to climb the stairs, but once I got curious about what was going on up there in them rooms, and I spied through a keyhole and got myself caught. Madame Nellie, who was a big woman, caught me by my ear and dragged me hollering out to the cookhouse. She told Mama what I was up to, and Mama walloped me to an inch of my life. I didn't go up them stairs no more after that.

So it all continued until long about the time I turned ten or so.

Like I said, I was never hungry and I ate a lot, too. I begun to sprout up like a weed. Grew out of my silk India suit twice that winter. My arms poked out the sleeves of my jacket from the elbow down. Worse than that, I got real clumsy. I'd stretch out my hand to pick up a glass of whiskey from the piany, misjudge it altogether, and knock it off instead.

So I couldn't be a little prince no more. Time come when the men callers started to notice I weren't small no longer, and they didn't like it that I was among the ladies carrying drinks. Colonel Georges thought to move my duties entirely out back to the cook-house again, but Madame Nellie had a gentleman caller named Berger from Natchez, who said he had a pair of twin Negroes about five years old and that I would grow up to make a fine drover—

strong. He supposed I could be trained to work with the stock in no time.

"I got no use for the two young'uns," Berger told the colonel. "Their mama died, and they're no good to me on the plantation. I'll make an even swap of them for this young buck of yours."

Colonel Georges puffed his cigar and took a sip of whiskey. He looked at me down on my knees, cleaning up something I had just spilled.

Madame Nellie said, "Ophilia won't be happy about it."

"Jim is half grown," the colonel observed, sipping his whiskey. "Maybe it is not wise for him to remain here. You told me yourself that you caught him peering through a keyhole at Suzette and the mayor."

"That was a year ago. Jim is still just a child!" Madame Nellie fought hard to keep me on, but it didn't do no good in the end.

The colonel said that Mama would get used to me being gone, because he would put the two little niggers in her care and she would be comforted. And besides, they could wear the silk knickers and turbans I'd growed out of, so it wouldn't cost him a thing. I ate as much as two or three young'uns put together, and it seemed like a more than fair trade to him.

And so it was that I was sold away from Mama forever. I never did see the two young'uns that took my place there at Madame Nellie's bawdy house. Mr. Berger sent a foreman named Ward to fetch me away the day after my eleventh birthday. They made the two young'uns wait on the porch whilst I said my farewells.

Mama was crying fit to bust. "My baby boy! My baby! They'll bow your straight back pickin' cotton. Draggin' a sack! I ain't never gonna see my Jim no more this side of heaven!"

Madame Nellie wiped a tear from her eye and put a hand on Mama's shoulder. "Now then, 'Philia, honey. He's practically grown. You gotta let him go sometime. Mister Berger's a fair man. Said he'd put Jim to apprentice with the drovers." Then she looked at me. "You won't mind, will you, Jim? Learn to drive a team? Workin' with the mules? A man's work for a real man. And maybe one day you'll drive a team right into New Orleans and come to see your mama."

It sounded interesting. I said I would not mind, and truth to tell, anything sounded better than cleaning up cigar ash and serving whiskey to a batch of drunken old men. It had the sound of adventure to me.

Mama said that she supposed it would be better for me to be out in the fresh air than working in a house of temptation after all. "No offense, Madame Nellie," she added.

"None taken, 'Philia," Madame Nellie said. "Altogether right. My own child is off to a private school in Charleston. I wouldn't let him near the place myself."

That was the first time Madame Nellie had ever mentioned she had a child of her own. Just like some slave, that woman had give up her little baby. The thought of that made me sad inside for her.

She took my face in her hands and kissed the top of my head. "You're a good boy, Jim. You'll make a better man than the men I've known." Then Madame Nellie told me to work hard and never to peer through keyholes.

Mama told me not to forget to say my prayers like she had taught. Then she give me a poke full of vittles to feed me on the way, kissed me good-bye, and I left with the foreman, Mr. Ward.

✼ ✼ ✼

It didn't matter a pin what Mr. Berger promised Colonel Georges about putting me to apprentice with the drovers. I can see that clearly now. Once that foreman tucked my bill of sale into his carpetbag, I didn't belong to the colonel or Madame Nellie or my mama no more.

It was February. We wasn't more than three blocks from home when it started raining the way it always rains in New Orleans in February: hard.

I had me an old blanket to cover my head, but my feet was bare. Ward had himself a black oiled rain slicker he put on over his tan suit. He told me to carry his valise and to walk behind him respectful-like. He said that I should use my blanket to cover up his valise and that it better not get wet.

"You call me Boss, y'heah?" Boss Ward shot me a mean look that made me forget all about the adventure.

"Yessir."

"Yessir what?"

"Yessir, Boss."

"You ain't with your mama no more, boy. Colonel Georges don't own you no more, nor Madame Nellie, neither. Don't think you gonna have it so easy as you had livin' with them gals."

"Nawsir, Boss."

"You think you're somethin' better 'cause you're a half-breed mulatter, but to my way of thinkin', a mulatter is one step lower than pure black. You're somethin' I wipe off'n my boots, boy, an' don't you forget it."

I plumb lost my voice after that. He smacked me once across the face and told me to answer when I was spoke to. I said, "Yessir, Boss."

I had me such a feeling of hate inside like I never had before. All this and I weren't no more than ten minutes' walk away from my mama.

174

Boss Ward was a small, wiry man with sunk-in cheeks on account of he had lost his back teeth. His four front teeth was all yellowed from smoking black cigars. His eyes was small and sharp beneath the shadow of his hat brim. Truth to tell, I thought he looked like the rat I had caught in a bucket when it had been sneaking eggs out in the henhouse some time back. Mama had killed that rat with an ax handle and had said how there weren't much in the world more wicked-looking than the face of an egg-sucking rat. I thought about this when I looked at Boss Ward. It made me shiver inside, and not because I was cold, neither. I thought about that ax handle. I had felt sorry for the rat, but I wouldn't feel sorry for Boss Ward if he got hisself caught in a bucket somewheres.

The sky grew darker, and the rain poured down heavier than I ever remembered. Maybe I just hadn't noticed how hard the rain could fall before this. Afar off, the lightning forked across the sky and stabbed at the water of the gray delta. Seconds passed and the rumble of thunder rolled over the city and pounded inside me like a big drum. I worried what would happen if Boss Ward's carpetbag got wet. By and by we come to the wharf where a big stern-wheeler was to take us to Natchez the next morning.

The downpour did not slow the work on the docks. Ragged black-skinned men without coats kept on with their work while their white overseers gathered beneath the shed roofs and smoked and talked and warmed their hands over open fires. Great huge crates and barrels and bales come rolling in and out of the warehouses and up and down the gangways of ships and off and onto the freight wagons. Like an anthill, it was. And those workers that did the lifting and the hauling were of no more consequence than the team of mules hitched to the freight wagons.

Through the center of all this bustle there come a line of twenty black men chained together hand and foot. They shuffled on past the dockhands whilst two white men with guns pushed and cursed them. The shackled men was loaded onto a stern-wheeler and chained to a post on the open deck.

Of course, I had seen such things before. New Orleans was the center of the slave market . . . auctions every day. But I had never thought on it much. Folks being bought and sold and taken where they didn't want to go? What did that have to do with me? What I mean is, I never felt like I was any kind of a slave until just that minute when Boss Ward said what he said about me being a mulatter and so low and all.

I wanted nothing so much as to turn tail and run back to Madame Nellie's bawdy house. Wouldn't do me no good though, I figured. Boss Ward would just find me, take me back, hide me good, and brand me with a hot iron like I heard tell was done to runaways.

I was still half numb at discovering my kinship when Boss Ward gave me a shove toward the tavern called the Three Bales. A painted sign with three cotton bales hung over the door. A plume of woodsmoke rose from the brick chimney, and two men dressed in seafaring clothes went in just ahead of us.

The room was dim and hazy, but what I noticed first was that it was warm from a great open-hearth fireplace that blazed at the back of a room crowded with long tables. The hum of conversation and laughter nearly drowned out Boss Ward's words, so he leaned his pointed face down close to me.

His breath was foul. "You wait here with the baggage, mulatter, whilst I have me some refreshment. And don't get no ideas about runnin' off." He popped me hard beneath my chin, then shook his slicker off and tossed it at me. "Hang it up."

I did as I was told, all the while keeping my eyes fixed on that fine blazing fire. I thought about the big fire in the cookhouse at home and how if Mama saw me this wet through and through, she would scold me and strip me and wrap me up and make me drink warm milk in front of the fire. Only one hour separated me from my old life. Poor Mama. If she could see me now, looking like a half-drowned puppy.

Boss Ward bought a pint of rum and sat hisself down at the table nearest to me. I suppose this was so he could be within one long stride of catching me up by my hair should I take to my heels. Three swells sat across from him with their backs to me. Boss supped his rum and talked with the swells, pointing to me and telling them that he had to keep a close watch on me because I was just sold and never been away from my mama before now. He said that once he got me on the boat to Natchez I wouldn't be no trouble because there weren't no way off except to jump in the river, which was a mile wide.

The three turned around like they was one face and looked my way; then they turned back and begun to talk about what was happening in California in the goldfields. By the time they had drunk three rounds, they was all red in the face and loud and excited. People was picking up nuggets by the bucketful just off the ground, they told Boss Ward. And millionaires was being made every day. They had paid their passage to Captain Vickers of the *Flying Witch*, a three-masted schooner set to sail that very night around the Horn to San Francisco. Only fools and cowards were staying behind in the States and missing such an opportunity to strike it rich!

"You're a strong, capable-looking young fellow," said one of the men to Boss. "Why don't you come along?"

Boss said he didn't have money for the fare or he would join them in a minute. He was twenty-seven and felt like he was wasting his life. He allowed how he was weary of tending niggers and running the plantation of a rich man and having nothing of his own to show for it. He reckoned that his employer owed him a lot more than just wages and that he would never receive what he was truly worth to the plantation.

Now I was sitting there beside the valise, sort of drowsing in and out. I would just begin to get warm when someone would open the door to come in or go out and I would be hit again by a blast of cold air. I missed the part of the conversation that was to seal my fate and set me on a course that was altogether different than I imagined.

One minute I was staring at the flames of the fire and the next minute I was lifted by the scruff and poked and pinched and examined by half a dozen men in fancy coats.

"Mulatter."

"Quadroon or half?"

"Half." Boss had the look of a man who had made up his mind about something. "I've got the bill of sale. It says he's half. Good combination. Smarts of a white man and the strength of a—"

"Mulatters sometimes get high-minded. Uppity," argued a man with a heavy gold watch chain draped across a dark red silk vest.

"He does as he's told," Boss Ward snapped. "Don't you, boy?"

"Yessir, Boss," I said.

The big-bellied man leaned closer to me like he was going to sniff my head. "Wait a minute . . . ain't this the child from . . . don't I know you, boy?"

I had seen plenty of swoll-gutted gentlemen around Madame Nellie's, but I never looked at their faces much. "I don't know, mister."

"Ain't you the child from down at Nellie's? All dressed up in the turban and the Persian slippers? Carry the tray around?"

"Yessir, I is," I told him.

"Well then." The big-bellied man seemed pleased. "I know this child." He turned to Boss. "Colonel Georges let him go to you?"

"A trade." Boss Ward fumbled for the bill of sale, which said plain as anything that one male slave aged eleven years had been traded for two five-year-old male children and that Frank Ward had taken possession thereof. "Now all I want is enough cash in hand to buy my fare to San Francisco and one hundred dollars besides. You can put this boy on the auction block in the morning and make a clear one-hundred-dollar profit on the deal."

I looked up at the face of the big-paunched man. He tugged his mustache and scratched behind his ear while he thought the proposition over. I was hoping he would go for it. Anything would be better than spending the rest of my life under the fist of Boss Ward.

Big Belly sucked his teeth awhile and squeezed my arm like I was a hog on the hoof. Then he reached into his pocket and took out his money belt. He made me stand and warm myself by the fire lest I catch pneumonia and die before he could sell me. The papers was drawn transferring ownership to him. This was signed by witnesses, including a judge who also recognized me from Nellie's and said I ought to fetch a good price.

So it was that Boss Ward sailed away to the goldfields and I was put on the auction block after only one night away from my mama.

✳ CHAPTER 2 ✳

Next morning the auctioneer asked the fella what bought me from Boss Ward what kind of experience I had. The auctioneer thought he said I was well mannered and hardworking and had spent my entire life working around the "horses" at the house that belonged to a certain famous colonel of the War of 1812.

Of course, four-legged critters ain't what was meant. All the same, as I stood on the block I was passed off as a first-rate stable hand to that crowd. Yessir! By the time that auctioneer got finished calling off my bona fides I was most convinced myself that I could handle a team and hitch any harness to a rig in less time than it took to say, "Whoa!"

Because of this misunderstanding, I fetched a high price, and also because my teeth was good and I was big for my age, which meant I was sure to grow bigger and stronger, and there was a whole lot of life in me and long years of service.

The hammer come down hard on the table. "Sold! To Mister Hezikiah Green, of Green Freight and Livery, Flora, Missouri, for four hundred thirty-seven dollars!"

Young Hezikiah Green counted out the money in gold coins, and the papers was signed. He looked me over real good as we loaded up to get on that riverboat. "Ain't I seen you someplace, boy?"

I looked him over real good, too. He was a tall, strong, youngish sort of man. He had dark side-whiskers and a tall beaver hat, which made him even taller. He wore a long black-and-tan checkered coat with matching trousers. His jaw was big, and he had the sort of face that the girls at Nellie's would have called handsome, I reckon. He had a happy, befuddled way about him—like a proud hound dog trotting home with a varmint to lay on the porch. His eyes was bright blue but bloodshot, and he smelled of the drink. Other than that I could not see that he had any disgusting habits.

"I don't rightly know if you seen me," I answered truthful.

"It'll come to me." He scratched his head under his hat and shielded his eyes against the sun, which had just busted out and made a rainbow over the river like some kind of sign. "My lucky day." He rubbed his hands together.

I decided to take my chances and keep my mouth shut that I had never been around horses. I was afraid he'd take me back to the auctioneer and turn me in for his money, and I wouldn't get to learn to drive a team after all.

It was getting on toward noon when the lines was cast off and that big old paddle-wheel boat took to churning up the muddy Mississippi. I still had most of a whole fried chicken in my poke that Mama had sent me off with. Hezikiah Green stood at the rail as New Orleans slid away, and I sat down on a crate. I offered him a piece of chicken and a corn dodger. He took them and was right congenial about how good they were and how it was seldom that a man could find chicken cooked this good.

"My mama fix it for me," I told him.

"This your first time away from your mama?" He chewed the last bit of chicken off the drumstick and flung the bone into the foaming water behind the wheel.

"Yessir. My mama is the cook at Madame Nellie's bawdy house. Some say she is the finest cook this side of . . . It just slipped out.

Green got a real peculiar look on his face. "I know your mama's chicken, boy. And I know Madame Nellie, too." He crossed his arms and stuck out his lower lip.

"Mebbe that where you seen me before."

He got real quiet. I gave him another good piece of fried chicken, and he ate it slow, then wiped the grease off his chin with a kerchief. "You growed up some. Growed right out of that silk turban and them

Persian slippers since last time I come to New Orleans. I was there at Nellie's last night, and there was these two little scrawny young'uns wearin' your outfits. I heard you got traded off."

The thought of it made me real sad. "Yessir. I growed too big, and they got shed of me. Now I'll never taste my mama's fried chicken no more, I reckon."

"But you ain't never been a stable hand." He said this with a sideways look to his face.

"Nawsir, I ain't."

"Uncle Trueblood ain't gonna like this much. Told me to get on down to New Orleans and pick us up a groom. Now what?" He looked miserable.

"Mama says I learn real quick. I know my ABCs and how to cipher."

He didn't say no more to me for most the rest of the day. Night settled in cloudy, black, and starless. Inside the bright parlor of that riverboat they was playing banjo and piany just like back home. Hezikiah Green was inside, but I wasn't allowed. I waited where I was told. I listened to that music and the rushing slap, slap, slap of the paddle on the water, and I must have dozed a bit.

After a while he come out and went into a sleeping cabin on the upper deck. I could smell he had been drinking, and I settled down on a blanket outside his door.

I was mighty lonesome away from Mama, so I finished off the rest of my grub. Except I saved out one last corn dodger, which eventually petrified, so I could carry it for a lucky piece like a yeller chunk of rock.

When the morning come, I woke up inside the cabin of Hezikiah Green. Sometime in the night he had moved me in to bunk on the floor beside the steam pipes where it weren't so cold. It was good of him. I have always thought so.

I woke up hungry as Daniel's lions in the den.

Hezikiah was already up and dressed and pulling on his boots when I come round. "Well, it only figures you'd be a late sleeper comin' from where you come from." He nudged me with the toe of his boot, then took hold of the blanket and gave it a jerk, spilling me out. "It ain't gonna do when Uncle Trueblood gets hold of you. You'll be up before the sun and no breakfast 'til you've finished feedin' the stock."

I sat up and looked at my empty poke. I wished I hadn't ate all my grub. "How long 'til we get where we going?" I was thinking about food.

"A few days."

"I'll be dead by then if I don't eat."

"You got chores to do, boy, before you taste anythin' but sawdust in your mouth."

He jerked me up and threw me out of the cabin. It was bitter cold. The day was slate gray, and everything in the world seemed to blend into the wide river. He gave me the boot forward to where a wood crate was marked *Green Frt. Co.* in black letters.

"What's that say, boy?" He pointed at the letters.

I got the part that spelled *Green* but botched the rest, and he give me another kick.

"Green Freight Company! And don't you forget it!" he hollered. "And inside that box is your road to breakfast. I got me four fine, filthy, used saddles in there. Bought at auction where folks know the difference 'tween a horse and a bawdy house!" He pried up the lid. "Now, boy, here's saddle soap and a brush and a rag. I'm gonna show you how to clean a saddle proper, and then you're gonna do it before you get your mouth around one spoonful of grits. You gonna know how it's done before you meet Uncle Trueblood, or I'm gonna pitch you in that river one piece at a time and use you for catfish bait."

There was other people on that boat, but they didn't pay his hollering no mind. I was his and they didn't butt in. It was clear to everyone that this man had hisself a no-good and that I needed to be taught a lesson.

I was sorry I shared Mama's chicken with him.

Before noon I learned how to soap a saddle proper—four of them. I finally ate me a piece of bread with two slices of bacon, and then Hezikiah Green started me on the harness, which I finished too late for supper. After that I didn't think so kindly of him no more, but I reckon he was just trying to save his own skin from the shock of when his Uncle Trueblood met me and found out I didn't know nothing about what I was bought for.

By the time we reached Missouri, I had cleaned every piece of tack six or seven times and knew the name of everything from cinch to singletree. I count myself lucky that there weren't no horses nor wagons on that riverboat, or he would have had me driving a six-up team full gallop around the deck.

Young Hezikiah Green's uncle was named Elwood Langford Rupert Trueblood Green. It was a mighty long name for such a little, sawed-off old man. He had a streak of mean and ornery that matched the length of his name.

To his face, most folks called him Mr. Trueblood Green. Behind his back they called him Bloodhound, Bloodsucker, or Old Blood-and-Guts, depending on which one of his businesses they was involved with. And once he got it in his mind he wanted something, most everyone just called him Uncle and give in to him.

183

Old Trueblood owned near half of everything in that little town. Not that Flora, Missouri, was much to own. It was a little collection of white clapboard buildings all snuggled together behind the levy. There was the Rupert House Hotel and Flora's Restaurant just beside the Elwood Cotton Gin and Warehouse. Folks drew their meager earnings at the Langford Bank and spent them at the Trueblood Mercantile and Dry Goods. Then there was Green Freight and Livery.

That took up every family name of the old skinflint. The only one I didn't connect right off was Flora's Restaurant. Young Hezikiah explained that Flora was old Trueblood's mama. She was long passed on, but Trueblood memorialized her cooking in that eating house with the most pitiful-tasting food cooked from her own recipes. A man had to be half starved or a stranger or in debt to Trueblood to eat a meal at Flora's.

The town was also named after Trueblood's mama.

There was three churches for the white folks who lived in and around Flora. The Methodist church was attended by Republicans and that minority of the town that weren't owned by Trueblood. The

Catholic church was downright deserted except for the priest and a handful of old coots and widows from the days when there was a French outpost along the river. The most crowded church in Flora was the Free Will Baptist, which was different from Southern Baptist and Primitive Baptist.

The Free Will Baptist church of Flora, Missouri, was chock-full of Democrats and was attended by everyone who worked for old man Trueblood or owed him a penny. The old man would foreclose the mortgage and repossess the property of a Republican Methodist without blinking an eye. On the other hand, he'd give special dispensation to debtors who were Democrats, provided they were also regular attending members of the Free Will Baptist congregation.

And then there was what Trueblood called "the darkie church, set up for those hapless sons of the mark of Cain, where no white man dast put his foot." This was the one place in Flora where those of us that was slaves could congregate peacefully on the Sabbath day. We could sing and glory and study how the Lord freed the Hebrew slaves and contemplate sedition according to the Good Book.

But I am getting ahead of my story.

On the day I stepped off that Mississippi riverboat onto the levy of Flora, I didn't know none of this.

All I knowed was that Hezikiah run the livery and freight office for his uncle Trueblood. Hezikiah had bought me for his uncle Trueblood's business. Hezikiah had drummed terror into my head about Mr. Trueblood, and I landed expecting to see a Goliath of a man with a long black bullwhip who would beat me if I didn't know the difference between a hame and a halter. Hezikiah told me to stay behind him until he had a chance to tell his uncle that I weren't fully growed. His uncle Trueblood would be expecting someone bigger than me, Hezikiah supposed, and he wanted to explain what a bargain I had been.

I was looking all around for someone big and mean-looking, but all I seen was a bent old fella with a cane that come shuffling toward me and Hezikiah. He wore a black suit dusted with dandruff and a high collar that cut into the flesh of his sagging jowls. His elbows was turned out and his knees was bent like he had tried to sit down and got stuck halfway.

He waved his cane. "So, Nephew!" he hollered real pleasantlike. "Where's the new man?"

Hezikiah gulped and blinked, and sweat popped out on his brow even though it were cold. "I got fine saddles and English-made harnesses at the—"

"Where's the new man?" Trueblood's toothless mouth screwed around in a squawk. "Old Dimmy's gonna die one of these days, and I ain't gonna leave that room at the stable empty, I told ye! Now, where's my new slave ye brung?"

"I got a good'n, Uncle Trueblood. He'll work out real good."

Trueblood was squinting at the deck of the boat, where a big, strong, ebony-colored man was hauling down the crates marked *Green Frt. Co.* "How much did he cost, Hezikiah? That's a nine-hundred-dollar slave if he's a penny! I tole ye stay in the budget I give ye!"

"And I did, Uncle! Four hundred fifty! And he's—"

"What is he? A contraband? Is he stole from somebody else? I tole ye I wouldn't have no contraband property! If ye got that man for four hundred and fifty . . . He shook his cane in the face of the big slave, who scowled at him and dumped a crate at his feet, then turned back to the boat.

"It ain't him," Hezikiah muttered and stepped aside. He reached back and grabbed me by the scruff of my shirt. "This is him. He's smart as a whip and strong. Young enough so as to be trained proper."

Trueblood turned white, then red, then purple as he sized me up.

Hezikiah repeated the yarn the auctioneer had told about how I spent my whole life around horses and worked for a famous colonel who fought with Andy Jackson in 1812. He explained what a willing lad I was and that I could do nothing but become a credit to the business.

Trueblood whacked me on the arm with his cane. "Ye paid that for this?" he shrieked at poor Hezikiah. "Ye're tellin' me that this is gonna replace old Dimmy when he's gone over yonder?"

"Now, now, Uncle Trueblood! One day, if I handle it right and do right by it and manage the business in a prudent manner, you have promised that Green Freight and Livery would be—"

"I'll see the lawyer about yer part in my will and change it tomorrow!"

"I like this boy! He's bright, I say! Ask him anything you want about how to harness—"

"Ye are a fool, Hezikiah Green! Paid twice as much as ye should for a mulatter child who anybody can see has soft hands! Look at them blisters!" He grabbed my hands and then flung me back.

I fell on the levy, then jumped up and went around out of the old man's reach behind the crate of saddles. I noticed folks was looking with pity at poor Hezikiah.

"He'll work out," Hezikiah pleaded. "Dimmy will teach him, and look at the long years of service we're sure to get out of him!"

"And I'll be long gone by then! What profit is there for me in that? A bad bargain!"

"He'll learn quick."

"He'd better. Yessir! Or I will see about my will!"

As Trueblood shuffled away, folks on either side tipped their hats and greeted him like he were the king or something. But he paid them no mind. Just muttered and grumbled on down the board-walk. Then I seen everybody wagging their heads and looking over at Hezikiah Green and me.

I do believe that Hezikiah would have sold me right then and there at a loss if anybody had been willing, but it was plain to see that owning me would be a liability in a town like Flora. The old blood-sucker was sure to curse and spit every time he cast his dim eyes my way.

Hezikiah turned round, give me a hard look, then jerked his head toward the street, which led right to Green Freight and Livery. "Let's go see what Uncle Dimmy can do with you."

And so it was that I come under the watchful care of old Uncle Dimmy.

Now Uncle Dimmy was probably older than Uncle Trueblood, but he was the exact opposite in nature.

Hezikiah called Trueblood Uncle because of blood kinship and that legal tie-in with the old skinflint's last will and testament. It was more a political decision than one of affection.

Uncle Dimmy, however, was called Uncle because everybody liked to consider him some sort of family member, even though he was as black as a beetle and ancient as Methuselah. Uncle Dimmy always said that after a man gets older than everybody else, white folks don't remember no more what color he is or where he come from; they just admire the fact that he lived so long. They come by and say howdy in hopes that some of that long life and luck will rub off on them.

Well, when I first seen Uncle Dimmy, I reckon I didn't think about being an old man myself someday. Mr. Hezikiah told me as we walked toward the barn that Uncle Dimmy had been a boy my age in Virginia when the Declaration of Independence was writ. That didn't mean much to me in them days. It had nothing to do with *my* freedom, did it? And he was still a slave, weren't he?

He was real old. I guess that's what I'm trying to make clear. Even so, he was in better shape then Trueblood, who owned him, just like he owned the horses and mules at Green Freight and Livery.

"Now listen to me, boy," Hezikiah warned. "I'm turning you over to Uncle Dimmy, and you'll do everything he tells you, hear?"

"Yessir."

"He'll make you fit enough to suit Uncle Trueblood Green."

In the yard, all the wagons and buggies was parked in a large covered shed. Three shaggy horses milled around in a corral beside the barn. One of the animals give another a kick, laid back his ears, and chased him off the feed, as they will do. Truth to tell, I hadn't been much around horses, and they looked mighty big and intimidating to me. I missed my mama.

The barn doors was wide-open, and it was dark inside. We stood there a minute, and I couldn't see nothing. But I heard the stirring of the animals in their stalls, a soft nicker. I inhaled the sweetness of horses and hay. A warm, friendly scent it was. I love the smell of a barn to this day. Then the sun come out and shined on the barn roof. Shafts of light beamed through some missing shingles. Specks of dust swirled around in the air, and I could see the hayloft above long rows

187

of stalls and the fine strong heads of the horses looking out at us as we come in. There was a small office just to the right of the door with a desk and a potbelly stove. To the left was a long, low-ceilinged tack room dripping with harnesses and horse collars and lined with rows of fine saddles sitting on barrels.

"Uncle Dimmy!" Mr. Hezikiah hollered. "I brung you a new colt to break!"

There was more stirring in the stalls. A black-and-white cat come out carrying a mouse in its jaws. It run over toward a door beneath the shadow of the hayloft, and there I seen my first look at Uncle Dimmy. His face was so black I couldn't make it out in the shadow, but his hair was as white as the stripe on that cat's nose. He was tall and lean and only bent a little at the shoulders—in good shape for a fella as old as the United States of America.

"Well now, Pickle," he said to the cat, "I thought you said you brung me a colt to break. Dis ain't nuthin' but a leetle ol' mouse." Then he laughed and picked up the cat and rubbed its ears while the mouse still dangled there.

Hezikiah give me a little shove forward into a patch of light. "It's me, Uncle Dimmy, and this is what I brung you."

The old man took a step toward me. I felt like a rabbit must feel when a lantern gets shined in his eyes in the night. I didn't move a step, but I tried to see the man's face.

"You back, Hezikiah?" he asked. "And you brung me a colt?"

"This boy. This here child is what I mean."

"I thought 'twas Pickle talkin' to me." He laughed again, and it was a pleasant laugh. "Well now. Well, well, well. Will you just look at dis!" He come on toward me, stopping just out of the beam's circle where I stood. "Do he have a name?"

Hezikiah said, "Tell Uncle Dimmy your name, boy."

I answered that my name was Jim.

"Dat'll do." His ancient gnarled grip reached out and took my right hand to hold it palm up. "You ain't did much real work afore now, eh, Jim?"

Hezikiah answered for me. "He ain't never been away from his mama before this. He come out of the kitchen of a bawdy house in

New Orleans, and I got him by mistake. But here he is, and you have to do somethin' with him, Uncle Dimmy, or Trueblood is gonna have my neck. I worked on teachin' him all the harness parts and cleanin' the saddles fifty times. He's smart enough, but he's a complainer. Must be 'cause he come from a kitchen an' his mama let him eat whenever he want to. Got an appetite like a half-starved goat."

Uncle Dimmy stepped into the light. His eyes was smiling, and his face was all lines like the rivers and roads on a map. The whites of his eyes was pale yellow, same as paper turned with age. He didn't have no teeth, but he grinned with his gums.

"You'll do," he said, and he patted me on the shoulder kind of like I was a quivering colt about to bolt out the corral gate. "Easy now, chile. You do as Uncle Dimmy say an' we's gwine t'git on fine."

I said I would, and that was that. He pointed up the ladder to the hayloft, then told me all the straw in the stalls needed turning and the manure shoveled. There was a wheelbarrow, and a shovel and a pitchfork hung right there on the wall. He said everything had a place and he expected that I ought to learn that place and put it all right where it needed to be when I was finished.

All of this made Hezikiah shake his head with relief. "He'll work out, won't he, Uncle Dimmy?"

"He will."

"I knew you could take him in hand."

I was ready to get to work, but Uncle Dimmy set the timetable in that barn.

"I gots me a skillet o' catfish t'fry up fust." He put his bony arm round my shoulder, then said to Hezikiah, "You get on home, Hez. An' don' worry y'self none. Me an' young Jim gonna have us a bite t'eat; then we's gwine t'git dis barn clean up afore bedtime."

✳ ✳ ✳

First evening, after the stalls was all clean and the critters fed, old Uncle Dimmy popped us corn and drizzled butter on it. He didn't salt it none because my hands was all sore and blistered.

We sat up awhile by the lantern light, and he had me tell him the very first thing I remembered about my life. So I told him about my mama and the way the kitchen smelled when she was making plum jelly . . . how the kettle boiled a deep red and how she skimmed the sugar foam off with a wood ladle and give it to me to lick. Whilst I tasted that sweetness she told me stories from the Good Book and sung me hymns and such. That was the first thing I remembered. It made my mouth water for that sugared ladle, and her voice come to mind clear as anything.

Uncle Dimmy said what a good woman my mama was. Then he done the same for me—telling me the first thing he remembered about his mama and what she looked like eighty some years before when she was taking the laundry off the line and how the sheets was stiff and how they smelled like sweet peas because they had dried by the garden.

It was something, hearing that old man talk on like that. I could almost smell the flowers and hear his mama talk to me, even though them sweet peas had bloomed eighty summers before!

He finished talking, and I didn't feel so lonesome no more. I was most tired I had ever been by then. Popcorn all ate up, he told me to go wash myself in the trough and brush my teeth with a twig. Then he slathered my blisters with bag balm, which is medicine for the sore udders of milk cows and such, but it works for blisters on humans, too. He stuck my hands into a pair of clean socks like to bandage them.

"Does you know how t'say yo' prayers?" he asked me.

I told him that my mama taught me and that she set great store by it.

"Sweet Jesus jus' as sweet to a man's soul as lickin' dat plum jelly ladle." He got down on his old knees and prayed like his mama taught him. I got down on my young knees and said my prayers like my mama told me to, and I was satisfied . . . body and soul.

✳ CHAPTER 3 ✳

So my life in Flora with Uncle Dimmy moved along day by day in the same way—winter, spring, summer, and fall—for six years. I growed into my big feet there at Green Freight and Livery Company. Uncle Dimmy fed me, taught me everything he knowed about horses and mules, and treated me as kindly as if I was his own child. We spent them years swapping stories until I knowed his all by heart. I have written all of Uncle Dimmy's life down in a separate book, and it is almost as thick as my own. But that is for another time.

February 1856 come round, and I turned eighteen years old. I was near to six feet four inches tall, and Uncle Dimmy said someday I was going to be stout as an oak, though I was still skinny as a birch tree. He told old Trueblood that young Hezikiah had got a bargain in me and that if Trueblood left the business to anyone else but Hez, Uncle Dimmy might take it into his mind to be a runaway and take me north with him!

Trueblood didn't pay Uncle Dimmy no mind. Business was mighty slow, Trueblood said, and he blamed Hez for its failing. He said Uncle Dimmy was too old to run anywheres, Hezikiah was a fool, and he didn't plan on dying anytime soon.

As I got taller, it seem to me that Uncle Dimmy just got more shrunk up. He was a little more bent, a little more hard of hearing, and his head shook from side to side like he was always saying no.

"Uncle Dimmy? You want a pan of corn bread?" I asked him.

His head wobbled no. Then he would say, "Shore would be good to have me some corn bread."

I had to ignore his head.

His hands shook so that I had to do all the cooking and such. It had been a long time since he tended to mules. I made him a willow rocking chair that Christmas, and he just set beside the potbellied stove and rocked and told stories and dozed.

White folks would come by and ask him if he was feeling well. His old head said no, but he would smile and say he was going home to see his mama and Jesus by and by. He would ask them white folks if they would like to have a last supper with him before he went.

Last suppers was usually whatever I had cooked up at the time. By now I was a fine cook. From all them years I had spent in my mama's kitchen and then with old Dimmy making me repeat every recipe I could remember, cooking come to me real natural.

Folks started dropping in of a morning to speak to Uncle Dimmy because they was certain he would invite them to have a last supper of my coffee, biscuits, and gravy. And then passengers off the riverboats would stop in for the noon meal because I had recollected the way my mama used to make fried chicken, and I could make it most as good as she had.

About this time a light come on in Uncle Dimmy's brain. He seen that folks in Flora and the people who got off the riverboats to get a bite to eat while the boats took on cargo was positively in revolt about the slop served at Flora's Restaurant. Biscuits there was as hard as meadow muffins baked in the sun. It was said that the chicken and dumplings served at Flora's could cause blindness because a fella could go blind looking for the chicken. So it come to Uncle Dimmy that folks who dropped in for a last supper maybe ought to pay something.

He set up a sign on an empty coffee tin.

UNCLE DIMMY'S BURIAL FUND

Under the sign was a list of prices for biscuits, fried chicken, jars of jelly, and the like.

It started out real small, but Uncle Dimmy emptied out the can every day and sent me down to buy supplies. Hezikiah caught the vision and hired a freeman to help with the barn so I could cook all day. He moved the tack and set up some tables and benches in the tack room. Hezikiah's wife, Nancy, made gingham curtains and tablecloths and napkins and such, and they brung their big cookstove down for me to cook on.

It was a wonder and a miracle. The hoot of the big paddle-wheeler whistle would sound, and I would get to frying because we knowed for certain that folks was going to swarm in like hogs to the trough!

Uncle Dimmy just sat in that willow rocking chair beside the pot-bellied stove and greeted folks as they come in. His can for the burial fund was still there, only now the sign for meal prices was posted big and plain above the counter. Uncle Dimmy would rattle his can and say howdy once again after the folks had already paid Miz Nancy for their meals. They all felt obliged to drop something in the old man's offering so as he might buy a fancy casket for his Great Gettin' Up Mornin'!

In this way Hezikiah Green got himself a real business. It was a going concern, I will say!

Another sign was painted and hung beneath the freight and livery sign. Big red letters spelled out:

UNCLE DIMMY'S TACK ROOM

Customers got to be real regular. On a certain day of the week we could just about tell who was going to show up according to the schedule of the riverboats. Pilots and deckhands alike marked Uncle Dimmy's Tack Room on their navigation charts.

One such customer was a young apprentice pilot, name of Sam Clemens, who showed up every Tuesday around noon. Whilst the others took their meals out in the tack room, Sam come back to sit beside the cookstove. That way he'd get a little extra and get to lick the chocolate-cake icing from the bowl. I didn't mind him none. He would talk about the old Mississippi and how she wandered all the way from St. Paul to New Orleans and what he seen on his travels.

This put a hankering in me to get on that paddle wheeler one day and leave Flora behind forever. Maybe I could travel north, where a man could not be bought nor sold because of his color.

I didn't tell nobody what I was thinking.

In them days there was whispers about the Underground Railroad taking slaves to freedom. Sometimes on Sabbath day the preacher would talk about men in bondage and how they was delivered to freedom by the Lord. Sometimes their slavery was of a physical nature, and sometimes it was the slavery of their hearts. Either way the Lord Almighty was in the business of setting captives free, and I was a captive. Just like that sweet sugar ladle, them stories from the Good Book and the tales that Sam told me made my soul hungry for freedom of both sorts.

Uncle Dimmy saw this in my eye, and he said to me, "Don't nobody get free 'less dey prays fo' an answer. Tell it to Jesus, boy."

So that's exactly what I done. I begun to pray for a plan and a way to get free from old Trueblood. I begun to ask every day that the sea would open and I could march on through, just like God's people in the Bible all those years ago, when they got shed of slavery in the country of Egypt.

But I didn't get the kind of answer I expected. When I first seen it, it didn't look anything like yes. It looked like a no. Worse than no.

This is what happened.

In all them years, I still hadn't got back to New Orleans to see my mama, and I took to thinking how fine it would be to just show up in her kitchen all growed up and surprise her. I told this to Sam one day whilst he was licking the icing off the bowl.

"Well, why don't you just go on down there then?" He was smiling like he knowed some secret. "You can leave with us. We're headed down to Orleans."

"You know I can't do such a thing," I told him. "I belong to old Mister Trueblood. He'd send the bounty man after me if'n I was to leave with y'all."

Sam leaned way back in his chair and sucked the chocolate off a wooden ladle. "Your mama has all those recipes, doesn't she? All the ones you talk about but can't cook?"

"I reckon she do."

"Mister Hezikiah is sure to let you go down and speak to her. You wouldn't be gone more than six days. When you come back, you'll have all the secrets to your mama's cooking, and there's no telling what that'll do for business here at the Tack Room."

I knowed Sam Clemens good enough to know that he didn't do something without expecting something in return. "What you want for carrying me all the way and back? I got no money for passage."

He twirled that spoon in his fingers and studied on it awhile. "Cook for me every day of your passage. I want chocolate cake and apple fritters and some of that . . ."

He listed every kind of dish I knowed how to cook, and then when his mouth was watering, he said he would go speak to Hezikiah on the matter straight away. He jumped up and went to fetch Hezikiah.

Hez and Miz Nancy thought it might be a real good idea for me to get on down to New Orleans and get all them secret recipes that my mama wouldn't give to nobody else. They told Sam that they would be right pleased to accept his proposal, but Mr. Trueblood Green had to be consulted on the matter. They said that they would give their answer next Tuesday when the *Mary Belle* stopped at the Flora levy to pick up fuel.

I took to praying real hard that Mr. Trueblood Green would see what a fine idea it was for me to travel on back to New Orleans.

But it was not to be. Same evening, Mr. Trueblood hobbled into the barn and started hollering for Hez and Miz Nancy to get on out of the kitchen and come have a word with him where they belonged . . . in the muck of a stall.

I knowed this was real trouble, so I snuck up into the hayloft and watched the sweet world unravel beneath me.

Trueblood was one mean old man; I can tell you that. He brung along two strong young fellas who sharecropped his land and went to his church. They didn't look none too happy to be there, but they stood just behind Trueblood to add some muscle to his threats. He begun to tell Hez and Miz Nancy that Uncle Dimmy's Tack Room had took all the eating business away from Flora's Restaurant. He said that the Tack Room was closed forthwith and that I was to go right back to my duties as a stable boy. He said if ever he caught me cooking in Flora again he would sell me down the river. All the folks at his Baptist church had been told that they was not to come round here no more unless it was to rent a horse and buggy. He told Hez and Miz Nancy that they was out of the will altogether and that they should pack theirselves up and leave Flora.

Then Trueblood snapped his fingers, and the two big shamefaced sharecroppers commenced to taking that little dining room apart. They broke the tables and the benches, throwed Miz Nancy's table-cloths on the floor, ripped down the curtains, and broke the crockery.

Uncle Dimmy sat there in his wicker rocker, and he cried like a baby. Miz Nancy run out of the place, and poor Hez cursed that old demon Trueblood and called him what he was. But it didn't make no difference to Trueblood. He owned the place, and he owned me and Uncle Dimmy, and he could do what he wanted.

He hollered at me to come out from where I was. I was scared he would sell me down the river right then, but when he took to shouting at Uncle Dimmy, I come down.

Trueblood whipped me with his cane. It didn't hurt none because I was big and he was an old evil man who had no strength left but his meanness.

"Clean this up, you sneakin', lazy nigger!" he shouted. "If it ain't clean and the saddles and tack all back in place 'fore mornin', you're gone, boy! I'll sell you for a field hand! Then we'll see how proud you are, doin' stoop work in the cotton fields!"

Thus ended my hopes. *Our* hopes. Everything was broke to pieces. I carried Uncle Dimmy into his bed and commenced to get to work on the tack room. I worked most of the night. I was real mad. It crossed my mind to go on over to Trueblood's house and climb through a window and put a pillow over his head. No one would be sorry. But I didn't do it. I just cleaned up them broken dreams and looked out the window as the sky got pale and perfect the way it does before dawn. And, because I was right scared I might do murder if I didn't find me an answer real soon, I prayed . . . a lot.

After everything was put back the way it had been, I went in and sat beside Uncle Dimmy's bed. He was sleeping the deep sleep that old men often sleep. Maybe he was dreaming about when he was young, because there was a smile on his face.

Then of a sudden he opened his eyes. "What you doin' up s'early, Jim?" Then he remembered. His face got cloudy. "You finish?"

"Got it all back the way Bloodsucker say to."

I told him what I had been thinking—about doing murder to Trueblood and going to see Mama. Then I confessed I had been thinking a lot about my freedom, too.

"Dat's right," he said to me from his pillow. "Light de lamp, chile. I done bin thinkin' 'bout crossin' dat river m'self real soon. Bin thinkin' 'bout goin' t' see my mama, too."

"Don't talk 'bout dying, Uncle Dimmy." I patted his hand, which was looking more like the claw of a bird lately. Thinner and thinner he was getting. "When you talk like that it scares me. What am I gonna do round here if you ain't here t' look after me?"

The old man smiled at me and waved his hand at the pine chest where he kept his things. "Plump up m' pillers an' hep me set up."

I did that.

Then he said, "Open de chest up, Little Jim. Get out my Great Gittin' Up Mornin' box dere 'neath my long handles."

So I done it.

Uncle Dimmy's chest was a cigar box where he hid all his savings from his burial fund. It had a picture of a red Indian on the outside, and he kept it closed by a little nail on the top. I knowed it was there all along because he had told me when his Great Gettin' Up Mornin' come that I was supposed to pay the undertaker, Dick Willis, with the money in that box.

So I give the box to Uncle Dimmy. He pried it open and let loose with a kind of cackle, then slammed the top shut again. He cradled the cigar box like it was a child.

"Gonna go out in style!" he said. "I done had a word wif Undertaker Willis jus' las' week. Done ordered me up a cherrywood

197

coffin wif nickel-plate handles. Gots me a hearse wif six horses wearin' black plumes. You be settin' up on dat carriage wearin' a top hat an' boiled shirt. Brass band gonna play me 'Death's Harvest Time' real slow and march behin' whilst we rollin' out t' de graveyard, an' all de wimmin gonna cry and moan whilst I is laid low in de grave."

The image pleasured him, but it gave me worse miseries. "Uncle Dimmy, it ain't time to talk of such things. Please—"

"Oh yes it is!" He put up a hand to silence me. "I s'pose I is gonna be watchin' all dis like the Good Book say from among dat cloud of witnesses!"

"You got a long time still."

"No, boy, it ain't so."

I was feeling like I was gonna bust with grief, although it ain't even happened yet. But Uncle Dimmy always did tell a good story and paint a tale good enough so as a fella's mind saw it clear as anything.

"It'll be a mighty fine going home," I said to him. "And never mind yourself none. I'll be sure it's all like you want. I'll take your Great Gettin' Up Mornin' money and pay the undertaker just like you want."

He busted out laughing. "No, boy! Dat's what I'm a' tellin' you. I done paid Willis fo' ever'thang!" He pried open the box and waved a receipt from Willis Undertaker's Parlor marked *Paid in Full*. And there was everything just like Uncle Dimmy told me: casket, hearse, horses, plumes, top hat, and brass band. And at the bottom of the list was a solid granite headstone set to be inscribed with these words:

RIP
Dimmy Canfield
b. 1764 d. 1856
Beloved Father of
Jim Canfield

"I didn't know you had a young'un," I said.

"Yessir. I does." He was looking at me, wanting me to catch his meaning, but I did not. "You is my young'un, Jim. Dere it is set in stone. It gives you my name."

When I understood the sentiment, I commenced to cry. I laid my weary head in that old man's lap, and I bawled like to bust. I never had a father before. And now he give me a name.

He let me bawl awhile, then patted me on the shoulder and told me to set up and listen up because he had more to tell me.

He shoved that cigar box into my hands and told me to open it. Which I did.

Inside there was ten double-eagle gold pieces staring me in the face. A double eagle was worth twenty dollars in them days. So Uncle Dimmy had two hundred dollars left over from his burial fund! And everything was already paid in full.

He begun to laugh at the look on my face. "Dat hide o' yourn is worth 'bout nine hunert dolluhs, Jim. I had hopes t' buy yo' freedom, but it ain't gonna happen. I knows it. Dere ain't enuff time, chile. But I see yo' frien'. I bin watchin' young Sam Clemens, de riverboat pilot. He's took a shine t' you."

"Yessir. He likes my cake all right."

"It's enuff. He don' cotton t' Mister Trueblood."

"Nobody do."

"Dat's a fact. But Sam'll hep you when de time come. Dem double eagles b'longs t' you, Jim. I mean fer you t' have dem fer a legacy, chile. As any good pappy ought, I bin savin' fo' my chile. Hide 'em now, an' set tight. When de time come an' I be gone over yonder, fetch up dat treasure an' pay dat riverboat man one double eagle t' carry you north."

✳ ✳ ✳

After all that talk 'bout death, I was powerful weary. I had not slept for near twenty-four hours, but all the same I cleaned the ashes out of the stove and went to fix biscuits and gravy for Uncle Dimmy's breakfast just like he liked it.

He called to me from his bed, "Little Jim, sing me 'Roll, Jordan, Roll.'"

So I sang "Roll, Jordan, Roll," which was his favorite song because he figured the Jordan River must be something like the Mississippi, and he loved the wide, slow waters of that river.

Whilst I was cooking, he called out, "Dat smell real good, don't it?" Then, "Dis de mos' perty mornin' I ever seed!"

The biscuits and the gravy didn't take no time at all to cook, but when I brung that plate to him his soul had flown away yonder. His face was all smiling, and he was looking out the window at the sun coming up in a glory of pinks and purples in the east.

I set down the tray and just climbed in beside him and put my arms round him. And I watched the sunrise and knowed that this was my pappy's Great Gettin' Up Mornin'. In the light and color of that dawn I swear I could see a young Dimmy, tall and straight and all aglow, walking on up those clouds, and his mama there with her arms wide to greet him. I seen this, though most folks think I'm crazy when I tell of it.

So the old man left the troubles of this world behind, but he left me behind, too.

I must have fell asleep there beside him. When I waked up, Hezikiah were standing over the both of us and my dear Dimmy was cold as a stone.

"Uncle Dimmy has died, young Jim," Hez said.

"I know it," I told him and I got up.

Hez moaned and sat down hard in the willow rocker. He hung his head in his hands and were a pitiful sight.

I laid Uncle Dimmy out straight on the bed, covered him with a quilt, and sent to fetch the undertaker. Then we set down and Hez said some fine words about Uncle Dimmy and how today marked the end of lots of good things.

I did not say so, but I was thinking that this was a day Uncle Dimmy had been looking forward to for a long time and that for him it meant a new beginning. And it was the same for me. I had me a name, and I had me an inheritance and a plan. Like the Hebrew children, I was about to depart from the land of Pharaoh Trueblood forevermore.

"Where are you and Miz Nancy goin'?" I asked Hez while we waited.

"West. I've got a little money saved. I've got my own team and a wagon. Trueblood don't own everything. We'll head to St. Joseph first. Then, come spring, we'll make for California." His eyes was real sorrowful when he looked at me. "Wish we could take you with us, Jim."

"Don't worry yourself, Mister Hez. I'll be fine."

"I want you to know that me and Nancy talked it over long time back. If this trouble ain't come about the will and such, me and Nancy had meant to set y'all free . . . both you and Uncle Dimmy when the property come into our hands. But it weren't meant to be. Uncle Dimmy died a slave."

"Well, he be free now, Mister Hez," I told him. All the while I was thinking how I was going to be free soon, too.

"So he is."

"I'd rather be Uncle Dimmy. Rather live a good life like he done than be rich like old Trueblood when he rises to pass through them pearly gates."

CHAPTER 4

The funeral come off just like Uncle Dimmy pictured it in his mind. Old man Trueblood spoke harsh words to the undertaker about it. He said Uncle Dimmy weren't nothing but an old slave and that it was a waste of money to send off a nigger in such a way. Trueblood claimed that Dimmy's money belonged to the freight company and to Trueblood.

That undertaker just give Trueblood a long solemn look like he was measuring him for a coffin. "The late Uncle Dimmy saved his funds for years in anticipation of the occasion of his demise. I know it and so does everyone in Flora who contributed to the send-off."

To make a long story short, Trueblood did not manage to wheedle even one cent out of the undertaker. There were six prancing horses with plumes, a brass band, and me wearing a top hat and a boiled shirt and riding atop a carriage. It was real fine. The preacher preached a real good send-off; then the white folks went home and all of us folks went on back to our church, and you might say we devoured the fatted calf in Dimmy's honor!

I hardly ever had such a feast in my life! It was announced that Uncle Dimmy, always thinking ahead, had bought up Fanny Brown's whole litter of weanling pigs for the event. We had us pit-barbecue pork and catfish cooked up the way Dimmy liked it. Makes my mouth water to think on it even now. I suspect that the white folks of Flora was sorry they could not join us that day! We sung and there was more hallelujah preaching and everybody gave testimony on into the night. Oh, glory! What a day!

And then it were over, and we danced home by lantern light. I didn't feel sorrow no more. I sat opposite to that willow rocker, and I told Dimmy thanks for everything and what a good time everybody had.

I talked to that empty chair quite a bit for the next few days.

Everybody were run off from the barn but me and the livestock. Mr. Trueblood fired the stable hand. Of course, Hez and Miz Nancy was long gone. I stayed there working alone, cleaning the stalls and feeding the critters and mending the corral gate whilst I thought about my gold double eagles and hoped nothing bad would happen before I could tell Sam my plan.

On Monday morning, Mr. Trueblood hobbled in with the town constable at his side. Constable Hobbs was shamefaced, so I knowed something was up. He had leg-irons in his hand. I'd been raking up straw, so I looked up and leaned on the handle and smiled real friendly, like I hadn't noticed them leg-irons.

"How're you gettin' on?" the constable asked me. He shuffled his right foot in the dirt.

"Right fine," I answered. "Mister Trueblood, you looking well."

Trueblood scowled and spat. "I figgered ye to be gone. Figgered ye'd hightail it outta here."

I did not look at them irons. "Where would I go, Mister Trueblood? Everybody in Flora knows I got no life but this. Got these critters to tend, and I done took over all of Uncle Dimmy's room. Got the bed all to myself now. Ain't that fine?"

Trueblood's lower lip stuck out. His eyes got real skinny and mean. "Happy here, are ye?"

"Right happy, Mister Trueblood. Real glad that freeman got hisself fired. It bothered me some to have him doing my chores."

This seemed to satisfy Trueblood. He mumbled to the constable that maybe they wouldn't be needing to restrain me. All this time I was thinking about Sam and that riverboat stopping at the levy the next day. I was sweating whilst I was playing dumb and smiling like a fool.

Trueblood cleared his throat. Constable Hobbs looked relieved. He put the chains behind his back.

Trueblood turned on his heel and said as he walked out, "I've hired me a business manager for Green Freight Company. Expect him soon from St. Louis."

They left me then, but I could still hear the clank of them irons. I knowed that I did not have much time and that I had better make good my escape the first time or nothing could free me except I go by the way of the grave, like Uncle Dimmy.

That night I stayed up talking to the willow chair and to the Lord about my freedom. I prayed that Sam would come on back here, even if he had heard that the Tack Room restaurant was closed down and that there wouldn't be no icing to lick from the bowl nor chicken to eat.

By the time the morning come, I was altogether done in. All the same, for fear Trueblood would come back, I took to my chores. I fed the horses and the mules and polished the tack, saddles, and such. Just the same stuff that I had done since the day Hez took me onto a riverboat and brung me here. I picked up the first saddle I ever cleaned and remembered how my hands was blistered when I finished. Now my hands was strong and tough. I could jerk down half a ton of misbehaving mule with one arm. I could drive an eight-up team hauling three freight wagons. Mr. Trueblood had got a bargain in me after all, hadn't he? I had earned my keep a thousand times over.

It come to me that if Sam did not come that day I would steal Redman, Trueblood's racing horse and the fastest horse in Missouri. I figured that if I was going to get hanged for being a horse thief, it might as well be for stealing the best horse.

I begun singing that old hymn "Steal Away to Jesus." By verse three I was most sure of what I was going to do. I heard the hinges groan on the barn door, and I looked up. There stood Sam Clemens in his blue apprentice river pilot coat and his cap. He was toting a bundle in a carpetbag.

I stopped singing, right glad he had come but not so desperate to see him now that I had a second plan.

"Howdy, Mister Sam," I said to him, right cheerful.

"Well, this is a fine thing." He looked around at the emptiness. "Nothing for me to eat?"

"Not unless you want to share a feed bag with Redman."

He come on in and climbed on the top rail of the stall to watch me curry Redman. I didn't talk about what had happened, but he knowed it all anyway. "So things have gone sour."

"A mite."

"Old Trueblood tossed everyone out?"

"Everyone but Dimmy. Dimmy flew away and I'm left."

"You staying?"

"I ain't been sold down the river yet, if you know what I mean."

Sam had a sly look in his eye. "Uncle Dimmy had a word with me about you before he passed on."

"Is 'at so?"

205

Sam looked over his shoulder and crooked his finger for me to come closer so as nobody could hear him. He dug into his pocket and pulled out a shiny double-eagle gold piece. "Your uncle Dimmy gave this to me. He said that there would be another for me if I helped you go north. News of the old man's demise and the closing of the Tack Room is all up and down the river. I thought I should keep my promise to him about you. We had figgered to get you on board the *Mary Belle* by pretending to take you to visit your mama. Then you were supposed to fall overboard or some such thing, and I'd come on back to Flora and tell everyone you drowned."

I was surprised at all this. I did not figure that an escape had been discussed before time.

"Y'all is something, Pappy." I spoke to Uncle Dimmy and that great cloud of witnesses who was watching this. Then I said to Sam, "It might have worked last week. But Trueblood is on the warpath."

Sam tossed his bundle onto the haystack. "I brought you a present." He was grinning big and motioned his head at the carpetbag. "Open it."

Inside that bag was a new suit of white man's clothes and new shoes big enough to fit me. Along with that was a bowler hat, round spectacles, a light brown wig, a bottle of bay-rum toilet water to make me smell like a Mississippi gambler, and face paint that Sam had bought off a lewd woman in St. Louis.

"Shave close. Smear this greasepaint on your face. It'll lighten your skin enough so you'll look and smell like a dandy off to see the sights. Not even your own dog will know you. You'll walk onto the *Mary Belle* at my side and . . ." He clouded. "You have that other double eagle? and expenses?" He named off the costs of the clothes and the wig and the face paint.

I told him I could meet the price.

He was satisfied. "The *Mary Belle* is headed north today. If it all comes off, you'll be free by Sunday!"

I thought about New Orleans and how I wanted to go and see my mama.

Sam saw the thought go through my head. He told me to forget it because in the far-off chance that anyone did think about me going south, they might remember my mama was there and send the law to question her. The only thing to do was head north, as far from Flora as I could get, beyond St. Louis and all the way up to Iowa.

"Get dressed," he said. "I'm going to eat down at Flora's Restaurant as my alibi, and then I'll wait at the back stairs of the hotel. You meet me there."

I done all that I was told. I shaved and doused myself with bay rum so as not even Lester Smith's prize hound would have knowed my scent. I dug up my gold pieces and put them in a sock and tied it round my neck. Then I dressed up in all that St. Louis finery and put my feet into them fine patent-leather shoes. Wig, greasepaint, and powder come next, and finally the spectacles. I looked in the looking glass but hardly knowed myself. Even so, I was feeling half sick with the fear that somebody might spot me. I looked at my hands and knowed what Sam had forgot. I needed a pair of gloves!

I was figuring what to do when I heard footsteps behind me. I turned around and there was Mr. Trueblood and another fella who I did not know. I plunged my hands in my pockets and acted like I was admiring Redman.

Trueblood hollered past me, "Jim! Where are you? Jim! You sleepin' in the hayloft? Get down here, lazy no-good! I've brought your new boss!" His weak old eyes was just glaring with fury. He cursed his slave Jim as if it weren't me at all. Then he stared right at me, and I seen he didn't know who I was.

I lowered my voice and put on a deep Southern accent. "Nobody heah, Mistah. There ain't nobody in this barn but me. Ah heard y'all had the fastest hoss in Missouri in this barn and ah figgered to have m'self a look whilst the rivuhboat was stopped. This must be that hoss," I told Trueblood.

At this, old Trueblood started sputtering and turning shades of red into purple. He blasphemed something terrible and begun to shout that his nigger had run away. He said most likely that shiftless no-good had stole a horse and took to his heels in the night. Probably had run off to find Hezikiah Green and make good an escape to California, where they would open a café!

Now the fella beside Trueblood had never seen me as a stable hand. For all he knowed, I was just what I looked to be—a gambler come to look at a horse. The three of us walked out together, and I said to both of them how terrible it was that the old gentleman's stable boy had lit out like that. I told them how once my daddy in Natchez had a pair of slaves who lit out together because they was wearing leg-irons and how they fell into a pond only six feet deep and drowned because of the irons.

It was a fine story. It set Trueblood off on how he almost put that no-good Jim in leg-irons, but the constable had talked him out of it because he thought Jim was too dumb to run.

Trueblood was apoplectic. I was hoping he'd turn to stone and drop dead just like old King Herod in the Good Book. He waved his cane like a sword. I remembered the first time he beat me with that cane and then the last time he done it, and I had to calm myself because it got me riled inside all over again. Not looking back, I strolled beside the new fella until we turned the corner toward the back of the hotel.

There was Sam, smoking a pipe and standing on the step. He looked up at the three of us coming at him, and then he looked away because he still hadn't seen that it was me. He coughed on the tobacco smoke and looked back in wonder that I was walking beside old Trueblood and clucking my tongue and telling him that he would surely catch his nigger by and by.

"Howdy, Sam!" I said real big.

"Hey, James!" he said back to me.

"This poor gent has a runaway slave," I said in my deep voice.

Sam joined the chorus of sympathy. I made as if to walk on with Trueblood and the new man, but Sam caught me by the arm. "We'll miss the boat, James. She's due to cast off in five minutes. I thought you'd never come." Then he tipped his hat to Trueblood and bade them a fine farewell, wishing them good luck with the runaway. We went in the back door of the hotel, through the lobby, and out the front door.

From there it was the longest walk I ever took in my born days, even though it weren't but a block to the boat. I kept my hands down in my pockets. My knees was shaking. Me and Sam strolled easylike on down the street past folks I had known for years. Sam was talking all the while about the price of cotton and the weather and such. Nobody looked twice at me. Together, me and Sam climbed up the gangway. I set myself down in a wicker chair on the deck and pulled my hat over my eyes and pretended to doze whilst the *Mary Belle* cast off and the big wheel begun to churn upriver toward the North and freedom. I count that moment as the real beginning of my life.

I stayed on deck until the *Mary Belle* was an hour out of Flora. A strong wind swooped down from the north, and the skies clouded over. It was dark as night, even though it was the middle of the afternoon. The lightning begun to flash, and the thunder rolled over us like a bass drum. It begun to pour down rain—fierce and mean it streamed down—carving little rivulets in the clay of the riverbanks and nibbling away the levies. If it weren't for fear of washing the greasepaint off my face, I would have stood out in it and let it baptize me in the pure water of freedom!

It come to me that even if I got caught by the bounty man and hung from a tree, this one day would be worth dying for. I never felt so fine as that afternoon watching the lightning bolts split the dark sky and strike earth and water all around us!

Some on board that riverboat was scared that we would be hit, but I had no such fear. It felt like the Almighty Himself put on a show just for me on that day of my jubilee. A kind of celebration, it was, and more than that.

Some may doubt my word, but I am telling the truth. As I watched and listened to the thunder, I plainly heard a voice of great and terrible wrath, of things that would come upon the North and South. I seen a terrible vision of blood and glory in the lightning that day.

Later, when the war come and the nation finally split in two, I was not surprised by it, for I knowed from that day on the *Mary Belle* that it was coming like a mighty storm.

I was the only passenger who did not beat a path into the main salon or into a sleeping cabin. Night had come by the time Sam found me out on the deck. He looked surprised to see me still in the deck chair . . . like he had forgot where he put me. He told me to get up and follow him, which I done. He led me down the stairs to a small sleeping cabin on the lower deck and told me I should get in there and not show my face until he said I could come out. He brung me a red flannel nightshirt and said he would bring me my grub morning and night. If anyone else come by and knocked, I was to make like I was sick and say I wanted to be left to myself.

So I done what he said. In the daylight hours I slept in the cabin. Sam brung me plenty to eat and emptied my chamber pot. When night come and the white folks gambled and danced and caroused in the fancy salon, I sneaked outside and stood in the blackness by the rail from time to time. Nobody noticed me there, and Sam never knowed I done it. I watched the lights of little river towns slide on by, and I studied on all the folks in them towns like me who would soon be free and all the young men who would die trying to hold them captive. The vision had showed me these things, and I never doubted that war was coming.

In this way the time on the *Mary Belle* passed quickly for me. We come to St. Louis and moored up among fifty other paddle wheelers on the quay.

Passengers left, and around noon Sam stopped by my cabin with word that the Mississippi had rose so high that the levies was near to breaking, and the rain was still pouring. "We're going to take on fuel and head right out. We'll be evacuating women and children all along the way north, no doubt."

It was plain to see that he was nervous on account of helping me get away from Trueblood. The strain was beginning to wear on him. Soon enough the riverboat would be full of folks, women and young'uns in need of shelter, yet here I hid with a cabin all to myself. Other menfolk traveling on the *Mary Belle* had already removed their traps from their cabins to get ready for the folks going to be evacuated.

I looked out the round window, and there stood the city of St. Louis—all brick and stone and fine buildings with tall smokestacks. "I have a notion that I don't want to go no further north without seeing St. Louis first," I said to Sam.

"Are you crazy? I figured to take you all the way to Iowa. Dubuque. Iowa's a free state. Even with the Fugitive Slave Law, folks don't take kindly to the bounty hunters there. They don't give those fellas any help with their dirty business. Iowa's a safe place to settle."

"I fancy seeing St. Louis myself."

"I couldn't let you go without saying that half the folks in Missouri still own slaves. This is a border state, Jim. You still aren't a freeman here."

"I aim to see St. Louis." I put on my starched shirtfront and my suit coat. "You done carried me as far as I aim to go."

Sam studied to see if I was in earnest about my plan. "I see you mean to do this thing, although I think you are a pure fool for it."

"I'll buy me a team of mules and a freight wagon here in St. Louis and drive myself north to Iowa. Nobody gonna stop me, even though I ain't white. When I be driving a team of mules, no bounty man looks twice. I done it a thousand times for Green Freight Company, and nobody ever stopped me and asked my business whilst I got a team in my hands. The bounty man will be looking for some ragged, footsore scarecrow flapping through the brush toward the North. Hide in plain sight; that is my intention."

Sam did not know that my knees was shaking when I got ready to leave him at the docks in St. Louis. I figured that by getting off the *Mary Belle* whilst she was still in Missouri, it would be less likely that the bounty man could pin anything on Sam if the question of my disappearance should ever come up. A white man could go to prison for helping a slave get free. That was the law of them days, and Sam had broke it for me. He had risked enough already, and I knowed that he had not done this for me only on account of the money.

He shook my hand the way one freeman does with another, like equals. I felt mighty proud to know him. I would say that Sam was my first real friend, though he was white and me colored.

He wished me good luck and Godspeed on my journey and told me that he felt sure since I had made it this far, I would make it all the way to freedom in safety. When we said farewell, I did not figure I would ever see him again.

I did not wear my greasepaint to cover the color of my skin that day. Even so, I kept them specs in my pocket in case I should see someone from Flora who might be in St. Louis.

I felt mighty sorrowful when I turned around and waved one last time to Sam. I might have been on the road to freedom, but that did not change the fact that it would be a lonely road for many a year.

✣ CHAPTER 5 ✣

It was the summer of '61. The War between the States had yet to amount to much. The Rebs had took that fort down South Carolina way. Some battles had got fought, and some young men had got theirselves killed, but most everybody up north was certain that it would get over double-quick once it got rolling.

Then in July the secesh whipped the boys in blue at a place they called Manassas. It made old Abe's generals take a long, hard look at the thing, kind of rethinking it all. Both sides settled down to growling at each other across the Virginia line, and that's the way she sat. Except worse luck in Missouri, right where I was about to be smack in the middle.

Folks in Missouri weren't clear for one side nor the other, and tempers boiled as high as the July sun baking down on the dirt roads. Both North and South allowed as how they would have Missouri and no two ways about it. Union soldiers plumped down in St. Louis, and when they declined Governor Jackson's request to leave, he made a fire-eating speech and called them invaders. He give a call for fifty thousand men to join up in militia and throw the Yankee soldiers out, and that sure enough stirred the fire under the powder keg.

I had me a wagon and a brace of mules, and I was making out pretty fair, hiring on to cart folks' stuff, hauling firewood and the like. At the time I was living in Keokuk, that corner of Iowa that snuggles up next to Missouri. I was most trying to ignore the war and carry on with my business when it jumped up and bit me.

I got a contract to haul supplies for the Union boys. Seems they were headed down the Mississippi, digging out Rebels as they went. To go along weren't exactly my decision, neither. They said they needed the use of my rig, with or without me. That made up my mind for me, and the next thing I knowed, I was in a line of wagons heading south.

For a long time we didn't see no Rebels to speak of. Sometimes a lean, hollow-cheeked, proud-eyed farmer would lean over his rail fence and spit louder than necessary when the soldiers went by. But for most of two weeks we traipsed from place to place, always hearing about a pack of Rebels here and a hand of raiders there but never catching hold of any what would hold still to be shot at. I believe it had something to do with what General Lyon caused to be tacked up on the trees all around: yellow playbill-sized notes what said that anyone caught bearing arms against the United States government would be hanged as a traitor. Kind of took the glamour out of the vision.

Then late one afternoon we come up on an old sugar-maple camp. It had not been used for a great many years, but there was signs all around that a bunch of men had stayed there and left not long before. There was still a handful of grain in the splintered trough from where they fed their horses, and hollowed-out places in the dirt inside the corncrib showed where twelve or fifteen had been sleeping.

The colonel, man named Grant—him that was later general and then president—said that the Rebels was right close and the men should look sharp. He got word from his scouts that the trail led toward a farm not more than three miles away. He figured to creep up on that farm in the dark. At daybreak, when there was light enough so as not to shoot friends, they'd pounce on that nest and bag the lot.

I weren't no soldier and didn't carry no gun. So it was just fine with me when a captain told us teamsters to stay at the old sugar camp 'til morning. He left us in the charge of a sergeant, a red-faced Irishman who swore something colorful, and all of them soldier boys went off sneaking through the brush.

213

Long about midnight, I was under my wagon sleeping when something woke me. At first I couldn't make out what had roused me. Then I heard a noise, a low cough, just up a brushy ravine from where we was. A minute later I heard it again.

I crawled over to the corncrib and shook the sergeant awake. "Sergeant, there's somebody up that little canyon back of us."

He grunted and snorted like a steam engine pulling up a grade and started cussing me in a voice that probably carried clear to St. Louis. "What are you waking me up for, you no-good . . . and me trying to shush him.

Instead of getting quiet, he got louder, what with telling me at the top of his lungs that even a wooly headed nigger like me shouldn't be scared of some old cow out in the woods.

Well, about the time the sergeant had cussed his way back five generations of my family, a raspy voice yelled, "Charge!" and a pack of Rebels came whooping and hollering out of the canyon.

The sergeant fumbled a Colt Army out of a holster hanging from a nail over his head and managed to drop the thing. It went off with a roar, and then the party really got rolling.

"Form a line!" the raspy voice called out. "Fire!" Half a dozen muskets went off pretty close together. A mule got hit and give an unearthly scream, and a couple of lead balls whizzed through both sides of the corncrib just over my head. Outside, I heard the other mule skinners tearing off into the woods.

The sergeant didn't even wait to try to locate his pistol. He crashed headfirst into the wall away from the Rebs and busted out like a bull. I couldn't think of nothing better to do than follow his example, so I snaked through the opening he made and took to my heels.

But my livelihood, my team and wagon, was back there by that camp. So after doing a hundred yards in the dark, I slid to a stop behind a clump of soapberry bushes to catch my breath and figure out how to go back after my belongings. The Rebs could have the supplies for all I cared, but I really needed that team.

I found the bottom end of the same gully that pointed back toward the maple camp and crept up quiet as a mouse. I calculated on being able to get my mules at least, on account of I had picketed them a short ways off from the camp where a little seep of water had raised a patch of grass.

When I got close, I could hear that same grating voice ordering men to hurry. He was after them to round up the stock and all the equipment they could, especially guns and ammunition. The farm folks thereabouts would feed Southern militiamen for free, so they did not need the cornmeal, but their weapons were few and of poor quality, and they prized the mules.

Working myself around to the east, I come to the clearing where I had staked the team when a regular bust all broke out again. From the shots fired and the angry yells, I guessed that the federal soldiers had been right behind the Rebs and had jumped them in turn just as they had jumped us.

It weren't going to get any quieter, so I sprinted toward the mules, unfolding a barlow knife as I ran. I figured to slash the picket line, not slowing to even pull the pin, let alone untie the knot. Them mules was already most skittish from the musket fire popping around, because when I come up under Shadrach's nose, he reared back and busted the tether.

"Whoa, boy," I said, trying to keep it low and make him mind at the same time. But Shadrach, he weren't having none of it. I made a grab for the scrap of rope trailing from his headstall, and he reared again and spun me half round from a swipe of his hoof. He clattered off into the blackness, leaving me feeling stupid and fearful I might still come up empty.

Meshach was tethered on the other side of the clearing. I couldn't see him exactly, except for the flash of a white blaze on his face. "Easy, Meshach," I called out to him friendlylike. "Just me. Don't be scared." That didn't even sound convincing to me, because no more than two hundred yards away the rifle fire was still rattling and everybody yelling at once.

I got my hand on the rope all right. He was a sure enough tall mule, but I was a big man, and I reached up my arm and grabbed him around the neck. Then I cut the line gentlelike so as not to spook him.

Thinking I had it made, I went to lead him off at a fast walk toward the southeast away from the fight. That's when something slapped him on the rump. I heard it plain as day. His head whipped around like a snake striking, with me holding on and my feet flying through the air. I had no time to give it thought right then, but it must have been a spent rifle ball that come sailing through the trees and give him a whack.

I might still have wrestled him down, but just as he was slinging me around like I was a rat in a bulldog's mouth, I come face-to-face with somebody who that very second broke free of the brush. I do mean face-to-face, too. Our skulls bashed together. The fella gave a groan and fell down like a hog knocked on the head with a sledgehammer.

I weren't far behind, neither. I stared for a minute at the thin gleam of moonlight shining on the blade of the folding knife still clutched in my hand. Then the ground of them Missouri woods opened up and swallowed me, and down into the brush I crashed.

* * *

The morning sun was warm on the back of my neck. I could hear a mockingbird yelling, "Get up! Get up!" But when I made to rouse myself and look around I got a fierce pain over my eyes, and I squinched them both tight shut again. I thought how I'd just go on laying in the brush awhile longer, before aiming to see.

Trying to sort out what had happened the previous night and how I come to be where I was, I didn't pay no mind to a little rustle in the grass down by my feet. The second time it come, I had to pay closer attention, because something slid up across my leg.

Now I've always heard that if a snake gets on you, you should lay real still 'til he gets tired and goes on about his business somewheres else. People what says such foolishness have never had a cottonmouth chase them cross a pond.

I jumped six feet long and four high, just like a jackrabbit. When I lighted again, I grabbed the first stout branch that come to hand and whirled around to thrash that snake for frighting me so.

That sun was powerful bright! So peering through one squinted eye and then the other, I raised my club and kind of sidled back toward the spot.

It weren't no snake at all! There was a man lying there! He was squirming and rustling around and had throwed his arm over my leg. Then it all come back to me with a rush—how I'd most nearly got clear with Meshach 'til crashing into somebody. This had to be that selfsame fella. Since he didn't have no uniform on, just a little gray cap laying beside him, he was one of the Rebel bunch.

Keeping the tree branch at the ready in case he come to feeling as rough as me, I called out to him, "Mister . . . wake up. You ain't dead, I reckon."

He shook a head full of curly brown hair and groaned. Then, after two tries, he pushed himself up on one elbow and rolled half over.

"Mister Sam!" I said, startled when I seen who it was. "It's Jim. Jim Canfield. What are you doing out here?"

In a real dry tone, he said, "I could ask you the same thing, couldn't I, Jim? Was that your mule that kicked me last night?"

"It sure enough was," I lied. What with the blood dried on his forehead, it didn't seem the right time to tell what really happened. "I'm powerful sorry. You all right?"

"I will be when my size-twelve head quits feeling like it's crammed into a size-six hat." He sat up, rubbing a lump on his noggin the size of a goose egg.

I told him how I come to be out in the Missouri woods.

Then he explained his part to me. "Marion Rangers," he said with a snort and a careful shake of his head. "We must be the most expert bunch of soldiers in the military maneuver of retreating in the whole of the Confederate cause. All we've done for the past three weeks is fall back, retreat, withdraw, and fall back again. We would have carried out our twenty-second successful retreat last night if it hadn't been for that new Captain Clayton."

"Him with the voice like a file rounding off a horseshoe?"

Sam nodded. "That's the one. Got the bright idea to outflank the federal army boys and seize the supplies. Wonder if anybody got killed." Then his forehead creased with more than just pain. "I'm not going back. I'm going home. I only joined up because all my friends did. But you know I don't hold with slavery, Jim, nor secession either. Last night, blasting away in the dark like that, I might have gotten killed or killed somebody . . . might have even shot you. I'm through playing soldier."

"That's good, Mister Sam," I agreed. "We can head out together. I'm living in Keokuk. Got me a business . . . or did have 'til I lost my team and wagon last night."

"Keokuk, eh? My brother lives in Keokuk." He stood and wavered a little like a pine swaying in a high wind, putting his hand to his head.

"Just set down again for a minute," I said, and I tore a strip off my shirttail. I soaked the rag in water from the seep of the spring and tied it slantways across his head.

He said it helped some, even if the moisture did open the split a mite. A spot of blood the size of a half-dollar soaked through the cloth.

"Your mules are smarter than us," Sam said. "I bet they left for home last night . . . probably halfway there by now. Maybe we'll catch up with them. Let's just get clear away from here so nobody decides to shoot at us."

Leaning together, we looked like an old A-frame shanty where one wall holds up the other. We navigated north by the sun until we come to a road and got our bearings. Climbing a knoll, we kept to a ridge of high ground where we could watch out for other folks and my mules, too.

By and by, we heard some wood chopping coming from a bowl-shaped hollow up ahead. The dip in the earth was ringed by trees, and we couldn't see down into it, but the noise of firewood being split had a homey sort of sound, peaceful and untroubled. Not war-like at all. Besides, Sam and me reckoned it was bad enough to miss breakfast with no remedy, so we didn't plan to miss dinner, too, if it could be helped. We swung down into that hollow, busting through branches and making all kinds of racket.

Half a dozen grim-looking Rebels popped out of nowhere all around us. Their hair and beards was scraggly and their guns naught

but squirrel rifles, but they were convincing enough. We walked nice
and easy down to their camp.

The leader was a brute of a man with coal black hair down to his
shoulders and a curly black beard all mixed up with a mat of chest
hair that overflowed his flannel shirt. He was as tall as me but half
again as heavy as my two hundred pounds. He seen us being brought
in, but before he came over he said to another bunch of three fellas,
"Go on with your practicin'."

Mr. Sam's eyes most bugged out of his head when he seen what
their practice was. The sound we had took for chopping kindling was
made by bowie knives full thirty inches long. Them men was swinging two-handed, hacking great chunks out of a tree stump. I seen that
the leader had one of them blades hanging from his belt like a sword.

"Who are yuh and what are yuh doin' here?" he demanded.

Now this didn't look like no time to say that I had been hauling
freight for the Yankee army, and Sam, he was tongue-tied on account
of he was a deserter from the same side these folks was with.

I put on my slowest field-hand drawl, so as to sound like I come
from the Deep South. "Please, Cap'n, suh," I said real respectful-like,
"dem Yankees so'jers clubbed Massa and took de wagon. Kin you he'p
us, suh?"

All at once he was just as friendly as he had been fierce before.
He took Sam over to his shelter (though it weren't but a brush arbor
built over willow poles). He sat Sam down on a three-legged stool
and fussed over my bandaging job with clumsy, sausage-shaped
fingers. Then they fed us both plates of catfish and corn pone and
offered to recruit Sam into their outfit.

A new alarm was raised with the cry of "Horseman comin'!"
There was an exchange of signs and countersigns, and then the newcomer was allowed to ride right straight up to the fire. "Greetings,
Colonel Pike," said a slick little man in a city suit and an elegant
pair of tall, shiny boots. "Captain Abner Grimes at your service. My
compliments to your organization. General Tom Harris requests
that your men be ready to join with his in an action down near
Springfield within the week."

Pike, with his heft and brawn, looked more like a country

blacksmith than anything I ever saw called colonel down New Orleans way. He stood and pulled that two and a half feet of knife out of his belt. He swept it across in front of him, then brought it up to his shoulder in salute, as if he were wearing gold braid on a parade ground. "Tell the gen'ral we'll be thar," he promised.

"And who might these be?" asked the smart-dressed fella, staring at me and Sam.

"This gentleman an' his boy was set upon by Yankees," Pike offered for us. "We're just patchin' them up some an' fillin' their bellies 'fore we send 'em along home."

I didn't like the look that horseman give us. His eyes got real narrow and suspicious, and he smoothed his blond mustache. "Do you think that's wise, Colonel? Yankee spies have been operating hereabouts, and now these two know the location of your camp."

Pike looked doubtful, and things might have gone bad for us if Sam had not found his voice at last. "I resent the implication, sir!" he said, jumping up from the stool. "I have sustained a wound, an honorable wound, in combat with the enemy, and suffered serious deprivation of property in the encounter. I do not see any such marks on you. . . . How have you suffered for the cause? I demand your immediate apology!"

A growl of approval came from Pike at this statement.

The dapper man raised an eyebrow and tilted his head. "I meant no offense," he said at last. "These are perilous times, to be sure, and one cannot be too cautious. Now I must be off to other encampments."

I was right glad that when Abner Grimes headed out, he went away south, direct opposite to us.

Sam Clemens said good-bye to Colonel Pike, declining once more the offer of a commission with his group. Pike said he liked Sam's spirit and that this tone would add some class to the company. But even the promise of high times to come down Springfield way could not induce Sam to stay, so he thanked Pike for the hospitality and we pushed off.

Walking all the rest of that day, we slept in a barn, then rose at dawn the next morning to put some more miles between us and the recent skirmish. We was just outside of Hannibal, which was the town Sam called home, when a young U.S. cavalry officer in a dusty blue uniform clattered up with a detachment of horsemen. He demanded to know our business and where we was going.

Sam said, truthfully enough, that we were headed for Keokuk. He added that his brother lived there and that I had a business there.

"How did you come by that head wound?" the officer inquired. "It looks like a bullet grazed you. Have you been in a fight?"

Sam laughed and touched the bandage. "Total stranger got mad when I told him the secesh Rebels are traitors to their country. Hit me with a chunk of stove wood and made some unkind remarks about my partner, Jim, here."

Partner! That clinched it for the soldier boy. No secesh would call a mulatter his partner. "Mind you get on your way then," the lieutenant urged. "There are roving bands of Rebel militia accosting travelers after dark."

"You don't say," Sam said. "Can anything be done about it?"

"Certainly." The young officer laughed. "We hanged a pair of snipers in Hannibal yesterday. Belonged to some guerrilla outfit . . . rangers or something. We mean to string up some more soon as we catch them."

Sam shuddered as the detail rode away. I knew he was picturing the same things as me: some men swinging bowie knives and other men swinging from the ends of ropes.

"Well, partner," he said at last, "I don't think Keokuk is far enough from Missouri to suit me, but it's a good start."

✳CHAPTER 6✳

S am's older brother Orion had him a law office in Keokuk. That is to say, he had a rolltop desk beside a window and a row of law books over the fireplace mantel in a little downstairs parlor. The two-story, pale yellow clapboard house where this parlor was located actually belonged to his wife's ma and pa.

Sam always said that Orion was the most truthful fellow what ever lived, and such character traits was a defect in a practicer of the legal profession, to quote him more or less. Said Orion was so able to see both sides of an issue that by the time he got done defending a man, even his client would have voted guilty. Sam said this broadmindedness was why Orion's law firm didn't have any business to speak of and why him and his wife and their little girl didn't have a place of their own.

Orion was a fine-looking man, square jawed, to my mind favoring Colonel Grant as to his face and neat-trimmed brown beard. He was a soft-spoken man who always treated me square and never seemed to get into the kind of scrapes that Sam fell over just by walking down the street. Any troubles Orion run into come from believing any old outlandish tale. Sam said that his brother was the single most gullible man on the planet, and I seen it myself.

When we got to the house, Orion was acting excited, pacing in front of the fireplace and wringing his hands. Sam tried to tell him the story of the Battle of the Sugar Camp, no doubt expecting to puff up his part some, but Orion had a story of his own to tell.

"It's come, Sam," he said with satisfaction in his voice. "You said it would never amount to anything, but here it is for real. All that time I put in stumping for Bates's election in the last campaign is finally going to pay off."

I guessed from the look on his face that Sam had heard his brother get worked up over things before. Sam told me that Orion was always helping out folks for free instead of charging, and everyone thought of Orion as an easy mark when they needed a loan to back some harebrained scheme or other. I saw that Sam was having thoughts such as these when his brother continued.

"Bates has joined Lincoln's cabinet. One of the positions in his patronage is secretary, and he's offered it to me."

Sam's jaw dropped. "Secretary of what? You can't mean in Lincoln's government. Do you mean undersecretary? Of what? Treasury? Or do you mean private secretary for Bates?"

Orion got the biggest grin across his face. I could tell he was going to play this moment for all it was worth, probably because he didn't manage to impress his brother very often. He waited 'til Sam had loaded and fired a whole salvo of questions before he answered. "Grander than any of those! I am to be the secretary for—" he drew himself up on his toes and thrust his hand under his jacket in a right distinguished pose—"the territory of Nevada!"

Letting fly a blast of air like a blacksmith's bellows, Sam give out with a single laugh. He sat down, laughed still more, and wrapped his arms around his ribs, as if he figured that laughing so hard would bust something loose. "Nevada!" he said when he caught his breath. "Secretary to a hunk of desert that has more Indians than white folks? What will you report on, Mister Secretary? The condition of this year's crop of sagebrush? The alarming invasion of horned toads?"

Orion looked right taken down a peg. He tried to give it back to Mr. Sam, but it was halfhearted at best. "It is a terrific opportunity! You have heard of the huge silver strike, haven't you? It's like the gold rush of '49 all over again. Thousands moving there, striking it rich! Why, it'll be a state in no time! I could grow up with it, maybe be governor someday!"

223

Sam growled, "Grow up is right! When they find more sand than silver in those holes in the ground, where will you be then? What about moving your family out to the desolate wilderness? Disease, savages, drought, wild animals . . ."

Easing down into a chair across the room from his brother, Orion's chin drooped on his chest, and all the excitement seeped out of him like a pat of butter oozing over a plate in the summer heat.

It weren't my place to speak, but I couldn't take no more. "Mister Sam, you did ought to let your brother tell you more before you go to bad-mouthing his chance. Go on, Mister Orion, tell us more. What do the job pay?"

Getting regular pay was not something that had often happened in Orion's past, and my question struck the right tune with Sam. "Yes," he agreed. "Tell us what it pays."

"Eighteen hundred," Orion said simply.

"Dollars?"

Orion nodded once.

"A year?"

He nodded again. A man thought himself well paid if he took home five dollars a week. So eighteen hundred a year was not the riches of Solomon, but it was a substantial sum.

Sam looked astonished. "Well, I'll be . . . I owe you an apology, Orion. This sounds like it might be for real after all."

It was a wonder how much Orion's face brightened at them words. Ain't it amazing how much joy and how much sorrow can be caused by things as unsubstantial as words?

Orion got back some of his enthusiasm. "And you can go with me. The job provides for me to have an assistant. I'll not try to bring Mollie and Jennie out until I've built them a house. What do you say? Shall we be old bachelors together for a year or so?"

This offer was made so earnest and with such plain longing for approval that even Sam bit back the harsh words that I seen was straining his throat. "No," he said. "It's not for me. But thank you, Orion, for thinking of me."

There was a knock at the front door and Orion left to answer it, asking Sam and me not to leave yet and for Sam to think it over before deciding.

Sam made a pouty face and shook his head at Orion's back. His mind was already made up. No desert for him, no sir!

How our plans and God's do surely fall out with each other.

Orion came back into the parlor with a tall, rail-thin cadaver of a man. He had a hawk's beak for a nose and the deep-set, brooding eyes of an undertaker or maybe a hangman. Orion introduced him. "James Redpath, I'd like you to meet my brother, Samuel, and our friend Jim Canfield."

"How do you do?" Redpath said in a jovial voice that was far from matching his looks. He shook my hand before taking Sam's.

"Mister Redpath was one of John Brown's lieutenants," Orion said. "Now he is aiding the government in ferreting out Rebels and traitors in Missouri. I have a letter here from Washington giving him extraordinary powers of arrest and trial."

225

"And find them I will," said Redpath cheerfully, as if daring anybody to argue. "I'll put a rope around every Rebel's neck until they tell me all about their leaders . . . and when they have told me all, I'll haul them to the top of the tallest tree I can find, may God have mercy on their slave-abusing souls." He said this as happily as if he were talking about going varmint hunting or some other sport.

I heard Sam swallow hard. He muttered something about how evident was Redpath's dedication to duty or some such truck and then acted like he didn't trust hisself to say more.

Orion fetched a letter from a pigeonhole of his desk and handed it to the abolitionist. "I wish you success," Orion said. "You may have heard that I am leaving these parts for my new position in the territory of Nevada. No need for your services there, I imagine. No dangerous Rebels in Nevada."

Redpath got a funny kind of crooked smile and said no, he imagined not. With that, he shook hands around again and took his leave.

Most as soon as the door closed Sam was up and out of his chair. "Is that offer still good?" he asked, grabbing Orion's arm. "I feel an intense desire to see Nevada." As he said this he run his finger around the inside of his shirt collar as if it had right sudden got too tight for his throat.

✳ ✳ ✳

Sam invited me to come along to the new territory of Nevada. Never did find my mules, and of course the wagon was long gone, not that it would have made no difference without a team. Not having any business no more nor any family in Keokuk, I couldn't see no reason not to go. It come to me that if I struck it rich, I could own a freight company entire, and if I busted I could still find work driving team for somebody else.

I think Mr. Sam was grateful I said yes. He had remarked more than once that keeping an eye on Orion was a full-time job, and since Orion felt the exact same way about Sam, I was fairly nominated to play nursemaid to them both. Only three days went by between the time we made the acquaintance of Mr. Redpath and the moment we left Keokuk to hook up with the westbound stage.

It was a hot, dry, dusty day when we took passage with the Overland Stage Company out of St. Joseph, Missouri, bound for Carson City, Nevada Territory. The fare was one hundred fifty dollars each, and nothing discounted for me having to ride outside the entire way on account of being black. I had only about half of that amount saved, but Mr. Sam paid the rest for me, saying I could pay him back out of the first shovelful of silver I dug up. He paid all of his brother's passage, too, since Mr. Orion didn't have no savings to speak of and the government didn't allow him no traveling funds.

The Concord coach had seats inside for six passengers, three looking forward and three facing back. There was also little jump seats inside of the doors so the coach could haul eight inside at a pinch. Besides the driver, there was a conductor fella who rode beside of him, and then on the roof of the whole affair they crammed as many other folks as could hang on, which included me.

That vehicle was pretty as a picture. It was sparkling clean, dark red trimmed, with yellow wheels and running gear. On the outside of both doors was a drawing of a right smart, Spanish-looking gal and the name *Esmeralda.* Up on the box sat the driver, pulling on a long pair of new buckskin gloves and never so much as sparing one look for the passengers nor the hostler standing at the head of the six-up team. The driver had a tall, shiny boot setting casual up on the brake and a coiled rawhide blacksnake whip lying beside him on the seat.

Right then I got such a hankering to be a stage driver I thought I would die happy if ever I climbed to such a lofty position. I studied on it some waiting for Mr. Sam and Mr. Orion to get their baggage sorted out.

Neither one of them had reckoned on the fact that all you were allowed to take was twenty-five pounds of gear. Now that weren't no bother to me. After selling the little tack I had left from my freighting business, I could put all my worldly goods in what the old-timers called a possibles bag, about the size of a small carpet satchel.

But them two brothers! They had to unload all of two trunks and ship it back home. The conductor nearly laughed hisself silly watching them two dig out fancy dress suits and such.

They managed to pare it down at last, and then their valises and my bag was throwed in the boot on top of about a half a ton of mail. The canvas cover was cinched down across the lot, and the passengers, which also included a lady and another gentleman, climbed aboard.

I climbed up behind the driver, and the conductor took his place. He looked at a big watch and give a little nod. That driver uncoiled his lash, and with a single crack of the whip the coach jumped forward and we was off, leaving the States behind and headed out on the first leg of a three-week journey that would carry us over two thousand miles.

✳ ✳ ✳

Three-quarters of our travel passed without incident. We reached Nevada Territory and was winging along, skirting the Humboldt River. It was late twilight when we rolled into Warbonnet Station for a meal and to take on a new driver, or jehu, as they preferred to be called. Warbonnet was called a meal stop, but the only thing I found to eat was stone-hard pone with more than a handful of sand in each bite. The other fixings was fried bacon that was more white fuzz than pork and coffee made with well water already so brown that the ground-up Arbuckle beans seemed pointless.

The new driver, whose name was Frank, was of medium height and frame, with wide shoulders spreading a buffalo-skin coat. He wore a broad-brimmed Texas hat above a blousy shirt and a wide leather belt topping buckskin breeches. His chin was stained from a mahogany dribble of tobacco juice. The old driver was bending Frank's ear about how some station keeper named Jules had got hisself fired because he had been too loud once too often about how the South was going to whip the Yankees. Now Jules had turned renegade and was leading a band of Northern Shoshones in raiding the stage line.

In an unnatural deep voice, the way a man will speak when he's trying to sound tough, Frank allowed that this fella Jules was a thief and a cutthroat on the run from the law. He said that none of them as fought for the Confederacy would welcome such as Jules.

Frank remarked that they was all better off now that Jules was given the get along and that he expected to see Jules swinging from a gallows most any day. Our conductor said that if Frank talked much thataway, then he had best keep his six-shooter close to hand, as he was soon going to need it. That was all I heard before we commenced rolling again.

I didn't pay much mind, having heard rough-talking folks before and knowing as a general thing that nothing ever come of it. Besides, the plains country was right pretty. A big, round, silver moon soared into the sky behind us and kind of swarmed upward like the searchlight beam of a giant riverboat bent on overtaking our puny craft.

Heaven's lantern lit the open spaces 'til I could pick out rocks and scrawny bushes half a mile away. From my perch on top, I could hear the conductor and Frank talking in low tones. Snores ripping out of the windows proved that Sam and Orion was sleeping.

I drifted off myself, lulled by the rocking of the coach on the leather straps called thoroughbraces when we pulled into another little station—just a corral and a lean-to hut, really—to change teams. Frank and the conductor had both got down for a minute while a skinny hostler swapped the horses for a six-up of mules. The conductor was back on the box and Frank was stepping up when somebody grabbed him from behind. Frank ripped off a string of swearwords that would have raised the eyebrows of a mule skinner and swung back around. That's when I heard him say, "Jules!"

I heard a dull thud, like that of a wooden club landing on flesh, and Frank give a cry of pain and then called out, "Help!" Looking over the side of the coach, I seen one big, bearded ruffian swinging a pistol butt and that skinny wrangler weighing in with kicks whenever a clear shot presented itself.

The conductor never moved an inch, just set still like a wooden Indian in front of a cigar store. He was scared of Jules hisself, too scared to go to the aid of his friend. The mules spooked when the club whacked again, and Frank give another call for help. The coach lurched forward, and the conductor fell off into the middle of the fight, whether he wanted to or no.

That team was sure enough off to the races. They kept to the road for fifty yards or so before the right rear wheel hit a rock or something and we went bowling off across the desert.

I vaulted into the driver's box and took up them ribbons like I was born to it. I figured that team would be right sassy when they sensed an untried hand at the reins, and right I was. For the first minute of sawing back and forth, they paid me no mind at all.

Up ahead, a bright patch of moonlight was sliced in half by a long, black line. That could mean only one thing: a dry wash, or arroyo, lay ahead, with us heading straight for kingdom come.

But I had already found out what I needed to know. No matter how well matched a pair of mules, one will always exert hisself a little more, be a little stronger. And of the two leaders, it was the right-hand critter.

So I hooked up a double handful of reins and cranked the leaders to the right, knowing I could use the natural ability of the stronger mule to pull the coach around in a circle. And wheel about we did, with the rear of the coach sliding over shaley rock and spurting up gravel, and me having no time to pay any attention to any boulders smaller than the size of my head. We did bounce some, right enough.

We did not really come close to flying over the edge of that canyon, but we whipped by near enough for me to spit into it, and that ain't no lie. We come flying up on the scene of the battle again. I heard the blast of a six-gun, and I knowed things was serious. I steered that team right into the thick of the fight, just missing where the conductor had landed on his head. We scattered folks to both sides, and when the shoulder of the right-hand leader mule knocked Jules down, the pistol went flying out of his hand. Then I give a whoa, and them mules stopped as sweet as if they had knowed me forever.

Maybe it was the two against one or the blindside nature of the attack . . . or maybe it was the scared, higher squeak to Frank's voice that come out when he yelled for help that made me do what I done. I pitched off that coach, right on top of Jules just as he was getting to his feet. It was like dropping a watermelon on somebody's head, catching him sudden and knocking him down again.

The other fella scrabbled in the dust, looking for that gun, and Frank give him a good right to the chin. Then Jules, who'd got hisself up quickly, punched me in the gut. He let me know I was going to live to regret interfering, if ever I lived so long. I was already enlisted for the whole of the war, too late to reconsider, so I folded my fists together like I was swinging a bat and uncorked a two-handed swing that Jules walked straight into.

The blow knocked him down on one knee, but he come up with a flurry of punches, and all I could do for a time was protect myself. I slipped in jabs that cut his lip and pasted his eye. He hollered for the other fella to throw him the gun. Things looked bad.

Frank and the other bushwhacker rolled over on the ground, and it scared me when I seen Jules's partner come up with the revolver. He swung it round to draw down on Frank, but Frank knocked the gun aside just as the trigger got pulled.

There was another blast and a spurt of flame that most blinded me; then Jules give a grunt of pain and stopped swinging. A second later, he keeled over. He was dead—shot in the back by his pard.

When the skinny fella seen what had happened, he throwed the gun down and took to his heels, and we never saw him no more.

Now about this point, another gunshot come from inside the

coach. It didn't hit nobody, thank the Lord. I ducked down anyways, and when I peeked I seen a hand waving a tiny .25-caliber pistol out the window. Seems Sam and Orion, being the only two passengers in the coach, had undid the curtain flaps just enough to poke the gun through but not enough to aim.

"Put that thing away 'fore you hurt somebody," I yelled.

The pistol disappeared like it was sucked back inside, and then I heard Sam's voice real quaky-like. "Jim? You out there? Is it Injuns?"

I told him everything was all right now but to stay inside and not to shoot no more.

The conductor was coming around, so I loaded him into the coach and told Sam and Orion to tend him, whilst I went and checked on Frank. I was afraid to go into the station, on account of not knowing if Jules had any more accomplices lurking about.

Frank was breathing real hard and ragged, hunched over, with a hand pressed to his side. About the time I got to him, he give a lurch and held out his hand to me for support. Even though the moonlight made it look black, I knowed that hand was covered with blood. He passed out then, so I throwed him over my shoulder and made for the hotel that passed for a station, danger or no.

Once inside, I swept some dirty tin plates onto the floor and laid Frank down on the rough-plank table. I got a lantern lit and a basin of water laid by; then I turned to Frank. With my jackknife I slit Frank's shirt up the side to examine the wound.

I found the wound, right enough. The first shot had ripped through Frank's flesh, between rib and hip bone, just above that broad belt. It was not a deep wound, more of a furrow than a hole, but it had bled considerable. It was a wonder Frank could have done all the fighting he did, with that gouge bleeding all the while.

But the other wonder was what else I found. Frank was a woman! That wide leather belt and blousy shirt had concealed it, but without the disguise, there weren't no mistake.

I went on washing and bandaging the wound, and when I was most done, Frank (and I don't know no other name to use) come around. First thing she said was, "You know, don't you?"

I nodded.

231

Then she said, "Does anyone else?"

I said, "No, ma'am. I reckon not."

Right then and there she made me promise not to let on to nobody never. She didn't even ask me how bad she was hurt or what happened to the others until after I swore to keep her secret.

I drove the team on to the next change of drivers, where we said good-bye. "Never mind what you hear folks say about the Injuns," Frank offered by way of advice. "They're mostly peaceable. Bushwhackers like Jules will try to get them blamed or at least rile things up. Watch out for the others of his kind."

CHAPTER 7

The last stage stop before we reached Carson City was outside Fort Churchill, about twenty-five miles east of our destination. The fort—not a real stockade, just a dozen buildings built of adobe bricks—stood in a bend of the Carson River. The fort got its start in the summer of '60, a year earlier than my arrival in Nevada Territory. The Paiute Indians, also called the Washoe tribe, had gone on the warpath and killed some folks at a place called Williams Trading Post. What followed the massacre was something called the Paiute War or the Battle of Pyramid Lake.

The killings had started when some white men stole a couple Indian girls. First the Indians whipped up on the whites, and then the whites hollered for help from the U.S. Army in California, and they scared the Washoes into clearing out.

But the miners and other folks of the Washoe mining region wasn't certain that the Indians wouldn't try again. They got the army to set up Fort Churchill, so as to keep some defenders nearby.

Things was not entirely calm yet, what with the war only being a year old and feelings pretty sore on both sides. There was two companies of Yankee infantry and one of Yankee dragoons at the fort. The dried mud-block barracks was naught but half done—the other half still building. But there was a couple hundred men plus weapons and ammunition stored there.

The stage depot hard by the fort was called Bucklands. The soldiers spent their spare coins there, friendly Indians traded, and miners coming to the Virginia City diggings passed through. Bucklands was on the

Pony Express trail and the route of the new Overland Telegraph. All in all, a right busy place for a flat spot amongst the sand and sage.

We stopped at Bucklands only long enough to swap the teams. A big, swaggering, red-faced man, two-thirds drunk and louder than a brass band, hung on to the rail of the Bucklands porch like it was a pulpit and held forth for the entire territory to hear. "Blast the Yankees and blast Abe Lincoln and blast the abolitionists! All the South wanted was to go in peace, but oh no, old Abe wouldn't let 'em. Well, he'll regret it, mark my words, yessir! Long live the Confederacy! Long live Jeff Davis! Hurrah!"

Sam poked his head out of the coach window and asked the driver who that fella was and weren't he scared to be so loud, what with the Union soldiers so close and all?

"Pay him no mind," said the reinsman. "He's drunk. But, stranger," he added in a real serious manner, "don't cross him, neither! That there is Bill Mayfield. Him and Ruff Hardy and Sam Brown and them other secesh Rebels, drunk or sober, they ain't scared of nothing. And they don't carry them pistols just for looks."

Sam pulled his head back in then, but not before I heard him remark to Orion, "What was that you said to Redpath? Out west there aren't any dangerous Rebels?"

The driver touched up the team and off we spun, so I never did hear if Mr. Orion made any reply.

✳ ✳ ✳

We had the expectations that Carson City, being the capital of the territory and all, would be a sight more imposing than it was. Between Salt Lake City and Carson, there weren't anything big enough to be called a town, let alone a city, so I was ready for something that looked a mite civilized.

The stage swung up over the last rise that separated us from our intended home and dropped down into a sink. The road churned with alkali dust like it was steam boiling under the wheels. Due west was the peaks of the Sierras—a great big, spiky wall, eight, nine, ten thousand feet high, like God had to build a mighty big fence to keep the desert from overrunning the world.

The driver hollered over his shoulder to me, "There's Carson!" He pointed with his whip.

I wiped the dust out of my eyes, best I was able, and I strained to see what he was pointing at. I made out some white specks at the bottom of them mountains. I thought I was looking at beehives or chicken coops, so I hollered back, "Where are you looking?"

And he said, "Right there!" and pointed again.

Them beehive, chicken coop–looking things was Carson City! The town was all built of whitewashed boards, and they was so puny compared with what God did out of granite, I had to laugh.

We rattled into the center of town, and I do mean rattled, because the dry air and alkali dust had leached all the moisture out of the wheels, and the spokes was fairly fixing to give up and turn loose. Our coach shared the road with a pair of freight wagons, hauled by ten pair of mules each. That's how they moved fuel, food, furniture, and the other fixings of civilization over the mountains. Pulling up in the middle of the downtown block of buildings, the driver whoaed the mules. Our journey across half a continent come to a sudden end.

I climbed down off the roof of that coach for the last time and stepped onto a plank boardwalk. I helped the station hands unload the bags out of the boot, and then I took a shot at shaking myself free of the dust.

That's when I noticed some fellas looking at me and pointing and others laughing right out loud. I even turned around to see what was so funny, but there weren't anything to be seen. I said to Sam, "What's so all-fired humorous? What is these folks laughing at?"

He looked me up and down and answered, "Jim, I expect they are watching you emerge from your alkali cocoon. You are, without a doubt, the whitest black man I—or any of them—have ever seen!"

Such was my arrival in the Nevada Territory.

✳ ✳ ✳

Sam and Orion fetched up at a boardinghouse run by an Irish lady, joining fourteen other fellas what was already staying there, all in one big room. I couldn't stay inside the rooming house, and no other place would have me, neither.

Sam said that this was only temporary 'til him and his brother got themselves a place of their own. I could stay with them when they did, and in the meantime, they fixed me up a tent out behind Mrs. Flannigan's place. She said she'd feed me all right, if I would chop the sagebrush branches for the cook fire, wash the dishes, and such. Which is exactly what I did for two or three days.

Now there ain't nothing dishonorable about washing dishes for your keep, but it seemed to me that I didn't come west to work as no house slave. My aim was to catch enough money quick to get me another team and go to freighting again. What with flour selling for fifty dollars a barrel, people was paying jewelry prices to get stuff hauled in from San Francisco. But first I needed a bankroll. There was all kinds of stories about folks striking it rich in the silver mines of Virginia City, and I made up my mind to ask Sam to stake me to some prospecting gear. He showed up outside my tent looking mighty down in the mouth himself.

"What's the matter, Sam? You look like somebody done stole your joy."

"That's about the size of it, Jim," he said. "You remember when my brother said that he was authorized to have an assistant?"

I nodded with the recollection.

"Well, what my brother forgot to find out was how his assistant was supposed to get paid. Seems he overlooked the little detail that if he hired a helper, it would come out of his own one fifty a month."

"That's bad, ain't it?"

"It is since Orion is trying to save enough money to get a house for his wife and daughter. I can't ask him to support me, too. I'll have to think of something else. Matter of fact, I got an idea."

It was just about sundown, and what they call the Washoe zephyr was kicking up. That wind blows regular in the afternoon, ripping down the east side of the mountains and playing rough with shingles and loose boards and careless chickens. My tent flapped so bad that I could hardly hear, so I said to Sam that we ought to go round to the front of the boardinghouse and stand to the lee of the breeze.

When we found a quieter spot, Sam lit his meerschaum pipe, so I commenced talking instead of him. "What about prospecting? Why don't you and me team up and find us a silver mine?"

He raised them bushy eyebrows and studied the bowl of the pipe for a minute. "Thought of that. But from what I hear tell, everything in Virginia City has already been claimed six ways from Sunday. There are new diggings down south of here, but I don't know yet if it's for real."

It was my turn to look glum. I really counted on making a silver strike. "Guess I could hire on as a miner for someone else. Or maybe a driver or a cook."

About that time, a fella come sailing down Main Street like a little boat driven by a storm. His coattails blowed halfway up his back, and he needed both hands to keep his hat squished down on his head. He was aiming for the boardinghouse, but he had to line himself up and come over on the slant a good deal upwind; otherwise he would have missed it.

He lit in the middle of Mrs. Flannigan's porch, near bowled over Sam and me, give a gruff "'Scuse me," and pushed on inside. But not before I seen his pointy, ratlike face.

"Quick!" I said to Sam. "Do you know who that fella is? And what he's doing here?"

"Met him at supper," Sam answered. "Name's Ward. He's a new roomer—fifteen of us in happy intimacy upstairs now—but he says he's just here a couple nights on business, then back to Virginia City. Why? Do you know him?"

I nodded. "His name is Ward all right! He was the slave boss what sold me and stole the money. Lowest man next to old Trueblood I ever met."

"Did he recognize you?"

"Doubt it. When he last seen me, I weren't but eleven or twelve."

"So? What's your worry? Even if he did remember you, what's he gonna do? Turn you in as a runaway and put his own neck in a noose?"

I shuddered like the wind was chill, only it wasn't. "I dunno what he might do. He has a real wicked feel about him. What's his business that he come here for?"

"He's a foreman on the Comstock Lode. Some kind of boss for the Chollar Mine, I think he said."

That killed any thought I had in my head of going to work in a mine, if that was the kind of foremen they hired up Virginia City way. "What was your idea," I said, "the one you started to tell me about?"

"Oh," Sam said, remembering. "Governor Nye suggested it. They use a lot of squared-off timbers down in the mines for bracing and so forth. Anyway, a man can stake a patch of pine trees up on the mountain, just like a mining claim. What do you think?"

"How far we gots to go?"

"Just due west. If you're game. We can go in about a week."

"Can't we leave tomorrow?"

238

Waiting to get on with our timber claim, the nights was long and lonesome, and the wind howled down from the mountains and made me feel restlesslike and dissatisfied in my soul. When that dark feeling come upon me, it seemed like there was some piece of myself that had gone missing, and I just had to find it. Trouble was, I didn't know what *it* was or where I had mislaid *it.* That being the case, I did not know where to begin looking.

Orion and Sam had found us a place to live, a little two-room house, so I weren't out back in a tent no more. But that was all that happened worth remark.

About another week passed in boredom and unease. Then one afternoon the Washoe zephyr again come swooping down on Carson City, carrying the scent of sage and pine and dust onto the valley.

Carson were only four blocks of white clapboard houses with the blue Sierra mountains rearing up in the west and all the wide desert stretching out to the east. One-story buildings bordered a town square on three sides. The fourth side was open to the desert. In the center of the square stood a sixty-foot-tall flagpole. In this space, teamsters parked their wagons whilst they went into the Ormsby House for a snort of whiskey to see them on their way.

On that afternoon the wind blowed so fierce that Old Glory stood straight out from the pole like the canvas were a slab of wood painted red, white, and blue. Such a wind could blast granite smooth and suffocate man and beast alike if they was to be caught out in it for long.

Carson was packed with wagons and teams of mules and horses whilst the mule skinners took shelter. Critters stood with heads drooping down, eyes closed, ears laid back, and tails to the grit and wind.

From the window of Orion's house, I could see all this misery. The zephyr moaned around the corner of the little building, and my soul begun to stir and pace and groan inside of me. Then that voice come to me, telling me that something was out there just beyond my vision, behind the curtain of dust.

"This is like to last awhile," Orion said to Sam and me. "There was supposed to be a wagon train headed our way from Fort Churchill. Let's hope they had the good sense to linger there."

239

Sam and Orion went into the kitchen whilst I stayed looking out at the dust storm. I could hear the two brothers talking about the war. The Union Army of the Potomac was taking a licking from the Rebs and Jeb Stuart's cavalry in particular. The news weren't good.

From that dismal topic the two brothers took off talking about the silver strikes in the mountains away south and up Virginia City way, but none of it held my interest. Deep inside I was listening to another voice, but I could not understand the meaning of it.

I must have stood at that window for an hour or better. I seen two freight wagons roll in. The drivers, bent against the wind, faces covered with kerchiefs, tended their horses and then beat it into the hotel. I knowed that there wouldn't be a bed to be had in Carson City that night unless a man was willing to share with half a dozen others. As for me, I would bunk right there in Orion's parlor on the floor and be grateful for it.

I heard Orion say, "A man can't know who to trust in these parts. . . . The place is crawling with secesh. . . . Captain Moore at Fort Churchill doesn't believe it, but I say we'll have the Rebel army rising up here in our own backyard before the year is out."

"That only makes sense," Sam said. "The Rebs can make as good use out of Nevada silver as the Union can."

So they talked on about Union spies and secret cells of Rebels intent on capturing Nevada for their cause. I thought that anyone crazy enough to want Nevada ought to take her and welcome. I was yearning for a long, cool look at the green Missouri countryside and a bath in Mississippi River water.

About that time I seen something just out beyond the brown curtain of swirling dust. First off I thought it looked something like a sail on a ship all billowed out in the gale. Then I figured it were a critter trying to make its way into the lee of a building across the square. There was a flash of red, and I seen that I was looking at a woman's hoopskirt and petticoat, which had blowed up over her head. There was two legs, covered in ruffled bloomers, stumbling against the wind. The fabric of the skirt pushed her back one step for every two she took.

"Glory be!" I said out loud.

Sam hollered out at me, "What do you see?"

"A female woman just blowed into the square!"

She fell down on her back in that same instant, and I was out the door and sprinting across the square and through the tangle of wagons and teams to her side.

She was making choking noises, sort of angry and scared and flustered at the same time, as if she had fell into water and was trying to swim. Them hoops was all the way up and over her shoulders, and she was trapped just like as if she had a gunnysack tied over top of her. Them long legs was kicking against the wind, but it didn't do her no good.

So she commenced to hollering, "Halp! Somebody halp me!"

Sam come along behind me. His voice was near drowned out in the wind. "What has blown in here, Jim?"

"A hoopskirt with a woman trapped inside," I said. Then I bent down and grasped the bottom hoop, which was at the top. I gave it a tug until I could see the crown of the female's head.

"Is she a keeper? Or do we throw her back?" Sam shouted.

In spite of the state of upheaval she was in at the time, I could see that beneath the coating of alkali dust she was young and beautiful and colored same as me. Later I found out that she was a child of a union between a runaway slave and a Cherokee Indian in the territories.

My soul rejoiced! All my life I had the feeling the wind was going to blow some good fortune my way, and here she were all in a heap, sitting at my feet.

She stuck out her hand. "Don't just stand there, you fool! Halp me up!"

I done as I was told, but I could not find any voice in me to speak even one word to her. I stepped back out of her way as she pounded on her red dress until it become obedient and stayed where it ought.

"Folks call me Sam." Sam made as if to tip his hat, but it had blowed away.

"They call me Lark," she said, giving a little dip with her knees, "because I sing."

I thought I had never seen a bird so beautiful. I tried to tell her my name, but I just sort of croaked at her.

She asked, "What ails him? Is he struck dumb?"

Sam answered, "Only smitten by the sight of unexpected beauty in such a place as this. His name is Jim."

I grinned and got sand in my teeth. She turned away from me before I could think of anything to say.

Sam knowed just what to say though. "Now, where have you come from, madam? And tell us how you happen to arrive here on foot and in such a condition." He bowed and offered her his arm to escort her back to Orion's house lest she be blowed back the way she come.

"There is a wagonload of helpless women out there. We were bound for Virginia City to perform at the Virginia House Hotel."

A wagonload of females broke down in a dust storm outside Carson City, Nevada? I had heard tell of the Virginia House Hotel from a Union soldier on the porch of Ormsby's. It was a hotel that served as a meeting place for the Rebel sympathizers in Storey County. It had a new saloon and dance hall that was all ready and waiting for a troop of hurdy-gurdy girls to arrive from the South. So this gal was one of them. I knowed about such females. They was girls who danced with men for a dollar a dance. Some of them would do more with a man than just dance.

Sam looked Miz Lark over real good. "Well, this ain't the Virginia House Hotel."

"Our wheel broke. They sent me on ahead to fetch aid." This event were a sort of miracle to the teamsters gathered in the corner bar at the Ormsby House. In no time at all there was dozens of teams and wagons charging through the Washoe winds in search of fair ladies in distress. There was more wagons racing through the storm than there was ladies to rescue. As it turned out, there was one dozen stranded females and three dozen freight wagons and buckboards. In some cases, this led to violence among teamsters who had been good friends and companions for many years. Something like the Civil War, it was.

Whilst the rescue was being made, I had the good sense to stay put in Orion's parlor alone with Miz Lark. She had lived most of her life in Louisiana and knew something about good food, so I whomped her up a quail-egg omelet and fritters, and at last I found my voice.

I told her all about myself and where I come from. I told her about my mama and Uncle Dimmy's inheritance and Sam and the riverboat and finally how I come to be here in Nevada.

"I'm a freeman, and I aim to stay free," I said. "I aim to make my fortune out here in the silver mines."

She smiled at me real sadlike, as if she knowed about dreams that sometimes come true but mostly do not. "I hope you find everythin' you want." Then she looked down at her empty plate. "You sure do know how to take care of a gal."

I sat down across the table from her and took her hand. "I know I am making bold, Miz Lark, but I got to tell you everything I been thinking." I nearly lost my voice again as them sweet thoughts crowded in my throat trying to get out all at once. "Well, you know when I seen this place I was wondering why I ever left the green fields of home. Then the wind blowed you into town, and I says to myself, 'Jim, that there is the very reason why you come so far.'"

She pulled her hand away. "Please don't . . ."

She tried to put a stop to my declaration, but it were too late. I had started, and now there weren't no halting me from telling all.

I grabbed her hand again. "What I mean to say is this: I ain't never seen a woman so purty as you are. I ain't never heard any lark sing so sweet as when I first heard your voice."

"Please, Jim." She stood and turned her back to me; then she went over and looked out the window. "You don't know nothin' 'bout me. 'Bout where I come from or what I am doin' here."

"I don't need to know no more than that I could love a gal like you."

"I ain't what you think. Ain't no sweet little lark."

"It don't matter to me." I went over to her and stood close enough so as I could have touched her, but I did not. I knowed well enough what sort of life she come from, and I did not want her to get the notion that I was like every other two-legged male critter who thought of her as something to be bought and pawed and wrestled around a dance floor.

She stared out at the dust blowing through Carson City. "I ain't free."

"Yes, you are," I said. "There ain't no slaves in Nevada. All that we left behind us. Every man and every woman gonna be free, no matter what color. Mister Lincoln is fighting over that right now."

"No. I ain't free to love a man. Can't sing for whoever I want." Her voice was soft and sad like someone telling of sweet dreams that couldn't ever come true.

I wanted to take her in my arms. Didn't she understand that nobody had a hold on her now that she had come west?

I told her this again. Told her I knowed women who had led a hard life who had been redeemed. I said that her soul was all that mattered to me and to the good Lord. We could make a new start. I would treat her good, and she would learn to love me.

She shook her head, then put her hand on my cheek. "Jim." She said my name so tender that I knew her heart was listening to me. "I bought my own freedom."

"You see!"

"But listen . . . freedom had a high price. The boss of this troupe,

Mister Ryeman, he bought me at auction. Put me to work in his place back in Natchez singin' and dancin' as a hurdy-gurdy gal. You know what such things mean. . . . When he heard tell of the war and the silver strike out here, he gimme a choice. A chance. Said if I wants to be free I can work my way to freedom. Seven years here in the West. Work off the price he paid for me and some more; then I can go where I wants to."

"That don't mean nothing!"

"I put my mark on his paper, Jim! Don't you see? That contract says I owes him all this money. Says I gots to work seven years or pay him five thousand dollars."

"Lark! Five thousand . . ."

"It was that or stay in Natchez with no hope of ever bein' free. One man the same as any other, I tole myself! Don't matter if I be in Natchez or Virginia City. Only here I figgered I could have some hope! Figgered I could cross off ever' day 'til seven years gets by. When some man paid his dollar for me to dance, I figgered to close my eyes and dream of the day . . ." She begun to cry soft and sorry like a young'un who done wrong and was shamed of it. "But now here you come along . . . big and strong and sayin' you could love me! An' I'm thinkin' mebbe I could love you, too. I didn't 'spect it, Jim! Not so soon! Not b'fore I even start . . ."

I put my arms round her, and she leaned against me. Her tears made my vest damp, but I let her cry. I was remembering them girls on down at Madame Nellie's in New Orleans when I was a young'un. Sometimes they would come out to the cookhouse and cry whilst my mama would hold them like they was children. By and by their broken hearts would find comfort to face whatever they must. So I held Lark in my arms just like Mama would.

Then I remembered how Uncle Dimmy said most folks was slaves of one kind or another. Didn't matter what color they was, most folks was owned by something and needed to be set free.

The old man's voice spoke clear to my heart as if he was sitting right there in his willow rocker. "Glory be, chile, listen up. Listen t' Uncle Dimmy now. You knows it only be love dat cut dem chains loose, Jim. Ain't nothin' but love kin set a soul free! Does y' love dis gal?"

He was telling me something! Like always, he was saying that there were some way to open that cage and let Lark fly free. I couldn't see the way clear yet, but it were there waiting for me.

"What you telling me, Uncle Dimmy?" I whispered.

Then Lark looked up at me. "What you sayin', Jim?"

I looked her square in the eyes. "I'm sayin' I loves you, gal, and I'll get you free!" I blurted this out, though I did not know how I would do this.

"If you try to steal me away from Ryeman, he'll shoot you dead! I seen him do it to a white man who tried to take away one of the girls from the house in Natchez. The law said Ryeman was right. No, Jim! That man would just hunt us down. Kill you and take me back . . . Seven years and then I be free. Ain't no man wait so long as that. Not when a gal sells her soul to buy freedom. Not when my contract is owned by a man like Ryeman."

"I'll get the money."

"How you gonna do that?"

"I loves you, gal. I come all this way just to find you and love you. Such things don't happen by accident! I'm gonna find some way; that's all."

I had made up my mind by the time the women come back to Carson. We watched them through the window. In the lead wagon there was a coarse woman with dyed red hair and paint smeared all over her face from the wind.

I made as if to hold Lark from going, but she pushed me away and dried her eyes.

"I can't let you go," I said in misery.

"Stay here, Jim!" she told me. "They can't ever know I met you! You hear me? You're a black man! Ryeman will shoot you dead if he 'spects you have an eye out for settin' me free!"

I held on to her hand. No man was ever so filled up with the miseries. "I'll follow you."

"No!" she shouted. "Stay away from Virginia City! Can't you see how it would kill me to know you was so near? to know that you was watching other men come and go into that saloon and that I was there? ... If you loves me, stay away from me. Clean away, you hear? You gonna break my heart with hope that can't come true!"

I let her leave me then. I watched her walk back to that life because I knowed what she was saying was the truth. First I had to make the way to set her free. Five thousand dollars! I would make my fortune and come find her and pay the price and take her with me.

⁕CHAPTER 8⁕

Early the next morning Sam and me gathered rucksacks crammed with one change of clothes each, canteens, axes, bacon, corn-meal, beans, coffee, sugar, and salt. We rolled up the canvas that had been my tent and lit out for the mountains and the timber claim that was going to be the start of our fortunes.

The lake we was headed for was named Lake Bigler, after some California politician. But there was already a move afoot to change its name on account of Bigler not only had Rebel leanings, he was a crook to boot. Most folks around the Washoe area called it by its Indian name anyhow: Tahoe.

In Paiute, Tahoe means "Big Water" or "Sky Water." Either handle fits it right well. Sam said Tahoe means "Grasshopper Soup," because the Indians had named it after the meal they liked best in the whole world, but I knew he was joshing and just made that up.

Anyway, Lake Tahoe, or Lake Bigler, was only ten miles or less away, but it was nearly straight up a mile of mountain! We figured to be a day just hiking there and setting up camp.

The first half of the trip was up a narrow, rocky gorge full of boulders and sagebrush. It was so still and hot in that canyon that I would have been grateful for a Washoe zephyr to come by, but it seemed even they didn't have no truck with that place. It looked and felt like a hunk of desert, only tipped up on edge.

We got to the head of the canyon, finally above the chaparral and into the start of a pine forest. Sam allowed we should stop and rest;

it seemed he was wore out with guiding. I have to smile when I think of it, because I was carrying both axes and all the supplies. He was toting only his clothes, but I reckon the responsibility of being pilot tuckered him out.

We sat down on a big rock where we could look out across the Carson Valley. We munched on some biscuits saved from dinner the night before and calculated how far we'd come and how far we still had to go.

Sam looked around at the hillside of pine trees and said, "What's wrong with right here?"

"Ain't it claimed already?"

Sam fished around inside his shirt pocket and pulled out a map the governor had give him. He studied it a minute. "No. All the claims are inside the bowl of the lake. These trees haven't been claimed yet. This is perfect! We don't have to climb any further at all."

"But I thought the idea was to cut timber so as to float it to the sawmill on the lake. What are we gonna do here? If'n we cuts logs on this hill, they'll sure enough roll clean back to Carson and no way to stop 'em."

"Don't you see?" Sam said, excited. "That's the beauty of it. We claim this grove or the whole hillside even! Then we show some businessman down in Carson what a great opportunity it would be to have a sawmill right there. Think of all the transportation costs that would be saved! Somebody will come along to buy our claim in no time."

"Buy our claim? Ain't we gonna work it ourselves?"

Sam looked shocked. "No, no. We're prospectors, don't you see? We locate a great opportunity for someone else to buy off us. First come the prospectors, then the investors, then the developers, then the laborers, and along in there somewhere are speculators. But see, we get paid before anyone!"

"So what does we have axes for?"

"Because we have to work the claim first to prove it's ours. Then we can sell it!"

I begun to understand why he had been so all-fired eager to have me for a partner. "What kinda work?"

"Oh, nothing much!" He waved his arms like a scrawny white bird not quite making it off the ground, which was his way of letting me know that the amount of work required was most next to nothing.

"Uh-huh," I said. "Like what exactly?"

"We have to mark the boundaries, put up a dwelling, and show that we have begun to log it. . . . That's all."

"Uh-huh."

"Really, Jim! We can start right now. Let me have one of the axes. I'll do the hard part, lopping off limbs around our claim to mark it, while all you have to do is start felling trees to build a cabin."

"Whatever you says, Mister Sam. But say, is you sure these is the right kind of trees? They look pretty small." I pointed behind me on the ground to where a chipmunk run up and grabbed a little pinecone. "'Sides, these here cones must have something in 'em worth eating." I busted a cone with a rock and picked out some seeds to chew.

When I offered a couple to Sam, he weren't interested. "So some squirrels will have to go someplace else for dinner! Come on. Let's get started."

I seen there weren't no arguing with him, so I took up my ax and found a likely looking tree close by on the only flat spot there was on that hillside. I reckoned to drop the first trunk right where I planned the door of the cabin to be.

I made the first cut about halfway through on the side for the tree to fall. Then I changed sides and made the second cut above the first.

Sparing a glance back up the hill, I seen Sam "marking our claim." He would go to a tree, chop off the tiniest limb he could find, then step back to admire the effect.

I went back to work, shaking my head. With a flurry of chops, I got through the trunk, and the tree leaned. It gave a big groan, and the fall speeded up. Next there was a big crack and a great crash as the pine smacked into the ground, busting off all the branches on that side but landing right where I planned. The thud of the tree and the noise made by the shattering limbs bounced down the canyon in the still air.

249

When the echoes of the crash died away, there was still a high-pitched howl that I could not for the life of me place. Then the sound of rocks spattering underfoot reached me, and the howl turned into Sam yelling for help!

I thought it must be a snake. Couldn't figure what else there might be to be afeard of out there on that hill. When I spun around, Sam was slipping and sliding back down toward me. Ranged across the hillside a hundred yards or so higher was a line of half a dozen Indians, men and women. I seen a couple rifles in the group, and the biggest man had a hatchet in his hand. He wore floppy leather pants with a sash around his middle and a buckskin shirt decorated with beads and crow feathers on the shoulders. His hair, dark and straight, just touched his shoulders and framed a broad, stony face. His eyes was watchful, though. I seen him look us over, checking that we had no guns and that there was only two of us. If their aim was to jump us, I meant to give a good account of myself with my ax before getting whupped.

But first I aimed to try to talk.

Sam skidded to a stop more or less behind me. I held up my hand, palm out like I seen traders do with Indians at stage stops. "We come in peace," I said.

"So do we," said the Indian in better speech than me. "My name is Numaga, but a lot of folks call me Little Winnemucca since my father is Chief Winnemucca. What are you planning to do with that piñon tree?"

It was right interesting how fast Sam got all his courage back. He hopped out in front and introduced hisself. "This is our timber claim. For the mines."

"I thought so," said Numaga. "I saw your boundary marks."

One of the squaws giggled at that.

"You know, these trees are too small and the wood is too full of sap for good lumber. I think you need to go up by the lakeshore," Numaga said.

Sam bristled up like he was gonna argue, but Numaga went on. "Show you something, too," he said, and he whipped that hatchet toward the nearest tree. Sam jumped back about a yard, but all

Numaga did was knock down a couple of pinecones and bust them open. "See," he said. "These are nut pines. My people gather the seeds to grind for flour. That's what we came here for."

I seen then that the womenfolk all carried woven straw baskets. Fact is, the men was setting down, having a smoke, and two of the women had begun to gather cones and shake out the seeds.

Sam looked a touch embarrassed, but he never was much good at admitting a mistake. "I'll scout up ahead," he said, real abrupt and huffylike, and he took off up the trail toward the lake.

Numaga helped me gather our tools, and before I set out after Sam, I shook his hand. The name Winnemucca was familiar to me. The elder of that name was chief of the tribe whose menfolk had taken the warpath against the whites just a year earlier. And this was his son!

I kept the connection to myself. There was always some things it was better for Sam not to know.

✼ ✼ ✼

Sam moved out some faster after the meeting with the Indians, and it was not because the trail was easier nor the mountain less steep. We arrived at the summit overlooking Lake Tahoe in just two more hours.

In spite of the teasing Sam done later about its name, I knowed he was just as thunderstruck with the beauty of the scene as I was. It was a picture of the purtiest lake ever—and big: twelve miles across and twenty-five longways. It was ringed with forests of pine trees and cedars and firs, each a hundred feet tall or more, and circled with mountain peaks that jumped up three thousand feet from its very edge, some still capped with snow. And all them pinnacles and trees and snow reflected in a perfect mirror, so they was doubled and I could hardly tell up from down.

I still ain't even begun to explain what Lake Tahoe looks like. I haven't even said a word yet about how many different colors of blue there is in the water, from pale blue green at the edge to the very darkest blue black out in the middle. And critters? Deer raised up from the meadow where they was grazing to look us over, then went right back to feeding. Squirrels and raccoons in the trees and beaver in the streams. Black bears and cinnamon bears and birds of so many colors they was like a feathered flower garden.

All this we seen not ten minutes' walk down from the summit, before we ever even come to the shore. Sam said it was "the noblest sheet of water on the planet" or like that.

I don't know what makes water "noble," but I say this: The bowl of Tahoe is one of God's private places to rest Hisself and admire what He done. When He gets tired of messing about with people, I'm certain He goes right on up there and sets down awhile to ease His mind. It made me smile just to consider it.

Sam checked the map again and waved his hand toward the northwest. "This way."

I didn't know if he was right or not, but truth to tell, it didn't matter to me none. Every which way was purty.

We followed a stream downward through a canyon. That creek was lined on both sides with aspen trees, their leaves already turned as yellow as the sun, and fluttering in the thin breeze.

We reached the lakeshore at the place where the stream emptied into a rocky little cove. Right by the mouth of the creek was a row-boat. It was made out of planks, and its nose and tail was squared off 'til it weren't much to look at, but the oars was there and the seams was tight. Sam said we had come to the right place, since some of Governor Nye's boys had left the skiff there on purpose and it was for us to use.

The shoreline circled on northeast a ways before turning west, and since the place we was headed for was due northwest from where we stood, rowing across instead of walking around made perfect sense.

We loaded our gear. For a time neither of us spoke. Just stood looking at the oars. Sam pulled out the map again.

I caught his drift. "I know," I said, setting down backward and grabbing them paddles. "You has to navigate."

So off we went, me leaning my back into each stroke and Sam busting hisself to navigate proper. We did not make much progress at first. The water of the lake was so clear that you could see the bottom down fifty or a hundred feet, same as if it was ten. I pulled a half dozen strokes and Sam hollered out, "Look at that!"

That naturally put me off my rhythm while I whoaed up to take a look.

Sometimes it'd be a rock as big as a church that'd slide by beneath, same as if we was a bird flying over top of it. Other yells would mean that he had spotted another one of them monster trout schools. One time we counted over eighty before we realized we was only counting the topmost layer and there was more under those. Finally we give up counting them and begun to wish to arrive at camp. Sam let on that there was a cache of some supplies, fry pan and so forth that included a fish pole and some books. Every time we seen more fish and remembered the fish pole, it did speed us up again some.

Halfway across the lake the bottom dropped away off into the deeps. We couldn't see nothing down there no more, just darkest blue, the color of ink. There's something mighty disquieting about knowing that when you *could* see bottom it was farther than a church steeple is tall, so when you can't see bottom no more . . .

253

Long about that time, Sam looked up from studying his map. "What's that?" he asked and pointed ahead of us.

I fetched around in the thwart, and at first I didn't see nothing to remark on—just the same line of trees and one bare patch of rock we had been aiming for most of an hour already. Then I noticed a line of blue water a darker color than the rest of the surface, not so pale, more like the deep parts.

"What is that?" I said, not mocking Sam's words but in real puzzlement. I stopped rowing, and we studied on it some. Either that line was getting bigger, fatter some way, or else it was getting closer.

Sam said, "You know, back in my steamboat piloting days, if the river water up ahead changed color, I knew it meant a sandbar or a shoal. But that was always a change that was lighter in color, not darker. Besides, there can't be a sandbar clear out in the middle here; it's too deep."

"Sam," I said as I kept on watching, "I can't see the rocks as close down to the waterline as I could before. That line must be a wave, coming right toward us."

Sam and me looked at each other, and then I commenced to rowing hard, giving it all I had. Navigating was plumb forgot. We just aimed ourselves at the closest piece of land we could see and got after it.

We had not covered another quarter mile before that wave was upon us. The good news was that first wave that come did not amount to nothing over a foot high. But behind him marched rank on rank of his bigger and bigger brothers!

That skiff begun to slip and slide and roll and bob, and I seen that we were right quick gonna ship more water than it could handle. "Sam," I yelled, "gotta turn back into the wind or she'll swamp!"

He just bit his lip and hung on to both sides.

Spray blew off the tops of the waves by then, and what had been smooth water was now all foamy. White crests—what the Indians call white horses—raced by on both sides, except for the ones that slapped us square on the bow and soaked me through in no time. "Bail!" I shouted to Sam, and he snatched off his hat and scooped up water to toss out.

Quick as he flung out a hatful, the wind throwed it back again and more besides. I strained into the teeth of the blow and made precious little progress. So little headway, in fact, that I did not want to sneak a look at the shore, because once I did and it was so discouraging that I felt like giving up entire.

Instead of looking over my shoulder, I looked up. How bright and cheerful the sky was! It weren't black nor threatening. What few clouds there was raced by like to say, "'Scuse me, but I can't stay floating around here. I gots to be in Missouri by morning." It was awful, because it didn't look like an evil day at all, to be so scary!

I said, right out loud, without minding that Sam was overhearing my private conversation with heaven, "Lord Jesus, don't let me die on such a purty day as this!"

Truth is, I'd made my peace with God a long time earlier. I was ready if Jesus did decide to take me from this boat and whisk me on up to the heavens. Maybe I'd even see my mama there. But I couldn't stop myself from thinking that I was not done with what I needed to do down on earth yet. And what about Lark? What would happen to her if she had to work out her freedom for seven years? Would her master keep his word?

But the rest of those thoughts would have to wait. I was digging into every wave something fierce, clawing my way across the tops. Most every stroke pulled us down a roller; then we was pushed up the next whilst I recovered, and I done it over again. I reached back for another pull, dug in with the oars, and nearly shot myself right out of the boat!

Sam's mouth was open, and I was mighty amazed myself. Just at that second, we arrived at a span of flat water, just like there was no wind at all. Sam, he allowed as how the currents of air were blocked by one of them tall peaks and sheltered us, just like cupping your hand around a candle flame to keep it from getting blown out.

He was mostly right—only it weren't just the mountains that was cupped around us that day, no sir. When I remember it even now, I am certain God Himself must have decided He still needed the two of us to have our feet squarely on this earth. There is no other way to explain the miracle.

Along about fifteen minutes later we pulled into the purtiest little harbor you ever seen, exactly what we had aimed for. It was stunning how calm it was there, if such a thing can be. If we hadn't wrung two buckets of water out of our things and built a fire to dry them, we might not have believed how much danger we had come through.

We did no boundary marking that night, nor did we cut any timber, save what we chopped up to keep our fire going. Autumn it might still have been on the calendar, but at six thousand feet, when the wind shifts around and blows off the lake straight into camp, you feel like the Sierra might decide to go right to winter.

Next morning I discovered that Sam had not only wound hisself up in all the canvas we had for a bedroll, but he had curled around the fire so as to keep it all to hisself. When gray light come along about five o'clock, I woke him and pointed this out.

He looked at the few remaining coals of the campfire and said I should stir around quick and put some more wood on before it went out entire. Then he pulled his head back in and went to sleep.

I rustled up enough wood to get the blaze going again, which made me not only plenty warm but also wide-awake.

By then Sam was getting overheated, so he wriggled out far enough to tell me it was my turn to fix breakfast. Then, scooching back a bit, he told me to wake him again when the coffee was ready!

I took the coffeepot from the cache of our supplies, filled it from the lake, and toted it back to the fire. I wanted so bad to dump that jug of icy water over my partner's head, but I resisted somehow. Instead I threw a double handful of coffee in and put the kettle on to boil.

By the time the coffee was bubbling, I had bacon sliced and fry-ing. The trotline set the night before had a big fish on it, and right soon he changed his skin for some nice cornmeal and was smoking in the pan, too.

256

Sam told me that in order to show we done the work required to "prove" our claim, we had to build us a dwelling. He allowed that a nice log cabin with a rock fireplace would be very pleasant and could be used as a hunting and fishing lodge after we sold our claim for a tremendous sum of money.

I let him know that he weren't going to do no boundary marking then if he wanted a cabin built. He was going to have to pitch in and help.

"Sam," I said, "there's a right straight sugar pine there that'd make a fine start. Whyn't you go on over and fell him?"

"What about you?"

"I'll be along after I clean up the dishes. You just get us started."

"I'll do that," he said and shouldered an ax. He studied the tree that was maybe two feet through the middle, and he give a swing that stuck the ax in the trunk to where he could not horse it out. Three or four hitches and he finally wrestled it loose.

"Sam, less'n you plan to drop that tree into them rocks where we can't do nothing with it, you'd best move around some," I said.

He give me one of them I-knowed-that-already looks and circled on around, like a fighter sizing up the other fella in the ring. He give a little chop that wouldn't hardly have busted an egg, then reared back on his haunches to look the situation over. "When did you say you were coming?" he asked me.

"Quick as I get everything cleaned up. You just go 'long about business," I said. "Don't worry about me."

He was most teased enough, so I finished the cooking gear and took after a tree myself. I found a likely stand of ponderosa pines and got to work.

When I got the first one ready to drop, I glanced over at Sam and give a yell. He had a right nice pile of shavings where he was standing, but he weren't very close to cutting through. He stood and watched my tree fall; then he dusted off his hands like he was really ready for work and goes back to swinging.

I dropped the second and the third before I heard him yell, "She's gonna go!" Sure enough, that sugar pine come flopping down. 'Course, it landed spraddle of our campfire and flung the fry pan most twenty yards through the air, but I told him he done good anyhow.

Sam looked right proud of hisself. "Now how do we go about piling these up to make our cabin?"

I scratched my chin for a minute and calculated on it. "Well, we got enough here for half of one wall, I reckon, after we trim all the branches off and cut 'em to length."

Getting a real narrow look to his eyes, Sam frowned and said, "You know, building a whole cabin just to prove the claim isn't necessary. Not at all. Why, we could build a lean-to and cover it with a brush roof, and that would answer the needs of the law."

So that is what we done. By that afternoon we had a two-sided affair of poles and cedar boughs. The back side was a big rock, and the front was left open toward where we planned the fire to be. We covered the top with more cedar branches, and there we were.

Sam said it was good enough and would serve no longer than we needed it before we sold the claim. Then he said we had to stop working for the day and go catch more fish for supper.

✳ ✳ ✳

By sundown our second night at the lake, we not only had a skillet of trout frying but a kettle of beans simmering and a pan of corn bread baked. I could not see that we had made an awful lot of progress toward being rich, but I also could not see how any rich man on the face of the earth could be any more comfortable than we.

Sam insisted that we build the fire up big and blazing after the cooking got done. He said he was cold, which is likely enough, but fact is, he was scared of bears. Whatever the real cause, our campfire was a beacon that could probably be seen clean across the lake, some twenty miles away. Most anybody could've steered by our camp that night.

And that is exactly what happened. Half the corn bread, half the beans, and all the fish had been ate up. Sam was stretched out by the fire, smoking his big bowled pale yellow pipe. He was spinning yarn after yarn about what he would do with the money from the timber claim.

First it was a trip around the world; then it was a home in San Francisco, and afterward a sea voyage. Next he allowed how he could invest in the stock of up-and-coming silver mines and get so wealthy he'd have all them things and never work a lick in his life.

I contented myself just letting him spin. It didn't cost nothing to dream thataway, and where's the harm? His ramblings didn't call for no response from me, so I was left free to dream about Lark.

Anyway, he went on to have a debate with hisself about whether he'd build his home out of stone or brick, and midway through the discussion he took off his little round spectacles and give them a wipe with his shirttail.

The debate come to a sudden halt, and I seen him peering out into the dark of the hillside. Then he slapped his glasses back on and squinted again.

I had heard strangers coming for about ten minutes before Sam took notice. It didn't worry me none, since we didn't have nothing worth stealing. Besides, anybody who wanted to sneak up on the camp would not have allowed theirselves to make noise. I heard a dog yapping and the soft tread of several pairs of feet. Mind you, they weren't noisy in the white man sense of the word; they just wasn't trying to be extra quiet.

Sam slithered into the lean-to and caught hold of his pistol. "Jim, there's somebody creeping up on us!"

"Put that away before somebody—most likely me—gets hurt," I said. "Somebody has just seen our fire—prob'ly seen it from Salt Lake City." About that time we heard Numaga's voice hallo the camp. "Come on in," I yelled back.

Presently a file of Indians appeared out of the dark. Numaga and his wife—whose Washoe name I forget, but it meant "Twilight"— had their son with them. The boy was only five or six, and he had a puppy yapping at his heels. The fourth Indian was another brave we had saw the day before. His name was Echapa, meaning "Coyote."

"Come and set," I offered, "and help yourself to the beans and corn bread. We've already ate our fill."

Sam laid his pistol on the ground but kept his hand near it. His eyes stayed fixed on the hatchets belonging to the Indians.

259

"We are on our way home," Numaga said, gesturing at a cone-shaped straw basket that Twilight carried on her back with the aid of a strap across her forehead. "We saw your light."

Twilight pulled bowls out of a sack slung at her waist and commenced dishing up the beans. She fed Numaga and Echapa first, then the boy, and last of all took some for herself. They used pieces of corn bread to sop up the juice and scoop the beans into their mouths. Even if I couldn't understand what they was saying, they seemed to be enjoying my cooking.

Presently Numaga belched and patted his belly. "You are a good cook. Sometime you must come to our village, and Twilight will feed you."

Numaga and me talked quiet about the silver strikes and the new flood of white folks coming to Washoe and about the war back in the States. He was a right well-informed man, anxious to see his people survive against what he judged was superior numbers and force.

Sam called the boy, named Togoa, over to him. Though the child, whose name means "Rattlesnake," understood little of what Sam was saying, he still looked up wide-eyed at the paleface with the curly brown hair.

Sam explained to his audience how he'd chopped down all the trees and built the lean-to and caught all the fish in the lake. This took a while before he finally gestured toward the one true accomplishment of his: cutting down the sugar pine.

Togoa's mama looked at where the sugar pine lay across the old campfire pit and said something to the boy in their own tongue.

Right away Togoa jumped up from beside Sam and run over to the tree.

"Washoes like the sap from sugar pines," Numaga explained to me. "Fire makes crystals that are good to eat."

Twilight and Echapa left off listening and went after the pine syrup too. Sam, looking sour at losing his listeners, shrugged and got up to watch as the young'un picked up a rock to bust the sugar crystals off the tree trunk.

All at once the boy screamed and throwed the rock down. Then he run to his mama and hid his face in her skirt.

Sam scrambled to where the pistol was lying. When he was nearly there, he tripped over a rock, stumbled, lost his glasses, and kicked the campfire apart. A boot toe of embers rolled straight into our lean-to, but nobody paid no attention right then.

Echapa also run back and grabbed a burning stick from the fire. He said something to Numaga whilst I grabbed Sam by the arms and shook my head, telling him to hold on a bit. The scrawny pup run around in circles, yipping and getting underfoot.

Whilst we watched, Echapa dashed back to the sugar pine and thrust his torch around on the ground like he was looking for something. He give a yell that I admit started the prickles up my neck, and he pounded the earth with that torch. Finally he stood and called to Togoa something that must have been "It's all right now," because the boy looked around from hiding his eyes.

"Scorpion," Numaga explained. "Washoes think scorpions are the most wicked spirit creatures there is. Had to kill it quick or we would all have evil dreams tonight."

Now I don't know how wicked that particular insect was, but he sure was the bearer of bad news for us.

Sam coughed and said, "Did you throw some green branches on the fire? Where's all this smoke coming from?"

The smoke was coming from them hot coals smoldering in the cedar boughs of our shelter. Sam and me grabbed two hatfuls of water from the lake to douse the fire, but it was too late before we got back.

When we were still twenty feet away, one side of our lean-to busted into a sheet of flame and roared up into the sky. Worse yet, hanging over the boulder that was the back wall was another big cedar with its branches drooping down.

Them flames licked that standing tree and must of liked the taste, because it ate straight up into the crown. Sam and me knowed there weren't nothing to be done, so we grabbed up our gear and went down to the waterline.

261

The evening wind off the lake blowed the flames into a nearby pine and then another and another. Pretty soon pinecones was exploding like bombs and launching theirselves in all directions. And everywhere they hit, another fire sprung up.

It was powerful hot! We loaded all our belongings in the skiff and the Indians put their things in, too. There weren't room enough for all the people, so we piled Togoa and the dog in on top and the rest of us held on to the sides of the boat and waded out waist deep in the water.

The wind held so steady that the fire marched right up the canyon back of our camp and climbed the hill. We watched it chew our timber claim just like a giant glowing orange worm.

"I don't really mind," Sam said as we watched the fire disappear behind one ridge, then start up the next one north like it ain't gonna stop before Canada. "I don't really care. . . . Having a timber claim is too much work. I just wish—" He stopped.

"Wish what?" I asked.

"I wish the boy would quit yelling 'Whee!' every time another tree explodes," he said.

✳ ✳ ✳

That were the end of our plans to be the timber barons of the Sierra Nevada. We didn't burn the entire mountain down, but only because about midnight, God took pity on such fools as we and sent over a thunderstorm.

That downpour lasted only an hour, but it took care of the fire. Trouble was, when we come out of the lake, all the dry timber near at hand was already burned up, and what wasn't charred was soaked, same as we, so we spent the night huddled together with no way to either dry out or warm up.

Come morning, we headed out early on. The Indians had already departed without a sound or a good-bye, after the fashion of their kind.

I asked Sam if he wanted me to row us back across, but he said no. "Now that there is light enough to not fall off a cliff, I want to find some brush that didn't burn up so we can cook breakfast!" His boots made squishing noises when he walked, and his hat flopped down over his ears like he'd been in the mountains a hundred years already.

262

We left the skiff and trudged along the shore. First little divide we crossed, we turned aside up a runnel where the fire had not gone and stopped for a mighty poor breakfast. The coffeepot got burned up and the cornmeal, salt, and sugar was wet through and spoiled. I had salvaged the fry pan and the bacon, and that was our meal. Sam had saved his pipe and his pistol in the ruckus but had lost his glasses, so even dried out and warmed up, he were in a don't-cross-me mood.

When he proposed taking a shortcut over the mountain instead of following the lakeshore back to the main trail, I let him have his way. It started out well enough, with the stream's path climbing a gentle slope headed east, which agreed right enough with my own sense of direction.

Pretty soon though, the little creek come to a fork, with neither branch running true east. I favored one and Sam the other, and once more I let him pick.

Halfway up the slope the banks was steeper, rockier, and narrower, and we had to climb up out of there or face backtracking later on. We scrambled straight up the mountain with no stream to follow and the hillside given over to low tangled shrub called manzanita.

There ain't scarcely a way to hold a line through brush that thick, especially when it gets taller than your head. Sam would never admit that the other way might be better. We wandered backward and forward on that slope, gaining a few yards, then giving it back to get by the next big thicket.

Eventually we did fight clean to the summit and come out on a bare rock ridge that looked back toward the lake on one side and out across Carson Valley on the other. Sam was right pleased, and he picked out the route for us to follow down.

I didn't see that any humans had ever come up or down that way, at least not in long years, but there was a deer trail and the east side of the mountain was more sparse of brush, which suited me. We come down the slope sliding in some places and eventually fetched up in a cottonwood-lined draw near the bottom.

263

By then I knowed we was going to come out on the rocky divide just north of Carson City, so Sam didn't do so bad after all.

We sat down in the shade of a cottonwood and rested a spell.

I leaned back against that tree trunk and pulled my hat down over my eyes. My thoughts was full of dishwashing and such or taking my chances with the mines and a foreman like Boss Ward. It come to me that there weren't no way to strike it rich and probably no white man would give me a job driving team, so my possibilities was limited. The urge to steal Lark and run away was powerful strong.

Brooding on this and that, I didn't pay much mind when Sam set up and stared over the streambed toward a brushy thicket on the other side.

Real low, he said, "Jim. Jim. Wake up."

"What is it?"

"There's a bear in the trees. He's looking this way. I think he's seen us."

"So? Old bear ain't interested in us. You're too scrawny and I'm too tough."

"He is so! I see him staring straight at us. I'm gonna scare him off!"

Before I could stop him, out popped his peashooter and he loosed off three rounds.

"Quit that!" I said. But without his glasses, he was a better shot than with them on. He actually hit what he was aiming at. Except instead of a growl or such, the thing he was shooting went *clang, clang, clang.* "That ain't no bear," I said, "but I don't know what it is either. Just don't shoot no more, whilst I go see."

Under the trees, back in a hollow made by the overhang of a cottonwood, was a humped-up shape that did sort of look bearish, at least to a man what needed glasses. There was a canvas covering over top of something, and it was plain from the place it was located that whoever put it there intended to leave it hid. By purest chance, we had sat down in the one spot it could be seen from.

It was a cannon.

264

When I stripped off the cover, there was a small bore weapon made to go into rough country, judging by the mount and the small size. It didn't look like no toy just because it was small. It looked plenty murderous all right. Something else: It looked new, meaning never used. The brass fittings was dulled but not overly so, and the wooden carriage and wheels was dried out but not so as to spoil the thing for use. In short, it looked like whoever left it there was planning to come back and fetch it.

"Who would hide a cannon out here in the brush?" Sam wondered.

"You figger Rebels? Or maybe somebody stole it from the army to sell to the Indians?"

Either of them possibilities sounded bad. Whoever belonged to that killing machine would not like to find us nearby when they come after it. So we pushed along then, pretty sharp, aiming to bring up the matter to Governor Nye when we got back to town.

✳ ✳ ✳

The fifth man in Orion's small parlor was not known to Sam or me. He come in with Governor Nye but stood quietly, shylike, near the door.

"So, Sam," Nye boomed in his running-for-office voice, "you do not intend to pursue riches as a timber baron, eh?"

"No, Governor," Sam said. "What with the war and all, these are uncertain times. The bottom might drop out of the lumber market tomorrow, and then where would I be? Besides," he continued with a sly look in my direction, "Jim is allergic to high altitudes. I don't see how we can pursue the claim."

Nye snorted. "I suspect you are the one who is allergic, but it's a reaction against hard work and not elevation!"

Sam bristled, but when Orion and the governor burst out laughing, he begun to chuckle, too.

"There, that's better," Nye continued. "Don't take it serious, Sam. I have the same aversion myself. Why do you think I went into politics?"

"Governor!" Orion gulped with alarm. "Did you forget we have a guest?" He indicated the silent man.

"What? Oh, Willie won't quote that, will you? Sam, I'd like you and Jim to meet William Wright, better known as Dan DeQuille to the jackrabbits who read his column in the *Territorial Enterprise*."

The thin fella with the sparse sandy hair and scraggly pointed beard leaned against the door with an easy grin on his face. "I don't know, Governor. We scribblers can't pass up something newsworthy."

I seen mock alarm on Nye's broad features. "Won't any of my loyal constituents help me? Someone come up with a bone for this newshound to draw him off my scent."

"I've got one," Sam volunteered. "I have . . . Jim and I have discovered an interesting artifact."

"Really?" DeQuille said. "What might that be?"

"Jim and I have found a cannon—a mountain howitzer, to be precise—that has been lost for close to twenty years."

"A cannon?" Nye rumbled. "Where? And how do you know so much about it?"

"Not so fast," Sam warned. "First, I want to know if the *Enterprise* will publish the story if I write it up. I published some letters back in Missouri."

"Certainly," DeQuille agreed. "If it's good we'll even pay you for it."

When the business doings was settled, Sam explained how he and I had located the cannon, leaving out the part about the imaginary bear. Then he said how he remembered something he read from Colonel John Charles Fremont's explorations back in the forties— how they had been dragging a cannon with them until forced to leave it behind because of the snow. "I checked Fremont's journal account, and the description matches exactly."

"We'll go recover it," Governor Nye vowed. "We'll set it up in front of the state capitol," he added with a wink.

The *Territorial Enterprise* ran Sam's story. He signed it with the made-up name Josh. Said that was what all the real correspondents done, not using their right names.

A few days later, Nye sent out a gang of his hangers-on to retrieve Fremont's cannon. They went right to the arroyo where Sam and I seen it, but the brassbound weapon was gone. They did find the canvas it had been wrapped in, lying in a heap, and the tracks where it had stood, but no trace of the cannon itself. Some folks said Sam planted the tarp and made the tracks hisself to give him something to write about, but Sam and me, we knowed different. But where it really got off to and who took it remained a mystery.

✷ CHAPTER 9 ✷

onths went by without me making much progress toward setting Lark free. I done odd jobs and saved a little money, but it looked like a terrible long road.

Then one day Sam tiptoed into the kitchen and motioned for me to follow him. He looked over his shoulder twice, like he was afraid somebody might be watching. "Don't tell a soul," he whispered in a real dramatic tone. "Don't breathe this to anyone, but the word is *Aurora*."

Since there weren't nobody but the two of us in Orion's parlor, this seemed like extraordinary caution. "All right," I agreed. "If'n you'll tell me what it means."

"It means our fortunes are made," he said. "Esmeralda mining district, little town called Aurora. Word just came today of a big strike there. If we head out tonight we can beat the rush and stake our claim."

I wasn't so sure. We had chased the timber claim and it had amounted to nothing, but I was getting desperate. "It sounds good, Sam," I said, "but I needs work that pays regular. I reckon I needs a steady job 'stead of a claim."

He got around in front of me and looked me right in the eyes. "Jim, I wasn't gonna bring this up unless I had to, but I can see you need more convincing. Do you remember the coach we came west in?"

"'Course," I agreed. "I ain't likely to forget a contraption I rode on top of clean across the country."

"What was painted on the doors?"

With a sudden recollection come the meaning he was driving at. "A Spanish gal, and her name was . . ."

"Esmeralda," he finished with a triumphant sound. "It's a sign, don't you see? We are going to strike it rich in Esmeralda!"

Aurora was even less of a town than Carson City. Of all the buildings in the place, maybe half was actually boards and a handful was built of stone. The others was canvas tents over dirt floors or heaped-up piles of brush or misbegotten creations of stone and brush and boards thrown together. And this was the biggest settlement in the mining district called Esmeralda.

There wasn't no main street, neither. Fact is, there weren't no streets at all. Folks just plopped their dwellings down wherever they felt like it, mostly beside what stretch of ground they thought was most promising.

Sam and me set up our tent in a howling dust storm, and I begun to have second thoughts about how good a sign that Spanish gal's name was.

We was huddled around a lantern, poring over a map of the place, when a voice hollered at us out of the storm, asking could he take shelter in our tent. The fella what come in dripping forty pounds of topsoil was an old prospector name of Billou. Dad Billou, everyone called him, because he seemed older than all the rest of the world. He had gray hair and a long gray beard. A short man, about shovel-handle tall, he walked kind of stooped over, but his disposition was cheerful. He had a choppy way of talking, as if he had only so much stock of words and didn't want to run out.

He'd been out to California in '49, made and lost a fortune in gold dust, been in the beginnings of the Comstock excitement, and been shouldered aside by the bigger companies. Now he was known as a beans-and-flour man, meaning he made enough from the diggings to live from one day to the next, but just barely. But he claimed to have a nose that could smell silver ore, and Sam and me was in no position to overlook any offer of help. Still, when Dad asked if we knew what to look for, Sam naturally replied that we did.

The next morning we went off in three different directions to look for prospects. We was to meet up again at noon and compare what we found.

I tramped over five miles of hillside. I found lots of squirrel holes and rabbit holes and sagebrush and weeds but nothing like what Dad Billou had told me to search for.

Sam was already back at the tent. He was grinning ear to ear and couldn't wait to spill his news. "I told you Aurora would make our fortune!" he practically shouted. "Just look at this." He pulled the pockets of his jacket inside out and dumped a heap of rocks on the upside-down bucket that was our camp stool. "Look at the crystals sparkle in the light. And see that streak of color through this one? We've found it for sure!"

"Where did you find these?"

"That's just it! They came from the ravine in back of us. I hadn't walked more than fifty yards before I found them all!"

Along about then, Dad Billou got back. Sam saw him coming and held his finger to his lips, meaning not to say a word. He wanted to just leave the ore samples out on the bucket and watch Dad's reaction.

Dad Billou come up to the tent flap and said howdy. "Seen nothin'. Followed a ledge. No good. Check far side later. That way." And with that he picked up the largest and shiniest of Sam's rocks and pitched it off toward the southeast.

"Wait!" Sam protested, snatching the other stones out of harm's way. "What kind of a prospector are you? Smell silver ore, huh? You can't even see it when it's right under your nose!"

Billou apologized for throwing the sample away, then asked Sam what he wanted with a worthless piece of granite with a streak of feldspar. Only what he said was, "Granite. Feldspar. Ten cents an acre."

Sam looked a mite crestfallen, but I had not expected it to be all that easy, so I weren't so down as he.

We decided that it might be smart for us to go together for a while 'til Sam and me caught on to silver prospecting proper.

For the next couple months, we three tramped the hills, canyons, and ravines around Aurora. Sometimes Dad would pounce on a chunk of rock and Sam and me would hold our breath, but he always flung it down.

Then one day we was just over the hill from the biggest strike that had yet been made in all Esmeralda. The mine was called the Wide West. The owners had dug a tunnel some two hundred feet into the hillside, following a ribbon of silver ore. They had been taking out several tons of rock a day and making only fair money. Then all of a sudden, while digging a new side tunnel or drift, they busted into a streak of pitch-black rock that crumbled to the touch. Dad said it was almost pure silver.

The ownership of the Wide West changed right sudden with its fortunes. Some fellas with secesh leanings—what they called Copperheads—moved in on the other owners. A .36-caliber suggestion was very persuasive, and the previous miners moved on somewheres else. The new head man of the Wide West was Bill Mayfield, the same loudmouth drunk we first seen at Bucklands station.

The reason that we come to the ridge in back of the Wide West was most mysterious to Sam and me. We had already prospected that knoll a half dozen times and not found anything. But Dad insisted that we go again.

We come to a place where a gully had washed slantways across the hill, exposing the rock layers beneath the soil. A dirty white streak of quartz showed at boot-top height, and in that quartz stone was the thinnest black line you ever saw, almost like a thread.

Dad flung himself down on the ground next to the rock face and put his nose against the quartz, just like a hound dog on a trail. "Dig here. Right here."

I swung the pick and busted the soil loose where Dad pointed his long, bony finger. Then Sam stepped in and shoveled it out 'til he come to solid rock again.

This kept up 'til I was standing in a hole about waist deep. 'Course, on Sam it was about chest deep. That time, when he took his place in the pit and flung up a shovelful of rock, the blade hit the shaft wall. It struck sparks, and the debris flew only a foot or two in the air and right down Sam's neck. He threw down the tool, jumped out of the hole, and went to shaking gravel out of his collar and the waist of his shirt. "That's far enough 'til you tell us what this is all about!" he said to Dad.

Dad agreed that it was far enough, and he jumped down in the pit hisself and went to sniffing the rock again. I could see that it was the fine, dark line that interested him and that it had widened to toothpick width.

He called for a knife, and I unfolded my barlow and handed it to him. Dad scraped that black streak 'til he had a little pile of mineral in the palm of his hand, about so much as a dime would cover. Then he touched it to his tongue.

Sam and me watched Dad Billou climb up out of the hole, still staring down at his hand. "That's it," he said in his normal allowance of words.

271

"I told you we had covered this hill enough times," Sam said.

"No," Dad said, flicking the dust in his palm with a dirty fingernail. "Found the indication. Boys," he remarked with a twinkle in his eye, "this ore is the same as the new drift in the Wide West. It's a blind lead."

Sam and I both looked at him in astonishment. It was the longest set of words strung together at once that we'd ever heard come from Dad's mouth.

Mining law said that when a claim had been properly registered, the locators had the right to follow the vein wherever it led down into the earth. But now and then, a second vein would run across the first at an angle; clearly a different streak of mineral entirely. If the second vein did not crop out on the surface it was called a blind lead, on account of no one would suspect that it was there.

The meaning of Dad's words finally sunk in to Sam and me. "You mean this is that real rich stuff they lately found in the Wide West?" I asked.

"And it's not part of their vein?" Sam continued.

"'Zactly," Dad agreed in his clipped speech. "Blind lead. Big rain the other night uncovered this top edge."

The miners working in the Wide West figured that they had just run into a rich body of ore on the vein they was following. But Dad was saying that this silver ore was from a different vein altogether and could be claimed by us as locators.

Sam and me danced around that four-foot-deep hole like we had plumb lost our minds. "We're rich!" Sam shouted. "Mansions and fancy carriages, here we come!"

Visions of a home with Lark flew around in my head. No mansion necessary, just her and me together.

Dad had a smile on his face when he said, "Celebrate later. Mark the claim now. Real work starts tomorrow!"

✷ ✷ ✷

The Monarch of the Mountains! I thought the name Sam give to our claim was a mite too grand. He said it was only fitting and proper, and we would be glad we had not called it Sweet Sue, Root Hog or Die, or Tres Hombres, like other mines thereabouts. I put it to Dad Billou to decide. He scratched behind one ear and said, "Good enough," so that settled it.

Dad ground up a pea-sized lump of ore in his mortar and washed it out in his horn spoon. He got the faraway look in his eye that he had warned us meant he was "calculatin'." Sam and I stood by, silent and respectful 'til the computing was done. Presently Dad roused hisself and said, "Three hundred a ton, I'll be bound!" Anything over fifty dollars a ton in ore paid the costs of transport and milling, so this was a powerful rich strike indeed.

The rules of the mining district give us ten days to prove our claim. Like the timber business, this meant putting up a shelter, which we already had, and doing a reasonable amount of improvements. Dad said all that was needed was to turn the pit we dug into a proper shaft. He said that once we showed that the vein we was following was more than a surface pocket, then investors would jump at the chance to buy stock—what they called "feet"—in our mine. He said that was how we would get the cash for the other necessities like a hoist, ore cars, and tracks.

Sam concluded that we was going to be nabobs of Nevada in no time. He wrote to the *Territorial Enterprise*, announcing the strike.

We knowed how Mayfield and his crew of Copperheads had moved in on the Wide West. Fact is, Sam had wrote another letter to the *Enterprise*, denouncing that whole crew for being sneaks, cheats, bullies, and thieves. He said the only reason his language was so mild was on account of a more accurate description would have scorched the paper. Even so, we figured they would be after the Monarch next. Sam and Dad and I organized ourselves into a round-the-clock guard. Dad said if we could keep possession just long enough for the speculating to get rolling, we could hire all the guards we needed from then on. But for the next ten days, one man was to be always aboveground with a sawed-off twelve-gauge, even when the others was working within call.

On the morning of the third day, Sam was on guard and Dad and me had blasted our way down twenty-five feet. The vein turned, getting wider all the time, and we drilled the holes in preparation for starting an inclined tunnel. Over his right shoulder Dad held the drill, a five-foot-tall bar of iron with a star-shaped point. I stood behind him, swinging the double jack, a ten-pound sledgehammer. Dad trusted me right well. After every strike, he'd rotate the drill a quarter turn so as to give the teeth a new bite; then I'd hammer away again.

We was about halfway done drilling our pattern of twenty-five holes to be packed with gunpowder and rock dust when the noise of a shotgun blast rumbled down to us.

My ears still ringing from the strike of the steel and the echoing boom, I kept the hammer in one hand as I swarmed up the notched planks. I come out of the shaft and seen Sam facing me, all alone. The coach gun was not in his hands. "What was that shot?" I said. "What's going on?"

Right then I felt a double circle of cold steel rings press into the back of my neck. "Only fired one," the boozy breath of Bill Mayfield informed me in a low tone. "Still got the other one for you if you don't behave. Now drop that hammer and go stand by your nigger-loving friend."

I wondered if there was any way to alert Dad, but a shake of the double-barrel in my face warned me off and backed me up to stand by Sam. A half dozen of Mayfield's bunch, grinning at their success, flanked him to either side.

Dad Billou's head emerged from the pit, covered in rock dust and looking like an old, bearded gopher. "What's the ruckus?" he managed to get out before he was given similar treatment to Sam and me.

"Now, boys," Mayfield said, "this here is part of the Wide West claim, and we aim to work it. Can't have you trespassing, can we?"

Dad Billou sputtered into his beard. "Your claim? Sidewinders! Skunks!"

"Now," Mayfield warned, "don't say nothing you'd regret later. Just turn round and start walking."

There was nothing else to do in the face of a load of buckshot and six fellas all packing iron. We started walking back to our camp.

"How'd it happen?" I asked Sam.

"I don't know," he said. His voice was shaky, but whether with fear, anger, regret, or all three, I couldn't tell. "I just leaned back against the rock there and laid the shotgun right beside me. The next thing I knew, one of Mayfield's buddies grabbed my arms and Mayfield took the double-barrel. He fired a shot to get you to come out, and . . ."

"Those stinking robbers!" I said. "They did this to the Wide West, but they ain't gonna take the Monarch. We'll get guns and fight back!" I was hot, boiling mad. It wasn't just that they were stealing silver from me; they was stealing my Lark! If I'd had a gun right then, I would have gone back to do murder without another thought.

Dad Billou cleared his throat and waited for me to cool down enough for him to speak. "Them fellas? Shoot you just for looking at 'em. Mayfield killed a sheriff. Ain't caught and hanged yet. Gonna face that?"

"But we can't just let them take it! Can't give up without a fight."

Dad coughed and said, "Live dog better than dead lion, reckon. More silver out there. Just go find another."

"Dad's right," Sam said. "If we went back they'd kill us. Then we still wouldn't have a mine, and we'd be dead. Someday this territory will have law enough to take care of Mayfield and his kind, but not now."

I give it up then. My partners weren't going to back my play, and the truth was, I knowed they was right. I was no good to Lark dead. I reminded myself that I was precious little good to her living, neither. I felt lower than low.

Dad said he was leaving that very day to go to prospecting again. Sam and me could have gone with him, but we didn't have the heart. Dad packed up his few things, wished us both luck, and took off down the trail toward the town of Bodie.

Sam and I sat and stared at the dirt or the sky—anywhere but at each other. Finally I could not stand it anymore. "I gots to know," I said. "Was you asleep when they snuck up on you?"

"No," Sam said. "I was writing another letter to the newspaper." After a time of misery, he asked, "So what do we do now, pard?"

275

I did not know if Sam was asking what we should do to make another fortune or if he meant that we should go set a spell and have a cup of coffee over the matter. The two of us did not have more than five dollars between us and just enough grub to whomp up something akin to Uncle Dimmy's last supper.

"Now that we are no longer rich men, I could use something to eat," I said to him.

"That is a start."

So I fixed our next-to-last pot of beans and throwed in our last bacon for flavor. We ate our supper without saying another word to one another, for we was both feeling pretty low, what with Dad gone and the Monarch up the flume. Worse yet, my misery was on account of letting Lark down. I recollected what she said to me that day about how having hope, if it were false hope, would break her heart. All these months and I was no nearer to redeeming her. I was a failure in the one and only thing that mattered to me. I was like a cloud passing over a dry and thirsty land without yielding even one drop of rain.

Sam's misery was different. I knew it was on account of the real probability that he might have to get hisself a job of some sort to stay alive. He lay beside the fire and smoked his last pipeful of tobacco. "It's all finished for me now. I do not intend to go back home to Missouri to be pitied and mocked behind my back."

"No need. You can stay here and get the same treatment."

Another half hour passed before he spoke again. "I could clerk. That's it. I was a grocery clerk for a day back home. I could—"

"One day?" That seemed to be as long as Sam kept interest in anything.

"I ate the proprietor's supply of stick candy, so I got the boot. I considered taking up the law profession, but that was wearisome. Once I was employed in a bookshop, but the customers continually interrupted my reading, so I left that position." He shook his head and tugged his beard, which was growed down to the top button of his shirt. "I got two hundred and fifty dollars a month on the river, but nothing called a river around here runs a stream of water bigger than a pump spout." He sighed. "What are we to do, Jim? It's hard to think of working after being so wealthy. I am as worthless as some of those giant gopher holes the boys call mines out there."

He was pretty worthless all right. I had never seen a man who worked so hard at not working. But as he felt so bad already, I did not want to heap my scorn on his torment. Besides, I had my own list of failures to consider.

"We'll sleep on it," I said, then turned my back to him and the fire and hoped he would shut up. I laid awake, considering everything that had happened. It crossed my mind to try and get our claim back. Or should I break my promise to Lark and come to steal her away anyway?

But Lark was right about all that. I knowed the truth. Being a black man, I'd have been strung up from the nearest tree and left for the buzzards.

So I just passed that long night in grief and pining for my gal. As long as Lark was still in debt, I was not a freeman neither. Thinking on these things was more work than working ever could be.

My soul grew weary with it, and no answers come from the heavens. By and by I fell asleep and dreamed of silver strikes and marching up to pay off Lark's debt. Them was good dreams to see me through such a black night.

When I come to, the sun was not up yet, but I could see a faint purple glow seeping through the clouds above the mountain. I thought that the pretty light was some sign of hope. It commenced to raining, but I was not put off.

It come to me that if me and Sam could strike it rich once, why not do it again?

"Sam!" I shook him awake.

"Leave me in peace," he moaned.

"Get up! There's plenty of silver to be had—and gold, too—if we'll just go dig for it!"

"What're you saying?" He pushed me back.

"If'n we found it once, why not again? Dad says he can do it. Ain't we as good as him? There's two of us and we is younger."

Sam was not altogether convinced. He pointed at the sky and told me that winter was coming and we would not have time to dig our own graves before the snows would come.

All the same, I was sure of it. Sam was going to be a wealthy man, and I would have my Lark! All we had to do was dig.

At last hunger roused my partner out of his wallow, and we ate our cold beans and commenced to climbing far up that mountainside, where I had seen the light breaking through the clouds. I took what I remembered from Dad Billou's lessons, found a likely spot, and we set to digging. Truth to tell, I went at it with a pick until a lot of dirt and rock was loosened up and there were a hole about eight feet deep.

"Big enough to bury us both," Sam said.

Then he climbed down in that hole with his long-handle shovel to throw out the dirt. He hated the long-handle shovel, Sam did. He still had not got the hang of it.

"Brace it forward and shove with the side of your knee 'til it is full; then throw it backward over your shoulder. . . ." I had showed him how a thousand times, but it didn't do no good.

He worked at it for a while, tossed the gravel just on the edge of the hole, and back it all come on his head and down his neck.

277

Sam did not say one word. He just clumb out of that shaft and marched on back down to the shanty, where he give up all hope of living. I pitied him a mite. He was a sorry piece of humanity: could not hold a job, could not study the law, could not throw a shovelful of dirt out of a mine shaft without hitting himself in the head.

"I am useless," he moaned at last. "In all the world there is no more worthless man than myself. What am I fit for, Jim? What sort of occupation can such an inept bag of wind as myself ever hope to hold?"

It was a tough problem, all right.

The answer to that very question, however, come the next morning in a letter from Virginia City. Sam opened it and hollered, "Eureka!" which was what some folks said when they stuck their pick into the mother lode and drew out a big nugget. "This is a letter from Joe Goodman, editor of the *Territorial Enterprise*!" Sam flapped the sheet of paper beneath my nose and gave a whoop that made most of Aurora reach for their sidearms. "My calling has called me at last! Mister Goodman likes my letters! He asks me to come to Virginia City and join the staff of his newspaper!"

To my thinking, this was the last hope of a desperate and hungry man. Sam had been offered twenty-five dollars a week with the *Territorial Enterprise* to work as a reporter in Virginia City.

"I'll never have to work again, Jim!" he cried joyfully. "I shall be a journalist!"

☀CHAPTER 10☀

T|hrough timber claims and mine claims and odd jobs, through true hopes and false ones and expectations lifted and dashed, I had kept my word to Lark and had not ventured to Virginia City. But after Aurora fizzled I had to ask myself the question: What was I to do?

Dad Billou had up and deserted us. Now Sam headed northeast across the dusty valley toward Mount Davidson, where the shanties, saloons, and hurdy-gurdy houses of Virginny perched on trembling ground above the warren of mine shafts. It seemed to me that I didn't have no choice in the matter, so I went along with him.

The clouds cleared off long about evening. Still a full fifty miles from our destination, I looked at the outline of that steep, treeless mountain rising seven thousand feet up, and I seen the glimmer of Virginia City's lights. It was altogether beautiful at such a distance.

The next day it was something else when we climbed the road. We passed through the rock pinnacles known as Devil's Gate and the dusty lawlessness of Gold Hill to come to the truth of the place: Mount Davidson was as steep as the tin roof on a Chinaman's washhouse. The town roosted on that slope about halfway up the mountain between heaven and sulfurous perdition.

The only thing that kept Virginia City from sliding on down to hell was the fact that the roads were terraced and braced. A man could walk into the front door of a west-facing building at street level, but by the time he reached the back side of the structure, the

279

floor was supported by tall stilts. Out the back windows were a view of the rooftops and chimneys of his back-door neighbor.

Farther than that were the mines and milling operations—smokestacks and tin buildings and hoisting works. Heaps of pulverized rocks from the diggings trailed away like the gravel of giant anthills. Beyond that, down Six Mile Canyon, a range of desolate mountains fell away into the same desert that me and Sam had crossed. It didn't look quite real from such a height, but it was beautiful, like glimpsing the Promised Land. I purely admired that view the first time I seen it and ever after.

There was a population of about eighteen thousand souls who lived there. Most were men. Twenty-four hours of the day at least one-third of them was underground working a shift in a mine. Wages for miners was world renowned. Men who never had two dollars to rub together was making the unheard-of sum of four dollars per day.

Nobody was a native of Nevada unless it was maybe a Paiute Indian or tiny babe what had the fortune to be born there. Every citizen of Virginia City had heard about the miracle of the Comstock and had come from distant lands to partake of that miracle. Every state and nation were represented: Chinese, Russians, Englishmen, Cornishmen, Irishmen, Frenchmen, Hungarian Jews, and Germans. In their homelands they most likely hated one another, and their daddies had marched off to kill each other on a regular schedule. On the boardwalks, the babble of blasphemy was in so many different languages and accents that it was positively biblical. They had all come on a pilgrimage to worship the silver god of the Comstock in their own language.

I reckon no place on earth had ever rose up out of the ground full growed like that place. When I first laid my eyes upon it, Virginia City was a new town of fine brick buildings. There was a fire brigade, fire chief, mayor, aldermen, a sheriff, and a tribe of deputies. To accommodate all this grandness was a Masonic lodge, Odd Fellows hall, hotels, banks, half a dozen jails, whiskey mills every few paces, saloons, gambling palaces, hurdy-gurdy houses, a street full of Chinese, a few Paiute campodie huts on the fringe, and even a church or two in the midst.

The only instrument keeping track of all this confusion was the newspapers. The papers, by which I mean Sam, reported on the doings of these establishments and momentous events—parades, politics, processions, occasional visits by acting troupes and singers, brawls, murders, uprisings, riots, hangings, funerals, births, deaths, and of course the news of what was happening in the mines. Compared to all of this, the War between the States seemed almost of no account.

That may have been what some foreign folks thought about that far-distant battle between North and South. The truth was that the Civil War was being fought hard right there in that town. And that great and terrible war would be won or lost according to what transpired right there in the Comstock.

All of this bustle was already in full swing by the time me and Sam entered Virginia City that first morning. It was like a carnival. Boardwalks was so tight packed with people that it was hard for us to trudge against the tide. The dirt streets was just as busy. Teams of mules pulled ore wagons. Buckboards and buggies rattled up and down C Street. Crossing on foot was a peril.

I glanced down the slope that led to D Street, where the soiled doves of Virginia City lived in small cabins. It was plain to see that men on their way back from the mines was enticed to stop awhile. The sight of miners peeling off to find their way down D Street made me feel a mite uneasy. Many of them women had begun their fall as hurdy-gurdy gals and had ended up living in a place like that.

I tried not to think on it no more when I spotted the sign of the Virginia House Hotel. I hoped Lark was there, yet I dreaded the fact that she might be still there.

Sam plunged ahead, his mind evidently fixed on fighting through the crowds to get on down to the office of the *Territorial Enterprise*. Then, all of a sudden, he stopped cold and nudged me hard. "Look there!" He pointed back down the slope toward the D Street cribs.

I was afraid he had spotted Lark. Although I had not told Sam how I loved her, I was sure that he would remember her from the day she blowed into Carson.

But it weren't Lark or the ladies he was gawking at. There, tied to

a rail just where Chinatown started, was a string of twenty or so camels. Some of them was kneeling down and resting, chewing their cud
just as peaceful as any milk cow. I had never seen such critters before
except as pictures in the Good Book, so this was a curious sight. Me
and Sam was thunderstruck by the vision.

Sam had heard in a letter from Orion that camels was being used
to haul salt across the flats from the desert. When Sam had read the
letter out loud, me and Dad Billou had laughed and thought that
Orion had gone crazy or that he meant this as a joke. But Orion
recounted the details about how the U.S. Army had bought them for
thirty thousand dollars and brought them there to patrol the western
vastness. They was not much use to the Union troops, so now they
just trudged back and forth across the desert carrying their burdens.
They scared horses and mules to death and was not well liked by the
citizens of Storey County. They might not have been anything more
than furry freight wagons, but they was miraculous to me. It took
some time before I was willing to follow after Sam.

We come to the door of the *Territorial Enterprise*. Sam shook
my hand and asked me what I intended to do. Without thinking,
I blurted, "I'm going to visit down to the Virginia House Hotel."

His eyes got narrow and he give me a grin, which was his way of
saying that he knowed what I was up to. "You gonna get drunk and
have a dance with that little hurdy-gurdy gal?"

Now Sam knowed I did not drink tangle-leg. Never a drop
touched my lips since I was a child and lived with Uncle Dimmy. Nor
did I hold with dancing, except the kind Uncle Dimmy had done in
church when the Holy Ghost fell upon him. "I just want to go see
the place."

He laughed. "Well, I do believe you're blushin', Jim Canfield."

"Ain't possible."

"That may be . . ." He smoothed his mustache. "I hear tell there is
a beautiful blackbird over there who sings like a lark. . . . You talk in
your sleep, you know."

I shrugged like it didn't matter and told him to mind his own
business.

After this he said to me that I ought to mind mine as well, because everyone in Nevada knew the sort of men who hung around the Virginia House Hotel. By this he meant the Rebel sympathizers who had pledged their oath to the Confederacy. He also told me not to look any one of them in the eyes lest I get myself shot and lynched and afterward killed. Those types did not cotton to free blacks, not even in the West.

I thanked him for his care; then he went on into the newspaper office. I felt mighty alone. He was the most lazy and shiftless man I had ever knowed, but he was likable and I had grown accustomed to seeing after him.

So there I stood on the edge of that muddy boardwalk. I stared at the outside of the Virginia House Hotel, hoping for some glimpse of Lark through a window. But I did not see her even at a distance. It was quite a while before I crossed the street and walked back the other direction. I considered that just being there was breaking a promise to her. Maybe there was some way to see her where she would not see me. Then I put my hand to my face. I had a full beard, I wore the rough red shirt of a miner, my pants was tucked into muddy boots, and I was all over in need of a good bath, brush, and curry.

"Even if Lark sees you, she ain't gonna know you," I said to myself. I felt in disguise and was glad of the mud.

As I walked on, piany music tumbled out the doors of every saloon. Though it were not yet noon, men bellied up to the bars and gathered round the faro tables to buck the tiger and lose their hard-earned pay. Businesses was open round the clock to accommodate the three shifts in the mines. A man could get off work at six in the morning, drink a bottle of tarantula juice before seven, dance with a girl at seven-thirty, lose what was left of his wages by eight, and still get plenty of sleep before he had to go back to work that night.

I walked past all that. A white man grabbed up a Chinaman by his pigtail and flung him off the boardwalk. Nobody paid no mind but me. Just ahead a drunk got throwed out of a saloon. He laid there on the planks, and three men stepped over him. I stopped just long enough to drag him off and prop him against the wall.

A man in a checkered coat and trousers laughed at me. "New

around here, ain't you? You'll never get anywhere if you stop and pick up every drunk. Care to play a little five-card draw?"

I thanked him kindly and pressed on.

As the piany music played, it was accompanied by a deep bass booming in the bowels of the mountain as miners blasted away in the shafts. The earth trembled beneath my feet, and I half expected the ground to open and swallow up the whole of Virginia City in one eruption of fire and brimstone. Along with all this business was a roar from the mills and mines that sounded like thunder and cannons all in one.

Then in the rabble and the crush and the noise I spotted Lark half a block up the way. Her high-collared dress was the color of wine. She had a cape around her shoulders and a black-felt bonnet on her head. I could make out her profile: long lashes, high cheekbones, full mouth. If anything, she was more beautiful than I ever thought a woman could be. She was standing just outside the window of the Kroeger's Dry Goods store and looking through the glass at what was on display.

I stopped dead in my tracks and pulled my slouch hat down lower over my brow. Someone bumped into me, then another, but I did not budge 'til Lark went into that building.

Sneaking up on the place easylike, I peeked through the window to see what she was looking at: a pale blue satin bonnet with flowers on it—daisies. The kind of thing a lady would wear out on a drive in a buggy with her favorite beau. I thought, *Now this is what Lark was gazing at. She'd like to have that bonnet.* I wondered if she come to this store often and how long she had been wanting that bonnet.

My whole heart begun to ache, and I wanted to rush on in there and take her in my arms and hold her against me like I had been thinking about for months. But I did not do that. Dumb and dirty, I stood there outside that glass and looked in at her the way she had looked at that bonnet. And there was some pleasure in the looking and the wanting. There was some filling of the empty place in my soul where only she could fit.

She bought some fabric, red-and-black checked, and some thread and needles. The clerk, a mousy little man, did not smile back at her when she said some friendly word to him. I saw her smile fade away. She looked out the window, right at me. Away she turned, then quick back again. She studied on me for a heartbeat, and then her face filled with amazement. She recognized me under the mud!

I started to run, but she was out the door and hollering my name. "Jim! . . . Jim!"

I took a few more steps and ducked round the corner of the building.

She followed. Next thing I knowed she were glaring at me.

"Howdy, Lark." I took off my hat.

"What you doin' here?" She was riled.

"Claim got jumped . . . gotta get work . . ." I begun to babble on about Sam and Dad Billou and how we almost had it.

There was no hope for her redemption in them words. I was just as bust as any poor miner on the Comstock. I would have to go down in the shafts if I could even get hired. Four dollars a day. Six if I got lucky. Where was hope for her redemption in that?

I seen the light drain out of her eyes. That's when I knowed she had been dreaming of me as much as I had been of her. But dreams were not going to buy her freedom.

"I come to get you," I blurted.

She put her fingers on my mouth. "Hush now. Not another word like that. They'll kill you and make no mistake! Get out of Virginny."

"Not without you." I started toward her.

Lark pushed me away as a fellow walked by, then turned around to look back. She said in a loud, brassy tone, "You want to spend time with me, it'll cost you plenty, honey!" Then she whispered in a voice so full of pain I thought she would break and me, too, "Don't try to see me. Please, Jim! I loves you and they'll kill you if they know it! Don't . . . don't, Jim! You don't know how it really is!" One warm touch on my brow. At that she turned and fled back to the Virginia House Hotel.

I was feeling as low as I ever had, watching her go. After that I stood beside the window of the dry-goods store and gazed down at the satin bonnet and thought of her in it and me setting beside her in the best buggy at Green Freight and Livery.

Dreams . . . vapor . . . nothing at all.
I left to find me some place to sleep out of the cold.

✳ ✳ ✳

"Can't use you," the mine superintendent said, turning his back on me and walking away for the third day in a row. It had nothing to do with the lack of work. It was only because I was black. That was enough to get me sent to the back of the line of men waiting for employment at the Mexican Mine. It didn't matter if I stayed there all night and was the first one at the foreman's office window the next morning. As long as there was one white man looking for work, I got set back behind him and behind the next that come and so forth till another day had passed.

What with winter coming on, Virginia City's mines had plenty of workers to choose from. When the weather turned cold, lots of fellas who thought they was prospectors just naturally headed toward finding work that would keep them warm and fed. Four dollars a day was what the mines was paying, but not for me. It wasn't just the Mexican, neither. The story was the same at the Ophir, the Gould and Curry, and all the rest.

Sam saw to it that I got shelter and grub, but that couldn't keep on forever. He was just getting started as a reporter, and his twenty-five dollars didn't stretch awful far. Even he was sharing cramped quarters with Dan DeQuille and other newspapermen.

I was living way below D Street, down in Chinatown. Had a pallet on the floor in a back room of Sing Woo's laundry. Sam talked his boss, Joe Goodman, into giving the laundry free advertising in the paper in exchange for the tin roof over my head and three bowls of rice a day. Goodman was a staunch Union man, and Sam explained how we had lost our claim in the Monarch to some Rebels.

Goodman also had the newspaper's Chinese cook feed me some. If not for that and Sam buying me meals besides, I would have plumb starved to death. But it could not keep on that way. I had to get work. I was not even able to help myself, let alone Lark.

Joining the day shift from the mine that just got off work, I trudged along C Street toward the brick building that was the

286

newspaper office. Noyes, the printer's devil, give me a big hello and shouted over the noise of the press that Sam was in his office.

He meant that Sam was across the street in the Delta Saloon, but I met him out in the street. He could tell from my face that I had still had no luck finding work. "Jim," he said, "I've been giving your situation some thought, and I think I know the answer."

I looked off toward the flag fluttering over the top of Mount Davidson and thought how if this was a joke, I'd strangle him. "Tell me," I said.

"Tomorrow morning, you go up to the superintendent and tell him you'll work for nothing." He stood there grinning with his eyes and mustache the way he always did, like he'd said something really clever.

"Sam, I ain't in the mood for none of your—"

"I'm not joking," he said. "You tell Superintendent Duncan or whoever that you love to work, can't live without it, and you'll work for free, for the pure enjoyment of it. He'll hire you on the spot just to see if you're serious."

"How do that help me? I still don't gets no pay that way."

"That's not the end of the scheme. Listen: You not only work for nothing, you work harder than anybody, the way I saw you swing that pick in Aurora. Word will get around, and people will start pointing you out and asking the foreman about you. By the end of the week, two at the outside, the foreman and the superintendent will be so embarrassed that they'll offer to pay you. But don't you take it."

"No?"

"No! Because by then you'll be famous. Other mine superintendents will be bidding for your services. They'll all want to have the famous Jim Canfield working for them."

"How am I gonna get famous so fast?"

"Because I'm going to write a story about you for the paper that will make you stand like Hercules and Atlas and Samson all rolled up together!"

And that is exactly what happened.

✳ CHAPTER 11 ✳

I was down at the six-hundred-foot level of the Mexican Mine. We was opening a new chamber, working along a drift, and once again I was half of the double-jack team. It might seem that swinging a ten-pound sledge for eight hours straight was no cause for rejoicing, but I was right proud of myself. When I was working for nothing, like Sam had suggested, miners stopped to watch. Pretty soon they was bringing their friends by to look, even men off shift from other mines coming down to see if it was true.

There was some grousing at first amongst the diggers what had Rebel sentiments about me being black, but even that stopped when they seen how hard I was working for nothing. The crew boss, Irish fella name of Mackay, took special pride in me on account of how when I joined his level it started moving more rock than any two other teams. He took it on hisself to talk to Superintendent Duncan personal about getting me some pay.

It took ten days, but Duncan finally give in and offered to pay me. Seeing how the *Enterprise* was making special mention of the Mexican Mine and him in particular as being the proprietor of such a curiosity as me, what else could he do? What clinched it was when the superintendent of the Chollar Mine offered me six dollars a day to go to work for him—for the bragging rights, I guess. I was relieved when Duncan said he'd beat that offer by fifty cents a day in order to keep me. Besides, Boss Ward was still over at the Chollar, and the last thing I wanted was to work anywheres near him.

There was a Cousin Jack, which is what Cornishmen was called,
working on the same level with me. Him and me partnered to work
the double jack.

Truro was a square-built man and strong. His arms was most
big around as other men's legs. His given name was Bodmin, which
around Virginny was soon corrupted to "Bad Man," so Bad Man
Truro was how the Comstock knew him. Such a nickname often got
him into fights with those who wanted to try on the man behind the
name, which was odd for two reasons. First off, he was as mild a man
as could be and would never have picked a fight with no one. And
second, he always won. He'd stand his ground whilst the challenger
got in a couple licks that he felt no more than if hit with a feather.
Then Truro would wrap the fella in a bear hug and squeeze until the
other party either give up or passed out.

We was sitting a hundred feet inside the drift, just at the bottom of a winze, a slope leading upward to the level above. It was a
spot with a nice breeze blowing through for us to stop and have our
midshift meal. Truro wiped the dust off his face with a neckerchief.
I stuck my candlestick into the square-set timber overhead, and we
both opened our pails.

"And what have you got today?" Truro asked me.

Now this was a good question, since I was still picking up meals
from the newspaper's Chinese cook. He always fixed American vittles,
but he sometimes slipped in a Chinese treat as well. On this occasion,
it was dried shrimp.

"What unholy thing is that?" Truro scowled in disgust. "You've
taken to heathen ways for certain if you'll eat the husks of bugs!"

"He give me these before," I said, popping a shrimp in my mouth.
"Try one?"

"Not me. Never," he vowed. "Only good Christian food for me!"
Here he took out a block of yellow cheese, a handful of crackers,
and a jug of black tea. Before he carved himself a hunk of cheese, he
crumbled a cracker into a chipped saucer and poured a little tea over
it; then he set it on a small ledge in front of a clay doll.

"Tell me again what you call that thing."

"It's a tommyknocker," he replied, "or the form of one."

The six-inch-tall seated figure wore a peaked cap and had busted-off match heads in its face for eyes and the stump of a real clay pipe clenched in its grinning mouth. It looked odd, sitting there on the rock face in the flickering candlelight—not evil but mischievous.

"You ain't worshipping no idol?" I teased.

"Not a bit of it," Truro said. "I learned of them from my own father, who worked the tin mines in the old country. Tommyknockers are wee spirits that play games with miners like hiding tools and blowing out candles. But it is wise to be kind to them, since they rap on the walls to warn of cave-ins."

"Truro," I said, "do you really think some fairy will come out here and eat them crackers?"

"No," he said. "It is probably just the rats growing fat on easy pickings. But you never know. Down here in the belly of the earth, we need all the good luck we can muster."

I agreed with that. It didn't pay to think too hard on having wooden timbers holding up six hundred feet of rock over your head. Or how pitch-dark it was when the candles did blow out.

"Did you hear we'll be getting a new shift boss? Meanest man on the Comstock, or so they say," Truro remarked around a mouthful of crackers.

"How so?"

"Makes the men work in air so hot and foul that they pass out. Says if they can stand up, they can keep working. Hard driver, he is, and will give a man notice for going to the water barrel without per-mission. Killed a man, too."

"A miner?"

Truro nodded, remembering the story. "Welshman, it was. Seems the boss ordered him to go into a drift full of steam and the miner refused. The shift boss cursed him and give the man a shove; then the Welshman took a swing. The foreman was ready for him though, because he always carries a sawed-off drill about two feet long. Cracked the Welshman's head like an egg."

"And this shift boss walked away clean?"

"Coroner said it was self-defense."

"And he's coming to work here? What's his name?"

Truro tied the bandanna back around his forehead to keep the sweat from running into his eyes as we got set to go back to work. "I heard his name from a cousin of mine who works at the Chollar. My cousin said we were welcome to him, too. Now if I could just recall . . ."

"From the Chollar," I repeated, feeling a sudden dread. "Is his name Ward?"

"That's it exactly," Truro agreed.

✵ ✵ ✵

Even though I was finally making good, steady wages, I kept my little room back of Sing Woo's laundry so as to save every cent for Lark.

Six days a week I labored. On the seventh day I counted up my savings, which come to thirty-six dollars each week after I took out three dollars a week for expenses like eating, which cost me fifty cents a day for six days. I skipped grub altogether on Sundays and set my mind on things above while I put aside an additional four bits a week.

291

By the end of four months I had over six hundred dollars in the bank. This didn't sound like much until I figured that in three years I would have the sum I needed to get my gal free. I dreamed only of that.

Then one afternoon, on the coldest day of winter, something happened that changed my life forevermore. I suppose it would not be too strong to say that on down the line that small event might have even changed the course of something as important as the war between the North and South.

I was coming back to Sing Woo's when I spied a silver dollar laying half stuck between two planks on the boardwalk. I stopped for a minute and looked around to see who might own it, but I didn't see nobody else, so I grabbed it with rejoicing.

From just round the corner of the alley, I heard Truro holler, "Jim, so you've had a bit of luck. Come on up with me and the lads and give the roulette wheel a spin on that lucky dollar you've just found."

For a minute I considered it, although I did not hold with gambling. Temptation reared up mighty powerful in me. But I did not yield to it.

"No, thank you kindly," I said.

"Then come have a drink with me. Just to be sociable."

"No, thank you kindly, Truro."

"At least come pay your dollar and listen to that little Lark gal sing for a while."

Now this stopped me in my tracks. I looked at that shiny new coin and wondered if it had not fell from heaven just so I could set a spell in the dance hall of the Virginia House Hotel and rest my eyes on Lark and hear her sing. But then I thought about what would happen if I was to find one stray silver dollar every week. Why, that would mean fifty-two a year! A tidy sum.

"No, thank you kindly, Truro," I said.

Somebody else behind me hollered, "What'cha gonna do with that, Jim?"

"Put it in the bank," I told him.

It was this kind of thing that had give me the reputation of a miser. Folks talked all around about how I hoarded my cash up in the Bank of California. They talked about how I was the man who worked for no pay, and now that I had wages, I never spent so much as a dime on the good life. Money meant nothing to me, they said. They figured I didn't care about a thing at all in life except working.

Well, they was wrong. I did not tell them that I cared for someone more dearly than my own life. They talked about the hurdy-gurdy gals down at the Virginia House Hotel. Every Saturday night Truro asked why I did not go on up there and listen to that little songbird, since we was of the same kind. I pretended like it did not interest me. Truth was, I often debated something terrible inside myself whether I ought to squander one dollar just to be near her for an hour or save that dollar to buy her contract.

While the other men rushed to lose their cash in the cribs of D Street or the saloons and gambling palaces of C Street, I put that dollar I found in my pocket with every intention of having supper, washing up, then going to deposit it.

I prayed that I would see Lark when I was out and about Virginia City. Sometimes I walked past the Virginia House Hotel at the time I knowed she would be singing, and I slowed way down and fussed with getting gravel out of my boots so I could hear her without getting into a brawl with the bouncer for loitering.

On the time when Lark and me did meet by accident, she was cool to me and I was tongue-tied. I figured she had stopped loving me the way a wildcat miner stops loving a fake vein of silver when it plays out after a few feet.

I did not blame her, but I knowed she would feel different once I let my true purpose be known.

So let folks call me a miser. I didn't care a pin for it. All I cared for was putting that silver dollar into my pocket and then in the bank with the rest of my dollars so they might be fruitful and multiply.

On that cold day, there was snow on the mountains, and a frigid wind begun to wail down from the top of Mount Davidson. I lowered my head and paid no mind to my companions as they trekked on toward the C Street saloons to warm themselves.

Passing the fallow garden patch of Sing Woo, I noticed someone hunkered down and digging in that near-frozen field. His back was to me. I could see he was a big man, and it was plain he was hungry. He give a happy little whoop and held up a scrawny turnip like he had found a sack of gold.

Curious, I walked toward him and hollered so as he would not think I had come to rob him of his turnip. "Howdy," I said in a friendly tone. "I didn't know there was any turnips left in Sing Woo's patch."

He quick stuck the pitiful vegetable into his pocket and jumped to his feet. Facing me, he looked like a grizzly bear: big, hairy, mean eyed, ready to pounce. His clothes was dirty but not ragged. His cheek was swollen and blue under his right eye. He looked to be in his early thirties. He growled at me, "This here is my turnip. Don't matter who owns this plot! It would have just gone to seed if'n I ain't found it."

I smiled. "Sing Woo won't mind. Keep it. Just that I ain't seen you round these parts, that's all. Seems a man's gotta be mighty hungry to go scrounging round in a turnip patch for his supper."

"I ain't et in four days." He relaxed some. "Got jumped and robbed just this side of Six Mile Canyon. It were dark as pitch. I made my camp. They pistol-whipped me, took my money, stole my horse, kicked me forty feet down an abandoned mine shaft, and left me to starve. I got out, though, and after I eat this turnip I'm goin' after the bunch what done it."

"You know who done it?"

He begun to walk back with me toward Sing Woo's place. "Not 'zactly. Their faces was covered, but I'll find them when I find my horse."

I told him my name and shook his hand.

"They call me Kettle Belly Brown," he said, rubbing his hand on a belly that were indeed big like a kettle. "I come from Missouri." He looked me over real good. "I don't reckon you're a secesh?"

I laughed. "Not last time I checked. But the woods are full of 'em hereabouts. A man can't hardly walk without stepping on a Copperhead here in Virginny."

294

He brushed off the turnip and put the whole thing in his mouth in one bite. He kept talking while he chewed. "That's what I heard . . . secesh . . . Copperheads . . . all over the Comstock. Most as many as any place except them that rides with Jeb Stuart, I hear."

"They don't cause no trouble out here."

At that he nearly choked on his turnip. "Well, I aim to catch me a certain Reb."

I asked him to come in for a real meal—one of Sing Woo's Chinese dinners.

Sing Woo did not like Kettle Belly from the first look, however. He said right out in plain pidgin, "Stink! Stink like pig. You don' eat 'less you go wash. You don' eat 'less you pay now!"

"I reckon I'll have wind soup and snowflake stew for supper then." Kettle Belly turned his pockets out to show they was empty.

"One charity case enough!" Little Sing Woo, who weren't but half the size of Kettle Belly, gave the big man a shove. Sing Woo shook his finger at me. "You bad enough! Cheap! Miser! All the time pay me nothing! Why now you bring hungry tiger for Sing Woo to feed! Pay my one dollah or you don' eat!"

I put my hands in my pockets and backed off from Sing Woo. He had hit me with a washboard once before because I did not roll up my pallet in the morning. He was small but tough as a banty rooster.

I felt the dollar in my pocket. I don't know what come over me, but I pulled out that dollar and held it up for Sing Woo to see. "There's your dollar, you little Chinese pirate! Now shut your trap and go fix us something to eat. This man has been robbed and pillaged enough. He is near to dying with hunger! So git!"

Sing Woo's eyes widened. "You! Where you get that? Cheap! How come you never pay Sing Woo dollah for meal before?" Snatching the coin from my hand, he went back in the laundry and hollered out, "Pig! Pig! Go wash or no eat!"

So we washed up while he cooked the biggest platter of Chinese grub I had ever seen. Kettle Belly was so hungry that he ate the whole heap without commenting on the way it looked. While he wolfed down his food, he told me the story of how he had come to leave Missouri and go west.

295

On his mother's side, Kettle Belly was kin to old John Brown, who had tried to free the slaves and got himself hanged and nearly started the war single-handed.

I thought to myself that if John Brown were anything at all like Kettle Belly Brown, then the old man must have swung his sword of retribution with a mighty rage against the slavers.

Seems that in all the battling back and forth in them days of the massacres at the Kansas border, the wife and sister of Kettle Belly got in the way of Reb bullets and was killed. He knowed the voice of the man who done it during a midnight raid but not the face. Since the fateful day of the killing, he had set out on a trail of revenge against the murderer, and the trail had led him west to Virginia City.

"He's finished when I lay my hands on him." He bit through the bone of a pork rib. "He thinks he's gonna get shed of me by hiding out in these mines, but he's done for. By the time I get through with him he'll beg for mercy, and that's a fact. Not only has he murdered my loved ones . . ." His words trailed off like he had thought of something and almost said it when he was not supposed to.

It were a sad story and I pitied him, but I didn't ask him no more about it. It were plain that he was nearly ate up inside with hating this faceless Reb and wanting revenge on his life.

I had seen such things before. Sometimes hate kept a man alive but ate him up inside at the same time. Most likely it were hate that helped Kettle Belly to climb out of that mine and then stagger up the mountain to where I found him, but to what end? It were better, I thought, not to talk about it no more for fear of it boiling over right then and there.

It was late afternoon when we finished eating. Whilst I went out to bring in an armload of wood for the stove, Kettle Belly took off his filthy clothes, wrapped himself in a blanket, laid down on my pallet, and fell fast asleep. Snored like a hog, too.

Sing Woo heard the snoring and stormed into the back room. He shook his finger at Kettle Belly and tried to get another dollar out of me if the giant was going to room with me. I told him if he threw out a man who had just been robbed and beat up, then he had no kind of heart.

"That's right! Sing Woo got no kind heart! Sing Woo businessman! If big man stay, people think Sing Woo keep pigs in back room! They no bring laundry!"

He had a point, but I threatened him all the same. "I will speak to Sam about Sing Woo's cousin who is cook at the paper, and I will get the cousin fired. Then Sing Woo will have to support him, and there will be no profit in it!"

Sing Woo muttered Chinese curses at me, but he gathered up Kettle Belly's clothes to launder and left the poor man to sleep off his ordeal and the Chinese dinner.

✳ ✳ ✳

I ducked my head against the Washoe zephyr that was blowing rain straight into my face. Even with my hat pulled low and tied in place with a bandanna, the drops still smacked hard enough to sting.

Pulling up in the lee of the *Territorial Enterprise* office, I reckoned to stop in and visit Sam for a minute before chancing the waterfall that passed for the road down to Sing Woo's.

As fast as I could, I got inside and slammed the door shut again, but not before a whole chorus of yells erupted from the newspaper folk. "Close that! Hey, where'd page three blow off to? Keep that cussed thing shut! Bolt it!"

I stamped my boots to knock loose some of the mud before I tracked it all over the office, then untied the bandanna and looked around. That room looked like a whole herd of crazy spiders had taken up residence. The roof leaked in more spots than the alphabet has letters. To keep the water from dripping on their precious compositions, the reporters had stuck tacks in next to each leak, then run strings down to tin cups, buckets, and pails. Just to go across the room without running foul of that web took a mess of navigation.

"Where's Sam?" I asked Dan.

"In the basement. He thinks it's drier down there. 'Course, he doesn't know how the floodwaters are rising." This last comment was uttered in a voice loud enough to be heard below stairs, just so's Sam would hear.

"Whoever wants me, come on down," Sam's words floated up to me from below.

I found him bent over a desk with a pocketknife in his hand. He was slicing out columns from Eastern papers like the *New York Tribune* and the *Boston Globe*. "Jim!" he said. "Welcome. Come in and set. I'm almost through picking out the article we'll reprint tomorrow."

He flung the remains of the *Tribune*'s front page onto the floor and uncovered the desk blotter. It was a mass of scars, cuts, and slashes from the enthusiasm he brought to his work.

"Anything of note?" I asked.

"More of the same," he replied. "Lincoln's fired another general. He still can't locate anybody to stand up against Lee."

"Any of that war affect the territory?"

He plumped down in a chair and frowned. "I've been giving that some thought. Foreign correspondents are full of how close Britain is to selling arms to the Confederacy. It seems that they are just waiting for two things."

"Which are?"

297

"Reports claim that Britain wants to see if the Rebs can win a big victory on Northern soil . . . push the thing to a finish, you see."

"That surely could not have anything to do with us way out here."

"No, but the second condition does. England still wants proof that the South has money enough to come shopping at their store—real money, not paper—which means the Confederacy needs . . ."

"Virginia silver and California gold," I finished for him.

Sam nodded. "And not just picking off a stagecoach here and a single shipment there but the whole output of the mines."

"Anybody back in the States figure this out yet?"

"Publisher Horace Greeley says Lee is planning a big campaign in the North to give the South its major victory. He also says that with so much attention focused on the threat from Lee, nobody will think about protecting us way out here. Maybe both things will happen at once."

"Has this Greeley convinced anybody yet?" I asked.

"Only one I know of," Sam said gloomily. "Me." He opened his poke of tobacco and thumbed a palmful into the bowl of his meerschaum. When he pulled a pencil-sized object out of his waistcoat pocket and begun to tamp the load, I jumped over the desk and snatched it out of his hand.

"Don't you know what this is?" I asked with alarm.

"Found it on the street this morning," he said with a shake of his head. "Why?"

"It's a blasting cap, you dunderhead. One good tamp too many and you'll be counting your fingers by subtracting the ones in the next county!"

"Oh," he said. "In that case I won't use it as a pipe tool. I'll just keep it as a lucky piece."

I never did know if he was really careless or just playing the fool with me.

✳CHAPTER 12✳

The work in the mines went on, unrelieved by little in the way of entertainment. I still would not part with so much as a dollar that could be set aside toward Lark's redemption.

Amongst all the rest of the population of Virginia City, the favorite entertainment was gambling. The miners bet on most any kind of sporting proposition, so long as there would be one clear winner. They staged wrestling matches, fancy shooting exhibitions, and jumping contests between bullfrogs brought up from the river. There was competitions between teams of men drilling with double jacks and drinking marathons where the winner was the one still standing after guzzling bottles of Twenty Rod whiskey.

For a time the hands-down favorite was the dogfights. These was carried out in a big room downstairs below the Sazerac Saloon. There was a circular pit with wooden walls and floor and space around the outside for the spectators to stand. Men come from all over the territory with their snarling and vicious mutts, everyone eager to prove that his beast could take on all comers.

But after a space, even the excitement of that bloody sport wore off. The simple, honest miners had been gulled into thinking that the contests were on the level, that the best dog won. Then one night one of the promoters was seen dousing the ruff of the favorite with something from a small blue bottle. He claimed it was liniment, but the suspicions of the boys was aroused.

They told the gambler they wanted to see him rub it on the challenger dog's coat, too. When he refused, they give him the choice of
either that or drinking it. Well, that busted up the contest. It seems
that the professional handler had been dousing his dog's fur with
strychnine, right where the opposing critter would take hold.

That promoter was given a brand-new suit of tar and feathers and rid out of town on a rail. He did not seem to appreciate the
honor, though. Anyway, that experience soured the boys on dogfights
and left them hankering for a new and novel way to lose their cash.

One night Truro come by where I was staying and wanted me
to go with him to the Sazerac. He said there was an announcement
being made there of a new entertainment. Right away, Kettle Belly
said he'd like to go.

I didn't gamble, of course, being too tightfisted with my dollars
to risk even one on the chance of winning more.

But just then Sam stopped by. It seemed he had the same thing
on his mind, and he was dressed to impress folks what were newly
arrived in town. Ever since being made the editor in charge of local
doings—or what they called "the local"—Sam tried to look the part.
That evening he wore a bright green necktie inside a gold-colored
waistcoat, and his hair was slicked back with a pomatum that smelled
of lilac water.

"Come along with us, Jim," he urged. "This new idea is said to be
a Goliath among sporting events—a real sockdolager."

I could not see the harm in tagging along to hear what was being
announced, so I agreed to accompany the other three to the Sazerac.
At the time, it did not seem suspicious to me that every one of my
friends showed up at once.

When we arrived at the saloon, the place was already packed out
to the street.

Sam announced in a real loud voice, "Press! Make way for the
Enterprise, boys. I've got to get the story straight for tomorrow's
edition."

And the miners parted for him like the Red Sea done for Moses.
Truro, Kettle Belly, and me swum along after, straight to the stage.

Already up there was a fight promoter, a swell by the name of

Hobie Piper, who liked to refer to hisself as an "impresario." Beside
him was the little Arab fella who had accompanied the first shipment
of camels to the U.S. back in the fifties and then stayed on. What his
right name was, nobody could pronounce, so he went by the handle
of Hi Jolly.

Piper motioned for quiet and, when the buzz slacked off, begun
his pitch. "My friends, the greatest kings the world has ever known
were the fabulously wealthy sheikhs and sultans of the mysterious
deserts. Now those men, who could buy and sell the likes of Virginia
City and command all the wealth of the Levant, had a favorite sport
to which they were even more addicted than gold. Do you know what
that was?"

"Harems?" Sam called out.

Five minutes of laughter went on before the groups settled down.
Just when it would start to get calm, some latecomer would ask his
neighbor what a harem was, and the ruckus would start again.

"No, no!" Piper finally admonished the crowd into silence. "The
most excellent of all pastimes, straight out of the marvels of the
Arabian Nights, the sport for which sheikhs would part with all the
wealth of the Indies, was—" he paused for the drama to build up—
"camel racing!"

If the earlier joke had set the walls of the Sazerac to shaking,
this declaration touched off a chorus that was like to raise the roof.
"Them things?" was the shout. "Horses built by congressional committee! Spare parts left over from creation!"

Newfangled ideas always do take some time to get accepted.

"Now here's the game," Piper continued, unfazed by the mocking.
"I have hired the use of Hi Jolly's string, ten prime ships of the des-
ert in top-notch racing form, to be used in a contest one week from
Saturday. The prize will be one thousand dollars."

All of a sudden my head swum, and the room seemed to spin.
A thousand dollars? One-fifth of what I needed to redeem Lark, for
winning one race? I begun to get excited, but my emotions plunged
the next second.

"The entry fee will be one hundred fifty dollars per rider. I will naturally be giving odds and entertaining your bets as race time approaches."

I half turned toward the door, not wanting to hear more. One hundred fifty dollars? It was crazy to even consider.

Sam caught me by the arm. "Is it true that the first rider to pay his fee gets first choice of the camels?" he yelled to Piper.

"Quite right," Piper agreed.

"Well then, here's your first entrant: Jim Canfield!"

"But, but . . ." I stammered.

"You are the best hand with a team I ever saw," Sam said. "There is no beast with four hooves that you can't master. Truro and Kettle Belly and I believe in you. We put up the money and you be the jockey. What do you say?"

What could I say? I shook hands with my friends, who had somehow nosed out the secret announcement beforehand and hoodwinked me into coming. The money was paid over, and I stepped up on the stage.

✳ ✳ ✳

What I had not known the night I was volunteered as a jockey in the first-ever Virginia City camel race was that Sam had finagled his way to an inside track. Before even deciding to invest in me, Sam did a little snooping. From an hour's conversation with Hi Jolly, Sam discovered that one of the camels, Daisy by name, was by far the strongest and most likely runner. By being first up with the deposit, Sam had guaranteed our use of her for the race.

"Ain't that cheating?" I protested.

"Not at all," Sam responded, sounding shocked. "I just did a little journalistic research. Anyone else in the room could have stepped forward, same as us. That applies to the other . . . advantage . . . I have secured."

"What other advantage?" I asked drily.

"We have hired the service of Hi Jolly to be your exclusive trainer from now 'til race time. Every spare minute you have I expect you to be practicing."

So I come to learn the ways of riding camels from nearly the only fella in ten thousand miles who could teach it proper.

"Most riders will not know how to manage their beast with only one rein," Hi told me. "They will try to hook up two, as with a horse, but this will only confuse the animal. And when a camel is confused, he will not race."

"Sensible," I said. "Same thoughts as me. How do I steer with only one line?"

"Oh, you must carry a stick, like so," he said, offering me a broom handle. "The rein offers only little control. The stick is used to give direction by tapping lightly on the side of the animal's face opposite the route desired and saying, 'hut-hut-hut.'"

"Uh-huh," I said. "Or uh-hut. And I'm going to learn this in one week?"

"No," Hi said. "Daisy already knows how to do all this. You are going to learn how to stay on."

At least he was being truthful.

I got my introduction to Daisy that same day. She was seven feet tall at the withers and weighed three-quarters of a ton. Covered with coarse brown fur on her hump, neck, and shoulders, she was lighter tan colored on the rest of her. When I come into the paddock, she swung her neck round to face me and chewed her cud thoughtfully.

"A very good sign," Hi said. "If she did not like you, she would have shown it."

"How's that?"

"She might have spit in your eye, or she might have chased you out of the pen while trying to bite you. She would not allow anyone she did not trust to be this near her baby."

That's when I noticed the buckskin-colored small version of mama that snuggled up next to her on the far side. He peeked around behind her to look at me, then ducked his head back, shy.

"His name is Sultan. Daisy will run all the faster in the race to get back to him."

I coaxed Sultan to me with a handful of grain and soft words. He hung back at first, but soon enough I had him nibbling out of my palm. He let me scratch under his chin and made baby camel sounds of happiness, mostly bawling and grunting. Next thing I knowed, Daisy's big brown head was laid across my shoulder, and she batted her long eyelashes with maternal pride. I was accepted.

We spent the week practicing hut-hut-hut. Learning to ride that pack frame that passes for a saddle was tougher than I expected, and I ate my share of red rock dust, but by the end of the seven days, I was ready.

The day of the race was a fine spring morning, with a cold breeze blowing off the Sierras and the Stars and Stripes snapping proudly in the wind on top of Mount Davidson. The contest was set to be run at noon, and the start signal would be the midday blast of the Ophir Mine whistle, whose works was closest to the course.

For want of an actual track, the camels was to race south down C Street to the firehouse at the far end of town, around it, and back to the starting point. The distance was about two miles.

I was already mounted up. Truro and Kettle Belly stood by Daisy's nose, keeping her calm. Sam, as befitted the promoter of our entry, was in the stands, placing last-minute bets and acting the part of a nabob. I heard a rustle of silk and spotted Lark in the stands with some other ladies. I did not dare wave, but I do believe I seen her smile at me.

Truro joshed me some when he seen where I was looking, but Kettle Belly's attention was elsewhere. Three entries further along was Ryeman, him who owned Lark's contract. I thought, not for the first time, how he reminded me of someone I had seen somewheres besides Virginia City, but there was no time to think on it then. The Virginia House Hotel and Ryeman also sponsored a rider, and it was no secret that the jockey was a secesh. The Copperheads was vocal about not letting a black man beat a true son of the South. Ryeman was giving his fella instructions in a loud and exasperated tone as their camel danced around in a circle.

"Hold him still!" I heard Ryeman yell.

All at once, Kettle Belly disappeared.

"Hey!" I hollered, but right then the steam whistle shrilled and we was off.

Daisy jumped into the lead right way. We was followed by the entry of the Excelsior Volunteer Fire Company, the Knights of Columbus critter, and then the Virginia House Hotel beast.

We made the first turn onto C Street proper, flying past the hoisting works of the Ophir and the Howling Wilderness Saloon. Throwing a glance at my competition, I seen the Knights of Columbus animal refuse to turn altogether and carry his hapless jockey up the slope toward the tailings dump of the Andes Mine.

Past the International Hotel and the Bucket of Blood and on by the Delta Saloon, the race still belonged to Daisy. The bells of Saint Mary of the Mountains and of the Presbyterian church rung in salute. I leaned forward in the saddle, tapped easy on Daisy's right ear to guide her more to the middle of the road, and flashed by the office of the *Enterprise*.

305

Another glance showed me that the Excelsior camel and another one had collided, knocking both riders sprawling into the street. The Virginia House Hotel fella was gaining on me, though, so I hunkered down close and urged Daisy on.

Up to now, things was according to plan, and I was already beginning to savor victory and my share of the winnings. But some of the local rowdies, aiming to add to the fun, had gotten to the livery stable by the fire station that marked the halfway point. They opened the corral gates that let out onto the road.

Blasting away with six-shooters and hurrahing and flapping their slouch hats, the boys drove ten head of mules and horses out into the path of the race. Daisy never slowed, but we spent a couple anxious minutes dodging amongst the bucking and plunging beasts.

When we circled the station and headed back up C Street, the confusion had grown even worse. By then the rest of the camels had reached the scene, and the mules were all in a frenzy. They set to kicking everything nearby, including some of the camels trying to come through.

I pulled Daisy to the side, finding myself clattering along the boardwalk in front of the Queen of Silver Saloon instead of on the road. Onlookers scattered in all directions. A sign hanging over the planks almost knocked me out of the saddle, and when I righted myself that's when I seen the child.

Up ahead, no more than a block in front of the rampaging mules and Daisy's flying hooves, was a little boy. He had pulled loose from his mama and gotten between the packed spectators when they jumped back inside the buildings.

I could hear his mother screeching even above the other noise. Being on the sidewalk, Daisy and me would miss him clean, but what about all them coming after?

Daisy was startled when I whapped her sharp on the jaw and turned her between two hitching rails. We spun round in the middle of the street, with her bawling and pitching like a ship in a hurricane. We was crossways to the stampede, twenty yards upstream from the herd with just a few feet separating us from the child.

I jumped from the saddle, caught my foot in the frame, and landed on my face in the road. Struggling up, I barely had time to grab the little boy to me and stagger back to huddle in the shelter of Daisy's bulk. The flood of mules and other camels parted as around a rock and raced by.

Giving the child back to his mother, I limped back to the finish line to apologize to Sam and the others. I had lost the race and with it all their money and my chance to get ahead on Lark's redemption. But I just couldn't see that little boy hurt . . . or dead.

Sam and Truro met me at the top of the hill. "It's terrible! Terrible!" Sam said.

"I know," I agreed, "but I'll make it up to you somehow. You and Truro and Kettle Belly."

"No, no!" they both yelled at once.

"Kettle Belly is dead!"

"He was knifed behind the grandstand!"

✳ ✳ ✳

The murder of Kettle Belly Brown caused almost no stir at all in the lawless life of Virginia City. When robbery, beatings, and even killings happened daily, the hearts of the people was hardened unless it touched them close. For Sam and me and Truro, his death filled us with both sorrow and guilt, because we had been so close by and yet unable to help.

Lark knowed how hurting I was. Once, passing near me on the street, she said no word but pretended to stumble so's I could catch her. She murmured thanks and passed on but in the brief touch passed me a note. It said she was praying for me and that I should be extra on my guard. But against what, she did not say.

And all the while my brain spinned out tale after tale of who done it and why. It was said to be robbery, since Kettle Belly had no cash or watch on him when found, but I knowed that weren't really the cause. His death was linked to a war and other killings on the other side of the continent. There was at least one other who knowed the truth as well: the killer.

As hard as it may seem, life still went on after Kettle Belly's murder. More grim and silent than before, I drew back into myself and tried to give over to the work as a way of getting on with my life.

The Mexican Mine was one of the richest diggings on the lode. Some of its ore assayed out at over one hundred fifty dollars to the ton. What that meant for us miners was that the money was there for improvements to take the work deeper, further, and grander.

Even while I was following the drift at six hundred feet, digging was going on to deepen the shaft to close to a thousand feet straight down. What followed was a new tunnel at eight hundred feet, hitting the vein that much lower. It never failed to prove out that the deeper on the lode a mine went, the richer the ore.

The other thing that was always true is that deeper works meant more water flooding in, hotter conditions, and greater danger for the miners. As the fastest-working crew in the Mexican, Mackay's group—including me and Truro—moved down to the new level.

I seen Ward at least twice every day, at the beginning and ending of the shift and sometimes during the workday when he come round to inspect. He didn't never recognize me as the young slave from New Orleans, not growed up and amongst a hundred other men, but once or twice I thought he looked at me funny, as if trying to place me. I figured to stay clear of trouble with him by working as hard as always and keeping my head down when he passed by.

My plan worked well, until the day come when we was drilling on the main face at the eight-hundred-foot level. Because of the slant to the vein of silver, the new works had yet to cut into the lode. Tons of worthless rubble had to be carted off before the tunnel again reached pay dirt. Ward give the order to cut straight ahead at full speed, drilling, blasting, and hauling out.

Now on that particular day, I was hammering and Truro holding the drill, same as always. The little tommyknocker doll set by our feet. We cut the first three of the blasting holes, but when Truro pulled out the bit to set up for the fourth hole, I heard him say, "The devil!"

"What is it?" I asked.

"Take down the candle," he requested, "and hold it where I can study the bit!"

When I done what he asked, we seen the last six inches of the drill was wet. "Go get Mackay," he said. "We'd best be testing this before we blast."

Water in the mines was often found in pockets, like bubbles trapped in the rock. Most times it could be drained away into the sump at the bottom of the hoisting shaft and then pumped out.

But sometimes the pocket would be immense in size and holding terrific pressure. Blowing it open could flood the tunnel with boiling water and steam. Sometimes the liquid was poison, blinding men it touched or even killing them.

When such a pocket was suspected, work was stopped until test holes, deeper than the blasting holes, could be drilled into the rock face to tap the pocket. Then it could be safely drained and the pressure released before the drilling and blasting continued.

John Mackay, being the crew boss of our level, understood right away what Truro was saying and agreed to stop work on the drift. He sent for the extra long drill, the one as had to be carried by two men instead of just one. Truro was one of the men, and a Swede name of Borger was the other. I was picked to do the driving, which Mackay said was to be done just above the floor level.

When the long bit was fetched, Ward happened to be standing

near the rigging loft, and he come along to see why it was wanted. After Mackay told Ward what was going on, Boss Ward had a fit. "I tole you to go ahead full speed with this here drift," he yelled. "Now you go and do the opposite! That drill ain't wet! Why, I spit more'n that! Get on with yer blastin'!"

When Mackay protested that it weren't safe, Ward really got riled. He swung that short steel bar around and hit the wall of the tunnel, throwing sparks. Then he cursed and said if he had to say it again, he'd fire the whole level and get men who would take orders.

Real soft, Mackay said for us to go back to work, drilling the blasting holes. Him and the Swede went back to work on a crosscut to the main drift, around a corner from Truro and me. Ward stayed and watched us work 'til he seen that we wasn't going to slack off; then he went on up the way.

Truro and me finished the drilling, packed the powder and the rock dust into them holes, and strung the fuses from the blasting caps. Then we went into the other chamber and told Mackay we was ready to blast. He said that after we lit the fuse, we would all go up the hoist to the next level, instead of just staying in the crosscut, so as to be good and safe. Him and the Swede and the others working at that level headed on up. Truro and me was to follow as soon as the fuse was burning.

309

When the level was clear, we set fire to the cord, grabbed our candles and the tommyknocker, and run like crazy for the lift. It weren't there!

"What can Mackay be thinking?" Truro said. "Ring for it, Jim."

I give the signal to lower the car, but nothing happened. Twice more I done it, and there was still no motion in the shaft to show that the cage was coming. "Quick," I said, "we'd best get around in the crosscut, so as to be out of the way of the blast."

No sooner had we reached the corner of the side passage than the charges exploded! Blasting rock sounds like a cannon going off, but the first noise was followed by more of a deep rumble in the earth. There was a rush of air into the crosscut as the blast pushed a breeze out ahead of it. The lanterns and candles all blew out. That was not unusual, and I was already fumbling in my pocket for matches. My ears popped and then rung like bells, but everything seemed normal. I could hear the sound of boulders being rolled along the main drift and smaller chunks bouncing off ceiling and walls, but over that was a high-pitched hissing sound, like a locomotive pulling into a station.

I struck a match, but before I could relight the candle, around the corner of the chamber come a boiling cloud of steam! Truro was closer to the entrance than me, and he caught the first blast square in the face and give a scream. I flung my arms across my eyes and felt the rush of burning vapor scorch my ears and naked chest.

The match blowed out again, of course. "Come on," I said. "Back to the hoisting shaft."

The rumble and the hiss was followed by something even more scary—the crash and gurgle of a mighty stream of water.

"Wait!" I hollered. "Keep back!"

I could not see it, but I could hear a rushing wave course down the main drift. If we had stepped out right then, we would have been in its path. As it was, a bubbling torrent swept along the tunnel and plunged in an underground waterfall over the edge of the shaft. A small wave bounced into our chamber, swirling around our ankles and making us jump from one foot to the other.

"Jim!" Truro shouted back. "Help me!"

He was mad with the pain. His eyelids was burned, and his whole face blistered. In the pitch-black I couldn't see no more than him, but I weren't panicked, at least not yet.

"This way," I said, like it was clear to me. I grabbed on to his arm and pulled him out into the drift. We coughed and gagged from the sulfur smell in the steam and splashed through scorching pools that even after the first wave passed was again several inches deep and rising.

The next danger was that we would overrun the drift and fall two hundred feet down the shaft. Then we would be torn to flinders by the rocks and scalded to death in the sump.

With my one hand locked on Truro's wrist and my other feeling the wall ahead of us, we scuttled sideways along the tunnel. At one point I slipped and fell down, dragging Truro with me. As my hand plunged into the hot water, it clenched tight of itself and brought up a lump of rubble from the floor.

The cascade dumping off the lip of the shaft warned me we was close. I could hear the pouring over the rim. A light appeared ahead. The cage dropped down into sight with Mackay aboard. He slipped his arms under Truro's and dragged him into the lift before he turned back to swing me in. Up we soared, toward light and air.

"What happened?" I gasped out. "Where was the car?"

"Ward," Mackay said. "He found us on the level above and said we were wasting time again coming that far away from the charge. He wouldn't let me send the cage down for you, said you'd be all right in the crosscut." Mackay shook his head, looking at our blisters and Truro's swoll-shut eyes.

I forced my hand to unclench. The lump I had picked up still had its match-head eyes, but the rest of the tommyknocker's body was gone, busted to pieces and washed away.

311

☀ CHAPTER 13 ☀

It took some time for my hands to heal up enough from the burns for me to swing a hammer again. The blistered places on my head and chest was sore but didn't slow me none. Truro was worse off than me. His eyes was wrapped in bandages, and while the doc said he would not lose his sight, it would be a time before he could go back down in the mines.

Ward never admitted no wrongdoing, said it was an accident. And who was going to risk his own job arguing with him? Mackay did stand up for me in one respect, though. Since I couldn't work the double jack, Boss Ward was actually fixing to lay me off. Mackay stood right up to him about that and told him that he would keep me on as a watchman 'til I healed.

A watchman in the diggings is kind of a free-roaming spirit. The job is to keep an eye out for fire, for timbers that need shored up, for cables that need replaced, and so forth. Since he's not part of a regular crew, the watchman is also supposed to spy for the mining concern, keeping track of supplies and seeing to it that nobody steals company property. As such, he is not liked by the other miners, since he can turn them in for smoking and other forbidden practices. But because I were only fixing to do the work temporary, I didn't figure to have no trouble of that kind.

Sam reported the accident in the Mexican Mine. Even wrote me up as a hero for dragging Truro out of the drift.

"Sam," I said, "there weren't nothing special about what I done.

Truro or any of the others would have done the same for me. 'Sides, I was saving my own skin at the same time."

"Give it up, Jim," he replied. "This territory has precious few heroes to brag about, and for the moment you are one. Might as well enjoy it."

Funny thing was, most folks showed their appreciation by stopping me on the street and offering to buy me a drink, which of course I had to decline anyway.

I might have got even more attention if it were not for the new fuss with the Washoe Indians. It seems that some miners had gone to chopping firewood. Now this weren't ordinarily no cause for discussion, but this time they took it into their heads to cut piñon trees.

Sam said that was right foolish because everyone knowed that pine-nut trees was too full of sap to burn, and the Indians needed the nut trees for food. He even wrote a column laying out all this information for the uninformed public.

Old Winnemucca and Numaga, his son, made a trip to Carson to ask Governor Nye to stop the tree cutting. Nye couldn't do nothing hisself, so he sent the Indians over to Fort Churchill to ask the army for help. This is like killing a gopher by burying him alive. It sounds workmanlike, but it don't accomplish nothing. The army was not about to defend the Indians that they was there to defend against.

"Besides," Sam explained to me and in the paper, "more than that, the tree cutters are all Copperheads, led in fact by Bill Mayfield. Captain Moore will not provoke the Rebels into a general uprising by arresting Mayfield and his crew. Not for doing something that only Indians care about."

So nothing but a lot of talk got done, but it occupied a mess of space in the newspaper. Sam said it made his job right easy.

❋ ❋ ❋

The worst thing about watchman duty in the Mexican Mine was the hours. Miners worked eight-hour shifts, and there was three shifts each day: seven in the morning 'til three in the afternoon, three 'til eleven at night, and graveyard from evening 'til morning. Everybody got to be aboveground during some part of daylight.

But the watchman's job, not involving swinging hammer or pick, not loading ore cars, was considered light work. There were only two shifts a day: six in the morning 'til six at night and the other the reverse of that.

Them hours meant that even though the days was at the longest of the year, since I had the daytime spell, I barely glimpsed the sun at all. It was right depressing to spend all my work time in the gloom of the pit and, when I come up, to find gloom above as well.

Couple that with the fact that watchmen work alone, and the darkness was inside of me as well as out. I had lots of time to reflect on Lark and our future together, which now seemed not even bright enough to be called uncertain. I brooded as I done my job, kind of chewing on my thoughts with half my mind.

One day Mackay sent me down in the secondary shaft of the Mexican Mine to a platform at the one-hundred-foot level. This passage had earlier been used for ventilation and to haul ore. As the hoist brought up rock from below, it was dumped automatic by a device at the landing, spilling the contents of the bucket into cars. At the time of my arrival there, the station was not in use because that shaft was waiting its turn to be deepened. It was supposed to operate again soon, to join in the development of the lower reaches, and that is the task that took me there.

My job on that particular day was to inspect the machinery at the platform, to see what might need replacing. I checked the hopper and the cables, the mechanism of the dumper, and the bracing.

The inclined tunnel down which the ore slides after being dumped is called a winze. It slanted down away from the station to another drift where the tracks for the ore cars set. Now Mackay had not asked me to check the winze or the rails below, but I figured to save myself a return trip and so took my lantern and started down the incline.

Intermediate between the landing and the drift was a disused crosscut that connected with another mine. This weren't unusual; most of the mines bumped into their neighbors underground. Some even shared shafts or main drifts. The works of the Mexican inter-sected those of the Union Consolidated at this point.

But at that shallow a spot, none of the tunnels in the next-door mine was being used and it was all deserted. It was whilst passing the opening to the crosscut that I heard the clank of metal on metal coming from the darkness beyond.

Mines being what they are, some noises are natural and to be anticipated, like small chunks of rock that drop unexpected from the ceiling. The groaning song of the timbers, the drop of water, or even the scurry of rats is soon recognized and paid no heed. But the noise of steel meant tools, and tools meant men, where none was supposed to be.

I stopped by the cleft and paused to think. It weren't none of my business what might be happening in the Union Consolidated. On the other hand, if anyone had been stealing tools or supplies from either the Mexican or the Union, this deserted passage was a likely spot to keep the secret.

That nothing honest could be happening in the drift was shown as soon as I crossed the threshold. The floor was half choked with sticky porphyry clay. In some places on the lode, the vein of silver ore is surrounded by this clay, a kind of real thick mud. It stays put until tunnels or drifts cut out the solid rock that holds it prisoner; then it oozes out of its seams from the weight of the stone above. Like squeezing the custard out of an eclair, it seeps into open spaces and has to be dug out and carted off. If anyone were planning to make use of this drift for mining purposes, the very first thing they would have did is taken care of the clay.

And if that weren't enough evidence, when I stepped over a mound of porphyry farther back in the passage, I seen the brand-new print of a boot, plain as anything in the wet mud. Right then I shielded my lantern down to a small glowing circle to keep it from being so easy seen, and I crept along quiet. It never occurred to me to go get help. Being watchman was my job and nobody else's.

I held the lamp up to guide me and to inspect the tracks left by the muddy boots. There was two sets of them—both small men to judge by the size of their prints—and they had walked along side by side. The glow also revealed to me the run-down state of the timbers and the vault of an upraise as I passed beneath it.

315

After going fifty yards or so, I could hear voices speaking in low tones, and I aimed to find out what the speakers was up to. If possible, I would creep close enough to learn their scheme and their identities. At least, such was my intent.

Abandoned mines is lonely places at any time, but when moisture is present, like with the oozing mud, they get downright uncanny. The timbers, which in an operating portion of the works are seen after and replaced as needed, quickly become the haunt of weird fungus that grows on the wood.

When the light of a candle or lamp strikes such a coating, it glows in fantastic shades of green and yellow or even orange. That was what happened around the next bend in the Union tunnel. When I turned the corner, I jumped back sudden, because right in front of me was a hideous, gleaming face, leering at me with its dark yellow mouth and looking at me from coal black eyes between orange pointed ears. I stumbled over to a loose stone, banging the lantern against the wall as I made to catch myself.

I knowed right away that the evil image weren't no demon but an illusion formed by some of that fungus on an upright timber. But in the start it give me, the damage was already done. Whoever was up ahead of me must have heard the noise. There was a sudden ruckus.

"Someone's there!" a voice shouted. A clatter of footsteps come toward me.

The fact that they was approaching told me something right away: They felt strong enough to deal with whoever had chanced upon them, rather than running the other way. So it seemed clear to me to take myself off instead of sticking around.

I blowed out the lantern and run back the way I had come. Getting rid of my light kept me from being spotted right off but made it impossible for me to get away very fast. When the shine of another light reached the tunnel wall beside me, I knowed there was no chance of me getting back to the winze and clear, so I started looking for a place to hide.

I was right then in the passage with the upraise. An upraise is a vertical dig that climbs from a drift to tap an ore body overhead. In the dark, I could not see how far the upraise went, but I hoped that it were high enough to be above the glimmer of the lamp.

Climbing them slippery beams was tough. I hoisted myself up on the first timbering all right, but then I had to crouch on the very edge of the beam. I needed to get higher out of the passage, but to go further I had to stand up sudden, with my boot toes on the very edge, and thrust my length upward into the unseen.

My fingertips barely caught the next ledge, and I somehow lifted myself. My burned hand was shrieking with the strain, and I couldn't have gone no farther.

Two men stormed into the cavern below and stopped directly beneath me. "There's no one here," said one. "And no one has gone out. Look, the only footprints in the clay are ours made coming in."

I thanked the Lord that fella didn't count them tracks too close.

"I s'pose it's nothin'. We's just jumpy is all," the second man replied.

The voice was that of Boss Ward.

"Let me finish what I was saying," the first man instructed.

I strained my eyes to see if I could recognize him, but he wore a hat, and from my angle there weren't no way to make out his features. His speech did have a familiar ring to it, but I concentrated on the words.

"My girls tell me that the Union officers have gotten in a shipment of two hundred rifles from California. Besides that, they have confiscated eighty weapons more from the militia headquarters at Carson in order to keep them out of secesh hands." The speaker chuckled at that, like it was humorous someway.

"When do we move?" Ward asked.

"Right now. The first act of our little tragedy will put the Yankees in motion tonight. The whole territory will be ours inside a week."

"An' the nigger? He's still askin' questions about what happened to Kettle Belly. Shall I finish him off?"

"Leave it be. It's too late for him or anyone else to stop us now. We can deal with him after."

My arm muscles was in spasm from the awkward position, clinging to the wall like a lizard, so I was right glad when they concluded their walk and headed out of the tunnel. I waited 'til they went clean back into the Mexican drift, and I heard the rattle of the hoist as they left the level. Then I finally eased myself down to the floor of the drift again, dropping the last six feet with a crash.

My mind was awhirl. "My girls," the fella had said. Ryeman! What was Lark caught up in? That they were Copperheads bent on mischief was obvious. But what was their scheme and who should I warn? Who would take my word against Boss Ward's? These were all things I needed to know, and from the sound of things, time was short.

I did not know where to turn. I could not find Truro. And Lark? I was scared to see her. For one, it might put her in danger. Nagging at me was the thought that she was mixed up in it someway.

Sam was the only one I could count on, and he was the only one I could tell what I seen. Soon as my shift was over, I located him in his "office" in the Delta Saloon. He was at the bar, bending the elbow with a bunch of his newspaper cronies. It was clear that some kind of celebration was going on.

"Sam," I said at once, "I gotta talk to you."

He acted real glad to see me. "Jim! Finally left the world of moles behind, have you? Come on, break your rule this once and have a drink."

"No, thanks," I said. "Anyways, I needs to see you. It's important."

"Why, so is this occasion." He waved two fingers to the barkeep the way he always done when he was buying drinks for hisself and a friend. "Mark twain," he called out, telling the barkeep to add two more to his tab. "You have to join me this once. I've been promoted. Joe is leaving Virginia for some business in San Francisco, and I'm to be editor in his absence." He said this last sentence real loud, as if all the folks in the saloon hadn't heard it twenty times already. But he was buying the liquor, so they give him a hurrah again anyway, to which he bowed.

I caught his elbow midbow and dragged him off of center stage and over to a corner table. I had first planned to talk with him outside, somewheres private, but with all the commotion in the Delta, we was in less danger of being overheard right there.

Sam was still smiling and waving to his crowd when I got right in his face. "Listen!" I hissed. "This is serious."

He swallowed twice and pursed his lips, and his head bounced a little as he tried to focus his eyes. It come to me that if this celebration had been running for very long, he would be worse than useless. I had to try anyway. "Hear this," I said. "I have got wind of a Rebel plot, right here in Virginia City."

"A Rebel plot!" he said at high volume, half standing up from his chair.

"Shhhh!" I said. "Don't talk—just listen. Ryeman is in it and so is Boss Ward. They plan to steal weapons from Fort Churchill. They say they have a scheme to take care of the soldiers. We gotta stop 'em."

Sam thought a minute, suddenly serious and blinking like a goggle-eyed owl. "You're right. We'll go together, you and me, to see Captain Moore. We'll warn him. He can arrest those two and lean on them 'til he finds out the rest. We'll go tomorrow."

319

"No," I said. "Tonight."

✳CHAPTER 14✳

The quickest route from Virginia City to Fort Churchill lay down the winding trail that went by way of Six Mile Canyon. Most of the freight and the travelers for the Comstock used Gold Canyon, farther to the west, so Sam and I had the road all to ourselves. It was late to be starting on the trip to the army post but no help for it.

The slope from town to the valley of the Carson River was steep. The looming bulk of Mount Davidson stayed spiked on the horizon behind, but the twinkling lights of the Comstock got quick swallowed up. And all too soon the twisting road dropped behind the cone-shaped mount called the Sugarloaf, and the shadows within the arroyo was very deep indeed.

Down below Flowery Peak, there was a trail that turned off the Six Mile Canyon route to a small trading post. A battered wooden sign read Drinks and Vittels. A hot east wind swirled the dust and moaned down the canyon. All at once our horses stopped of themselves and stood with their ears pricked forward, in the direction of the side path. Slower than our mounts, Sam and me picked up the clatter of hooves.

Then a horse and rider busted out of the dark ahead of us and come down the road at a gallop.

Sam and I barely had time to rein apart before the unknown horseman split between us, so close that his stirrup touched mine.

"Hallo," I hollered. "What's the trouble?"

But the strange figure answered not a word. The echoing hoof-beats bounced off the rocks before facing into the whining of the wind.

"Who or what was that?" Sam said. "Could you see his face?"

The collar of the rider's pitch-black duster was pulled up close and his floppy-brimmed hat tied down with a bandanna. I could not even make out that he had a face, much less remark on his features. "No," I said. "But nobody rides in that big a rush unless there's calamity. Come on!" I didn't give Sam no choice but put the spurs to my livery nag, and on toward the trading post we charged.

There was no light ahead and nothing to show where the promised food and drink could be found. We located the saloon only by spotting a darker mass against a black cliff side. The door stood partly open. A faint, rust-colored glow from within showed that there had been a fire on the hearth, but it was burning mighty low.

"This don't look good, Sam," I said. "Did you bring your pistol with you?"

321

He made no reply but fumbled under his jacket, and I took the action for a yes. Whilst I dismounted and walked cautious to the doorway, Sam kept his horse in motion, spinning around like to watch every single direction at once.

"Anybody there?" I called. I crept up on the entry from the side, my heart pounding in my ears. I had no weapon at all, and as I come closer to the door, I seen what I took to be a piece of stove wood laying on the threshold. Stretching out my reach, I stooped to pick it up.

It was a man's arm! I had mistook his dark blanket coat sleeve for a tree branch. "Sam!" I shouted. "Come here quick!" The body lay facedown in the opening, and it didn't take no genius to know he was dead.

Inside the post, which was no more than a single-room cabin with a wooden counter running across the far end, there was another dead man. By the poor light from the fire, I seen him lying just below the edge of the counter.

I found the stub of a candle and lit it, whilst Sam hovered outside the door, muttering under his breath. "What have we got here, Jim?" he asked in a gulping voice. "A double murder?"

"Looks like it," I said. "This fella," I added, pointing with my boot toe, "was likely the owner of this place." I showed Sam the greasy apron knotted around the man's neck. "Looks like someone come to rob him."

"Who's the other?" Sam hissed, stepping over the body in the entry with as long a stride as he could manage.

"Maybe one of the attackers or maybe another victim." I dragged the body back inside the cabin and turned him over. It was an Indian. In fact, it was Echapa—"Coyote"—the Washoe we had met by the lake.

✵ ✵ ✵

It did not matter that the heavy dust obscured the road or that we had to trust the good sense of those unfamiliar horses to keep us from flying off a cliff. With two dead bodies behind and the unknown phantom—possibly the killer—ahead, Sam and me hurtled down Six Mile Canyon like our lives depended on it.

As we galloped, I tried to piece together what we had found. Echapa had been gunned down. The hole just to the left of his breastbone had put paid to him. Fact is, he could not have moved an inch after that wound. How come we found him to be lying facedown in the doorway, a streak of blood stretching ten feet back to where his hatchet lay on the floor?

And what about the proprietor of the place? His skull had been split open, likely by that selfsame hand ax. But had he shot Echapa after receiving such a blow? It did not make sense.

On the face of it, it seemed plain enough. Echapa and perhaps other Indians had jumped the saloon keeper. The barkeep and Echapa had exchanged wounds, from which both died.

But Echapa was stone-cold dead—had been for some time— while the barkeep was still warm to the touch. I pondered that difference but come to no answers.

And over and under and intruding on all these thoughts was the puzzle of the lone rider. Who was he? He weren't no Indian; that much was plain. Could he have found the bodies and lit out for help, same as us? If so, he might have feared that we was the murderers returning. That would explain his desperate flight.

The only thing to be done was to tell Captain Moore and the army at Fort Churchill. For the time, even thoughts of Rebel schemes was forgot.

We turned east when we hit the stage road, which was marked plain. Following the curve of the river for another five miles, the lights of Bucklands and the fort come into view.

We rode straight to the officers' quarters, a low adobe building on the north side of the compound. We wasn't challenged at all. Near as I could tell, the only sentry on duty was across the parade ground in front of the arsenal. There sure weren't no sense of urgency about the place.

As we drew rein in front of Captain Moore's quarters, Sam leaned over in his saddle and said to me, "Jim, I know Captain Moore. Orion introduced us. So I'll start off explaining, but you jump in anytime you see me leave out anything important."

We knocked on the door, and a burly Irish sergeant opened it.

Sam explained who we was, asking to see the captain, and we was taken in.

Captain Moore was seated at a desk, writing by the light of an oil lamp. He glanced up and I seen him do a double look, almost like he couldn't believe what he saw. "Well, this is a surprise. Come in and sit down." He motioned to a pair of ladder-back chairs fronting his desk. "Sergeant, would you please get Lieutenant Jewett and our other guest and return here at once? At once, you understand?"

The sergeant give a snap of his head and a salute, then hustled out.

"Now," Captain Moore said to us, "what can I do for you?"

"Captain," Sam said, "I hardly know where to begin. We actually came to warn you of a Rebel plot to seize the arms stored here. But on the way, we discovered a murder, or perhaps it's two murders."

At the word *murder*, the captain stood up and drew his sidearm, a Colt Army revolver. He didn't exactly point it at us, but he didn't lay it down either. "Perhaps you'd better tell me everything." There was a cold edge to his words, and I begun to feel right uneasy.

"It was at the old Six Mile Canyon trading post," Sam begun. "One white man, perhaps the owner, has been killed. There is also a dead Indian, a Washoe named Echapa."

At that instant the door burst open, and the sergeant and the lieutenant fairly rushed in. They grabbed Sam and me by the arms, pinning us into our chairs.

"What is this?" Sam sputtered. "What are you doing?"

The captain ignored him. "Come in, Mister Ryeman," he said to a figure lurking in the doorway. In strutted my worst enemy in the world, though he didn't know me from Adam: the man what held Miz Lark's bond and the chief of the Rebel plot.

"Yes, that is the one," Ryeman said, pointing his finger at Sam. "I overheard him plotting with another secesh, but unfortunately I did not recognize the other. It is just as I told you, Captain. The Rebel gang are rousing the Indians to go on the warpath."

"But . . . but . . ." Sam stammered. "Jim here heard about a plot all right, but it isn't us. Tell them, Jim."

I craned my neck around to try and look into the eyes of the man known as Ryeman. "It was you," I said. "You're the fella I heard in the mine, scheming with Boss Ward. Captain, sir, you got this backward."

To do him credit, Captain Moore looked right sharp at Ryeman when I said Ward's name, but Ryeman come back quick. "How clever," he said, "naming a man with well-known secesh sympathy in connection with me." He laughed. "Come now, Captain! Are my papers in order or not?"

Moore looked a little embarrassed, and that was not good for Sam and me. "Mister Ryeman is a . . . works for the federal government. And you two are under arrest for treason, sedition, and murder."

"Murder?" Ryeman repeated.

The captain explained what we had just reported, then said it was his belief that we had killed both men and cooked up the story to heat up the bad blood between the whites and the Indians.

Right then something else clicked in my head. "I know where I seen you before. Back in Missouri. You changed your hair color and shaved off your beard, but your name is Grimes. I seen you when you was rounding up secesh militia for the fight at Springfield. You come to Pike's camp." Them last words slipped out before I seen what harm they could cause.

"There, you see, Captain. They admit being in a Rebel camp, with cutthroats of the worst sort. Just as I told you. I had already infiltrated the Rebel ranks, and that's where I spotted these two. When I saw them again in Virginia City, I knew they were up to no good."

I seen what the game was then. Abner Grimes was a Confederate spy, but he had somehow got papers to pass hisself off as a spy for the North. And we was being set to take the blame for his treason.

Sam was still unable to string two useful words together.

"Captain," I said, "does it make sense for me, a black man, to be helping the cause of the slavers?"

Captain Moore shot a look at Grimes again, but it was a nod of understanding and not questioning. I knowed that Grimes had planned for that objection, too. "Some men will do anything for money," the captain said. "Lieutenant, take them to the guardhouse."

Sam finally found his voice. "Wait. You know my brother is the territorial secretary. Let me at least write him a note. He can straighten all this out, I'm sure."

Now I was not in the least bit sure that Orion could straighten out a twelve-inch ruler, but I blessed Sam for coming up with a delay anyhow.

We was both stood up, ready to be marched off to the hoosegow, but when the sergeant who was holding me seen that his commander was going to let Sam pen a letter, he naturally relaxed. Being careful not to tip him off by tensing myself up, I let my shoulders sag.

Grimes smirked in the doorway, and the captain got paper and ink for Sam, who bent over the desk. The lieutenant stood behind the empty chair that had lately held Sam, and the sergeant was behind me.

I took a quick step to my right and back, turning toward the sergeant as I did so. I give him a shove that sent him sprawling into the lieutenant, and I whipped one chair after the both of them.

The captain reached for his pistol, and Sam wrestled with Moore, his two hands clamped on the officer's wrist. "Run, Jim," he yelled. "Get out of here! Go!"

As I started for the door, I seen Grimes reach under the skirt of the coat he wore and knowed he was going for a gun. I threw myself at him full force, knocking him backward through the doorway.

Grimes was smart. He grabbed on to my coat, knowing that all that was needful was for him to slow me down 'til the sergeant could recover and I would be caught.

So I didn't try to wrestle with him. I brought both my knees up to my middle, so when we landed it was with all my weight right in his chest. The air and the fight went out of him, and he loosed his hold.

I was up quick and dashed off into the dark, snatching the reins of my horse as I went and doing a running mount from alongside.

I could hear everybody yelling at once, "Corporal of the guard! Stop the prisoner. He's escaping. Shoot him!"

I didn't ever know if it was someone obeying that order or the captain hisself who fired, but a bullet zinged past my right ear as I crouched low over the horse's neck.

More shots was fired after that, but no others come close to hitting me. I lit out across the desert, scarcely knowing where I was going and only grateful for the dust storm that was hiding my tracks.

✴ CHAPTER 15 ✴

The howl of the east wind was at full force, whipping my coat and stinging my face. Night and the high desert closed in around me 'til I begun to feel as dark as being down in the mine. Sam was bound to get hanged as a spy, and the real spy was a snake being welcomed to the fireside. It looked hopeless.

Some vague notion of heading for Carson to find Orion kept me moving west. While I rode, I argued with myself that not even that would help. In the first place, Orion might be suspect, too, and in the second, he would surely be watched, and here I was a fugitive from the same gallows as hung over his brother. But 'til something else presented itself, Orion was my only aim.

The dust storm turned the sagebrush into heaps of piled-up sand. Distance was all distorted, too. A hill that I fixed in my mind as a far bearing turned out to be a mound of weeds only a few yards off.

That was when I first realized that I was truly lost. I did not know where I was nor how I had come there. I could not even retrace my own path, even if I had wanted to ride straight back to the fort and give myself up.

The wind had been steady out of the east. If I kept my back to the blow, I must surely run upon the stage road, or so I reasoned.

My eyes was so begrimed that it was difficult to raise the lids. Tied behind me on the saddle was a canteen. Getting off the horse, I used him as a windbreak to shelter myself from the gale while I splashed some water on my face.

I was also starving. I had not eaten since the noon meal because Sam and I left in such a hurry to reach the army post. I patted my pockets, but all I come up with was a little sack of them dried shrimp, left over from that day's lunch.

I left the packet inside my coat to keep it from blowing away and drew out one piece at a time. The tiny bites of food give me a black humor. What if my last meal on earth should be what Truro called "husks of bugs"? It beat gnawing on sagebrush though, and I thought of Kettle Belly snatching that woody turnip like it was a feast. Circumstances surely do change a man's perspective.

Crouching there, I debated whether to toss whole handfuls into my mouth and get substantial swallows or stretch the morsels out a ways. The reins was laying across my shoulder and my back was to the horse, so I was totally unprepared when the nag give a snort and jerked his head around.

The reins trailed across the sand, and I dived for them but missed. My spring put flight into the horse, and he slung his head around once more and took off trotting.

"Stop, you misbegotten—," I yelled and I took out after him.

But he was moving with a purpose now and kept out of my reach. His head was up and his ears pricked, like something called to him out of the bleakness. Had he scented another horse or the smell of hay in a stable, or was he headed clean back to Virginia City, following some bearing that only horses recognize?

I jumped over a dirt-clad lump that I took to be another bit of sage, but I was wrong. This mass of windblown grit hid a boulder, and there was a crevice on the other side that I had not seen before I leaped. My feet tangled up when I landed, and I sprawled on my face.

Though I snatched myself up quick as I could, the horse was gone, completely gone. I wiped the dust from my face and took off running again to follow his tracks. Then I seen it: a faint yellow light, low down on the horizon. Likely the horse had gone there for shelter or food.

Setting off toward the glow, I expected to come upon a prospector's camp, way out there in the desert and all. But when I got close enough, I seen the beehive-shaped mound of bark and earth. It was a Paiute campodie.

Stumbling straight into the cleared space in front of the hut, I spotted where my mount had gone. There was a makeshift corral, and my horse was craning his neck and turning his head sideways through the rails for a nip of bunch grass.

Now I did not know who or even what band these Indians was. Further, Sam and me had found Echapa killed dead but a few hours before, apparently in a fight with a settler. And if that was not enough, things was not exactly pleasant between the Indians and the whites over such matters as pine-nut trees. I wondered whether strange Indians would regard me as closer to white than they was. The best idea seemed to be to grab the trailing reins and ride off.

But the scrawny donkey inside the corral settled that option. He give a loud snort and then a bray that would have waked the dead. From inside the campodie, three Indian braves emerged to see what the fuss was over. One had an old double-bladed ax, and the other two was carrying knives. I was right surrounded, and they had not even been trying.

Not wanting to act suspicious or treacherous at all, I gave them a big howdy. Then I explained that my horse had run off and that I had followed him to their camp. I said if I could trouble them for directions, I would be on my way again.

It did not settle me that none of them responded. I did not know if they spoke no English or if they was sizing me up.

The question got decided when the one with the ax shook it at me and ordered, "Put up hands!"

I did. I think I could have run off right then and got away, but they was between me and my horse, and I would have been just as bad off.

The leader then gestured toward the entrance of the campodie. I had to duck to get through the low doorway and once inside was backed up against the far wall separated from the entry by a low, smoldering fire.

The odor of that hut liked to knock me out. It was half full of sage smoke, and the other half was mixed of rancid fat, spoiled hides, and none-too-clean bodies. There was no other of their kin there, just the three braves and me.

"I am a friend of Numaga," I said, trying hard to think of what might pass for a pleasantry. "You know him? Son of Old Winnemucca?"

The man with the ax sneered. "Old man and weak young man! Father and son more white than Indian."

"Well, I'm black," I said, pointing out the obvious.

"Enough talk!" said the leader. "You got money? tobacco?"

I quick checked my pockets to see if I had anything to bargain with, but all I found was that half-eaten package of dried shrimp. "Nope. But if you'll let me go . . ."

All three laughed, and it was not a pleasant sound. Catching a stranger alone out in the country made them ready to take out their anger without fear of reprisal. And I was that stranger. Were they going to kill me now?

They exchanged a look and give each other a sign of agreement.

"Take off coat and boots," the leader ordered, shaking the ax at me. "We let you go, but we keep clothes and horse."

I took a real long time slipping my arm out of the sleeve, my brain racing. The paper sack of shrimp crackled as I touched it, and I had a vision.

"You must not do this thing," I said in my deepest bass, singing-in-church voice. "I am a great sorcerer, and I will turn you into . . . scorpions!"

"Huh," the leader snorted, trying to sound unconcerned.

His two friends laughed also, but it weren't as hearty as before.

"You see this black skin?" I said. "I am a powerful wizard that you das't not mess with. Watch this!" I reached in my pocket and pulled out a shrimp. I flipped my hand around so that dried thing fluttered in their faces like it was alive. "Who but a sorcerer has scorpions that live in his pockets?"

"*Aiee*," the youngest of the three said, looking ready to charge out the door. I was gaining on them.

"And watch this!" I commanded. I opened my mouth wide and tossed in the shrimp.

I knowed I had them on the run then, because they backed way up by the doorway to get as far from me as possible.

While their eyes was still on my crunching jaws, I snuck my hand in the sack of shrimp again and brought out a handful. "Maybe you want some?" I yelled and threw the wriggling pieces.

In the flickery, smoky light, them things did appear just like scorpions. I almost couldn't blame them for screaming and clawing at theirselves to brush the crawly looking things off. The leader had the worst of it. Since he was closest, he got a half dozen stuck in his hair.

They all bolted and lit out in three different directions.

"And don't come back or I'll do something even worse!" I hollered after them.

I knowed that my little trick would not keep them away forever, but I could now retrieve the horse and go on toward the west. It worked.

* * *

With the coming of morning, the force of the wind died. As I hoped, the gray dawn that lightened the sky above one set of peaks confirmed my travels, and I struck out toward the northeast. As the day broadened, it weren't long before I struck the stage road and had my bearings again at last.

I dared not travel the road, for fear the army or some other might be set upon my track, but I could parallel it right easy and so kept my pace pretty steady. Twice I made out the form of travelers and hunkered down behind a sand dune 'til they had passed, but they was a good ways off and no danger to me at all.

Finally I was in sight of Carson and had something of a plan. Mostly what I had was a powerful hunger, since there had been nothing in the campodie that I felt inclined to eat and that handful of dried shrimp made far less impression on my belly than it had on the Paiutes.

Passing Carson City to the south, I circled round to approach the place as if I had only come over the mountains from California. Then I found a spot to hide 'til sundown, when I crept toward Orion's house.

Picketing my horse way out in the brush on the hillside, I slowly approached, bent low, until I reached a mound of rubble. That's when I discovered exactly what I had been expecting: namely two men guarding the house. They was nearer the building than I, talking in low voices. I gingerly raised my head above the level of the heap of dirt 'til I could peer over it. The two watchers was holding conference beside the little shack called the necessary.

"I'll go back to where I can see up the street," one of them said, giving orders. "You hang here."

"If he'd been coming, he would have been here by now," the other replied. "He must of figgered we'd be watching the place and gone somewheres else."

"He ain't that smart," the first returned. "Unless he just hightailed it out of the territory altogether, he'll be along by and by. He's got nowheres else to go."

I swelled up some, hearing my intellect discounted so casual, but I deflated again quick at the other remark. They had me reckoned square to rights. Just then I wanted nothing so much in the whole world as to snatch Lark over her protests and take us both far, far away.

Yet I knowed I could not do that, could not leave Sam to face hanging . . . could not let the Rebels succeed in their plan. A steely resolve formed in the pit of my stomach, and I shook off my cowardly thoughts.

I snuck toward the remaining guard, snaking from brush to brush 'til nothing remained but ten yards of open ground. I bunched up my muscles the way I always done before swinging the sledge down in the mine, drew in breath and held it, and clenched my fists tight.

Something hit me in the back of the neck. It was just a pebble, but it might have been the whole of Mount Davidson for the way the impact shook me. My pent-up air went out like a shot, and I almost twisted my own head off cranking it around to see over my shoulder.

At first I couldn't make out nothing in the darkness. Then a second piece of gravel looped through the air to fall next to my right shoulder, and I shifted my gaze some. Something small fluttered between two clumps of sage, like a blackbird flapping down near the ground. It was someone's hand, and they was gesturing for me to come back to where they was concealed.

Anyone with unfriendly intent would have nailed me with something stronger than a pebble or raised the alarm if they was afraid I was armed. With the studied deliberation of a cat moving toward a mouse, I rotated my face back toward the guard to see if we had roused him.

There was no hurt done there. He was still pacing back and forth and only rarely stopped to study the black hillside. Keeping my gaze fixed on him, I slid backward over the same ground I had just covered until a whole line of brush obscured my position from the house.

Moments later a dark form detached itself from the chaparral and silently crossed to me. When it was right next to me and the face full into mine, you could have knocked me over with a feather. It was Lark!

I plumb forgot myself, and had she not seen what was coming and put her hand across my mouth, I would've give us away for certain.

Keeping her palm over my lips, she brought her face right next to my ear and whispered, "Jim, I've been so scared for you!" Her nearness and the scent of her perfume made my head spin. I stretched my arms to embrace her, but she shook her head and whispered to me again, "Can you get us both inside the house?"

I was totally fuddled at what was going on, but we couldn't stay where we was and discuss it. My instincts was to get Lark away somewheres safe, but I knowed she must have some mighty powerful reason to be here.

Giving a quick nod, I signed for her to follow me, and back once more toward the house I slithered. I had no real plan except to rush the man and try to overpower him before he could use the six-shooter I was sure he carried. It had to be soon, too, lest his companion come back. I felt a light tap on my heel that let me know Lark was right behind and ready same as me. But still I delayed, not daring to hope for any better chance, yet waiting for some unknown signal.

It was fear for Lark's safety that made me hesitate, and that final pause was a godsend. In that short span, the sentry elected to light a cigarette, the lucifer match bright as a flare. It flashed to me that the lookout could not be holding a gun and had blinded hisself as well.

I was already sprinting toward him before these thoughts had finished hobbling to the surface. I seen the startled look in the guard's eyes as he heard my running feet and caught the compounding mistake he made when he instinctively shook out the match before dropping it. That split second cost him the chance to draw his gun.

Even before the hand-rolled smoke dropped from his lips and long before he had a chance to cry out, I was on him. My first punch went into his chest to silence him, and as he doubled up, choking and sputtering, I drove a second into his chin and straightened him up again. He went over backward, his cigarette spinning through the air like a penny sparkler.

Lark raced past me toward the house. I paused just long enough to help myself to the guard's pistol, then pounded after her. I had my shoulder lowered, ready to bust in the door, but no need. Lark had it open, and we both slipped in beside a startled Orion and Governor Nye.

"Douse that light!" I yelled at Nye, same as if I was the governor instead of him. He blew out the oil lamp, and the room plunged into dark. "Get down on the floor and keep quiet! There's armed men watching the house," I said. "Keep Lark safe. I clobbered one of 'em, and I'm gonna drag him in."

I heard Lark cry out, "No, Jim!"

But I wanted lots of answers, and the fella outside could supply some. Taking the Colt in my hand, I ducked low and eased open the door.

It was a good thing I bent down, because when the door opened, a gunshot split the night, and the slug splintered a length of door-jamb off the frame, right level with where my chest would have been.

I snapped off a shot in the direction of the muzzle flash, then slammed the door shut and flung myself to the other side. Two more shots from outside ripped through the door itself. I rose opposite to where I had just been and smashed the revolver into the window. I fired once, thumbed back the hammer, and fired again, then dropped back to the floor. This time, instead of more gunfire, a cry of pain responded.

"Orion, you got a loaded gun in the house?" I asked. Being down to three shots without the means to reload did not set well with me.

Orion made no reply, but presently a double-barreled shotgun slid over to me across the floor. I checked the hammers and found that it was indeed capped and ready.

There had been no further shots or sounds from outside, but even so I crossed to the opposite side of the door and used the muzzle of the scattergun to gentle it open.

No shots responded.

I poked the barrel out through the crack and waited.

Still nothing.

Gathering myself for a rush, I charged back out into the night, firing the last three bullets from the Colt Army left, right, and center. Throwing it down, I shifted the shotgun into position to do business and skidded to a stop beside the outhouse.

Dogs was barking up and down the main street, but no more shots came.

I hunted around to where I had knocked the man down. I found the remains of his cigarette makings and right next to them a little puddle of blood. I scouted clear around the front but found no watcher there either.

"They're gone," I reported to the three folks back inside. "But if you're gonna light that lamp again, let's do our talking sitting on the floor."

"What is this all about?" Governor Nye demanded as Orion rekindled the light.

"Them fellas was secesh, looking for me," I said. "But as to what this is all about, I reckon it's for someone else to explain." I looked straight at Lark when I said this.

"He's in the middle of it now, Governor," my little innocent songbird said. "He needs to know."

Nye agreed. "Lark here is a federal agent. She has been working undercover, getting information on the activity of a Rebel spy named Grimes. We know that they are behind the stage robberies, but we think there are bigger plans afoot."

"You don't know the half of it, Governor," I said, and I explained what I had overheard in the mine and what had happened to Sam and me since.

Orion laughed at the part about his brother being locked up at Fort Churchill. "Best place for him. Keep him safe for now."

"Yes, but Grimes was clear that something was about to happen soon. Maybe even tonight! And now they know that I made it to you with my share of the news."

"I can confirm what he says, Governor," Lark added. "First of July, Grimes got word of a Confederate move north into Union territory. The plot here is timed to match."

"All right then," Nye allowed. "We need to warn Captain Moore at once!"

Orion and the governor studied me, same as Sam done when it come to anything involving physical labor.

"I see how the wind blows," I said. "Just you write me out a letter to Captain Moore, Governor, so's he'll have something to read whilst he's fixing the noose around my neck!"

✳ ✳ ✳

There was not enough time. Now that I had found my Lark, I had to be torn apart from her again right after.

"Now you know what I could not tell you before," she said. "Why I was so scared for you to come round me at all."

"You mean 'cause I would have given you away?" I teased.

"Jim Canfield!" she said, sounding right wrathy. "You don't think for one minute . . ."

She never did get to finish what she was going to tell me, because I grabbed her in my arms, and we clung together like the secesh and the war and the Comstock could all hike over Mount Davidson and leave us be.

At last I heaved a great sigh and turned her loose. "You know I gots to go see this through to the end, don't you, gal?"

She nodded, twisting her hands together. The tears streaming down her face like to broke my heart. "Don't you get yourself killed. Or I'll never forgive you."

"Wipe your eyes," I said. "I'll come back for you. Besides, now that there ain't really a five-thousand-dollar contract to fill, we can take what I saved and get us a home of our own. I will never let you sing for nobody else long as we live."

She busted out crying all over again.

Borrowing Governor Nye's black saddle mare, I set out toward Fort Churchill, just as dawn was breaking. It were a most unpleasant-feeling morning, grayly overcast but with no promise of rain to settle the dust. I rode east into a strange half-light, while black clouds raced toward me. The day got darker instead of lighter.

I knowed where I was headed and how I would get there but had no idea what I was riding into. Nye seemed to think that once the word reached the Rebel leaders about their plans being uncovered, they would hightail it out of those parts. I was not as certain. Seeing how casual they had killed Kettle Belly and almost done for me and Truro made me believe they would not panic so easy.

Not that my doubts had any effect on what I was called to do. Carrying the warning contained in the governor's note to Captain Moore and seeing Sam set free was my job, and I aimed to get it done and take myself back to Lark as quick as possible.

Whilst I rode, I thought about what I'd heard. If it was true that a big battle would soon be under way somewheres in Union territory, then this must be the great push by the Confederates aiming to bust the Union spirit. I called to mind the opinion of Horace Greeley that Sam had shared with me: A big victory back east and silver from Nevada Territory and the Confederates could count on buying arms from England. If that happened, the North might be pushed into calling for a truce and ending the war.

The Union, the future of the country, was on a knife edge, and one length of that shiny, sharp blade stuck up right between the hooves of the mare.

✳ ✳ ✳

I rode past Bucklands at a high canter. The string of camels penned in the corral back of the stage stop looked like business was going as always. But even before I reached Fort Churchill, I knowed something was wrong. There were no companies of infantry drilling on the parade ground, no dragoons working with their horses, no sign of activity at all.

The first person I encountered was the same sergeant as had tried to capture me two days before. He come out of Captain Moore's office and seen me riding up. At first he gave a wave, friendly-like; then he seen who it was and whipped out his service revolver. Covering me with the muzzle pointed right at my brisket, he seemed astonished that I rode straight toward the porch.

"You again?" he said. "What are you doing back? I figgered you to be halfway to Mexico by now."

"Nope," I said. "Got an important message for the captain from Governor Nye." When I reached inside my shirt, that Colt suddenly touched the end of my nose.

"Don't even move," the sergeant said through gritted teeth. "I don't know what your game is. You may have put your head through the noose, but I'll blow it off before I'll let you get the drop on me."

"Easy, Sergeant," I said, my hands straight up and still. "Just you grab the corner of that writing you see poking out."

Without moving the barrel of the pistol one inch, his left hand stretched out toward my shirt, and two fingers snagged the message.

"That's it," I said. "Pull it on out. It ain't going to bite you."

"What'd you say this was?"

"Message for the captain. Say, where is he, anyway? Where is everybody?"

"I ain't telling you nothing, you Reb spy! Get down easy and step away from that horse!"

I did as I was told, then at a wave of the Colt, backed up into a corner of the porch whilst he unfolded the letter.

His eyebrows went up as he read the letter, and he looked at me over the top of it. "You know what this claims?"

"Yep," I agreed.

"How do I know it's genuine?"

"Well, now, you don't. You go ahead and lock me up whilst you and the captain sort it out. Just alert the guard so's no Rebs catch you by surprise."

The look of concern that passed over the sergeant's face did my feelings no good at all. "Captain ain't here. Message came at dawn that the Washoes attacked a stage between here and Williams. A massacre. Captain Moore ordered everybody to arms, and off they went in pursuit."

"Everybody?"

"All three companies. Left me here to guard the prisoner and look after things. There's two sentries and two more men down sick and that's it."

"What was Captain Moore expecting—a thousand Indians on the warpath? Who brought the report?"

"I did," said the voice of Abner Grimes from the doorway.

✳ ✳ ✳

Grimes relieved the sergeant of his pistol and, with the pair of us prisoners marching ahead, managed to take the two sentries unawares as well. He captured all four as easy as pie and now prodded us toward the guardhouse.

"You're crazy," the sergeant said. "The whole troop will be back soon as they find out it's a hoax. If you want to save your neck, you'd better take off now."

"I don't think so." Grimes chuckled. "See, there really was an attack, and now some of my men are leading Captain Moore on a merry chase toward Utah Territory."

"What do you think you'll gain?" I said.

Grimes, like most sneaks and scoundrels when they have the upper hand, did not mind bragging on hisself. "To start with, we'll have that whole stack of Spencer repeating rifles from California and enough ammunition to outfit my whole regiment."

"So you and your traitors," the sergeant sneered, "can use 'em to kill squirrels when you go hide out in the hills?"

"Hide out? No, no. My regiment is just waiting 'til I signal them to capture the fort. Then we will use the Spencers for a different purpose when Captain Moore returns."

The sergeant had been walking a little to one side of the rest of us, and perhaps his aim had been to distract Grimes with the talk. But the idea of his comrades riding right into a cold-blooded ambush pushed him over the edge. Giving a hoarse cry, he whirled around and jumped for the throat of the Rebel spy.

The Colt in Grimes's hand blasted. I don't know whether he was just quick or if he set the sergeant up on purpose to make him try something, but he coolly shot the sergeant in the throat and dropped him in the dirt. Ignoring the man writhing at his feet, he waved his pistol at the rest of us and invited, "Anyone else care to try their luck?"

Nobody spoke, and Grimes waved us on toward the guardhouse.

"He'll bleed to death," I protested.

"Let him," Grimes said, "unless you want to join him."

The guardhouse at Fort Churchill was a simple, adobe-block building that faced the parade ground on the far side of the compound. It had only two cells, and both of them opened onto the open air underneath a roof that gave some meager shelter to the guard's walk outside.

Even though the day had grown steadily darker from the ominous black clouds, up ahead I could see Sam. He grasped the bars of the window in the door of his cell, his face pressed against the opening.

"Hello, Sam," I called out. "Looks like we're going to be cooped up together for a spell. I hope you got your pipe and tobacco enough for us both." I prayed he would catch my drift while there was still time.

"Us both?" he said in surprise. "You don't—"

"And matches and your tool for tamping," I added hastily.

I could see Sam look down and fumble with something, then hold up the round bowl of the meerschaum to the bars. "Got it right here."

"I can hardly wait 'til we get inside," I said.

"Shut up and move faster," Grimes ordered. "This is no party."

Grimes ordered Sam to stand back from the door while he had me slide back the bolt on the latch. He motioned with the gun for the soldiers and me to get inside. I purposeful dawdled a mite to let the soldier boys get clear of the entry.

"Hurry up, nigger," Grimes said. "I've had enough trouble with you already. I'd as soon blast you as look at you."

"Me too," I said, flinging myself all of a sudden inside and behind the wall. "Now!" I yelled.

For a man who never hurried to do anything in his whole life, Sam acted right fast on that occasion. From holding his pipe up to his mouth casual, he whipped his hand forward like he was throwing a baseball, aiming that shiny yellow bulb at the feet of Grimes.

There was a roar as the blasting cap Sam had stuck into the bowl exploded, and pieces of stony meerschaum peppered the air like shrapnel from a six-pound cannon.

Grimes shouted and clutched his face. He triggered off one round that struck the adobe and whined away harmless.

Then I was on him. I kicked his arm hard, and the pistol flew from his hand. The left that I connected with his chin had more force behind it than was strictly necessary, but I were too impatient right then to hold back. Grimes lay sprawled across the walkway, blood streaming down his face from a dozen cuts.

"See to the sergeant," I yelled to the soldiers. "I'll take care of Grimes."

✵ ✵ ✵

I do not know what signal Grimes was supposed to give to launch the attack, but the explosion of the meerschaum grenade served the purpose. With Rebel yells and pistol shots, a troop of horsemen about twenty-five in number swept out of a canyon a half mile west of the fort.

There weren't no time for anything like strategy, just quick action to see to defense. "Barricade yourselves in the armory," I said to Sam and the two guards. "Hold them off as best you can."

"What about you?" Sam called out to me as I ran toward the governor's horse, still tied to the post across the square.

"Got an idea," I hollered in return. "I'll be back!"

Sam and the others would have to fend for theirselves, for as I vaulted into the saddle of the black, the front rank of the secesh boys spotted me, and the chase was on. Three of them Rebs peeled off after me, and the others took to circling and firing into the armory. Coming behind the horsemen were three empty wagons to haul off the plunder, and bringing up the rear, bouncing and jolting, was a small cannon. It didn't take no genius to figure out where Fremont's howitzer had wound up.

But that was all I had time to take in before I bent low over the mare's shoulder and laid on the quirt. I was never so glad of the use of any horse as in the mile or so that separated me from Bucklands station. That critter showed a turn of speed that served us well. A couple bullets whizzed past, but a glance over my shoulder showed we was pulling ahead, and another minute brought us within sight of Bucklands. The three Rebs changed their minds about me and doubled back toward the fort.

A stage was pulled up at the station, and the driver was setting on the box. It was Frank.

"Rebs are attacking the fort and the boys need help," I yelled.

Frank never argued nor questioned but just bellowed for all real men to grab their guns and get out there on the double.

One of those that bailed out of the saloon was Truro. "Saints above! Is it you, Jim? I thought you were killed for sure."

"Not yet," I called back, "but plenty of folks been trying. Pile as many as have rifles into the coach and head out. . . . The war has come to Nevada, but I mean to head it off."

✳ ✳ ✳

My return to Fort Churchill showed an amazing scene. At the center of the action but only dimly seen in the twilight at midday was the adobe-block armory. Through narrow rifle slits designed for just such a purpose, Sam and the two guards was giving a good account of theirselves, forcing the Rebs to keep their distance. The secesh fellas fired into the building, but the main threat was at the front, where they had planted the howitzer just opposite the lone entry. One poorly aimed round had already knocked a cornice off the building, and another had blowed a three-foot hole in the wall just left of the door.

The lives of those inside the blockhouse wasn't worth spit if the cannon continued in play, but so far Frank and Truro prevented it from being aimed better. Outside the circle of Rebs, Frank whipped the stage back and forth past the Rebel line, while Truro directed the rifle fire from inside the coach.

The short figure managing the cannon seen that he could not succeed 'less the stage were eliminated, so he ordered most of the attackers to mount again and assault the coach. That was exactly what I was counting on.

When I come over the ridge nearest the fort, I rode Daisy, and I led a pack string of six more camels at the fastest rolling gallop ever seen. I kicked Daisy into a charge as down the slope we bowled, with me hut-hutting for all I was worth. The rest of the string ranged theirselves alongside as if they figured it was a race.

My camel brigade struck the center of the Reb line of cavalry, and every horse critter within a hundred yards went to bucking and plunging. Such a mess of hollering and cussing was never before heard on the planet. Fighting a battle and capturing the fort was altogether forgot. It was all those boys could do to hang on with both hands!

That little fella that had been the leader was none other than Boss Ward. His horse, a genuine Mexican plug, jumped straight up and come down with all four feet planted together. That landing must of drove Ward's tailbone clean up to his neck. Next bounce, he shot up in the air with both feet out of the stirrups.

Most of the Rebel troopers was forcibly dismounted by the time I made my second pass through the line with the camels. Then Frank whipped the stage across the field again, and Truro's boys winged a

couple more of the secesh. The ones still more or less in their saddles
lit out for the hills.

About that time, Sam and the two soldiers come flying out of the
blockhouse and seized the cannon from an astonished Reb. Unlike
the halfhearted men Ward and Grimes had recruited with promises
of loot, the two Union soldiers knew how to handle that howitzer.
They spun it around and brought it to bear on the only group of
secesh that remained standing.

One of the Union soldiers hollered out, "We loaded her with
canister. If we fire at this range, there won't be enough of you left
to bury!"

"Yeah," hollered Sam, real warlike. He shook his fist, too.

That was the end of the battle of Fort Churchill. Frank swung
once more around them Rebs, dropping Truro's men off in a circle.
The Rebs throwed down their guns and raised their hands. At rifle
point, facing a cannon loaded with grapeshot, and with their mounts
still dancing like crazy critters, what else could they do?

Ward had finally bounced to a halt, but he had no intention of
being caught. He spurred his horse toward the armory, intending to
race back into the canyon from which the attack had come.

From the doorway of the blockhouse staggered the figure of
Abner Grimes. He waved both arms and yelled for Ward to save him.

Boss Ward jerked his horse down to his haunches in front of
the door and triggered off two shots that made Sam and the federal
soldiers duck behind the cannon. I seen Ward reach down to give
Grimes an arm up and seen Grimes yank Ward out of the saddle to
the ground.

As Grimes jumped into Ward's place and spurred the horse, Ward
run alongside tussling and pleading with Grimes not to leave him.
The two, comrades moments before, now fought over the means of
escape. A volley of shots rung out from the soldiers and Truro's rifle-
men, and both Ward and Grimes hit the ground, stone dead.

We rounded up all the secesh and locked them in the guardhouse.

All at once Sam yelled out that Mount Davidson was on fire.
"The Rebels have torched Virginia City!"

345

There was a tongue of flame, dark red, that streaked the sky in the black clouds swirling around the peak.

"Can't be the town," I said. "It's too high on the mountain."

"But something is on fire up there," he insisted. "Look at the length of that flame shooting out!"

I had terrible misgivings to see the brilliant fire in the middle of the pitch-black clouds. I wondered what it could possibly mean. Was it an evil omen of terrible import? I called to mind the danger the country was in. What if our little victory in Nevada Territory had come too late?

A shaft of sunlight busted through the clouds right then, straight to the peak as if aimed at the pinnacle of Mount Davidson. There, revealed to all in its true nature, was the reality of the flame on the mountain: It was the giant red, white, and blue banner . . . Old Glory . . . still waving, proud and free.

It wasn't 'til a whole day later that the telegraph brung the news. The Yankee boys had won a bloody and terrible battle at a little town called Gettysburg. General Robert E. Lee was whupped and turned his troops back toward the South. The worst danger to the Union was over.

✻ ✻ ✻

That was the end of that Rebel threat to the silver mines in Nevada Territory. There was still those who favored the South, but they was more quiet and Fort Churchill more alert after July 4, 1863.

With Grimes and Ward both dead, there weren't no leaders for the secesh. Bill Mayfield was the one who killed the saloon keeper and Echapa, meaning to stir up the Indian troubles. But others in the gang turned rat on him, and he fled to Mexico.

Grimes was the one who'd killed Kettle Belly's family back in the border wars, and it was the voice of Grimes that Kettle Belly had recognized on the day of the camel race. 'Course, that discovery ended up costing Kettle Belly his life as well. That I was connected with Kettle Belly is what put Ward on my track and what almost got Truro and me killed in the mine. I don't believe Boss Ward ever did recognize me for the child he stole and sold back in '49.

I have often wondered why Sam did not write up this whole story hisself. When I asked him that once, he said his made-up stories was easier to swallow than the truth of this one, but he would use bits and pieces of this tale in different yarns. And so he did.

✳ EPILOGUE ✳

The sun was setting behind the Sierras. The peaks southwest of Virginia City were outlined with a golden glow, while streaks of orange faded into pinks and purples in the gathering dusk.

Seth Townsend wiped his forehead and reached for the pitcher of tea. It was empty. This observation brought him to notice how late it had grown. Where had the hours gone?

"Sorry, Mister Canfield," he apologized. "I've taken up your whole day." Townsend looked at his watch. "And I've even missed all of the story about the train."

A slow grin crept across his features and was returned by the man seated in the porch rocker. "You are like . . . ," he began, then corrected himself. "You *are* a time machine. Could I borrow some of your pictures to run with the story? I promise to return them."

Jim Canfield stood and, despite his stooped shoulders and bowed knees, sped with remarkable ease through the screen door and into the house. He was back a moment later with an armload of fading prints. He passed several to Townsend—portraits of long-dead miners and views of buildings in Virginia City that had been swallowed up by fire fifty summers before. But one heavy silver frame he kept back in the crook of his arm.

"You can borrow any you like," Jim offered. "'Cept this one." Almost shyly, he turned the withheld photo so Townsend could see. It showed a proud muscular figure in tall boots and a shiny black suit who could have been Jim Canfield's great-grandson. Next to the young man in the portrait was a woman dressed in white, her lace veil pulled back to outline a face that glowed with happiness. "This one," Jim Canfield said with a catch in his voice. "It's of Lark and me on our weddin' day. I can't part with it for even one night."

Cumberland Crossing

Tennessee farmer Jesse Dodson is on
a desperate mission. He must cross the
Cumberland Mountains to find his son,
William, who has run away to join the
Union army. When Jesse passes through
Confederate and Yankee lines, he's plunged
into the midst of the Civil War. As the Union
advances on the Confederate stronghold of
Tennessee, will he be able to keep his
promise to his wife—to bring their son home?
This is the true story of Brock Thoene's
great-great-grandfather. . . .

To the memory of Jesse Dodson,
whose true story this is, and to
Jesse Wattenbarger,
Jess Thoene,
Jessica Rachel Thoene,
and
our granddaughter, Jessie

✷ CHAPTER 1 ✷

It became clear to me as I crossed over the Cumberland Mountains that the Confederate forces beyond the stronghold of my home territory of East Tennessee were in trouble.

Three days into my journey to Nashville I heard the tales of Southern defeat from a wagon train of a dozen refugee families fleeing the inevitable.

I introduced myself. "Jesse Dodson, McMinn County. What news from Nashville?"

"Nashville is doomed to be abandoned by the Confederacy!"

"They say a hundred thousand Yankees are closing in!"

"Nashville is no place to go right now, Dodson! There's a Yankee sharpshooter behind every tree!"

I thanked them for the information and the warning, then pressed on into the gathering gloom of twilight. I was dressed in civilian clothes and had little fear of Yankee snipers. Anyway, my boy was gone, the Union was advancing on Nashville, and I intended to fetch William back home.

As I rode on, the rain pierced me with a chill as sharp as a sniper's bullet. On the west side of the Cumberland Mountains I stopped at a coaching inn to rest and feed my horse, Trafalger.

The inn was no more than a large log barn with a fireplace at one end, a few plank tables where meals were eaten, and a separate room where boarders were given cornhusk-filled mattresses to lay on the bare dirt floor. All the same, it was shelter from the bitter winds that swept down from the slopes of the mountains. A night beneath the stars could be pure misery.

That evening a dozen soldiers in Confederate gray ate their meals in silence, scraping spoons against tin plates with such ferocity that I wondered how long it had been since they had eaten. These were no holiday soldiers. Their clothing was stained from hard travel. Gold braids were tarnished, and scarlet trim was faded from hard service in the field. They paid me no mind as they tore off chunks of coarse brown bread and sopped up the last drops of gravy from the venison stew.

The proprietor was a grizzled old woman. She carried the kettle of vittles around once again and told the men to eat up, for they would need their strength to fight the Yankees.

When she looked my way at last, I smiled in a friendly fashion and held out my bedroll to show my intentions.

She eyed me as if she did not approve of my civilian clothing. "Where you headed?"

"West. To Nashville."

The sergeant was a young man with chapped, windburned skin and fair hair and eyes. I figured he could not be much older than nineteen, yet I guessed he had seen far more suffering than any man should see in a lifetime. He raised his head and sized me up. "Going to fight the Yankees, are you?"

I replied truthfully, "The Yankees have my boy, and I will fight to get him back if I must. He is a child of sixteen."

"A prisoner," the sergeant said through a mouthful of bread. "Blue bellies are taking our boys captive every day. Taking them north across the line. You don't have much chance of finding one among them all."

"I promised his mother I would try."

The sergeant nodded. "You'll have a hard time getting through our lines and over to the Union side."

"I'm a civilian."

"It's plain to tell you're a Tennessean."

"McMinn County."

"We'll hold your part of the state all right. But Nashville?"

"It is not going well for the cause then?" I asked.

He motioned for me to come sit beside him and his companions, and he would give me all the news.

I paid the proprietor two and a half dollars in Union gold for my lodgings and a meal of stew. Taking a seat close to the fire, introductions were made, and the grim story of Union aggression against Tennessee was recounted.

"We hear Brigadier General Don Carlos Buell, in command of the Federal Army of the Ohio at Louisville, has been ordered to march against Nashville with fifty thousand men. Fort Donelson on the Cumberland River is under heavy attack. We twelve are friends and neighbors from Alabama and have been on furlough. News of this situation reached us, and we have been riding for three days to rejoin our unit in Nashville. These are perilous times. There is safety in numbers. You may ride with us tonight if you wish, sir."

I thanked the sergeant and explained that Trafalger was in need of rest and that I must stay until morning. Left unsaid was the fact that my son William was one of the blue-coated Federal troops.

It came to me that this serious but kindly natured fellow and his comrades might be the very men who would raise their rifles and fire upon my son. This caused me tremendous grief at the foolishness and waste of this war. Shaking the hand of each soldier as they departed, I wished them well for the sake of their families. They were fine young men, not much older than my son.

I spent a restless night with thunder rolling above me like artillery fire. Finally, I rose before dawn to resume my journey through the downpour.

From the start of the rebellion, William had been determined to join Lincoln's army against the wishes of his mother and me.

"This is not our war one way or the other," I told William after Fort Sumter was shelled. "We own no slaves and owe no loyalty to either batch of fools! The son of Jesse and Alcie Dodson will not raise a hand against friends and neighbors in McMinn County, Tennessee.

'Thou shalt not kill,' the Good Book says, and you'll join the Yankees over my dead body!"

Next morning, in spite of my threats, William was gone. He left his mother a note.

> *Dearest Mother,*
> *Father cannot understand, but I aim to fight to see Nashville beneath the banner of freedom for all in our country or die trying. I will not war with Father just to fight for the Union, so I am leaving quietly. You know in your heart it is right that I do this. Forgive me, dear mother. Pray for us and for freedom. Farewell until we meet again . . . perhaps on Jordan's farther shore.*
>
> *Your son,*
> *William Dodson*

William had never seen Nashville nor traveled fifty miles from our farm. I blamed his foolishness on an English Methodist abolitionist Sunday school teacher who preached Abe Lincoln. This London reformer had filled William's head with nonsense and then left with a vow to return some day wearing a Yankee uniform to set every slave free. Now so had William.

As for me, I had not voted for the Giant Killer, Lincoln, for president. But neither had I voted for the fire-eater, Breckinridge, nor for Stephen Douglas, the Little Giant. Instead I had taken my place with most of my state and county and voted for Bell, a well-spoken, moderate Tennessee politician of the Peace Party. (I shook his hand once at a Knoxville rally.) How I regretted that Bell did not win. Things might have been different.

Whatever the cause, William had broken the heart of my wife, Alcie, when he left. I promised her, whatever the odds, I would try to find him. This matter alone meant far more to me than the coming Northern invasion of my home state.

The muddy road was rutted from last night's passage of wagons and cannon and the tramping of army boots, but by midmorning the highway was nearly deserted. A dozen overloaded civilian buckboards passed me heading the opposite direction. From the passengers I learned that the Yankees had completely encircled Fort Donelson, eighty miles away, and it was only a matter of time before "The Bonnie Blue Flag" would be heard no more in Nashville.

Travel weary and hungry, I arrived in Nashville early on the morning of February 15. It was bone cold, gray, and drizzling. I led Trafalger to the livery stable where an agitated young stable boy, a slave of about sixteen years, introduced himself as Cyrus and took the reins. But instead of tending to the horse, he stood peering out the barn doors toward the direction of the market square.

Over the rooftops the mournful cadence of a bell tolled the call for assembly.

"I ain't never heard that bell make such a noise before," muttered the boy in a fearful tone.

"A church bell," I remarked impatiently. "It's the Sabbath."

"Nawsir. It ain't Sunday. It's Saturday t'day." He shook his head. "That there's the market-house bell. Don't ring 'less somethin' be burnin' down. Ain't no fire though."

"Where's the boss?" I asked.

"He done gone to the square. They's all gone. Reckon they intends to fight the Yankees. Boss man say our soldiers all a runnin' south away from them Yankees."

The voice of the stable boy was tinged with such sorrow over the imminent fall of Nashville that I was certain it had not occurred to him that the coming of the Yankees would mean his freedom.

I instructed him to stir himself and tend to my mount. "Yankees or no Yankees, that critter is hungry and so am I. Where's a good inn?"

He directed me to the Brown Hotel, where I hoped to find a hot breakfast and lodgings. A mob of ashen-faced citizens scurried past me to the square, where I supposed some momentous news about the war was to be announced.

The streets were full of activity. The lobby of the hotel, however, was completely deserted. Dining room empty. I noted full plates of breakfast left uneaten and abandoned. I considered the wasted food,

357

then scooped up eggs and ham between two biscuits and downed a cup of still-steaming coffee.

After satisfying my hunger, I joined the throng on the boardwalk. Making my way up the street, the tolling bell brought to mind the grim clang of a death knell counting out the years of an ended life. Today the bell tolled for Nashville.

The civilians formed a solemn conclave in the market square. The murmur of voices fell away as a man in a top hat stepped onto the back of a buckboard and raised his arms for silence.

The ringing ceased, yet a mournful echo resonated above us. It seemed to me that I could hear the deep, distant drum of Yankee cannon fire in counterpoint as the echo faded. Was it my imagination?

Beside me a young matron burst into tears. The life of proud, independent-minded Tennessee was coming to a close.

The man glanced at his pocket watch and removed his top hat in a gesture of regret. "Fellow citizens of Nashville, as your mayor I must tell you that we have this very hour received word that General John B. Floyd and General Gideon J. Pillow, the ranking Confederate officers at Fort Donelson, have escaped across the Cumberland River with Floyd's Virginia Brigade."

A moan emanated from the packed crowd.

I thought of young William among General Grant's boys in blue, storming the gates of Fort Donelson. For the first time in months I felt a surge of hope. If William still lived, he might be as near to me as the sound of artillery!

Again the mayor spread his arms in request for calm and order. His voice cracked with emotion as he addressed us. "General Buckner remains behind to yield Fort Donelson to the Northern aggressors. We are left in the hands of the enemy."

An agonized cry of collective grief, terror, and disbelief arose.

"Please!" shouted the mayor. "We must remain calm! Our gallant forces are retreating south across the bridge, and no private citizen will be allowed to cross until the army is over. It must be so. Our boys must remain free to return and fight another day!"

From that hour, a state of confusion reigned in the city. Markets were stormed by the citizenry. Women shouldered great slabs of bacon and rolled barrels of flour down the streets. They gathered bolts of fabric and clothing enough to supply them and their children for whatever might come. On every block, young Confederate recruits stopped at their homes to kiss wives and sweethearts and mothers farewell.

I withdrew from the chaos to the Brown Hotel and took a room while other guests hurriedly checked out and prepared to follow in the wake of the retreating army. Settling in a chair beside the window in my room, I observed the panic beneath me until night fell. The sky was alight with burning cotton warehouses. In spite of the eerie glow, I fell asleep, fully clothed, sometime past midnight.

Several hours later a series of terrible explosions shook the glass in the windowpanes. I woke with a start as three more horrific blasts issued from the direction of the river. I learned later that General Floyd had ordered the strategic destruction of the railroad and suspension bridges over the Cumberland after the retreat of Confederate forces. This action trapped thousands of terrified civilians in the city and in the path of the oncoming Union army.

359

I splashed water on my face, and without emotion I muttered, "So, the war is over in Nashville. Perhaps if we are lucky it will all end this quickly."

After that, Nashville was as silent as a tomb. Women, children, and those too old to fight huddled in their houses to await the dreaded arrival of Federal troops. There was nothing for me to do now but remain at my post beside the window to watch for the victorious Army of the Ohio and my son as they paraded down the main thoroughfare before me. I determined that when William passed my way, I would snatch him from the ranks and expose him to his officers as a runaway child. After that I would drag him, hog-tied if necessary, home to his grieving mother and the farm.

✶ ✶ ✶

For a week after the fall of Fort Donelson, Nashville watched for the expected invasion of the dreaded Yankees. To my great disappointment the Federal forces made no attempt to enter the city. I sent a letter to Alcie and the children expressing my hopes that when the Federals did occupy the town, William would be among them.

All the young men of military age in Nashville had gone south with the Confederate army. The mayor and most of the city council remained behind, fuming at the fact that Nashville had been left defenseless. The anticipation of the evil deeds that would unfold when the Yankees came caused that week to be called the Great Panic.

I awoke the morning of the twentieth to the sound of iron-shod horses trotting purposefully across the cobbles of the street. My first thought was that the Yankees had finally arrived from Fort Donelson. I was wrong.

The Confederate forces were on the way to Murfreesboro when it occurred to General Floyd that he had left a mighty heap of supplies back in Nashville. General Nathan Bedford Forrest, with a small detachment of cavalry, was sent to recover the army stores and get them south to the retreating army. I knew this was sure to cause a riot in the city because the people felt they had been promised the stores. What else would they have to live on when the fearsome Yankees took the city?

I ate my breakfast hurriedly as the swell of angry voices grew and a mass of wounded soldiers and citizens of all types swarmed toward the market square and the Confederate warehouses to take possession. Even black slaves were there, ordered by their masters to raid and carry away goods.

Last to arrive on the scene, I hung back as I witnessed Forrest's horsemen surround the crowd.

Forrest, six feet of lean and steely-eyed strength, rose in his stirrups and bellowed, "In the name of the Confederacy, y'all listen up and git on home! The Confederacy'll have these here supplies to fight the Yankees, and you'll not hinder us from takin' them neither!"

I noted that he spoke with an unschooled tongue. Word was that Old Bedford, as he was called, was looked down on by the majority of Rebel officers because he was not of the gentry. There was wild fury in Forrest's eyes, and I sensed he was dangerous.

One of his troopers shouted, "Git on home now! The general means what he says!"

Forrest enjoined, "I'll have this here square clear in one minute or by the Almighty, you'll be sorry in two!"

The mob remained steadfast, although women who had served the Confederacy these many months stared at one another in agonized disbelief. Many gathered their young'uns and made ready to run.

Forrest's gruff order went unheeded. The general stared at his pocket watch and raised his hand in preparation for the signal.

Then some fool civilian fired a shot into the air. At that moment Forrest dropped his hand, and the Confederate cavalry charged into the screaming women and old folks and slaves.

Ducking behind a column of the portico, only twenty-five yards from the line of action, I watched as Forrest's men rode down a group of slaves among the population. Rifle butts raised and slammed down, and the cries of the fallen were drowned out by the curses of the soldiers.

The incident was over in less than five minutes. The square was cleared of all except for two dozen slaves who had been injured too badly to walk or killed outright.

Sprawled in his own blood near the center of the square was old Samuel Burton, doorman at my hotel. I strode quickly toward him, thinking I would get him home to his quarters.

Samuel was ominously still, and I felt sick at heart. The old man was too fragile to be ridden down and survive. Kneeling beside him, I touched his hand and said his name.

He was dead.

The sharp point of a saber pricked the fabric of my coat between my shoulder blades. I raised my hands.

"Is this slave yourn?" I recognized the voice of Nathan Bedford Forrest, towering over me on his mount.

I managed to control my rage, no doubt on account of the sword. "I don't own a slave, General Forrest."

"You a nigger lover then? A black Republican? Where you know this here critter from?"

"Samuel is the doorman at my hotel."

"Not no more he ain't. He's rubbish now." Forrest laughed.

Anger rushed through me. "It didn't have to be done this way."

The blade nudged me harder. "Civil disorder. These here troopers only struck down the rebellious slaves." Forrest laughed in amazement at my concern. "Not one white woman or child bloodied. Just a mite humbled. And look here. Peace is restored. Don't tell me my business. Now git up off'n yer knees." He withdrew the sword.

I stood and turned to face him, burning his visage into my memory: deep-set gray eyes, chiseled features, neatly trimmed spade beard. "I'll get a wagon and fetch the body back to his home."

"Where would that be?"

"Brown Hotel."

"And what be yore name?"

"Jesse Dodson."

"You're a Tennessean; it's plain by your speech. Whereabouts exactly?"

"McMinn, east of the Cumberlands." Even just mentioning the county, I inwardly chided myself for answering so directly. Why was Forrest interested in such details?

He nodded and narrowed his eyes in thought. "I know that county. They lynch Yankees over yonder, I hear. Blue bellies won't get in there. You got you a good horse?" Forrest was grinning.

"Good enough."

"How about this here body? You got you a buckboard to carry it?"

"I will fetch one."

"Yes. That you will. You will fetch a buckboard and be back here ready to empty out that there warehouse and haul these here supplies where I tell you to. It come to me you are a mite too big and healthy not to be of some use to the South. You'll make a fine grave digger. I'll make you boss over a hundred darkies. Consider yourself swore into the army of the Confederacy. Yes, sir. Private Jesse Dodson. Be back in ten minutes, Private Dodson, or you will think a load of stone just busted loose on your sorry head. Keep in mind I shoot deserters."

I had no doubt he meant both ends of that equation to be personally taken.

With that, he rode away toward the heap of supplies and the wagons that had been commandeered to haul the goods.

With Old Bedford's warning ringing in my ears, it was all I could do not to spring to the stable, saddle Trafalger, and make a mad dash out of town. I was a mere ten minutes ahead of Forrest's firing squad. No doubt the general would be watching the time on his gold pocket watch and would indeed kill me if I was not far enough out of his grasp.

I walked toward the barn behind the hotel. Meeting up with Cyrus, the stable boy, I ordered him in the name of General Forrest to hitch a team of mules to the hotel buckboard. Then I rapidly went to work saddling Trafalger.

Cyrus muttered, "What the boss man gonna say 'bout givin' the buckboard to that Forrest?"

"He would not argue. Now get to it, Cyrus, or we'll all be in hot water."

"Yessuh," he said and then paused. "That Gen'ral Forrest? I just hear he kill some folk on down to the square."

"That he did," I replied over my shoulder, not wanting to tell him about Samuel.

"Samuel Burton be down in that square."

"Yes." There was no avoiding it.

"When he comin' home?"

"He is not coming home."

The boy's chin trembled, and hands dropped to his side. "Samuel be my granpap. What you mean, suh, he ain't comin'?"

"He's dead."

Now there erupted a wail of grief that I had not anticipated. "Forrest kill my granpap! I'se gonna kill that slaver! I heard 'bout him. He the one what sold half the slaves in Tennessee. Slave trader! Bounty man! I'se gonna kill him like he done Granpap."

The boy snatched a pitchfork and was heading toward daylight and death when I mounted Trafalger and loped out to stop him. "Drop that pitchfork, boy!" I commanded. "Whoa up! You aiming to get yourself killed? It won't bring your grandpa back."

Ten seconds passed. It seemed like my entire allotted time. I expected to see Forrest ride around the corner into the stable yard any instant.

"I can't go nowhere. Mistuh Brown, he put a bounty on my head, shore enuff."

"The Yankees are coming." I grabbed the fork and tossed it away. "There won't be no more bounty for runaways because y'all will be free! Tell you what: Let's both get away from Old Bedford and his cutthroats."

Cyrus almost smiled. With one backward glance, he latched on to my hand and swung up onto the saddle behind me.

With three minutes to spare, I spurred Trafalger out of the yard.

Clutching me tightly, Cyrus yelled, "Rebs be all 'long this a'way, suh! I show you where to ride straight to them Yankees!"

Following the directions of Cyrus, we took a shortcut across the fields toward the outskirts of Nashville.

I dared not look back, although I felt the rage of General Nathan Bedford Forrest following hot on our heels. Trafalger seemed not to notice the extra weight of his burden. He sailed effortlessly over stone walls and split-rail fences. The ease with which Falger put distance between us and the Rebels drew admiration from Cyrus.

"Must be a Yankee hoss!" said the boy after several breathless miles. "Run fast as any critter I ever see'd."

I reined Trafalger up under a hickory tree several miles away from Forrest. "My horse don't fancy joinin' up with ex-slave traders pretending to be gentlemen, I reckon."

For the moment we were safe from Bedford Forrest and his grave diggers. I could not imagine the terrible events that waited ahead for me and my family at the hands of General Forrest. Had I known the suffering he was to bring into our lives, I would have returned that hour to Nashville and shot him out of his saddle.

✳ ✳ ✳

With Cyrus to guide us, we rode out to the suburbs of Edgefield.

Cyrus said, "Yankees mos' likely come this a'way when they comes. Edgefield is the place they be comin' to, suh. Oughta wait here."

Finding a dilapidated and crowded hotel, I was told that "my boy" would have to sleep out of doors. I dared not leave the agitated young man alone after the death of his grandfather. So I stabled Trafalger and paid for two stacks of clean straw for Cyrus and me to sleep on in the barn.

I rested uneasily, with visions of Forrest's cavalry charge and of William being trampled by ten thousand horses.

Early Sabbath morning on February 23, I was awakened to the shouts of a large group of children who had been walking through the drizzle to Sunday school.

"It's them!" sounded the alarm. "The Yankees! Oh, Mama! It's the Yankees!"

"The Yankees are coming!"

"Run for it! Hide quick! The Blue bellies are ridin' in!"

I leaped from the straw as the bell of a church began to clang wildly. Pulling on my boots and dashing coatless into the street, I witnessed frightened women running to retrieve their children to hide them from the dreaded Federal troopers. Doors on neat frame houses slammed shut with sounds like the cracks of rifle fire. Window shades were instantly drawn on the ground floors, and an instant later the curtains of the upper stories were likewise closed.

The church bell fell silent.

Within a matter of moments I was the only human remaining on the rutted, muddy street. In the house across the way I saw the corner of a drape lift. Smiling and raising my hand in a wave of acknowledgment, I thought I heard a feminine shriek. The fabric instantly fell back.

Fear was the predominant emotion of the Edgefield townsfolk that Sunday morning. I was certainly the only person in all the area around Nashville who had been looking forward to this moment.

A surge of excitement coursed through me. Would William be among these first Union soldiers? Cold rain penetrated my shirt and gripped my bones, yet I was warmed with hope. William was coming! I moved to the bend in the road, waited, and listened to the approach of iron-shod horses.

A troop of about fifty Federal horsemen rode up and around me. Their eyes were alert to the rooftops and alleyways, but their rifles were not cocked nor their sabers drawn.

"Excuse me, sir," said a young lieutenant politely. "Do you know where there is a livery stable?"

I had seen one on our entry into Edgefield, and I directed the officer. "There has been some looting," I said. "Best go gently about what you take."

The lieutenant looked shocked. "We have the strictest orders to treat the citizens with the utmost courtesy and to pay for whatever we require . . . in gold."

This was certainly a different slant to the dreaded Yankee invasion.

"Specifically," the young, trim officer continued, "our supplies are still miles back, and we have some mounts in need of a blacksmith's attention and some tack in want of repair. Our company saddler is laid up with the grippe."

"I'm a fair hand at shoeing," I admitted. "And I can stitch leather."

"Well then," the lieutenant agreed, "would you like employment?"

For the next week I served the Yankees and was paid well for my time. Of the anticipated pillaging I saw none. Nor was I the only civilian who found the Federals to be agreeable taskmasters; many others swallowed their Southern pride after they compared the attitude of the Northerners to what they had seen of Old Bedford. I had plenty of opportunity to inquire after William, but no one heard tell of him.

When it came time for me to leave and report my failure to Alcie, the lieutenant asked me if I would care to enlist as substitute saddler for their company permanently.

"No, thank you kindly," I responded. "I'm sorry y'all have to go to the fighting, but me, I'm going home."

Just before leaving Edgefield, Cyrus approached me. "Them blue-coats say I don't gotta go back to Boss man. But if they leaves here, somebody might make me. What should I do, Mistuh Jesse?"

"Cyrus, it seems to me that the good Lord has provided you a chance to be free. You stay that way. Go farther north if you have to. As you go, you heed how you can say thank You to the Lord for what He has given you, and like the Good Book says, He'll direct your path."

The young man's face came all over serious and thoughtful. "I surely will do that, Mistuh Jesse. I surely will."

✳CHAPTER 2✳

O ver a year passed since the fall of Nashville, and still no word of William reached us. Battles raged east, west, and south of us, but around McMinn County in East Tennessee, the war did not seem to exist. The country was foraged by Rebel troops, but mainly they left things be, and the Yankees stayed away entirely.

I first heard the news about the runaway slaves from R. J. Ferguson, who was owner of Tellico Junction General Store as well as postmaster. Those of us who frequented R. J.'s store shortened the name of the place to Tellico Junk. The title fit the atmosphere.

It was well-known that in 1790 R. J.'s granddaddy had followed Daniel Boone into Tennessee to trade with the Indians and trappers. With the exception of corn liquor, which the old man made in a still out back, nothing much sold. "Tellico punch" is what kept the old trade in business in the early days.

R. J. had inherited the establishment before my time. He was a small and rowdy man with the temper of a fighting cock when he sampled too much of his granddaddy's punch. Then he got saved at a Methodist camp meeting and forsook hard liquor of every variety. He destroyed his granddaddy's still and burned the famous and secret family recipe for Tellico punch the same day. This was a great disappointment to many of the riffraff among the local male population who thought highly of Tellico punch.

As for all the items that had not sold in the long history of the store, R. J. kept the stuff. It remained where his grandfather had placed it. Though Tennessee was a goodly way from the ocean, a whaler's harpoon and a tangle of sea-fishing nets hung from the rafters. I always supposed that R. J.'s grandfather had crossed the Cumberland Mountains and expected to find the Pacific Ocean, then turned back east in disappointment. Leather knee breeches, powdered wigs, and ladies' garments from the last century were piled in a dusty mound behind other heaps of junk. There was too much to name and all of it useless.

In the center of the room were half a dozen cracked, desiccated saddles and a conglomeration of decayed bridles. King of the heap was an ancient Mexican saddle that someone had brought home from the war against Santa Anna. Being a saddler and a farrier in my spare time, I considered the Mexican rig to be the only item of interest. Pommel, swells, and cantle were built so high that a man could not be shaken loose and would only fall out if the horse was turned upside down.

There was little of value to be got in R. J.'s store, but he stayed in business because of the post office pigeonholes in the corner near the fireplace. R. J. had received the government contract to deliver the mail shortly after he destroyed the still. He considered this to be a divine reward from the Almighty. For as long as I could remember, R. J. Ferguson dispensed mail, wrote letters for the unlearned, swore affidavits, and witnessed wills from the caged corner. Of late, he posted casualty lists from the battles.

Although R. J. was technically an employee of the government, he was not in danger from neighbors with Southern sympathies. We all came to Tellico Junk to get our mail and hear the latest news of the war.

Like me, R. J. kept his mouth shut and his thoughts to himself about the follies on both sides of the Mason-Dixon Line. Our speck of earth was a parade ground for both causes. Some owned slaves. Many were abolitionists. It was rumored that a few in our county had helped contraband slaves escape north into Ohio.

Over the years I had begun to believe that R. J. was part of the

Underground Railroad. More than once I had heard sounds escaping from the trapdoor of his cellar. The basement was accessible only by shifting a heap of ladies' corsets off a second sack of barrels.

"Varmints!" R. J. growled on those occasions as he stamped his hobnailed boot hard on the planks of the floor.

I pretended to pay the stirring no mind. I had noticed, however, that unlike the other petrified stuff in his establishment, the unmentionables of the fair sex were in a little different position each time I came in.

Yet R. J. avoided taking a stand. He grieved with families who lost sons on both sides. Each faction believed that R. J. Ferguson was one of their number. Curiously, he knew all the verses of "Dixie" and could sing out with the best of them. I suppose he also knew "The Star-Spangled Banner," but at that time and place it was unwise to raise that tune.

It is enough to say that he went on doing what he was meant to do and nobody bothered him or Tellico Junk. He was a wizened old man by 1863, but then I could not remember him being otherwise.

His back to the door, R. J. was putting the mail in the letter boxes and shaking his head all the while. I supposed that one of the envelopes had the mark of the war department giving official notice of the death of some McMinn County son.

"Morning, R. J.," I announced myself.

He did not turn around. "Howdy, Jesse."

"It'll be William's birthday. His eighteenth. His mama thinks he'll send us some word when he comes of age. Anything for us?"

"Nope."

I leaned against the upright timber, ducking my head to avoid the dangling harness. "Any news then?"

"Yep." He continued sorting the delivery. "Big battle up Virginny way. A place called Chancellorsville." He completed his task and turned to face me. The usual twinkle in his faded blue eyes was gone. "What's it all for, I ask ye?" He rubbed his hand across his brow.

I knew he did not mean for me to answer the question. "Casualties?" I asked.

"Seventeen thousand boys in blue."

I shuddered and thought of William—just one boy, but he was mine, and my mind could not picture any other face but his. "So many? Lord have mercy, R. J.! Wounded and killed?"

R. J. grimly glanced at me. "That's just the first sum. Reckon they ain't counted all the wounded yet. Likely there will be more to die among those fellers. Three days that battle lasted."

I looked for a place to sit down. There was none. Until this time I had not heard of so many dying in one place. I remarked bitterly, "Lots of folks have something to celebrate. A great victory for the Confederacy."

"There ain't no place in this whole wide country that there ain't some mama gonna be cryin' for her boy. The South lost thirteen thousand. Don't know how many maimed or got shot and dyin' by inches. Don't know how it will all end."

I was suddenly angry at the waste. "When there aren't any more boys left to die maybe? When everything folks love is torn asunder?"

R. J. put his hand on my arm and lowered his voice, although there was no one else around to hear. "There's something else I got to tell you." With his rheumy eyes he studied my face. "Can I trust you, Jesse?"

"Yessir."

"Tuck Ringworth was a captain in the Confederate cavalry. He had been wounded in the arm and was home on furlough. His farm was nine miles to the south of my place. He had a reputation for cruelty toward his servants."

"I know of him."

"I reckon you do. And you know what he does to runaways." His glance flitted to the stack of corsets. "Law gives Ringworth the right to do whatever he wants. Kill 'em if he takes a mind to."

"They're no use to him dead."

"Crippled they can still work. You've seen it. Hamstring the men. Other things to the women. He's got his soldiers out lookin' for this bunch. Ringworth ain't up to the chase, but there's a number who signed on to his cavalry unit, and they're scourin' every hill and valley for contraband."

"Those slaves got to be a far piece off by now."

"Mebbe." He pursed his lips. "Most likely they're still around somewhere. And if'n they was . . ."

"I got a family," I said as a chill went through me. What Tuck Ringworth would do to runaway slaves, he would also cause to be done to those who helped them flee.

"Your farm is the last before the mountains. If'n the contraband was to reach your place, cross your fields . . ."

I knew with certainty that if I nodded, R. J.'s runaways would emerge from beneath the corsets and follow me home. Sooner or later doom would also come knocking at my door. Yet the dead of Chancellorsville urged me to not let their miserable deaths be for no reason.

I replied, "You know my left eye is a bit dim since that accident I had when I was a child. I just can't see out of that side like I used to. Why, a fella could walk all the way through my herd of heifers in my lower field, cross the creek, and disappear into the woods, and I'd never know if it was a human or just a cow."

R. J. grinned. "I thought you had that bull down in the lower pasture."

"You mean the one that chased John Dixon and tried to kill him last week?"

"The very one."

"Too dangerous. Kids want to try some fishing down at the creek. I don't want any one of them coming within reach of that bull."

"He's a mean 'un!" R. J. agreed.

"Yessir, he is. And that being the case I am planning on shifting that bull away off to the south pasture. Bringing the heifers in to graze. Tomorrow."

R. J. nodded absently and turned to stare into the letter boxes again. "Right smart of you to think of it. Some child could wander into the bull's territory, and something tragic might come of it."

✳ ✳ ✳

That evening, against the wishes of Alcie, I moved Ahab the bull out of the lower pasture.

"That critter is as big as a locomotive and will bust through the split-rail fence like it isn't there."

I explained, "Fishing down at the swimming hole is too good this time of year for the neighbors to pass up. Don't want Ahab killing anybody."

"Jesse! The lower pasture is rock wall on three sides and the crick on the other! Nothing else will hold him."

She was right. Ahab was as mean as they come. When he took a hankering to go visiting, there was not much that could hold him back except in that lower pasture.

I could not explain to Alcie that R. J. was bringing a wagonload of Tuck Ringworth's runaway slaves out to the farm, and the only safe way out of the valley was through our lower field and across the creek. With Ahab guarding the crossing, those folks would not have to worry about Tuck catching up to them. Nine humans—women toting babies; old, worn-out menfolk—they would not make it five yards into the field before the bull would run them down.

"Now, Alcie, you know there's only one thing that'll keep a bull critter from wandering. A sweet, little heifer on the straw. That's the trick. . . ." I slipped my arm around her waist and tried for a kiss, but she was not interested in testing my theory.

"Nothing so sorrowful as a lonely bull." She grinned at me in a teasing way, then grabbed the milk bucket and headed for the milking stool. "You know how it is. All right, then. Just be sure you leave a sweet, young cow in there to keep him busy."

For good measure and so as not to wear out one cow, I drove two good-natured heifers in with Ahab.

That night, young'uns prayed up and tucked in, Alcie reconfirmed my notion about why man critters give up a wandering life and settle down with one woman. I awoke the next morning convinced that Ahab would not have the will or the energy to break through that flimsy fence.

I was wrong.

Drawing water from the well, I chanced to look around. Ahab's female companions grazed contentedly on the tall grass, but Ahab had taken a notion and was altogether gone. A twenty-five-foot section of rail had been smashed to the ground.

Behind me Alcie remarked in a told-you-so voice, "I warned you. I'll have your breakfast waiting when you fetch him back."

I had just led Falger to the corral and left our second son, Loren, in charge of mending the fence when I spotted the dust of R. J.'s freight wagon coming up the lane.

"Howdy, Jesse! Loren!" R. J. bellowed while he was still one hundred yards away.

Surrounded by young'uns and with the baby on her hip, Alcie waved and hollered, "Morning, R. J. I got coffee and biscuits in the warmer if you're hungry."

Alcie always had a fondness for R. J. on account of his burning the recipe for Tellico punch. Most of the women admired him for making it just that much harder for the menfolk to get their lips on the rim of a jug of hard liquor.

R. J., who was a confirmed bachelor, also had a fondness for Alcie. He often remarked how amazing it was that a woman of Alcie's small size could have such a large litter of kids and not look altogether swaybacked, worn-out, and bedraggled. Mutual fondness aside, I felt it best that Alcie never know about our small part in the aid of Tuck Ringworth's slaves.

I rode out to meet R. J. alone. Coming alongside the wagon I said in a quiet voice, "You got them?"

"Yessir. You mind if I back the wagon into the barn?"

"I never told Alcie about his. Nor the young'uns."

He cocked an eyebrow at me. "You never told Alcie?"

"I don't want her in hot water if it should go wrong."

R. J. rubbed his cheek. "I reckon Alcie didn't mention anything like this to you?"

"Why should she?"

R. J. grinned. "Time you know'd. She's the one brought this idea to mind. Told me at church if the railroad was still running . . ."

"You mean she's known about all this?"

"You might say that. Your boy William first, then Alcie. Nigh on four years them two been helpin' out." R. J. slapped the lines down on the rumps of the mules. "Things was just fine until you moved that bull down to block the ford of the crick. Alcie know'd you wouldn't move the critter if'n she asked, so she asked me to ask, then argued with you about what a foolish idea t'were to move ol' Ahab. She was right certain if she crossed you about it, your stubborn streak would kick in, and you'd move the bull for sure."

I was dumbfounded. How long had Alcie been taking the bit in her teeth against my will? And William, too? "I oughta give both of them a good hiding."

"You might do that if'n you ever catch up to William. I'd think twice about layin' a hand on that woman of yourn. Alcie would take a chunk of stove wood to you if'n you ever tried t' whup her."

He was right. Alcie was prone to doing what was right and figuring I'd find out after the deed was done. "I should've known." I glanced back at the heap of manure in the wagon bed. It stunk. "All of them in there? Under the stuff?"

R. J. winked. "If'n you was, let's say, a Reb officer in a shiny new uniform, and your sweetheart just stitched on them golden braids and embroidered her initials next to your heart . . . would you go a'diggin' through a load of bull manure to find anything a'tall?"

"Babies in there, too?"

"They're all nine hid under a false bottom. Got water and vittles. It ain't so bad. We give the babies a drop of laudanum to keep 'em quiet. Just keep them young'uns of yourn out of the barn till nightfall, and no one will ever know."

"My young'uns ain't likely to go playing in bull manure."

"I was countin' on that. Now, speakin' of bulls, have y'all lost that big bull of yourn?"

"'Deed I did. Broke the fence just like I knew he would. And Alcie said he would. He's gone, all right."

"Yep. Well, I seen him back up the road a mile and a half toward Twizicks' farm. Best git on and fetch him back, Jesse, or somebody's a'gonna come after y'all for damages."

I brought Falger around and was spurring him to the road when R. J. called, "Hold on! I got somethin' for y'all!"

Too harried to turn back, I hollered, "Leave it with Alcie!"

Trafalger was a fine horse, and his long, easy strides fairly ate up the distance to Twizicks' farm. Ahab's tracks mingled with those of two dozen horses, but the busted rails on the Twizicks' fence led me to believe that the search would be a short one.

"He's gone that a'way," I mumbled to Falger.

The grass in that pasture was lush and belly high to Trafalger. Ahab had cut a wide swath through it that disappeared into the stand of pine trees at the far side. I could not think why that bull had not stopped to graze a bit.

We loped across the field. Beyond the woods I could hear the bawling of a cow.

"Well, now," I remarked, "Ahab's wasted no time at all. Twizick had a hankering to breed his stock to Ahab. Looks like God answered his prayers."

I figured I'd throw a rope on Twizicks' cow and use her as bait to lead Ahab back home.

Entering the thick, dark stand of trees, I paused to listen. The rush of the distant creek and a hushed whisper of wind in the trees nearly drowned out the murmur of men's voices.

I shook my head in defeat. Twizick had found my wandering bull before I had. I hollered, "Howdy, Twizick! I come to fetch back Ahab! Give a holler so's I can find you!"

Ahab's strong bellow issued from the trees on my right. I remarked to my horse, "He's down at the crick."

There followed the crack of a rifle, then two more.

"All right, Twizick!" I shouted. "No need to waste the powder. I got a fix on you!"

Falger snorted, neighed, and the high whinny of another horse returned to us. I let him have the lead, and he took me straight as an arrow into the camp of two dozen Rebel cavalrymen.

Ahab was in the center of the camp, hanging from a stout tree by his hind legs. He was bleeding fresh from a wide slash across his throat, and a lean, hungry-looking soldier was preparing to gut him with his saber.

I said, "That's my prize bull you've slaughtered."

Their picket, a boy of William's age, pointed his carbine at my head. "This was a stray. Busted through two fences to come to supper. He's the main course. Now raise your hands, mister."

I obeyed, determined to let the matter drop. After all, I was outnumbered two dozen to one.

"That ol' bull will feed half the Reb army," I said cheerfully. "You plan to eat him here or wrap him up?"

The captain replied, "Some of both." He motioned the boy to lower his aim and for me to drop my hands. He shoved his hat back on his head. "You look like a reasonable feller. Got one of them fine East Tennessee horses we come lookin' for."

Ahab was one thing. Trafalger was another. "You intend to eat him, too?"

"Nawsir. We intend to ride him." He sauntered toward me. "Us and General Nathan Bedford Forrest intend to ride him and chase down every Blue belly in East Tennessee. You got any objections?" He reached out to grab the reins.

At my cue, Trafalger tossed his head hard, knocking the Reb a staggering blow in the side of his face. The officer reeled back and fell, cursing, on the ground.

Responding to the pressure of my legs and a slight tug on the reins, Falger backed out of the camp. "This horse won't be rode by any man but me, fellers. Give my compliments to Old Bedford!"

With shouts and curses ringing out behind us, Trafalger lit out through the thick wood, running a course worthy of the best foxhunt in Tennessee. Only this time we were the fox.

Bullets buzzed past my ears like angry bees. Bark from nearby trees shattered on the impact and stung my face. Following the bank of the creek, I counted on the fact that my horse and I had ridden this land a thousand times, and the men of Bedford Forrest were strangers here.

At the ford Falger charged across without any urging from me. Instinct and fear somehow pushed him to speed and agility that I had never experienced on any horse before that day. He outdistanced the tired mounts of the cavalry, but I could still hear them behind us. They would not give up, no doubt, tracking back to our own front door unless I could outride and outfox them.

A series of high stone fences was ahead, spaced a mere twenty-five yards apart. Last autumn Falger had soared over two of the three chasing a fox when no other horse in the county had managed. The third was, in my judgment, too high even for Falger. I had pulled him up, though he had been game to try it. The fox had escaped through a hole.

Today, however, like the fox, there was no way of escape except through the wall or over it.

"They're eating our dust!"

The first barricade loomed ahead, standing at six feet high. My horse took it without hesitation.

And so with the second.

The Rebs likewise cleared the walls. Their yells echoed joyfully through the forest.

The third fence had been built to keep deer out of the corn patch of some long-forgotten pioneer. Fifty years had passed and still it stood, solid and seemingly insurmountable. I had never measured it, never thought to. No horse had ever jumped it.

377

But then, Falger was no ordinary horse. I could tell that he was eager to try for it. In his mind the fox that had beat him was probably still on the other side, and he would run him down. I felt him strain, so I let him go.

"All right then, you've been hankerin'. Take us home!"

At my words, Falger seemed to take flight. The stone loomed in front of my face, and I thought we'd smash it head-on, but we did not! For an instant I felt as if man could truly fly. Up and up we sailed! One moment of rush with wind—the top of the fence beneath my stirrups—and we began the descent.

Behind us came the shout of dismay, "He's took the fence!"

We were safe!

Then the unthinkable happened: the crack of the chestnut's left hind hoof resounded in the air. There was no mercy in that stone, no weakness, no give. Falger hung midair for a second while I flew out of the saddle and into a briar patch. With a terrified scream, his legs churning and finding no purchase, he crashed down.

I narrowly escaped being crushed beneath him.

The wind knocked out of me, I could only lie where I had fallen. Trafalger struggled to his feet. As if ashamed by his failure, he towered over my body with his head drooping and the reins dragging.

On the other side of the wall I distinctly heard the Rebs swearing in admiration.

One of them called to me, "You still alive, mister? That flyin' horse of yourn. Didn't kill him, did it?"

"No, sir." I brushed myself off.

"I'm right glad to hear that. Purely a horse to admire."

"'Deed he is!" I replied, running my hand down Falger's hock and grimacing at the split in his hoof. The blow had knocked his shoe clean off.

"I'm keepin' this here shoe of his as a memento, mister."

"You do that. That's all of him you'll keep."

The Reb laughed. "I don't reckon there's an easy way around this here wall?"

"Not a'horseback. It'll take y'all a few hours out of your way, and then my bull will be too rotten to eat."

"Well then. You win this one, mister. We'll drink a toast to you and Pegasus at our regimental wingding."

"Greet General Forrest for me," I said cheerfully, although a sense of dread settled over me at the thought of Nathan Bedford Forrest in my own county. Would Old Bedford remember the man from McMinn County who deserted him in Nashville over a year ago?

For now, at least, we were free to go. It would have been easy enough for those soldiers to scale the wall and shoot me dead. But from the way they treated Trafalger and me, I could tell they had a keen sense of chivalry. Trafalger had made a good enough fight that they were content to eat my beef and leave the rest alone.

I felt the satisfaction of a fox that had outrun the hounds. In the off chance the Rebs might change their minds, I led Trafalgar a dozen different directions and doubled back through the river three times before going home.

There was, at the end of the day, only one regret: Trafalger had been badly lamed by the stone wall. I would not be riding him for some time.

✳ ✳ ✳

It was near midnight when Trafalger and I came limping home. The light of a single candle shone through the window of our farmhouse.

"Alcie!" I called.

She fairly flew out the door and ran to embrace me. "Oh, Jesse! I thought they'd done you in!" She was weeping. Her tears dampened my shirt.

"R. J. came back for his wagon round suppertime. He said Twizick told him the Johnny Rebs had killed the old bull and chased you across the country! Oh, Jesse! I thought you were dead or taken, too! Not two in one day! Dear Lord, not two!"

"Falger is lamed. They never laid a hand on me." I tried to comfort her, too weary from the day to comprehend exactly what she had said.

"William's gone, Jesse!"

"Well, yes, Alcie. He'll come back, though."

"The letter! The letter! I could not have lived if they had taken you, too!"

379

And now the dim light in my brain began to glow a little brighter. Had not R. J. told me he had something for me? And had I not told him to give it to Alcie? Had the letter from William or about him finally arrived?

"Letter," I repeated the word dully. Alcie leaned heavily against me and sobbed harder. I managed to gather my wits. "Is it about William, then?"

She merely nodded in reply.

I muttered, "Falger's been lamed. Go inside and get my supper. I'll tend to my horse and be in directly."

A sense of anxiety filled me as I led the horse into the barn. So the news we had been dreading had come at last. I did not need to see ink on paper to know. The details were of little consequence. Perhaps the how of it would be explained, but I would never under-stand the why of it all. R. J.'s freight wagon was gone. I figured that meant the slaves were gone. Their freedom had cost me a bull and the soundness of my horse. Those things meant nothing to me. But the freedom of all their kind had most likely cost the life of my son and a million others. That night I cursed their freedom. Were a million slaves worth the life of my boy?

I fed and watered Trafalger. I did not have the strength to see to his hoof, although any other time it would have been the most urgent need I attended to.

Alcie was sitting by the fire when I entered the house. The glow of its light seemed to drain her face of all color. Exhausted, she stared blankly into the flames.

My plate was heaped with food. The letter was beside it. I washed my hands and sat down as if I intended to eat, but I could not.

The scrawl on the envelope was not in the hand of William. I took out the paper. There were two letters. The first was a brief note of explanation.

> *Dear Mr. and Mrs. Dodson,*
> *I was with your boy Billy from the first day of our enlistment until the day he was lost to the Rebs at Chancellorsville. He called himself Billy Dearson, but I see from his letter to you it ain't. He were a good friend, and I shall miss him. He were a good soldier, too, and done the Union proud. I reckon by this time you have got word from the War Department that he is gone missing and figgered to be dead by those of us who seen him and the others go down. They was surrounded on top of a ridge and cut off. Them Rebs come a'screaming and fell on him. We was out of cartiges. So was the Rebs, but it was hand to hand and they was more hands than we. Twenty-five or thirty 'gainst him and two others. Only three of us in the mess got out of that scrape. I am sorry it has happened. We could not get back to bury them. A lot of good boys died there.*
>
> *Here is the letter Billy ast I send to you if he was to die. Since he is most likely ded, I am sending it. Captain come and took his belongings and will send them along home. Billy often spoke right kindly of his mother. When he mentioned her cooking it always made us boys in the mess hungry.*
>
> *Yours truely,*
> *J. S. Hildebrandt, Private*

"Alcie?" I was shaking. My strength drained from me. I could not pick up William's letter to read his last words to us.

"They called him Billy," she whispered. "He hated it when I called him Billy."

"I asked in every camp of the Federals for William Dodson. Look here at the letter from his friend. Dearson, he spelled it. No wonder I could not find him."

Alcie kept her gaze locked on the fire. "Right I think that he called himself *dear son*, since he was indeed. Don't you think, Jesse?"

I managed to swallow, managed to make myself speak. "This feller didn't see the boy killed. Didn't see him fall! I . . . I won't read his letter of farewell to me until I know!"

Now she turned her pitying eyes on me. "Read it."

Suddenly angry, I scraped my chair back and left the house, slamming the door behind me.

I walked out onto the lane, not knowing where I was going or why. The stars made a soft glowing against the moonless sky. I had been so focused on finding my oldest son that it had been a long time since I had paused to look at creation and pray. Since William had left us, my conversations with the Almighty had become mundane and businesslike: "When'll it rain? God, we need rain."

Ah, but that night, my heart broke open as the heart of a father will do when his son is lost or dead. I fell to my knees in the dust of the road and cried out to the Almighty in my anguish. "Is my dear son dead, Lord? Have You taken him from us forever?"

I begged God for a different outcome to the tragedy. I asked God to take my life instead—if William was still alive and in some Rebel prison somewhere. "Take me, but do not let my boy die before he has lived! Let him return home to his mama."

I had resisted the battle, and had thought I was doing right. But my son, in his good conscience, had taken my place in the line. He was most likely dead, but through that terrible night I could not accept it. If he had died, he had died in my place. Would things have been different if I had gone to the battle in the first place? Would William be home still, safe on the farm? Or at least be fighting by my side, where I could have watched out for him?

I cannot say what time it was when I crept into bed. Alcie was asleep. Or, at least, she was quiet and still. My soul still churned within and would not let me sleep.

The Rebs had killed my boy or taken him prisoner. At last this was my battle. At last the Confederacy had given me cause to fight.

Next morning, Trafalger stood patiently as I tapped the last nail through the horseshoe. The force with which he had struck his left hind hoof against the stone wall had cracked the exterior laminate. The split extended nearly halfway up to the corona band at the top of the foot. The damage was deep and potentially dangerous, but with the special iron shoe I had concocted, I figured Trafalger would eventually heal.

Loren, manning the bellows of my forge, peered down with concern. "Will he heal up right, Father?"

I rasped the front edge of the hoof until it was perfectly protected by the iron shoe. "He won't be rode for a while. It'll take most of a year before I'll be hunting on him again, I reckon. But this rim we built into the shoe will keep the split from getting worse."

It is strange to say now, but I was almost grateful for the accident that had lamed Trafalger. Such obvious injury meant that I would not be riding him for a long while, but it was also a certainty that no band of Rebel cavalry or Yankee troops passing through our farm would be inclined to confiscate my horse.

This same thought had also entered Loren's head. The image of Trafalger and me outrunning the band of secesh cavalry pleased the boy. He stroked the muscled shoulder of the big chestnut. "We won't need to hide him from the Rebs no more, will we, Father?"

"Nor from Union foragers neither." I finished the job and straightened slowly. My back still ached some from the fall I had taken.

"And Trafalger will be well by the time this war is over."

I nodded. "We'll hope our boys are all home long before Trafalger is fit to ride."

We both fell silent then, and I supposed that Loren was thinking of William the same as I was. We stood listening to the hum of flies and the swish of Trafalgar's tail.

"Wish I knew," Loren said, looking at the horse but not at me.

I replied in a cheerful, offhanded way, as if I had not discerned his real thoughts. "Falger's fine and fit. No use to fret over him."

"Wasn't." Loren's face clouded. "I was . . . well . . . wondering about William coming home. Wondering if he was alive."

I lowered my eyes and without answering turned my back on Loren and set my hands to cleaning up. Gruffly, I ordered, "Don't let your mother hear you talk that way. Now take Falger back to his stall. Make sure the floor is mucked out. It's your job to keep it as clean as your mama's kitchen. Nothing worse for a cracked hoof than standing in filth. Sure way to give him an abscess, and then we'll have to shoot him."

I wish now I would have controlled the grief and anger I felt myself long enough to help Loren deal with the news of his brother. Loren needed to talk about it, and I was no comfort at all. Nor was I any consolation to Alcie or the little ones. I pondered on where William might be and what he would be doing and what I must do to find him.

Over the past months there had been dark moments, times when I saw the grief in Alcie's eyes, and I went outside and cursed William for doing this to his mother and his brothers and sisters. I had been bitter against him for the torment he had left us with. And, to be truthful, more than a little angry at God for allowing William to run off and then me not being able to track him. Yet now I knew I would have to leave my dear family behind while I joined the fight where William had left off.

That evening over supper Alcie spoke about William to the little ones, who listened to tales about their big brother with wide and awestruck eyes. Louisa, Loren, Harriett, and Howard joined in with their mother, but Robert and tiny Sarah were too little to remember William at all.

As for me, I ate without speaking. A knot like a fist formed in my gut, and it was all I could do to sit through the conversation.

At last I broke in with a voice that boomed like a cannon, though

383

I had not meant to speak so harshly. "There'll be no more talk about him! It was a cruel and rebellious thing he's done, going off to this war, and now he's left me no choice."

Alcie's eyes brimmed. "But, Jesse, it's William's birthday today. Can we not remember what life was for us before?"

"What's the use of it? Everything has changed for us now."

Alcie and Louisa began to weep.

I spat, "See there, Louisa? Look how William has broke your mother's heart."

The little ones, without knowing what the ruckus was about, added their wails to the scene. Loren sat pale and rigid in his seat and glared at me as if I alone was the cause of all misery.

I rose abruptly and went out to check Trafalger's newly shod hoof. It did not require attention, but I needed a little peace. I did not go back to the house until Alcie, in her nightdress and a shawl and carrying a pillow and blankets, came out to fetch me.

384

"Are you coming to bed?" she asked in a gentle, pitying tone like I was one of the young'uns and had fallen and scraped my knee. "Or shall I make you a bed in the straw so you can sleep next to Falger?"

My back was to her. I brooded against the gate of the stall and could not meet her gaze. I felt ashamed, indignant, and somehow wronged all at the same moment. "Falger's company suits me. He does not think me a villain."

"Nor do the children."

"And you?"

"You are as comfortable and kindly to me as an old shoe, Jesse Dodson. I do not sleep well without you." She wrapped her arms around me and pressed herself against my back. Her warmth, her softness stirred me, and I turned to embrace her. She was my friend, my love, the only other one who knew what I was feeling.

"Before he ran away . . . was I too harsh with William? Is that why he left?"

"You know he would have joined up when he came of age no matter what you said."

"We've been grieving nigh onto two years, Alcie."

"You hide your sorrow behind a wall of anger like you hide that horse of yours from the cavalry."

For the first time since I found his bed empty and knew he had left us I admitted, "I miss my little boy, Alcie."

Alcie sighed and buried her face against my chest. "It's been a long while since he was little. He never even knew he had a new baby sister. Doesn't even know about little Sarah."

"Don't speak of him as if he's gone forever. It breaks me to think I left so much unsaid to him." My heart became tender, and for the first time since William left, tears streamed down my cheeks.

"You're leaving home soon, aren't you, Jesse?"

I nodded slowly. "It's my war now. If William is dead, I cannot let his death go for naught. If he lives, then God help me, I'll find him!"

"Give me a few days. There's mending to do. You'll be gone awhile, I reckon. It's summer now, but you'll need your long handles come autumn. And there are things you'll need to tell the children. Parts of your heart you'll need to leave behind for them to cherish."

"It can't go on long."

"Even a day parted from you is too long. But the hardship for you is the fighting. For me it is being left behind. We will both be strong."

I kissed her and blessed her for knowing me so well. We made our bed up in the straw and passed the night talking about the first night after William was born. We were not more than children ourselves. I was eighteen and Alcie but sixteen.

Alcie said, "William is the same age now as you were when we made him."

"I imagined myself to be a man."

"I lay beside you and watched you sleep and never felt such love. I thought I'd break for loving you so strong."

"I supposed I was capable of accomplishing anything."

Alcie stroked my hair, and I did not feel any different than I had those many years ago.

"When you find him, tell him you were exactly his age when he was born. You were man enough to have a family and raise your children to stand up for what they believe in."

"I reckon that is so," I answered quietly as the bitterness left me and something else rushed into my heart. "I am proud of him. I just . . . didn't want him to run off and get himself killed in Mister Lincoln's army. When I held him in my arms the fist time . . . I never prayed so hard or feared so much or had so much hope. Easier for me to give up my life than to lose that boy."

"He is so like you."

"He's a better man than me, I fear."

"I never saw two better men nor two more alike. Stubborn, strong, fierce for the truth. Both of you. What would you have done at his age?"

"I would've fetched my rifle and gone to join up."

She buried her face against my chest. "Promise me you'll come back, Jesse. Promise me, and I'll believe you no matter what comes."

"How can I make such a vow?"

"Say it, and it will be true. Say it, and God will help you keep your word."

"God help me. I will come home to you, my Alcie girl. And I'll bring the boy back with me if I can." I kissed her lips, and we wept together.

✳ ✳ ✳

All too soon I waved good-bye and again traversed the Cumberland Mountains. I knew when I set out that once I wore the blue it might be a powerful long time before I could go home again. What I did not know was what a powerful change would be wrought in me by the crossing.

✳ CHAPTER 3 ✳

Camp Spear 1
June 1863

Ihad gone to Nashville on May 25 to enlist. Given my frame of
mind, I was prepared to join up with the first bunch of boys that
looked full of pepper and ready to scrap, be they artillery or foot
soldiers. Fortunately for me, before such a thing could befall me,
I was hailed in the street by Melvin Long, an old friend.

He was all kitted up, from the jaunty angle of his cap to the polished scabbard of his saber. His face split in a grin so wide that he like
to have dropped his pipe. "So, Jesse," he said, remarking on the determined set to my jaw, "you've finally had a bellyful and ready to lick
yore weight in wildcats."

"Came to enlist," I acknowledged.

"Got an opening for a saddler in our outfit," he said. "You being
handy with harness and such a farrier besides, Cap'n Briant'll be real
glad to get even so old a bird as you."

"What do you mean old?" I challenged, ready to give it right back
to him. "Are you calling yourself an infant? I'm thirty-six. You must
be most thirty yourself!"

"Twenty-five," he corrected, "and most of the fellers are not above
twenty-one. But don't take offense, old hoss; you'll add seasoning to
the meat." With that he clapped me on the back and led me off to the
city hall to meet Captain Joshua Briant.

Which chance encounter explains how I came to be part of Company F, Third Regiment, Tennessee Volunteer Cavalry. The regiment had been formed some time back. When brand-spanking new, they had guarded the trains from Nashville to Murfreesboro. Later on, they got bloodied at the affair at Stones River. Now they were at Camp Spear, just outside Nashville.

Captain Briant was a fine, tall man, three inches above my five-foot-eleven-inch stature. He affected bushy side-whiskers, but he was no dandy for all that. His wide-set green eyes studied me the way I examined a horse or a mule that I was considering. "For saddler, is it?" he inquired at last. "You'll get no special consideration for that, Dodson. In this outfit, everyone drills and everyone fights, from the blacksmith to the colonel's servant."

"Yessir," I said. "If it wasn't that way I would be looking somewhere else."

"Bit above the age to be playing at war, aren't you?" Briant was all of twenty-two.

I was getting a mite tired of being regarded as nudging Methuselah, and I said so.

The captain ignored my reply and continued, "Or is it that you've heard the draft is coming and you want to avoid being conscripted as a foot soldier? There are other regiments newly forming of all green troops. Why should we have to break you into our way of doing things?"

"Captain," I said, a little more forcefully than I intended; I came near to calling him Sonny. "I can ride to hounds, I can shoot, I can keep tack in trim, and I can doctor horses . . . but what I came here for is to fight. If that isn't what you are about, I'll thank you to excuse me so I can get on about my business."

To my right, Melvin Long made a strangled noise like he had sucked a gob of tobacco juice up from his pipe.

Briant nodded thoughtfully. "Ask me what happened to our last saddler."

"All right," I obliged, even though I had a pretty good guess. "I'll bite."

"He was killed on patrol . . . shot right out of the saddle by a sharpshooter he never even saw."

"Captain, do you suppose that Johnny Reb picked him off because he was a saddler? You got a job you want done, and I want to get into this fight . . . what else do we need to discuss?"

Standing up from his desk, Captain Briant extended his hand and shook mine. Then he addressed Long, who had stood silent through the whole exchange. Melvin probably wondered if announcing his friendship with someone who would back talk the captain was such a good idea. "Private Long," Briant said, "thank you for bringing this man to my attention. He will no doubt be a valuable addition to the regiment. Would you please take him to see the surgeon for examination and then to Sergeant Cate for mustering in?"

Long snapped a salute and led me away. On the way to the doctor's tent he kept saying, "Just don't talk like that to the colonel . . . just don't understand."

✳ ✳ ✳

Melvin took me to the office of the regimental surgeon, a man known as Dr. Souers. His name squared well with his preferred treatment, as Melvin told me that Souers prescribed quinine for every complaint. Melvin said he'd be back for me and left me in the good doctor's clutches.

Souers was a pig-eyed, flush-faced man, whose breath bore more traces of oh-be-joyful than of quinine. Almost the instant I met him, I wished he was in the market for a horse and I had one to sell; he was that eager to conclude his dealings with me. The entire exam consisted of his looking at my tongue and the soles of my feet. Then he stamped my papers *Approved* and signed his name.

"Don't you want to thump my chest or take my temperature or something?" I asked.

"What for?" he said with a dismissing wave of his hand. "You ain't ailin', are you?"

I reflected that any worry I had felt over the vision in my left eye had been wasted. My sight on that side was blurred some, on account of getting hot lead splashed in it when I was younger. But that was not the eye I aimed with when shooting, and I had been prepared to argue the point. It was just not necessary.

The next of my new comrades-in-arms was Sergeant Cate, who seemed to be of an age with me. Cate, having heard the report of my interview with the captain, squinted at the surgeon's paper. Then the figure with the three yellow chevrons on his sleeves spat a stream of tobacco juice and wiped his drooping mustache. "Company F is my bailiwick, do ya see? You jump when I holler, don't squat 'less I say to, and if you got something to say, you tell me. Don't be bothering the captain or Lieutenant Freel, and we'll get by. You don't look like an infant to need wet-nursing."

"No, indeed," I concluded.

"Well then," Sergeant Cate said, "sign or make your mark here."

On a camp stool was a book open to a page that read Company Muster-In Roll, on which I inscribed my name, age, and description.

"Got a horse?" Cate asked.

"No, sir," I said. "My family needs all the stock on the farm."

"No matter." Cate shrugged. "If you did, then the army makes note of its value, case it gets shot from under you. And don't be calling me sir. You say 'Yes, Sergeant' or 'No, Sergeant.' 'Sir' is only for buckos with the shoulder straps. Got a firearm?"

"Colt Navy thirty-six," I said, unwrapping and passing him the revolver, butt first.

"Hit anything with it?" he inquired.

"Been known to," I admitted.

"Younger recruits turn up with great horse pistols and no sense. I hafta take 'em away before they go hurting themselves or somebody else. Be like you can keep yours. Just don't wear it till I say."

"Yes, Sergeant."

"Saddler you're replacing already messed in with your friend Long, so you can just take his spot in the same tent. That's all."

I must have looked expectant or something, because Sergeant Cate asked, "You forget something?"

"Don't you have to swear me in or like that?"

"Signed is sworn," he remarked. "You're as in as you can get.

Draw your uniform and equipage. Oh, and, Dodson? Don't be leaving the post without permission."

Melvin Long took me to see the quartermaster sergeant. From him I drew a too-large blouse, too-tight pants, cap and boots that fit, a blanket, a gum poncho, and a cloth haversack.

Next Melvin led me to our quarters. My new home was a Sibley tent. These cone-shaped canvas affairs, designed to house twelve men, covered the field at Camp Spear so as to resemble a Red Indian village. The Third Regiment occupied seventy or so of those tents, and we were not the only outfit stationed there.

Melvin Long smirked at me and remarked, "New man has to sleep nearest the flap."

"From your canary-eating grin, that must be bad."

"Maybe not if you don't mind having the duty corporal stomp on your face every two hours all night when he relieves the watch."

I stowed my little sack of personal belongings in the tent, and then a bugle sounded. "What's that mean?"

"That's one you'll learn quick enough," Melvin said. "Chow call."

✳ ✳ ✳

The hours of my first evening in Camp Spear passed in a blur. Meeting many of the hundred or so members of my company, watering and stabling horses, and twice standing in rank for no apparent reason made it hard for me to sort out details. I do recall seeing the lights in hundreds of tents wink out just as the last notes of a mournful bugle call died away. The last sound of all was a drummer boy striking six slow taps on his drum.

I slid into slumber thinking of home . . . Alcie and the children. Then I thought again of William and wondered if he had been in a tent like the one I occupied. It made me feel closer to him somehow and reassured me that I was doing the right thing.

Despite Melvin Long's warning about the dangerous position I occupied in the tent, I did not awaken all night. If a corporal stepped on my face, I must not have noticed.

From years of before-dawn chores on the farm, I awoke ahead of daylight without anyone telling me to. Such was not the case for my comrades. Soon another bugle call sounded, this one strident and demanding, and the men began to groan and mumble to themselves.

A corporal flung open the tent flap and shouted, "Turn out, you men! All out! Ten minutes to roll call. Shake a leg!"

Since I had slept in my britches and socks like I saw the other veterans do, I had only to pull on my blouse and boots. Then I stood up.

The man sleeping next to me opened one eye and muttered, "Kill the bugler . . . no, kill that corporal first, then the bugler. What time is it, anyway?"

"Coming five," I judged, sighting the morning star.

"There is no such hour," my drowsy friend grunted, turning and pulling the blanket over his head. By this I judged him to be city folk.

On his way out the flap door, Melvin Long aimed a kick at the fellow's backside. "Get up, Cochran, or it'll be your last hour. This mess will not pull extra duty just so's you can get your beauty sleep."

"Go away," Cochran mumbled. "You ain't my mother nor a sergeant neither. I . . . hey, what're you doing?"

True to his word, Long was determined that our mess would not be in trouble, and he dragged Cochran upright by a handful of his long, greasy hair.

"Ow! Hey, that hurts. Let me go!"

"Soon as you're in rank where you belong. Come on here, Jesse. You, too, Dobbs. Lend a hand. There, you see," Long concluded as another bugle call sounded. "There's assembly already."

Norm Dobbs, an eager, lanky youth who seemed to be all willowy limbs and no body, helped me drag and carry Cochran out to line up facing the great, cleared square surrounded by tents. Cochran grumbled and slouched but caught Long's baleful stare and remained in line—barefoot and half-clothed but present.

I noted in the assembled ranks that there were others like Cochran, though most were dressed and presentable.

Sergeant Cate called the roll, noted absences of which there were a few, and made his report to the orderly sergeant. Then we were dismissed.

Cochran headed straight back toward the tent, no doubt to

resume his interrupted rest, but another bugle call rang out and Long announced, "Stable call. Let's go!"

It was the policy in mounted outfits to care for the stock before breakfast for the men. As Sergeant Cate frequently reminded us, it took sound, sturdy horses to make a cavalry unit, but the monkeys who sat in the saddles were not special at all. Each of us had three horses to lead out to water, then curry and groom, while the animals munched their morning rations.

Cochran hailed me from the next stall over, just as I was finishing. "Say, Dodson, you seem to know your way around these critters. How do you get them to hold up their feet for you?"

I joined him next to a big bay gelding. "They don't hold them up for you; you have to pick them up," I said, snorting at the ignorance of the city bred. "Look here." I squeezed the bay's fetlock. The horse obediently hoisted his leg and let me cradle it behind my knee while I used my pick to clean the sole. "See how easy it is?"

"I'm not sure," Cochran disagreed. "Let me watch another one."

On our way to mess, Dobbs tagged along beside me, his legs and arms going all different directions as if he had more joints than most folks. "Watch out for Cochran," he warned. "He's a beat . . . always trying to get you to do his chores."

"Here, Dobbs," Corporal Pym called after him. "Come back here and stow this rake away properly."

When Dobbs obligingly gamboled back toward the stable, he accidentally trod on the tines of the rake. The handle flipped up, but rather than hitting himself in the face, Dobbs succeeded in knocking the corporal's cap off.

Corporal Pym emitted such a stream of oaths that I looked to see the paint peel off the stable wall. But Dobbs was such a good-natured critter that he seemed to take no notice.

✳ ✳ ✳

The month of June that followed my enlistment was, as promised by Sergeant Cate, one of drill, drill, and more drill. The hours from breakfast till noon were filled with mounted drill with sabers, dismounted drill with carbines, wheels and pivots by company and such. After our noon meal it was regimental maneuvers, with close to a thousand mounted men swinging in lines, columns, and flanking movements.

In the twilight, when the last stable call had been performed and the evening meal was under way, the talk turned to the progress of the war in the places where it was really being fought.

"I hear Vicksburg is about played out," Melvin Long said, referring to the Union siege of that city on the Mississippi. He took a pair of hardtack biscuits from the salted water in which they were softening and slapped them into a pan of sizzling pork fat to brown. "It won't be long now before Old Man River is true—blue Union from Minnesota to the Gulf."

Many were of the opinion that Robert E. Lee, the Confederate general, would be up to something before he would let that happen.

"You watch," Sergeant Cate said. "Massa Bobby Lee will be trying something to take the pressure off Vicksburg. Here, put some pepper on that skilligalee."

"Try somethin' where?" Cochran asked.

"North, maybe, like around behind Washington. They say that the Reb General Longstreet is on the move."

"And what about us?" I inquired as I labored over a broken bridle. Recruits were always so hard on equipment that I was kept busy repairing tack whenever I was not obliged to drill. "What do you figure for hereabouts?"

Cate nodded gravely before answering, giving his one-word opinion as an old campaigner: "Forrest."

The Confederate chief of the army occupying the southern portion of Middle Tennessee was Braxton Bragg, but when the talk turned to the enemy, the figure most often raised was that persistent devil, my old nemesis, Confederate cavalry commander General Nathan Bedford Forrest.

Since Nashville had been retaken from the Rebs back in February of '62, Middle Tennessee was divided between the two opposing armies. We Federals held a line below Nashville that ran southeast from Franklin to Murfreesboro. The secesh faced off with us no more than a dozen miles away, along the line of the Duck River. There had been probes, reconnoiters, and even pitched battles but no significant changes in position.

Except for Forrest.

Old Bedford was as apt to turn up behind our lines as he was to raid forts on the Mississippi or strike into Kentucky, all of which he had done.

"So you figure Forrest will be coming this way again soon?" I pressed. "He hasn't been heard of for a month."

Cate nodded. "I can smell him, sure as you're born. But we're ready for him this time. We'll nail his hide to the barn, certain. It's our duty. Yes, indeed, our duty."

I wished I was as confident. For two years Union commanders had chased Old Bedford all over the state without ever pinning him down. He knew when to fight, right enough, and he knew when to withdraw. Three times I heard tell that his force had been reported "decimated and scattered," only to have him attack again in a week, none the worse for wear.

All of which masked the cause of my personal great grief: If we could not dislodge Forrest and the rest of the Rebs from Middle Tennessee, then there was not even any talk of kicking them out back of the Cumberlands, where my home was.

"Yessir," Cate repeated, "I can sure smell him, old slave trader that he is. But we'll bloody his nose right enough this time. Pour me some more of that coffee, Dobbs, and don't spill it on my hand this time."

CHAPTER 4

Well before dawn the next day, June 24, the bugles tore apart my dreams of Alcie and home. No reveille or stable call either, this blaring of brass horns. The buglers of all twelve companies of our regiment and a like number of infantry and four batteries of artillery commenced their calls to arms.

"Wake up, Cochran," I said, nudging the man next to me. "It's boots and saddles."

The sudden appearance of Sergeant Cate confirmed the alarm. "Turn out on the double, you men. We're going into action. Corporal Pym, have the men draw rations for three days, forty cartridges apiece, and be ready to move out in fifteen minutes."

Such was the effect of the constant drilling over the previous month that instead of half-sleeping men falling over their night-dresses, we were actually standing to horse in the required quarter hour. In that span we had dressed, watered and saddled our mounts, and received three pounds of hardtack and two of salt pork and twoscore rounds of ammunition.

At the cry, "Company . . . mount!" I swung aboard the tall black gelding I was allotted, and we trotted out of Camp Spear in columns of twos. Until that moment, I had not even had enough time to wonder what the cause of this alarm was or where we were headed.

Three miles south of Nashville, General Stanley, commanding the entire cavalry corps, drew us aside into a cleared field and passed the word. "The whole army is moving south. General Rosecrans is going to run Bragg and the Rebs out of Shelbyville. Our job is to find Forrest, and after we find him, to back him into a corner and kick the living daylights out of him. What do you say, men?"

We gave him three cheers and a tiger and three more for Rosy Rosecrans as we moved off south again, along the Murfreesboro road.

Cate rode by, and as he did, he wheeled his bald-faced bay alongside my horse. "You will admit I almost had the right of it," he prompted. "It's just that we are not waiting for Old Bedford to move this time. We're going out after him!"

It rained that day and all the next. The Third Regiment scouted ahead of the army and Company F was the vanguard. We did not have the struggles with the mud as did the artillery and the doughfoot soldiers who came after us, but it was mighty lonely way out front.

On the morning of the twenty-seventh, we busted through Guy's Gap and got the word that Bragg had not even waited for our coming but had withdrawn the Confederate troops south toward Tullahoma. Seems he saw that Rosy's strategy of encirclement was about to work, and Bragg wanted no part of it. Of Forrest there was no word at all.

That was the day on which I had my first encounter with the Rebs in battle.

Our company was spread out in skirmish lines, in widely spaced ranks of sixteen men across. As chance would have it, my messmates and I were in the first rank, with Dobbs, Cochran, Long, and me to the extreme left of the boggy trace. We advanced our horses at a deliberate gait, aware that we should be encountering the Reb rear guard anytime.

"Jesse," Dobbs sang out, "I see somethin' moving up ahead."

As he spoke the words there came the dry rattle of musket fire, and a lead hornet buzzed past my left ear.

"Have at 'em, boys," Long shouted. "This is what we came for!"

With that, our side of the line surged forward across a swollen creekbed and up a brushy hillside. I caught a glimpse of a gray-clad figure drawing down on me from behind a fallen log. He looked the age of my son William, and it surely did give me pause. Then the spell was broken, and we both fired and both missed. As he had only a single-shot weapon and no time to reload, he turned and skedaddled up the slope.

All of my comrades had similar experiences driving in the Confederate pickets, and we all burst into a clearing on the hillside at about the same time. Long was hollering like crazy, and Cochran had a big grin on his face as if we were about to win the war right there.

Across the intervening space of thirty yards of open ground we heard a voice shout, "Front rank . . . fire!"

The shadows under the limbs of a grove of black cherry trees exploded with the roar of mass rifle fire, and the view ahead disappeared in a cloud of smoke.

I heard Cochran yell, "I'm hit!" but had no time to spare him a thought right then, since my horse screamed and pitched forward at that same instant.

I let go of the reins so I could vault clear of the gelding as he tumbled, but my Sharps carbine pivoted on its strap, and the butt clobbered me on the back of my head. I ended up under the neck of the fallen critter, on the downhill angle. I could not have fought back even had I been in a position to do so.

Long, Cochran, and Dobbs wheeled for the cover of the brush through which we had come, and our bugle sounded recall. I would gladly have obliged, but the black horse was stone dead. What was more, exposed as I was on the open hillside, only the carcass lying between me and the Rebs kept me from getting my own share of minié balls.

As soon as I recovered my scattered wits, I crawled backward down the slope, hiding from view as best I could behind my fallen mount. Whether the secesh could see me or if they just guessed at my whereabouts, I kept hearing musket fire and seeing the jerk of the dead horse's body as the heavy slugs slammed into it.

Sergeant Cate grabbed me by the leg and pulled me down into

a gully. I tried to thank him, but he shut me up by telling me what a fool I was and using other, more colorful descriptions. "Our job is to scout the enemy dispositions and report back. You can't report back if you're dead, Dodson. There'll be no more charging unless you get the order, understand? I expected more control from an older man."

He was right, of course. I had come near to getting myself killed my first time under fire and to no purpose whatsoever.

"Drop back and see if you can pick up another mount," Cate ordered. "And when you return, be ready to do a job, not be a hero."

I caught a spare horse from Company D. Seems one of their troopers had taken a ball on the point of his knee. He was out of the fight and out of the war and more than likely going to be shy a leg.

When I rode to rejoin my outfit, I glanced down at my own uninjured shin. There, streaking the shoulder of the dun-colored horse was a fan-shaped stain of blood, right where the former rider's leg had been.

Cochran's wound was no more than a scratch along the line of his jawbone. It came to me as soon as I saw it that the scrape could have been made by a tree branch same as a musket ball, but to Cochran it was almost mortal. "Come near taking my head clean off," he told everyone who would listen. "I gotta get me to an aid station."

Sergeant Cate disabused him of that notion right away. The sergeant slapped a handful of stinging, camphorated goo on the wound. When Cochran yelped like a scalded pup, the sergeant told him to get back in ranks or he would smear the gunk around some more.

The report from the right side of our line was of greater importance than what my group had discovered. Tullahoma was ahead on a plateau. The single, wagon-width track that led there was covered by a battery of Confederate cannon, waiting for our troops to march up the defile. It was our job to root them out if we could, so as not to delay the passage of the infantry. We posted pickets on our end to watch out for a Reb flanking maneuver; the rest of Company F formed for battle.

Captain Briant told us what was up. "Men, we have to ride hard and fast. While the rest of the regiment keeps the Rebs busy here, we can outflank them by way of a canyon to the north and come up behind their guns. In columns of twos . . . by the left flank, ho!"

The rain had not ceased, though it had settled down to a steady drizzle that made my uniform stick to my body like I was a half-drowned cat in a gunnysack. Cochran's hair was plastered down over the sides of his face, and he winced every time he plucked a couple of strands loose from his wound. The horses were so soaked and mud-died that except for patches, blazes, and stars, they might all have been the same color.

We slipped and slid as we circled first north, then east, then back south again. We followed an unguarded canyon that Captain Briant believed would give us the drop on Johnny Rebs.

The last quarter mile was so steep and so treacherous of footing that Briant ordered us to dismount and lead our critters. I think he was afraid a horse would take a tumble and in that spot carry half his command downstream, so caution was the word.

Before we had reached the head of the gully, we heard the boom of cannon fire. This meant we were near our objective, but it also meant that our boys were caught under the falling shells that rained on the Tullahoma road below.

Captain Briant spread us out in line of battle just below the crest of the hill and had us mount up. So far it seemed that no Reb picket had spotted us, and our surprise attack remained a surprise.

This time I was in the middle of the line and about three rows from the front. "Steady," I urged Dobbs, who was showing signs of impatience. His horse, a great, tall bay, was champing at the bit and prancing sideways. "Remember the dressing-down I got from Cate, and keep your mount steady." Our carbines were still in their scab-bards—it being almost impossible to manage a galloping horse and aim a rifle at the same time. Every trooper had his sidearm cocked and drawn, the horses dancing nervously and sensing the excitement from the mounted men.

When Captain Briant hollered, "Charge!" all impatience was unleashed as we swept over the brow of the rise a hundred yards from the guns.

I could see it plainly. There was a battery of four Napoleons, five-inch cannons that could throw solid shot or canister. Each gun had a crew of four men, plus there was a company of infantry to protect the battery from just such an assault as ours.

As our charge swirled down from the heights, the Confederate gun captain coolly ordered two of his cannons to pivot in place to face us. The soldiers guarding the cannons were already on one knee, firing into our ranks. Just ahead of me a man threw up his hands to grasp his face before he toppled from the saddle. His horse plunged on, riderless. I fired my Colt until I emptied all six rounds, then replaced it in the cross-draw holster and drew my saber.

An instant later the pair of Reb guns blasted, and a flurry of canister tore across the field. Lead balls like giant shotgun pellets mowed through us. Twenty men in our front rank went down, but whether they were wounded or their horses shot from under, I could not say.

Forty yards away the cannons unleashed another volley. Like hail on young corn, the new leading row of my comrades disintegrated in blood and shredded uniforms.

Suddenly my rank was heading the charge. It was by God's almighty hand—and no other explanation—that there was no more time for the secesh gunners to reload. I rode down on the line of their infantry. A grizzled corporal in a floppy slouch hat drew a bead on my breastbone and pulled the trigger, but his powder must have been wet, for the gun misfired.

I swatted his bayonet aside with my saber, then brought it down backhanded across his shoulders as I spurred past him. I kneed my dun into a tight turn just as another gray-clad solider yanked the ramrod free from his musket barrel. The left shoulder of my horse hit the Reb in the chest, making him drop his weapon and sending him spinning into a two-wheeled gun limber. He flipped over a wooden-spoked wheel like he was vaulting a fence, but how he landed I did not see.

A third opponent, sensing that I would be on top of him before he could reload, clubbed his rifle and swung it at my chest, intending to sweep me out of the saddle. Holding the saber point downward to my left, I caught the blow on the guard and fended it off. Then, for want of any other stratagem, I released my foot from the stirrup and kicked him in the chin. The lean, long-haired private was knocked to his knees, but as he fell he was already drawing a knife that was half the length of my saber.

I was clear on the other side of the melee, and the fighting was all behind me. As I twisted the horse to the left, he snorted and reared. A bullet cut both reins just under his chin as cleanly as a blade would have done.

I still had only one foot in a stirrup and was without any control over the plunging buckskin. When he shied toward the trees I was instantly flat on my back in the mud. The saber was jarred loose from my grip and flipped away.

The secesh with the long straggly hair loomed over me, raising his knife with a two-handed grip. He looked like a butcher with a cleaver, and I was the hog carcass to be split.

There was no time to roll out of the way and no method to deflect the blow. There was only the barest instant in which I shouted out to God to save me, and then the weapon flashed toward me.

Midway in its descent, the Reb's swing checked abruptly, and he crumpled sideways. It has always seemed to me since then that I saw the impact of the bullet that struck him in the chest before I heard the pistol shot that had launched it, even though it came from only a few yards away.

Sergeant Cate leaned over and extended his hand to me, helping me to my none-too-steady feet. "Up you get then. You shouldn't drop your saber like that, Jesse. You might want for it." He kicked the heavy-bladed bowie away from the dead Rebel's hand as he holstered the revolver with which he had saved my life.

It seemed that Cate was mighty calm and easy for being in the midst of a battle, but the truth of it was, the fight was over. The remaining secesh fled down the slope, abandoning the cannon and their dead and wounded.

We had captured the battery, successfully protected our column on the road below, and taken a handful of prisoners as well. The Reb soldier catapulted over the gun limber by my furious charge was still cowering behind the wagon wheel. He was no more than fifteen years of age, and his face was as innocent of whiskers as a girl's.

"Come on out of there, son," I said. "You ain't hurt bad, are you?"

He rose with both hands in the air, and he was trembling like an aspen leaf in a high wind. "Turn round and march yourself over to that sergeant yonder," I ordered.

The boy stood rooted in place, as if he were wearing two hundred pounds of chains.

"What ails you? Are you shot?"

Shaking violently from blond head to bare feet, the boy replied, "You gonna shoot me in the back?"

I snorted. "I don't aim to shoot you at all! What foolishness are you spouting?"

"You ain't gonna shoot me?" he asked again doubtfully.

"Not as long as you behave," I snapped, tiring of the absurd exchange. "Where'd you get such nonsense?"

"Old Bedford . . . Gen'ral Forrest . . . told us you Yanks shot prisoners."

"Well, we don't!" Then a thought struck me. "But you say your outfit belongs to Forrest?"

The boy stretched upward with extravagant pride, in direct contradiction to his earlier alarm. "Morton's battery. Light artillery for Gen'ral Nathan Bedford Forrest!"

* * *

There was a hurried conference with Captain Briant. Cate and I were involved, while Melvin Long, Dobbs, and Cochran listened in.

"Morton's battery, by heaven!" Briant exclaimed. "Then we are on to Forrest, sure as sunrise."

"Yessir," Sergeant Cate agreed. "That young Reb prisoner . . . when he found out he was not to be shot, he was so full of hisself he couldn't leave off talking."

Since crossing Guy's Gap and beginning the assault on the slope leading to Tullahoma, there had been no certain news about Forrest's location. And as Captain Briant muttered to himself three or four times, keeping track of Forrest was still our main mission. "Tell me again what the boy said about Old Bedford's whereabouts."

"Said Gen'ral Forrest was coming from way over in Columbia, but he was gonna get here any time now and kick the stuffing out of us at Wartrace," I volunteered.

"Wartrace, eh?" Briant mused. "That's behind us already. We are overtaking the fleeing secesh so fast we'll pin Bragg's whole command against the Duck River at Shelbyville . . . and what will Forrest do about it? Will he strike us in the rear, or will he swing south and meet us head-on before the ford?"

It was not for a lowly private like me or even a sergeant like Cate to comment on these musings, and so we waited respectfully till Briant made up his mind. "All right," he announced finally, "we must prepare for both possibilities. Sergeant Cate, I want you to ride to General Granger with the infantry division. I expect you'll find his headquarters near Wartrace. Warn him about the possible flank assault. Dodson, you come with me."

"Yessir," I said, saluting. "Where are we going?"

"To see the colonel," he said, mounting his big chestnut horse. "If he agrees, the Third Regiment is going to ride like thunder for the crossing of the Duck River and be waiting for General Bedford Forrest to come waltzing into our arms."

It came as no surprise to me that Colonel Minnis was quick to leap to the same conclusion as Captain Briant. If our regiment could speed ahead to Shelbyville, we would cut off the Confederate line of retreat, trapping their forces between us and General Granger's foot soldiers coming along the road . . . and the biggest prize of all would be Old Bedford himself!

※　※　※

It was afternoon when the Third Regiment came to the outskirts of Shelbyville. A lieutenant of the First Middle Tennessee Cavalry raced up to our colonel. He was galloping full bore as if he would not stop till Nashville, but when he spotted the regimental colors, he set his gray horse back on its haunches. In the mud of the rain-soaked road, the beast skidded twenty feet before "whoa" became a reality.

"Colonel Braddock's compliments," he reported with a salute. "He asks that you come on ahead—double-quick. The Reb baggage train is still on Skull Camp Bridge, but we can't get at 'em on account o' the Reb rear guard."

The order to move forward at a quick trot was relayed down to company level before the words had even finished tumbling out of our colonel's mouth.

That shavetail lieutenant whipped his lathered horse around alongside and delivered the rest of his report on the move. "We've had us a runnin' fight since midmornin'. Been tryin' to come at the wagons, but a troop of cavalry plus about six hundred Alabama boys is between us and the bridge. The whole Reb army is gettin' away!"

As we drew nearer Shelbyville, we could see the truth of the matter for ourselves. The direct route through the town to the crossing of the Duck River was blocked with overturned wagons and heaps of grain bags. The other approaches were likewise guarded by grim-faced men in gray. About a quarter mile farther on, a thin streak of black smoke was creeping into the afternoon sky.

"Lieutenant," our colonel demanded, "tell your commander to stay in line of battle, firing so as to make the Rebs keep their heads down. When he hears our bugle sound, clear your men out of the way!"

The junior officer snapped another salute and spurred away.

"By gum!" Melvin Long said. "We're gonna see somethin' now!"

"Why, what's gonna happen?" a nervous Norm Dobbs hissed at me from his spot behind me in the column.

"Reb rear guard has kept our boys from lambasting their retreat," I explained, "but the bridge is still intact. If we can bust past, maybe we can head 'em off."

"But what about us?" Dobbs persisted, looking even more lean and scarecrow-like than usual.

"Well," I said, nodding at Sergeant Cate's order for us to check our sidearms and putting fresh caps on my Colt, "let me put it to you this way. Did you ever go on a foxhunt?"

"Me?" Dobbs gulped, fumbling with his tin of percussion caps and dropping a handful in the mud. "I never been near a fox."

"Well then, laddie buck," remarked Cate, coming back up the column on the other side and overhearing the conversation, "all I can say is, hold on to your hat!"

Before Dobbs could ask yet another question about what he meant, it was "Forward—at the walk . . . trot . . . canter," and we were off. We stayed in a column of twos as a pair of light cannons opened up on us from behind the makeshift ramparts of meal sacks. Fortunately, they were firing high. Our advance was so swift that they could not adjust quickly enough to bring the guns to bear. We rode forward with a rattle of musketry before us and the explosions of the shells behind us.

When our bugler sounded the charge, we were no more than four hundred yards from the Rebs. We saw the boys of First Middle Tennessee break their skirmish line and bunch up behind wagons so as to get out of our way as we thundered forward.

The next bugle call split our column of twos apart into two streams of mounted blue, then split it again so four lines of galloping troopers were attacking. One column each as to the left and right and the two in the center were aimed straight down Main Street.

There was one volley of concentrated rifle fire from the defenders, and then we were among them. Only we did not stop to mix it up in front of the town. Our aim was not to capture Shelbyville but to cut off the retreat or, failing that, to take the bridge before the Rebs burned it, protecting their retreating supply train.

At the head of the column on my left, Captain Briant directed his bay horse directly toward a barricading wagon bed. Firing his pistol to the right and the left, he jammed home his spurs and lifted the bay over the obstruction. Astonished Rebs actually held their fire as he soared over them and continued galloping down Main Street toward the river. After him two horses were shot down, but the next three riders also vaulted the barrier safely.

The eight men in front of me in file fanned out as we approached the line of meal bags. Our lead rider, Corporal Pym, was shot through the body and killed, but as his corpse tumbled over, his foot caught in the stirrup, and he was dragged alongside the frantic horse.

The panicked animal turned broadside to the firing line and ran parallel to the earthworks, spoiling the aim of the Johnny Rebs.

So it was that all of us who came after jumped the Rebel line safely and clattered on toward the bridge. I scattered four shots right and left so as to make the hurdle easier for those coming after me, and in that way most of Company F passed the Confederate line uninjured.

Just because we had crossed the first obstacle did not mean our fight was over. Ahead of us, filling the town square that opened before the bridge, was a tumbling mass of men. Mounted troopers swinging sabers clashed together and wove through dismounted men waving bayonets.

There were about a hundred secesh opposing us at the bridge, about half of them cavalrymen. At first they outnumbered us, but more of our regiment successfully passed into the town, and the sound of firing coming from behind us was slackening. I shot at one feller coming at me with a pigsticker and at another who was drawing a bead on me with a shotgun, thus emptying my revolver. I felt no perforations, so I must at least have made them jump back.

Captain Briant was engaged in battle with a stocky, dark-complected man of forty years or so. The Reb had a curly brown beard. He fought skillfully but almost negligently, as if his real attention was on what was happening around him. He kept sneaking glances up the river.

This was all I had opportunity to note before my own attention was diverted elsewhere. A brawny Reb sergeant with a coal black beard and eyes to match spurred straight at me. He was waving a heavy, straight-edged saber about as thick as a fence post. When our blades collided, I felt the blow clear up and down my spine, and it made my teeth rattle.

His weapon was much heavier than mine and as difficult to ward off as a sledgehammer, but mine was the quicker on the recovery. I slashed at his face, making him throw up his arm to protect his good looks, and thereby I nicked him below the elbow. He swung back at me with his sharpened club but missed when I ducked below the arc.

407

When my weapon flickered toward him again it pinked his sword arm, and his saber clattered to the ground.

Suddenly the bridge exploded with a roar! The far end blew apart in a shower of splinters. There must have been jugs of coal oil on top of gunpowder, causing flames to quickly devour the wooden structure.

From both sides of the fray came our other two columns of men. They had cut their way into town by other routes and now attacked the square from both east and west.

This changed the odds completely. Now we were about three hundred in blue against less than half that many graybacks. I heard Colonel Minnis call on the Rebs to throw down their arms and surrender.

To my amazement, the next sound that rang in my ears was the Reb bugler blowing charge! A column of twenty or thirty mounted graycoats, led by Old Bedford himself, hacked at full speed into our midst. The trapped Confederates—and there were about a hundred of them—massed together with the newcomers and busted through our encircling ring. Swinging sabers and clubbed pistols, the Reb troopers knocked us aside without fear of being shot. They knew that those of us who still had ammunition could not fire for fear of hitting our own men.

Skull Camp Bridge at Shelbyville was built on the edge of a twenty-foot limestone bluff. Without breaking stride, every one of those Confederate cavalrymen put his mount at the leap and launched into the air above the river. I had never seen anything like it, and judging by the expressions on the faces of my comrades, neither had anyone else!

About half of the escaping troopers did not land well and were knocked from their horses, and some others were shot down while swimming across. But about thirty riders, including the bearded sergeant, who I had thought was my prisoner, emerged on the other side to clamber up the rocky slope and disappear into the trees south of the river.

We made no attempt to follow.

Leading the band who made the successful flight, leaping his horse the farthest out into the stream and shouting hoarsely for the others to follow, was General Forrest.

Captain Briant reined in next to me as we watched the last of the Rebs disappear from view. Old Bedford stayed at the water's edge, heedless of the occasional minié ball that still spattered into the stream near him. When the last of his men had made the crossing, he, too, took his leave.

"Divided his force even in the face of our attack . . . held us off till the baggage train got across . . . destroyed the bridge so we cannot quickly follow in anything like adequate numbers . . . counterattacked and rescued his men," Briant mused to no one in particular. "That," he said, pointing with his saber at the back of the Rebel general, "was Nathan Bedford Forrest."

A dispatch rider galloped up and handed the captain a note.

He read it, grinned ruefully, and tipped his hat to the departing Rebs. "And if that were not enough, while we were engaged here, another five thousand secesh troops crossed unopposed upstream from here."

I could scarcely credit it, but Forrest's successful escape across the Duck River was the end of the Tullahoma campaign for the Third Regiment and nearly the end for all Union pursuit. Because of our losses, which were thankfully more to mounts than to men, we were withdrawn from the front lines and placed in reserve.

When General Granger arrived in Shelbyville with our infantry, he feared a counterattack by Forrest's cavalry and so put off for a day sending the troops across the river. This delay gave the Rebs the chance they needed to reform their columns and put some distance between the two armies.

There was some skirmishing that went on as other units of the boys in blue pursued the Confederates south, but no more pitched battles and no more chances to bring Forrest to bay. So an opportunity to inflict important damage on the Rebels was lost because of fear and indecision and, to give the devil his due, because of the cunning and courage of Bedford Forrest.

All of which is not to say that Rosy's offensive had not been successful. In nine days we had pushed Bragg and his graybacks out of Middle Tennessee and back into Alabama, kicked them out of territory they had held for a year.

* * *

Back in Camp Spear in Nashville, I got to read the first newspaper I had seen since the campaign started. I scanned the pages of the *Nashville Sentinel* for stories about our exploits. "Here it is," I said at last as Dobbs and Cochran peered over my shoulder around the campfire. "President Lincoln sent a telegram to Rosy Rosecrans to congratulate him, said to tell his men they did well."

"Page sixteen!" Cochran exploded. "Might as well have left it out altogether. How come we are buried back so far?"

The answer was there in black and white: Besides what we had accomplished, General U.S. Grant had accepted the surrender of Vicksburg at last, and in Gettysburg, Pennsylvania, a little town none of us had ever heard of, Robert E. Lee's push to take the war onto Northern soil had by heroic efforts been thwarted.

"Is that all it says about us?" Dobbs fussed, dripping grease from his bacon and hardtack sandwich onto the newsprint.

"'Fraid so," I agreed. "Seems Gettysburg and Vicksburg are more important stories than us."

"Humph!" Cochran pouted, fingering the nearly vanished scratch on his jaw. "I come nigh to gettin' my head blown off, and nobody takes no notice." He took some consolation from the fact that Sergeant Cate had boasted of skinning Old Bedford, but Cochran did not wave this in the sergeant's face, of course.

As for me, though the news for the Union cause was everywhere good, it gave my spirits only the smallest of lifts. There was still no word about the fate of my son; no amount of good news from the war could make up for that. More: The Rebs had been forced out of Middle Tennessee, but they still held the East, and I could not go home.

Worst of all: the letters from my Alcie gal—the perfumed epistles as dear to me as breath itself—stopped coming, and there was no wind from east of the Cumberlands to tell my why.

☀ CHAPTER 5 ☀

Camp Spear II
Late Summer 1863

Sunday as a day of rest had a peculiar meaning in the army. The Sabbath was the only day when no drill occurred and our duties were reduced to policing the camp and caring for the stock.

In the other hours that remained, we were allowed to recreate ourselves. Though gambling was officially forbidden, some men spent the entire day of relaxation with greasy, pasteboard rectangles playing bluff or challenging the monte bank or bucking the faro table. It seemed that some fellers had actually anticipated profiting from their enlistments and arrived at Camp Spear with all the accoutrements of gambling parlors. They had no difficulty finding lambs eager to be sheared either.

Others of us occupied our time reading, writing letters home, mending our clothing, or catching up on the laundry. There was at that time no chaplain for our regiment so Sunday services were not available in camp.

Now soldiers are not better and no worse than the run of the populace when it comes to spiritual matters. Those as were given to vice brought it with them to the army, and those of the Christian faith packed their beliefs along to enlistment too. It is true that many found their faith to be sorely challenged by their new surroundings and the temptations that come from being young and away from home.

I had just stabbed my thumb for the third time trying to darn the same sock. "Ouch," I muttered.

Melvin Long, newly made corporal, laughed at me. "You aren't cut out to be a seamstress, Jesse. Stick to mendin' saddles."

I inspected the drop of blood on the pad of the injured digit and agreed. With that I tucked needle and thread back into the cloth pouch called by the soldiers a housewife and announced, "Melvin, I am in need of something to take my mind off home."

"Card game?" he offered.

I shook my head. "I'm no gambler. I hate losing more than I like winning, so it's no fun for me."

"I already know you're not a drinkin' man, Jesse," Long acknowledged. "Well, it is Sunday. Care to go to church?"

"You mean we can?"

Melvin nodded. "Sure enough. Rosy Rosecrans made it a general order that any soldier who wants leave to attend services can have it. All we got to do is see the captain."

Visions of singing and good fellowship rose before me. "What are we waiting for? Let's see who else wants to go along."

We found Cochran and Dobbs trading haircuts. Cochran had been ordered by Sergeant Cate to do something about his straggly hair, said it might improve Cochran's shooting if he could see what he was aiming at.

Dobbs had already figured out that in an exchange with Cochran, one always made out better by receiving Cochran's contribution first. Otherwise Cochran could be very persuasive with reasons he could never pay you back. In this instance, Cochran had done a credible job of trimming Dobb's noggin. Aside from a few spikes that stuck up on his crown and the fact that his bangs marched uphill, it was not entirely without merit.

It was now time for the two to swap positions. Cochran took his position on a low round of pinewood.

"Care to go to church with us?" I asked. "Melvin says we can get passes to go into Nashville for services. He's off seeing the captain about it right now."

Dobbs scooted a three-legged stool close to Cochran's back.

Scrunching one of his long, spindly legs nearly to his chin, Dobbs contemplated the bushy thicket of hair as if surveying where best to attack it. He had a straight razor tucked in the pocket of his fatigue blouse. The other barbering tools lay near to hand. "Not up to me. Not 'less Cochran wants to wait on his haircut."

"I guess we'll pass, Jesse," Cochran said. "Gotta get cleaned up or Cate will have at me with the prunin' shears."

"I understand," I said.

Dobbs flourished a pair of scissors next to Cochran's ear and took a few practice snips of his hair.

"Ouch!" Cochran complained. "Cut 'em off—don't yank 'em out!"

"Sorry," Dobbs acknowledged. "Scissors must be dull. I'll use this other pair."

The second cutting tool applied to Dobbs had a similar result, except that while it would not cut hair, it did a fine job of nipping out a small piece of Cochran's ear.

"Great balls of fire!" Cochran spouted. "What are you playin' at?"

"Sorry," Dobbs repeated. "Must both be dull. I'll just touch 'em up a mite with the whetstone."

I passed him the stone, but in his present configuration as a human pretzel, Dobbs could not get purchase enough to sharpen the edge. He unfolded his limbs to stand upright, slipping in front of Cochran. "Won't take a second," he promised.

As Dobbs levered himself erect he somehow fumbled the whetstone and the two pairs of scissors. For an instant he looked like a juggler doing a particularly dangerous act. Then one after the other, he dropped all three implements.

The whetstone hit Cochran on the head. Both pairs of scissors fell point downward, impaling themselves in the top of the pine round, right between Cochran's legs. One of them pinned a scrap of trouser fabric to the wood.

Cochran blinked before yanking the scissors free. Standing up carefully, as if afraid to make any sudden moves, he eyed the razor still in Dobbs's pocket. "You know, Jesse, think I'll change my mind and go along with you to church. Guess I'll take my chances with Sergeant Cate after all."

There was time for us to get curried and combed and make it to the Cumberland Baptist Church of Nashville before the last verse of the opening hymn "My Faith Looks Up to Thee." Some of the parishioners looked askance at us as we entered. Two ladies whom we passed twitched their skirts aside, but little we thought of that.

The hymn singing continued through "Jesus, Lover of My Soul" and "Sweet Hour of Prayer," and then the pastor stood up to preach. My sweet meditations of home and family and our little country church vanished in an instant when the pastor began to speak, but for the sake of courtesy, we four remained in our places.

Pastor Bergman took for his text the deliverance of the Israelites from the grasp of Midian. "All the citizens of the sovereign state of Tennessee have an obligation to resist tyranny. Should we live like the unanointed Gideon, thrashing our wheat in secret so our oppressors do not steal from us? Shall we be forced to bow down in idol worship of the bearded pagan diety who sits on his throne in Washington?"

Murmurs of "No, no, never" echoed around the sanctuary, and we four received numerous piercing looks.

"The godless invaders," Bergman continued, "who would deny us our rights and despoil us of our property must be put down! They must and shall be expelled from our midst."

When he had finished at last, the congregation sang "There Is a Fountain Filled with Blood," but we left during the benediction.

"Well, Jesse," commented Melvin Long, "I don't think we'll be goin' back to their services."

"Naw," said Cochran. "There weren't none of them folks gonna invite us home to supper anyhow."

I returned to camp much sobered and worried about the outcome of the war. If the division of the country ran so deep, how could any side ever really win? Regardless of the result of battles, what could mend such a grievous breach? For how long even after the fighting stopped would the consequences of the rupture remain?

✳ ✳ ✳

Despite our hard knocks and long hours in the saddle on the Tullahoma campaign, our regiment lost but fifty men, who were killed, wounded, or captured. We felt real pert and proud of ourselves. Said Cochran, "They shoulda turned us loose. I woulda chased Old Bedford clean to the Gulf! I woulda kicked Braxton Bragg's behind clean to Mexico! I woulda—"

At this point Sergeant Cate interrupted by poking his head in the tent flap. "Fall in for fatigue duty. Turn to and police the camp. Cochran, me boyo, since you are in such fine fettle, you are elected for a special privilege: Draw a pick and fall in for road-building detail."

Cochran's groan and the smirks of the others at this statement were easily understood. When Camp Spear first received troops, it was no more than a bare field of dirt and brush. Different commanders determined to improve the surroundings according to their personal tastes. In the case of Colonel Minnis, it was resurfacing the dusty road that was the camp's main thoroughfare with cobblestone. Every day men were selected to haul, spread, shovel, and level chunks of limestone. Now in mid-July, the combination of sweltering heat and rock dust made road building a matter for regimental punishment details. Unfortunately for Cochran, there just were not enough men undergoing discipline to fill the labor company.

As the bugle sounded fatigue call, we formed ranks for the afternoon roll before being assigned the rest of the clean-up chores. It was at this lineup that Company F's replacements were introduced.

The single addition to our mess was a German recruit by the name of Johannes Blankenbeckler. He was swart, bullnecked, and as solidly cheerful of disposition as he was fractured of English. He was instantly rechristened Blanket, Cochran objecting that the German's other handle was too cumbersome.

Blankenbeckler grinned and agreed by saying, "Ja. Blanket iss goot. Easy to remember."

"Well, say then, friend Blanket," Cochran said, oozing good fellowship and camaraderie, "how'd you like to trade duty with me today? My lumbago is actin' up again, and I sure need the relief."

"Don't do it," Melvin Long warned the German. "Cochran is a beat. If he knows you are a soft touch, he'll be after you all the time, and he'll never pay you back neither."

Cochran's face was contorted between flashing his ingratiating smile at Blanket and giving Long looks sharper than any bayonet. The stitches on Long's chevrons had hardly clinched tight, but even so they already limited Cochran's response to the corporal's advice. "Come on, Blanket," Cochran pleaded. "What do you say?"

"I do not know what iss this soft touch, but I am new here and want to get along wit my new friends. I say ja, I will trade if da sergeant agrees."

When informed by Corporal Long of the proposed switch, Sergeant Cate surprised me. I thought he would insist that Blanket not be taken advantage of on his first day, but instead he agreed to the swap. In fact, he seemed rather pleased with the notion. "Sure, and a fine idea it is, too. Very well, Private Blanket, join the road crew by the flagpole. Cochran, come with me."

"Wait just a minute!" Cochran protested. "I smell a rat."

"I have just been notified," explained Cate, waving a slip of paper under Cochran's nose, "of the need for an additional fatigue party, and I bethought to send the new man. But as matters stand, it falls to you, Private Cochran."

"But what is it?"

Cate looked as innocent as new-fallen snow. "Did I not say? It's a funeral party."

If Cochran's moaning protest had been heard in Ohio before, his lament over this new situation likely roused sleepers in Canada.

The funeral to be conducted was of a horse, not a soldier. In the fight at the Skull Camp Bridge, more animals had been wounded than people, and of these, some had come away with festering sores. It took a week to carry them off. Cochran would be joining others in digging holes wide and deep enough to bury the fallen equine heroes. The corpses were dragged to the burial field by mule power, but once there, the graves had to be dug right next to each body so the corpses could be easily tumbled in. Given the ninety-five-degree heat and the fact that some of the horses had been in the field for a while, one can only imagine the horror that Cate's announcement produced in Cochran. But there was no way out. All of us had witnessed that he was the one who had suggested the swap.

As saddler, I was excused from most fatigue duty so as to get caught up with the necessary repairs to bridles and saddles. About five in the afternoon, my own business required me to visit the stores and draw some more leather and saddle soap. I deliberately adjusted my route to pass the funeral detail, taking care to stay upwind, of course.

Long quizzed me on my return. "Did you see Cochran? How was he gettin' on?"

"He was loving every minute of it," I reported. "Having a grand old time and shouting with excitement."

Corporal Long grabbed me by the arm. "Don't kid an old soldier, Jesse. What are you talkin' about?"

"It's the gospel truth," I maintained. "He was shouting 'Hurrah! Hurrah!'" But even my best poker face was not up to the occasion. "Well," I finally relented, laughing, "maybe he was leaving the *H* off his cheer. Truth be told, I think Private Cochran is trying to throw up his immortal soul!"

It was some time after Cochran had attempted to take advantage of Blankenbeckler and been outfoxed himself that Company F received one more additional recruit. This was John Quincy Hamilton III, age nineteen, who wasted no time in informing us that he was lately of Harvard University. He had only returned to his native Nashville to lend his dashing expertise to routing the Rebs. He was offended that there was no room in our tent for his two trunks of belongings and made several unkind remarks about the smell inside our home. Not that he was wrong, of course, but it seemed ungracious and lacking in tact for a newcomer to mention it.

I do not know what infraction Company F was guilty of so as to cause the colonel to favor us with Private Hamilton, but he was instantly a trial to all. If Cochran was a deadbeat and Dobbs a bad-luck Jonah, at least they were recognizable types, accepted and tolerated as such.

Hamilton was something else again. He was slender, vain, superior of attitude, and given to looking down his long, thin nose at all aspects of army life. Had he taken part in the grousing about the duty and the food, he might have had a chance for acceptance. But when every one in our mess felt that he was sneering at them as well . . .

So it became a kind of company pastime to give Hamilton plenty to be upset about.

On the very first day in camp, after drawing a uniform, it was every recruit's privilege to complain about how ill-fitting it was, how scratchy the tight collar was, how hot the wool jacket was, and so on. This response was expected and deemed commendable.

Not so from Private Hamilton. He brought a bespoke set of three uniforms—dress, undress, and fatigue—with him to the post. He held the tunic at arm's length as if it had lately been taken from a leper. Even worse, Hamilton set about criticizing the cut of everyone else's uniform: how sloppy we all looked, how unsoldierly. He concluded by saying that he would have his manservant take orders from each of us to supply made-to-order livery like his own by week's end. From the mirror gleam of his cavalier boots to the downturned, catfishlike set to his mouth, John Quincy Hamilton III was hated by one and all.

It was more than Cochran could bear, and this time he had Corporal Long's connivance in his scheming. Said Cochran to Hamilton, "You sure are right! Just look at Dodson there: grease marks on his trouser legs, tarnished cap badge . . . Jesse, you are a disgrace to the outfit. A disgrace! Ain't that so, Corporal?"

"Certainly is. Dodson, I'll bet you have even forgotten to put the shoeblackin' on your umbrella."

I hung my head in shame and remorse. "It's true, Corporal. Even worse, I don't know where I have mislaid it."

Hamilton's ears twitched. "Umbrella? No one informed me. I was not issued an umbrella. Why was I not issued one?"

Corporal Long looked shocked. "That quartermaster sergeant. How dare he shortchange you that a'way, and you a young gentleman of quality as you are. That is not to be tolerated! You march right back to that sharper and demand that he furnish you with your umbrella at once."

Being slighted did not square with Hamilton's opinion of himself.

Moreover, correcting the failings of someone he thought of as a clerk was securely in his brief as a rising member of society. Hamilton set out immediately to amend the wrong he had suffered. The rest of our mess trooped along to the supply depot to watch the fun.

Now the quartermaster sergeant bore more than a passing physical resemblance to a red-bearded grizzly bear. In addition, his usual demeanor was like to a bear also, only not as friendly.

Hamilton's life was in jeopardy, though he did not recognize his danger. Crossing Sergeant Jasper was always chancy, but it was particularly so when Hamilton called, pushing through a crowd of men to the head of the line and demanding Jasper's attention. Sergeant Jasper had only just been informed that instead of going off duty, he must attend to the mustering-in needs of two new and unexpected companies of troops. Also, Sergeant Jasper had partaken too freely of medicinal spirits on the previous evening, and he was experiencing a disturbance inside his head like all the church bells of Nashville ringing at once.

"Sergeant," Hamilton said politely enough.

"Get back in line," Jaspser growled without looking up.

"Sergeant," Hamilton tried again louder, "this will take just a moment."

To Jasper's credit, he tried to ignore Hamilton, showing his irritation only in the force with which he slammed a pile of clothing down on the counter and snarled, "Next!"

Then Hamilton made a fatal misjudgment. He snapped his fingers at Jasper, as no doubt he was in the habit of doing with inattentive waiters. "Sergeant!" he said imperiously. *Snap! Snap!* "You have made a mistake that must be corrected at once."

I do not know which aspect of this speech most infuriated Jasper—the imputation of an error or the demand by a lowly recruit that something be done immediately. Peering around the doorframe or peeping in the window, Cochran, Long, Dobbs, and I saw Jasper momentarily stunned into silence. It was like slapping a bull on the nose. The very temerity of it surprised the quartermaster sergeant, but as Cochran once remarked, the only safe way to slap Sergeant Jasper was with a sledgehammer.

419

In any case, here is what happened. Jasper gave a bellow that would have done credit to either bull or bear. Then, slamming his fist down on the counter, he broke the wooden planks in two, spilling a hundred pairs of trousers on the floor. The foremost recruits in line backed up and trampled on those behind while all men fled to get outside.

Hamilton was left confronting Jasper from three feet away. I tend to think that John Quincy Hamilton III may have had some reservations about going ahead with his complaint. Indeed, the rest of us wondered if *we* had gone too far.

"Now!" roared Jasper. "You have my full attention. What did you say you wanted?"

Hamilton cleared his throat with an audible quaver, but we grudgingly conceded that he did not shrink back as much as we expected.

To Dobbs I whispered, "I'd be heading back toward Harvard by now."

"Me too," Dobbs agreed. "When I see a runaway locomotive comin' toward me, I always skedaddle!"

"I did not receive my government-issue umbrella, and I want it," John Quincy Hamilton III stated.

"Your what?!" Jasper bellowed.

"Umbrella. You failed to supply me with an umbrella."

It was truly amazing to see how fast a three-hundred-pound man like Quartermaster Sergeant Jasper could move. Before any of us could blink, Jasper leaped for Hamilton's throat. Only the fact that the sergeant's feet tangled in the heap of trouser legs saved Hamilton from destruction.

Red beard flying over his shoulder like a regimental battle flag, Jasper landed with the force of a brick chimney blown over in a high wind. He most certainly would have crushed the life out of Hamilton, had he connected.

But Hamilton's determination had dissolved just in time. As Jasper came crashing down, John Quincy Hamilton III squirted out the door of the supply depot and ran for it.

"Most likely a track-and-field star at Harvard," Melvin Long remarked.

"Think he'll be back for his umbrella?" Dobbs wanted to know.

Cochran shook his head. "If I was him and I thought I would ever have to face Sergeant Jasper again . . ."

"Yeah?"

"I'd sooner go naked for all three years of my enlistment."

✻ ✻ ✻

"Jesse, pour me a skosh of coffee, will you?" Melvin Long suggested at supper one evening.

"You dunderheaded ninny, Dobbs!" Sergeant Cate shouted the next day on the target range. "Put your thumb down when you squeeze that trigger! You came within a skosh of putting your own eye out!"

"Hurry up, will you, Cochran?" I demanded on fatigue. "If you don't move a skosh faster shifting that tack we won't get finished before reveille tomorrow!"

It seemed that when the boredom of camp life became too great, one of the unacknowledged pastimes was making up or using new-fangled words. *Skosh* became a jack-of-all-words, meaning "a little, a small amount of anything." No one ever claimed to have made it up or even to have heard it somewhere else; it just made its appearance in camp and within two days was in common use.

After our rebuff at the local church a while back, the search for a meaningful way to fill our Sundays continued. Since I still woke up early, I always had a bit of time to myself to think on the services back home and to pray for Alcie and the young'uns. But the rest of the day it was hard to think on anything spiritual, what with all the goings-on in the camp. To card playing and the homely occupations of time off duty was added dime novels.

"Hey, Cochran," Dobbs demanded, "ain't you finished with the *Gold Fiend* yet?"

"Just a skosh," Cochran replied. "Here, look at this new one I got over to the sutler's."

"What is it?"

"A real gimcrack! See: *East and West, A Daring Adventure by Land and Sea*."

"All right," Dobbs acknowledged. "Give it here."

Into this stifled atmosphere strode Private Hamilton. Only a week had passed since the quartermaster sergeant had rubbed some of the shine off Hamilton's upturned nose. In that time the college student had sulked and by refusing to laugh at himself had put even more distance between himself and the rest of us.

His arrival this Sunday afternoon was different. He had a spring in his step, and he looked around eagerly. Behind him was another young man, this one in the uniform of a parson.

Hamilton focused on our little group and came directly toward us. "Ah, Dobbs, Cochran, Blanket, Dodson, and Long, I want you to meet a dear and distinguished friend of mine . . . the Reverend Morris Larson."

We all stood and dusted ourselves off, shuffling in an embarrassed fashion because of our relaxed dress. Cochran thrust the two yellow-jacketed novels into Blanket's hands behind his back, and Long nudged a pack of cards under the tent flap with the toe of his boot. We mumbled greetings.

Hamilton continued, "Morris—I mean Reverend Larson—is an old college chum of mine. We met most providentially, and he agreed to accompany me back to camp." He paused to let a gaze of deep concern linger on the face of each of us. "I want you all to know that I recognize how bad a start I got off to, but I wish to make amends. Realizing how hungry you are for spiritual nourishment, I have prevailed upon Reverend Larson to preach to us today."

"Truly?" I said at this unexpected development. "This is real kind, Reverend. You may have heard that we were not exactly made to feel welcome in the Nashville churches."

"Shocking!" Larson announced with a look of righteous indignation. "To deny you of spiritual consolation in your hour of need."

"There's just one thing," Hamilton said smoothly. "I have not yet approached Captain Briant to ask his permission to assemble the men, and in fact I don't feel that I am the one to do so. But if a deputation such as you five would go, I am certain he could have no objection."

I confess that I had some misgivings at this point, but Cochran and the others were so instantly enthusiastic that I felt guilty for my lack of eagerness to join it.

In any case, within fifteen minutes we had petitioned the captain for permission to muster the men for a sermon. Larson promised that it would be rousing and uplifting. True to our promise to Hamilton, he was not present at the officer's tent, nor was he credited with having sponsored the notion.

"Fall in for sermon," was the unusual command that followed the bugle-calling assembly.

We lined up in ranks facing the flagpole while the Reverend Larson mounted a wagon bed from which to address us.

"Men," Captain Briant began, "I know you will be pleased to give your attention to this man of God who has graciously come to share his spiritual insights with us. And I know you will also want to express your gratitude to those of your comrades who arranged this event: Long, Dobbs, Cochran, Blankenbeckler, and Dodson. And now, Reverend Larson."

Larson stepped forward, and then oddly seemed overcome with the gaze of the crowd. He appeared speechless, even thunderstruck.

"What's the matter, Parson?" called out some unknown in the crowd. "Can't you preach?"

"Can't I preach!" Larson roared. "I know this book from lid to lid! From Generation to Revolution! For the whangdoodle mourned for her firstborn and fleeth to Mount Hepsidam!"

That was all the farther he got, for an outraged Captain Briant started toward the impostor only one step in advance of us. The fictitious parson had his escape well planned, however, and sprinted ahead of our vengeance to exit on horseback from the camp.

The damage was already done. The five of us were each given three days' punishment for improper conduct. We were made to stand atop cracker boxes on one leg. Of course, the soldiers' code forbade us from laying the blame on Hamilton.

Worse even than the punishment were the reactions of the rest of our company. The other Christians were embarrassed and chagrined at the mockery, while the routinely profane found the whole thing a great lark . . . not at all the kind of witness we would have wanted.

Only the stoical Blankenbeckler seemed unfazed. He looked up from a thin red volume he was reading and observed, "In dis world you will troubles have. Sometimes a skosh more, sometimes a skosh less."

⁂CHAPTER 6⁂

McMinn County
September 1863

F or six weeks, from July to mid-August 1863, our regiment
drilled, rode guard along train tracks from Nashville to
Murfreesboro, drilled, went on scouting expeditions toward
Sparta, drilled, chased a false report that Old Bedford was moving toward Kentucky, and drilled. And in our spare time we . . .
drilled again.

Meanwhile, the war seemed at a stalemate. Bobby Lee had been
tossed out of Pennsylvania but was then allowed to escape unmo-
lested back to Virginia. Cochran said that the goggle-eyed General
Meade, who had stopped the Rebs at Gettysburg, had gone and
caught "Federal commander disease": the slows. Somehow it seemed
that no Union general was ever able to put two victories together
back-to-back.

By August 15 Camp Spear was so completely surfaced with cobblestones that its streets were in better repair than those of Nashville
proper. 'Course, truth be told, some of those selfsame cobblestones
had once graced Nashville's streets before being midnight requisi-
tioned.

When we finally got a true report of General Forrest's whereabouts, it like to broke my heart: He made his new headquarters
at Kingston, east of the Cumberlands and thirty miles *north* of my
home near Athens. Much was made of how the Rebs were now on

the defensive and how Rosy was getting ready to hit them again somewhere. But all the idle speculation chafed me. I still had no word of the location of my son and no news from my home.

Then, just when the inactivity of camp life and the anxiety over my family were about to make me despair, something happened. Colonel Minnis sent for Captain Briant to ride over to regimental headquarters to confer. In about an hour Briant was back, and though it was nearly supper he ordered the bugler to sound assembly. Here is what we heard.

"Men," he said, "General Rosecrans is ready to move again. This time we are going to boot the secesh out of Chattanooga and maybe out of Tennessee altogether."

There was a rousing cheer at this. In one instant, all the terrors of the Tullahoma campaign and all the tedium of Camp Spear were forgotten. Victory and glory were once more the order of the day.

When the shouting died, Briant continued, "The Third Regiment is to remain in Nashville, guarding the supply lines from here southward."

426

An audible groan swept over the ranks. What had been excitement changed again to gloom. In fact, the despondency was even deeper when it sank in that the rest of the army would be on the move but not us.

That was the moment at which Corporal Long nudged me and nodded toward Briant's face. The captain was wearing a sly smile rather than a scowl or frown. "He knows somethin' he's not tellin'," Long avowed.

"However," Briant acknowledged at last, "the guard duty will not include Company F. The colonel has asked and I have agreed that we should be temporarily assigned to General Crittenden's corps as scouts. Every man is to draw three days' rations. We leave tomorrow at dawn."

If the earlier cheers were enthusiastic, the later news produced an outburst that was deafening. Hats and haversacks were tossed in the air. Cochran, not content with pitching his own hat in the air, seized Blanket's and threw his skyward as well.

When the assembly was dismissed, Captain Briant sought me out and drew me aside for a word. "Jesse, what I am about to say will not become public knowledge for some days yet, so keep it to yourself. But since it concerns you personally, I wanted you to hear it at once."

Worries buzzed around my head like the cloud of horseflies around the stable. Chief among them was that I was to be left behind. "I know the other outfits need help with their tack, but Franks over in Company D has the makings of a fine saddler. Can't you get him?"

Briant laughed and shook his head. "Not that. Just the opposite, in fact. General Rosecrans wants to keep the Confederates guessing as to which direction the attack on Chattanooga will come from. Part of Crittenden's force, including our troop, is to cross the Cumberland toward the Hiwassee River. And that means—"

"Athens! My home . . . my farm?"

"The same," Briant agreed. "If all goes well, you'll see your place again in no more than two weeks."

Home. I had dreamed of it so often. Prayed for Alcie and the children. Worried about them. Soon I would know what was happening. If the ones I loved most in the world were all right. And if Alcie had heard anything else about William.

427

Setting out in company with a troop known as Minty's Horse, we were the advance guard of General Crittendon's Twenty-first Army Corps. We first contacted the enemy that same day, a party of opposing cavalrymen who were raiding near Sparta.

There followed three days of running fights, first along Wildcat Creek and later up into the reaches of Calfkiller Creek. We were pushing the Rebs back east over the mountains but at considerable loss to ourselves.

The skirmishes fell into a pattern: The Rebs would show themselves, fire a couple of volleys, and then fall back. When we pursued, dismounted sharpshooters would blaze away at us from ambush until we stopped to surround and eliminate each one. Every time we halted on account of one Reb, the main body would draw off in perfect safety and set up to do the whole thing over again.

On August 18, Company F was proceeding cautiously up a draw

to the southeast of Calfkiller Creek when we came under sniper fire. The stream wound out of a brush-choked canyon between two hillsides strewed with boulders and dotted with oak and hickory trees.

We were riding in a skirmish line across about a quarter mile of hillside in advance of the main body of the troop. We had seen Rebs about a half hour earlier, and some of them had gone up this draw. Long and I were near the center of our line.

"Look sharp," Long cautioned everyone. "There is plenty of cover hereabouts for bushwhackers."

We had not ridden more than another fifty feet before the crack of a rifle split the morning, and Long was knocked backward out of his saddle. His horse bolted and fled.

"Dismount! Dismount!" Sergeant Cate yelled. "Use your mounts as cover."

I looped the reins of the bay I was riding over a fallen limb and knelt beside Long. "Ah, Jesse," my friend sputtered through clenched teeth, "it hurts like blazes."

"Where are you hit, Melvin?"

"My arm . . . look for me, will you, Jesse? I think he shot it clean off."

Long's left arm hung limp, and blood pumped from a ragged hole in his sleeve. I whipped off the strap from his carbine and used it to make a tourniquet around his upper arm. Then I dragged him behind a rock. As I did so, another lead slug flew past and plowed a furrow in the leaf mold near my boot. "Take it easy, Melvin," I urged him, trying to sound calm. "I'll be back for you in a minute."

When he did not respond, I saw that he had fainted.

"Sergeant," I yelled, "Long is hit bad . . . needs help."

My voice drew a third round from the sniper, clipping rock splinters just above my head.

Cate shouted, "Anybody see where those shots are coming from?" Nobody replied.

Minutes passed without another cartridge being fired.

"Dobbs," Cate ordered, "when I yell, you, me, and Hamilton are going to move to that next clump of trees. Keep low and keep your horse between you and the hill. The rest of you, cover us."

I eased around the corner of the boulder and rested my Sharps in a crevice. Swinging the muzzle back and forth like the nose of a questing hunting dog, I attempted to aid my friends. But how could I when I had no idea where the sniper was located?

Cate shouted, and the three men burst from concealment to advance farther up the canyon. They had not covered more than a dozen feet before the Reb rifle boomed again and Dobbs's horse screamed, reared, and plunged over backward. We all sprayed the slope with return fire but blindly and without noticeable effect. Dobbs scurried behind an oak, and the other two dove to the ground.

"Where is he?" Cate demanded again. "Anybody see that time?"

There was still no response.

Cate swore. "We're gonna get picked off one at a time this way!"

I studied the hillside. Trees, rocks, and brush all provided some cover, but there was only one likely spot I could see. Halfway up the incline was the stump of a hickory tree, as big around as a dining table and about table height. If it was hollow as well, the Reb sniper might be inside it. I watched carefully but saw no movement.

"Blanket!" Cate yelled. "Move up!"

Private Blanket obeyed the command, but he was sensible about it. He drew his revolver and fired across his horse's back as he ran. When he had discharged all six rounds he jerked the horse down in a shallow depression in the earth and lay behind it. His sprint attracted another bullet that would have parted his hair had he not flopped down exactly when he did.

I had seen what I expected, but in the barest blink of an eye. At the instant of Blanket's rush, a brown-haired figure dressed in gray rose from inside the hickory stump, drew a bead, and fired. Then the sniper ducked down again, out of sight and protected.

He was visible for only a split second, and his perch gave him command of all the approaches to his nest. Every time he fired, he knew a charge was coming, and he stood erect and shot.

I lined up the blade sight of my carbine on the stump and reminded myself to adjust for the elevation. Firing uphill makes most shots go high. I could not afford to miss, because once he knew his hideaway was discovered, the Reb would sneak out to another, and the deadly game of hide-and-seek would continue. I could not even call out to my comrades for fear the sniper would hear and move.

So I waited.

"Dodson," Cate ordered, "move up."

What to do now? I could see from the positions of my friends that I was the only one with a clear line of fire. Snatching my cap from my head, I reached out for a nearby stick. I mounted the hat on the dead limb, this without moving the Sharps or taking my eye from the sight. Then I bellowed, "Now!" at the top of my lungs and thrust the cap aloft. A second later my headgear went spinning away toward the creek, and the Sharps bucked in my hands.

I studied the hickory stump for a long, long time. Then I stood carefully upright.

"Did you get him, Jesse?" Dobbs called.

Shrugging, I turned away to see to Melvin Long.

"Did you get him?" Dobbs repeated.

"He never come up no more," I said simply. "Go get the sergeant, will you? Melvin is in need of help."

Melvin Long was lucky, as lucky as anybody can be who has just been shot. Minié balls, being soft lead and about the size of the end of my thumb, had a terrible effect on bones they hit. Limbs were usually so shattered that taking them off was the only hope of saving a feller's life.

Long's arm wound was clean through the meat, without touching the bone. Once we got the bleeding stopped, he was patched up and sent back to Nashville. In the meantime, I was made acting corporal of the outfit. Others were not so lucky; thirty troopers of other units were killed dead or died soon after being bushwhacked on the Calfkiller or in the fight outside Bon Air.

Despite the losses inflicted on us and the other troopers of Minty's Horse, we pushed the Reb cavalry back over the Cumberlands and stood on the summit ourselves.

Captain Briant took special care to explain to us what was afoot.

"General Rosecrans has two corps to attack Chattanooga from the south, but he doesn't want Bragg to know it just yet. Us and the rest of Crittenden's corps are to make a big show of crossing the mountains north of Chattanooga and make the Rebs think this is the direction of the attack."

"And then what happens?" Sergeant Cate drawled.

Briant paused and reflected. He rubbed a grimy hand over his high forehead and picked an oak twig out of his burnsides. "Either Bragg will send his boys out to fight us and Rosy pounces on Chattanooga, or Bragg gets scared and calls his troops in from East Tennessee to help defend the city. If he calls them back, we retake East Tennessee from the secesh, and then both our columns squeeze Chattanooga like a nutcracker."

We knew from captured snipers that we had been fighting members of Dibrell's Horse, a local unit of secesh Middle Tennessee boys. But east of the mountains were regular Confederate troops.

"Who are we squaring off with tomorrow?" I asked.

"Can't say for certain," Briant admitted. "But we heard tell Forrest was headquartered in Kingston."

Forrest again! Kingston was the first town of any size we would encounter once we descended the slope.

Five days later, after a careful passage over the mountains but no more fighting, we discovered that Rosy's strategy had worked. Bragg had called his forces back toward Chattanooga as far as Loudon on the Knoxville and Chattanooga railroad. We rode into Kingston unopposed, except for a few small boys who spit on our shadows as we passed.

And there were not many of those incidents either. If Nashville regarded Yankee troops as invaders and Tennesseans who wore the blue as turncoats, often the situation was reversed here. We were looked upon as liberators, only quietly or even slyly.

Private Cochran and I were scouting ahead of the main body along the west bank of the Tennessee River. We found a small cross-roads settlement, searched it for Rebs, then turned back to report.

"'Scuse me, Granny," Cochran said to an elderly woman smoking a corncob pipe under an elm tree. "Can we water our horses from your well?"

Loudly she hollered, "You blue-bellied snakes think you can come in here and take all our possessions and make free with our belongings! You must ride on outta here and go off and get yourselves shot!"

"Granny," Cochran said, baffled at the vehement outburst, "we don't want to take nothing; we just want to water our horses a skosh is all."

Underneath her breath the silver-haired woman muttered, "Swear at me."

"What?"

"Go on—do it," she hissed. "Cuss me and tell me you'll take whatever you please."

I tumbled into the scheme at once. "Get away with you, you old crone!" I berated her harshly. "You skinny scarecrow of a no-good Rebel. We are going to water our horses and take whatever we've a mind to. Get back in the house, and if you're lucky, you won't get hurt."

Slipping her a wink, I reined my horse toward the pump at the side of the house.

Granny returned with a flutter of eyelashes and said softly, "God bless you, boys! Be safe."

"What was all that about?' Cochran demanded when we were out of sight of the main road. "Is she teched?"

I nodded and grinned. "Like a fox. The Rebs have held this part of the state for two years. Granny knows that to curry favor some of her neighbors would run and tell Old Bedford about how she willingly aided Yankee troopers."

"Woof!" Cochran acknowledged. "She's a sly old bird!" Then an unpleasant notion struck him. "Wait a minute! That means she thinks Old Bedford may not be really gone . . . that maybe we didn't kick him out for good!"

I dropped my chin and gave Cochran my best schoolmaster look. "You get a star on your composition this day, Cochran. Yes, indeed."

✳ ✳ ✳

General Crittenden's corps was putting on a great show, marching and countermarching and generally acting like there were three times

more of them than there really were. When we went into camp for
the night, every mess of eight men built three campfires, so as to convince any onlookers of the mighty host that was coming upon Chattanooga from the north. 'Course since it was so warm still, we ended
up sleeping way back from those fires. Men actually volunteered to
go on picket duty to get out of camp and cool off.

South of Kingston, the Tennessee River was the dividing line
between our forces and the Rebels. We kept to the west bank, the
secesh to the east. Now that we were across the mountains, the cavalry's job as the eyes of the army was more important than ever. Even
though the Twenty-first Corps was the feint and not the real assault,
it still made up one-third of Rosecrans's Army of the Cumberland. It
would not do to get pounced on unawares.

Wherever we could ford the river, and in late summer there were
plenty of places, we struck across into Rebel territory. We scouted
toward Loudon and Philadelphia and finally, on August 28, toward
Athens. Once across the river we would range as much as twenty
miles inside enemy territory.

Captain Briant cautioned us. "Men, I can't tell you the reason just
yet, but we have got something real important to do. We don't know
where Old Bedford is right now. He may still be up Loudon way, or
he may have already pulled back toward Charleston. We need information about troop movements and intentions. Corporal Dodson?"

"Yes, sir," I responded.

"This is your home ground, is it not?"

I nodded.

"If there are any little-used paths or deserted cabins that you
know about, I'd like you to point them out on the maps to Sergeant
Cate and me. We may need a bolthole before we get back. What do
you say?"

"Captain," I said, "I can go you one better than that. I been thinking about it for a day now. If you'll detail me a couple of men to ride
with me as far as Tellico Junction, I'll get you all the news you need."

When I had explained myself to the captain, he drew me aside
and tried to dissuade me. "If you are captured in civilian clothes,
you can be shot or hanged as a spy. No one is asking you to do this.

Why not guide the whole troop where we can make a fight of it if we have to?"

"Captain," I said, "we'd still be outnumbered, and it's a long way back to the river. 'Sides, I know folks who will talk if they aren't scared of being seen talking to Yankees." I did not think it the right time to tell Captain Briant of the price on my head as a Confederate deserter. It might have put him off my idea, and I was as anxious for news of home as I was concerned about Old Bedford.

"All right," Briant agreed. "Do you want volunteers, or have you got some men in mind?"

Blanket, Cochran, and Dobbs stepped forward.

"These are the ones I was going to ask for," I said. To my surprise, Hamilton stepped forward as well.

"Very well," Briant concluded. "Leave as soon as you're ready and be back here by tomorrow night."

About a mile above Tellico Junction there was an abandoned gristmill on the bank of Walden's Creek. I did not think anyone would have put the mill back into operation in those troubled times, and we could use the place to lay up by day. That's where our squad made for, arriving just past midnight.

"No lights," Dobbs hissed after reconnoitering up ahead. "I listened for a time, and I didn't hear nothin' either."

An owl hooted from the branches of a sweet gum, but no other sound could be heard except for the trickle of water over stones.

"Tie up the horses below the lip of the creek bank, just behind the mill," I said. "That way they'll be out of sight but handy to the back door."

We settled on the floor inside the mill and watched the stars pinwheel in the sky through the space of missing shingles. We dared not make a fire, so drank cold coffee out of our canteens and ate a cold supper of hardtack and cheese.

"Why do you not go to da postmaster's place now?" Blanket asked. "Why for daylight wait?"

"Ferguson may have folks staying over with him," I explained. "It'll look more natural if I come in when the sun is up than if I sneak in this time of night. You fellers just wait on me here."

"How long should we wait?" Cochran asked.

"If I'm not back one hour after sundown," I instructed, "you three hightail it back to camp."

"What'll we tell the captain?" Dobbs asked.

Shrugging, I replied, "Tell him I failed."

✳ ✳ ✳

Early in the morning, before the rays of the sun had outlined the highest leaves of the sweet gum, I swapped my uniform for a pair of overalls and a flannel shirt. I knotted a blue-and-white-checked kerchief around my throat and pulled a tattered straw hat well down on my head. The addition of a pair of down-at-the-heels, out-at-the-toes work boots completed my transformation.

Only Blanket was awake, on watch. The other two were tucked behind the millstones, Dobbs hugging the base of the grain hopper. "You want I should wake them?" Blanket asked.

"Naw, let 'em sleep. Just keep alert for trouble," I said. "Now that the owl has gone to bed, give an ear to that 'baccy bird across the hollow. If he stops singing sudden-like, it'll either be me coming back or somebody you don't want to meet."

"What iss a 'baccy bird?"

"Just listen a skosh," I instructed. "Hear that? Tobacco bird . . . 'baccy bird, we calls 'em. He says, 'Merrily we chew . . . merrily we chew.'"

East Tennessee humor was lost on Blanket.

"Never mind then. Just watch sharp if he stops saying that!"

I could be disguised, but there was no hiding a U.S. cavalry horse. I had no time to requisition a mule or some other homely local critter, so I walked the two miles to Tellico Junction.

There was no light showing at the front of Ferguson's place, but a trickle of smoke from the chimney at the back told me R. J. was up and getting his breakfast. I circled to the kitchen door and called in my most backwoods tone, "Yo, Mistuh Ferguson, is you at home?"

There was silence from within till I repeated my call, and then an elaborate throat-clearing vibrated the tools hanging on the wall beside the door. A rumbling cough mixed with a forceful snort put one in mind of a drowning bullfrog, if such a thing can be imagined. It was R. J. and no mistake. "Who's that callin' out yonder?" he inquired.

"Just me, Mistuh Ferguson . . . Ahab Trafalger."

"Ahab Traf . . . R. J. sputtered. Then to my great relief, he said nothing to give the game away. The screen door creaked open, and a spindly arm extended through the crack. "Well, Ahab, come on in. Haven't seen you in a coon's age. Set a spell and have some coffee."

I stepped into R. J.'s kitchen and asked nonchalantly, "Anybody else about? John Dixon mayhap or Jesse Dodson?"

"No one 'cept the cavalry officer sleepin' upstairs," R. J. said with a significant raise of his bushy eyebrows. "He's passin' through McMinn County, looking for deserters. His men is out in my barn right now."

So my instincts and a gracious God had kept me from a disaster! What would my story have been had I waltzed into Tellico in the middle of the night?

R. J. leaned his head close to my ear and hissed, "What are you doin' here, Jesse? The woods from Niota to Noneberg is crawling with Rebs!" Then in a louder tone he remarked, "You still runnin' 'shine up the Hiwassee?"

"And how!" I agreed forcefully. "Them army fellers is a right thirsty bunch." Then I murmured, "I've had no letters for months! How's Alcie and my babies?"

"It's bad, Jesse," R. J. whispered back. "Reb cavalry has run off all your stock and cleaned out your larder. Alcie is just scrapin' by." He almost blew my eardrum out when, without warning, he shouted, "You'll be wantin' sour mash then, Ahab?"

"Can I see her?" I pleaded softly. "Is it safe for me to visit?"

But R. J. didn't answer that question. Instead he continued loudly, "Too bad you don't have a supply of 'shine with you to sell hereabouts, Ahab. Lots of troopers hereabouts, up to Athens and so forth. Why, there's even a mess of them camped on Jesse Dodson's place . . . and more of 'em comin' down from the north every day."

The creak of the stairs out in the store warned that someone was indeed coming down. To seem as relaxed as possible, R. J. and I picked up our coffee cups and wandered out of the kitchen and into the store. I got the shock of my life . . . all the accumulated debris of generations was gone! Even the fishnet and the ladies' unmentionables.

"Yes, sir," R. J. remarked conversationally. "It sure is fine havin' so many of our brave boys around here. Why they think of uses for almost anything . . . even made springs for their cots out of old corsets!"

A pair of riding boots and pant legs of faded and indeterminate pale blue stomped into view from above. These were followed by a saber tip bouncing unsheathed from step to step and then the sleeve braid and collar tabs of a first lieutenant, Confederate cavalry. The short, beady-eyed officer was bald to about the middle of his head, but wore his remaining brown hair long and shaggy and tucked haphazardly behind his ears. "Well, Mister Ferguson, who might this be?"

"Ah, Lieutenant Clark, this here is old Ahab from up Hiwassee way."

"You look able-bodied," Clark asserted. "Why aren't you in the army?"

Why not, indeed? What could I say to this suspicious little man?

"Say, Ahab," R. J. interrupted. "What was you telling me about Yankees over on Walden's Ridge?"

Bless R. J. Ferguson! If there was one thing this Reb officer could profit from more than a hillbilly recruit, it was information about the enemy! "Yessuh," I avowed. "Powerful number of Blue bellies sweepin' over the hogback."

His attention diverted, Lieutenant Clark demanded, "How many is a powerful number . . . one regiment . . . two? More?"

"Oh, my stars, Captain," I said, deliberately raising his rank, "there's a tremendous more than that. Must be forty or fifty thousand men the other side of the river. And horses! Ten thousand cavalry if they's a dozen. And such guns! Why Joshua would not have needed no trumpets if he'd a'had sech guns! Yessuh, nothin' gonna stop them Yankees short of Chattanooga."

"By thunder, General Forrest will give them a tune to dance to!" Clark declared. But for all his bravado and pride in his commander, Clark still looked ready to dash off and report. "Much obliged for the

437

lodging, Mister Ferguson. Duty calls!" The lieutenant strode out into the morning, yelling loudly for his sergeant to saddle up; they were to move out at once!

When we were alone, R. J. said, "I'm right sorry, Jesse, but I guess you got the gist of what I was tryin' to tell you before. Alcie's got a rough row to hoe and no mistake, but there's no way you can get over there to see her. Not now—no way."

"It's all right, R. J.," I said. "When you see her, tell her I'm nearby and that I will see her soon."

✳ ✳ ✳

Despite my concern about getting back across the river, I could not leave Tellico Junk right away. My disguise might work from a distance or in the early light of day but would not fool anyone who knew me. If a neighbor recognized me, I would be putting myself and perhaps my family in danger.

So I holed up with R. J. most of the day. He fed me and filled me with tales of Reb foraging and how any antislavery sentiment was likely to get a man arrested. Three times during my visit he hid me in the cellar when folks came calling, then drew me out after the danger passed.

Finally I could not stand to wait any longer. Truth was, I feared that my troop would be getting antsy over my continued absence and might do something stupid.

So with the sun still a handsbreadth above the hills, I took my leave of Tellico Junk. Although I was concerned for Alcie and the children, I had learned that they were still all living, and my joining the Union side had not caused them to be put off the farm. I had also gotten the information the army needed: Rebel General Bragg was pulling his troops south from the upper reaches of the Tennessee River and having them fall back toward Chattanooga.

Now to get back across the river to safety.

I sauntered casually along the main road till I came to where the dim outline of the disused wagon track branched off toward the mill. Passing by the turn without so much as a glance in that direction, I continued on a ways before pausing. Loitering in the shadow under an oak for a spell, I kept an eye on things till I was convinced there was no one watching me.

When I got to the knoll in the bend of the creek below the mill, I stopped and gave a bobwhite whistle to let my friends know that I was coming in. It came to me that Dobbs might be on guard, and this might be the one occasion when he would actually hit what he was aiming at.

Instead of Dobbs it was Hamilton at sentry. He waved me in without a word and continued his watch.

"How'd it go?" Cochran demanded. "Any trouble? Can we head back now?"

"Simmer down," I told him. "Everything's fine, but we can't leave before dark. You know that."

"Sorry," he said. "I'm just all nerved up since those horsemen came by."

"What horsemen?"

Blanket explained. "Reb. Joost thirty minutes ago. I was on guard when harness jingle I hear . . . I think maybe three or four riders."

"Did they see you?"

The German shook his head emphatically. "They did not come so far up as da mill. I only catch a glimpse of them down at da ford below. Three mounted men, like I figger."

"Where did they go?"

"Up da gully acrost da creek, und then I lose them in da trees."

My mind was racing. It could be Lieutenant Clark and his men, or it could be another Reb patrol altogether. Either way, they had passed entirely too close to our hiding place for my liking, and it was not yet sundown.

There was nothing to do but wait, but I wasted no time in shucking the disguise and getting back into my uniform. Lieutenant Clark struck me as one who would be real pleased to hang a spy.

A few minutes later I went out to relieve Hamilton. "Anything?" I asked.

"Nope," he reported. "All real quiet."

He was too right . . . it was too quiet. "How long has it been since you last heard that 'baccy bird?"

There was not even time for him to reply before the unmistakable noise of approaching horses interrupted.

"Warn the others and then slip down to the bank," I ordered. "Keep our nags quiet and see that the cinches and bridles are all tight, case we have to make a dash for it."

Three riders appeared at the ford. They split apart on the far bank of the stream, with one rider remaining opposite the mill and the other two crossing and coming toward me. This looked for all the world like they had reason to be suspicious of the mill and were going to encircle it.

There was still a chance that they would look the place over and ride off. Because of the thick brush, even the rider on the far side could not get round the mill pond to where he could spot our horses. If everyone stayed real still and quiet . . .

But it was not to be. Hamilton, who had failed to note the signals of nature, could not keep himself in check any longer. His Sharps boomed, and the Reb across the creek whirled his mount and dashed behind the brush.

Our one chance now was to fight and win. If they got help, we were cooked. Dobbs and Cochran must have thought the same, because another carbine blasted out a window of the mill, and one of the riders bit the dust.

The two remaining Rebs returned the fire, booming away with dragon pistols. When the man on my side of the creek shouted across, I could tell by his voice that it was Lieutenant Clark. He called for the other feller to join him, and the trooper jumped his mount into the creek.

Midway over there was another shot fired from the mill, and the horse flinched and dumped the rider into the water. Clark triggered off one more round that smashed through the rotten boards of the mill, then swung his roan to flee. Two shots followed him, but neither took effect.

Just that quickly the Reb officer was around the bow of the creek bed and out of our view.

My first thought was *Good riddance, and we will vamoose too.* But it would not serve; I had no way of knowing how close reinforcements were. Clark had to be stopped.

Digging my boot toes into the dirt bank with short, chopping steps, I sprinted toward the top of the knoll. I reached the low peak in the center of the horseshoe curve just as Clark circled it below me.

My leap from the summit was not an elegant dive. In point of fact, I plunged into the air feetfirst. Effectiveness substituted for grace, though, when my boots struck the Reb officer in the shoulders, and we tumbled to the sand in a heap. His pistol boomed once more and went spinning away.

Clark was a game little Reb. Even knocked half silly and with me atop him when we hit, he was still trying to draw his saber when I brought my fists together on both sides of his head. That ended his resistance for the time.

By good fortune the reins of Clark's bay horse had tangled in some willows near the creek, and I caught him easily. By the time I toted the unconscious Reb back around the bend, Dobbs, Cochran, and Hamilton were saddled up and ready to ride. They had caught the other horse as well and had a Reb private tied into the saddle and gagged.

"Where's the third man?" I asked.

Dobbs shook his head. "Dead."

"All right then," I said. "Daylight or no, we can't wait around here to see who might have heard all the shooting . . . and we're taking these prisoners with us. Can't have this lieutenant asking around after someone of my description."

When we headed out, I led the troop across the creek, back across, then up the center a ways to throw off any pursuit. Next we rode hard up the slope between Tellico Junction and Athens till we came to where the dim outline of a deer rail forked.

"You go on up the west branch," I ordered the three men. "When you come to the summit there's a canyon on your right with water and cover enough to hole up in. Wait for me there."

"Where are you gonna be?" Hamilton demanded.

I pointed to the other fork in the thin path. "This curls around to a spot where I can look over our back trail. I want to see if anybody is following us. Now get along with you."

I had told the truth about the path I followed. It did give me a chance to study the ground back the way we had come. What I had left unsaid was of a more personal nature and no one's business but my own.

Reaching a place where the trees thinned and the game trail played out, I tied my horse to an oak. Bent low, I crept to the brow of the hill just as the sun was dropping behind Walden's Ridge. The last yellow light was washing out of the oaks below me, but it still lit the hayfield in the curve of the river.

My hayfield.

The crest on which I lay was just above my farm. It was to this very spot that I had brought Alcie when we were courting. I had stretched out my hand and waved it over an empty landscape and vowed to fill it with the good things of life and a place of our own.

Below me and across the stream stretched the pasture that I had not seen for months. The fences that divided the fields lined up with the dark green triangle of the late-summer garden. The arrow formed thereby pulled my eye to the barn and just beyond it to the white clapboard house with its climbing roses and surrounding porch.

My chest ached with the nearness of it . . . then Alcie stepped out on the porch. As though my presence had in some way called to her, she shaded her eyes and looked all around.

I wanted to jump upright, shout, wave, and caper! I wanted to run down the hill into her arms and never leave again! With a catch in my throat, I forced myself to lie still as two of my little ones ran to Alcie from the garden to clasp her about the knees.

Of the Confederate soldiers I caught no sign, yet their absence made things harder for me, not easier. The temptation to go to my loved ones was strong, yet I could not. Not yet.

Thank God the light faded then from her face and hair, veiling the nearness of my longing. When Alcie shooed the babies inside and reentered the house herself, I shook myself out of my trance and crept back to my horse, vowing to return as soon as I could. For now

I had seen enough. God was keeping them safe and well. I had to leave them in His capable hands.

Within the hour I rejoined the others and reported faithfully that there was still no sign of pursuit. From that point on we rode through brush so thick no one would figure a squirrel could penetrate it. Twice we hid in thickets while other riders went by close enough to touch, and once we had to backtrack near a mile to avoid a Reb cavalry patrol. At midnight we forded the river, and after being challenged by the sentries, we were led into our camp.

❖ CHAPTER 7 ❖

It was only three days later that I headed back over the Tennessee River. This time all of Company F was with me and a whole lot of other folks besides.

"Rosecrans has crossed the Tennessee below Chattanooga," Captain Briant informed us. "Now that the Rebs know where the real attack is coming, General Crittenden believes that Forrest will be moved south today toward Charleston."

Briant went on to explain that it was the job of our cavalry, including Company F, to get between Old Bedford and the road south. If possible, we were to prevent him from joining up with Bragg. At the very least, we were supposed to delay the secesh horsemen till Chattonooga had been secured.

Our objective for this move was a place called Jasper's Ford. Sitting atop the road south from Knoxville to Chattanooga, the place was also at a bridgeless crossing of the Little Hiwassee River. It was believed that if we set up at that spot we could deny Forrest the passage.

We drove off some Reb pickets that were standing sentinel on the road and invested the ford with about a hundred men. Since we were mounted troops, we arrived considerably in advance of the rest of the expedition, but we were expected to hold on till reinforcements arrived.

The September day was hot and dry. In contrast to the rain and mud of the Tullahoma affair earlier in the summer, the ground was parched to the point of choking dust. The ford of the stream was nearly all bare rocks.

The other contrast to my earlier campaigning was the fact that we were now on the defensive. Dobbs was assigned to keep the horses for Cochran, Blanket, Hamilton, and me while we formed part of the skirmish line. The actual ford was just upstream of us.

For a couple of hours we exchanged a few shots with Reb pickets on the other side of the stream but nothing very heated. In contrast to the lazy battle, the sun at meridian height was exerting itself to be stifling, and the air was still and ovenlike. Lying in the brush behind logs and dirt mounds made the presence of the trickle of the creek a terrible ordeal. When the water in our canteens soon turned stale, we could not refill them or help ourselves to a cool drink from the stream, since to move from cover was certain to draw a bullet.

At noon we saw a column of dust rising to the north of us and sweeping closer like that cloud that went before the Hebrew children. Cochran believed it to be our reinforcements arriving, but I said no. "Has to be Rebs," I explained. "Look where it's coming from."

So it proved.

We saw the movement of horses through the trees on the far side of the creek but nothing clearly. It seemed that there was not to be an immediate mounted assault. Within a few moments, however, the popping of sporadic musket fire increased in both tempo and volume.

We fired back, and I was soon lost in the rhythm of the drill for our carbines: Crank down the lever to drop the breechblock, blow the residue out of the barrel, load another cartridge, close the block, apply a percussion cap, throw up the weapon, fire . . . and repeat. Overhead a cloud of blue gray, acrid smoke settled into the streambed until nothing of the other side could be seen. It was as if the smoke was our enemy, and we were doing our level best to annihilate it.

Little aiming was ever done, apart from pointing the muzzle in the general direction of the foe. It was an article of faith that only constant firing would keep the enemy from gaining an advantage. Therefore, only speedy reloading mattered.

Bullets whistling above our heads and into the trees reminded me of my duty as a corporal. "Aim lower," I shouted both left and right on the line. Even as I spoke I saw Cochran trigger off a round while lying half on his side behind a log. The barrel of his Sharps pointed skyward. "Lower!" I hissed.

Screams punctuated the clatter of gunfire as bullets somehow found targets. Three places to my left a man gave a sudden groan and threw up his gun as if suddenly deciding to quit the battle.

A dozen Rebs dashed forward to the center of the stream. In their gray uniforms, they first appeared to be only darker swirls on the smoke. Even when they came to within twenty yards of us, they remained unreal until all were shot down and fell screaming or moaning or thrashing or heavily silent into the puddles in the ford.

There was a lull in the fighting. The barrel of my carbine was too hot to touch, and I reloaded it carefully, then set it aside. The sound of men coughing from the fumes and dust and heat replaced the noise of gunfire.

Down the line came Sergeant Cate. "Look sharp. Keep your heads down and keep your cartridges to hand. They'll be coming on strong this time. Don't fire till I give the word."

A line of black ants trudged over the rock behind which I sheltered. They had a regular highway from one side of the boulder to the other and were bent on moving house or something from the amount of twigs and dry leaves they were carrying. How could they be so oblivious to the life-and-death struggle happening around them? At first I was amused, but soon I was envious of their lack of concern.

A shell from a Reb cannon whizzed overhead, bursting in the trees behind us. Then another shell dropped in the creek, showering us with gravel. The third round burst upstream of us, right along the shoreline. One man had his leg torn off by the explosion, and two more were killed outright.

I heard the brush rattling and turned to see the cause. Though Hamilton was gripping his rifle with both hands, he was shaking violently and the barrel was thrashing in the branches of a bush.

"Easy, Hamilton," I urged. "You'll be all right."

"Corporal," he said, "are you scared?"

"Yes," I acknowledged. "A man'd have to be crazy to not be scared."

Hamilton nodded and licked his lips, smearing the stains of the smoke around his mouth. "I haven't been scared before. I didn't think I ever would be. I didn't know what . . . what it would be like."

"Take it easy," I said again. "You'll be all right."

A loud wailing cry from the far shore sent a shiver down my spine and made me doubt my own words.

"Here they come again!" someone shouted.

This time the streambed to the left and right was full of dark, wraithlike shapes. There were so many of them!

"Fire!" Cate yelled.

A volley from our weapons cut into the oncoming shapes, twisting them into even more grotesque forms. Then, from up the creek to our right, came a bugle call and the thunder of hooves. A troop of cavalry was hurtling on us, already on our side of the water.

"We're outflanked!" was the cry and "It's Old Bedford!"

"Fall back!" Cate ordered. "Fall back to the horses!"

Hamilton was already sprinting to the rear, his carbine forgotten in the brush. A bursting shell scored his face with hot iron, and he screamed and threw up his hands. Others were throwing aside their rifles in their haste to escape.

I fired once more in the direction of the pounding hoofbeats, then rose to go. "Come on, Cochran. Time to get."

Cochran triggered off one more round before standing to follow me. Something seemed to slam into him from behind, and he pitched forward and disappeared in the brush and the smoke. "Jesse," he called feebly from somewhere in the haze, "help me."

I reached for him, calling, "Where are you? Cochran, where are you?"

"Help me," Hamilton moaned. "I can't see! Help me! Somebody guide me!"

"Jesse," Cochran called faintly from the mist.

"Jesse, come on!" Cate demanded. "Get back now!"

"But Cochran . . . ," I said, knowing that I would never find him until the smoke cleared.

"Corporal Dodson!" Captain Briant ordered. "Fall back to the horses at once!"

The shapes of three oncoming Rebs loomed out of the smoke.

I drew my Colt and loosened three rounds at them before I left Cochran behind and fled. Hamilton's arm was wrapped around my neck, but for all that, he was still running faster than I was, practically dragging me with him.

Forrest's horsemen pursued us from the ford. We had held the crossing for exactly one hour . . . that was all.

We retreated down the stream and up the slope on the far side, looking for the high ground and a place to turn again on the enemy. When we pulled up our horses on a timbered hillside, it took me some minutes to recognize it as the same vantage point above my farm as I visited only days before. There was the same garden . . . the same house. I hoped my precious ones were inside and safe. I wondered if I was to die within sight of my home and family.

"They'll come at us from both sides at once," Briant warned. "Form an angle here with the point down the hill. Dodson, you and Cate anchor the ends of this line."

We could hear the Reb bugle calls gathering the troops again. Like a pack of hounds when the cougar is treed, the enemy horsemen circled and swirled at the foot of the hill on which we perched. Soon they would come for us.

I turned toward Hamilton. His scalp wound had bled into his eyes, but I could tell it was not serious. I wiped his face with a rag, then knotted the cloth over his wound.

Just then, to the note of the bugles was added another sound: a crash of exploding shells and the deep, bass rumble of cannons. The shouts of Forrest's cavalrymen turned to calls of warning as cannon fire dropped in their midst.

Then I heard Nathan Bedford Forrest shouting for his men to regroup and fall back. "On to Chattanooga! There'll be plenty more Yankees to kill down there!"

The arrival of our army and a battery of artillery saved our lives. Soon Old Bedford and his troopers were past us, undeterred in their move to reinforce the Rebs to the south of us.

I returned to the creek after the skirmish to seek out Cochran. He was not there.

✳ ✳ ✳

I cannot say how Alcie knew it was me coming across the meadow. I was covered with dirt, smoke, and the grime of battle. My beard had grown out grizzled in the four months since last I had seen her.

The horse I rode was lean and hungry. I could not spur him faster than a walk or he would have collapsed beneath me. And if the horse was thin and ragged looking, then I was double the vision of hardship. I might have been any stray Union soldier come riding in to look for a meal at the farmhouse. But somehow my Alcie knew it was me a'coming from half a mile off.

I raised my field glasses as I crossed the creek. She was barefoot and her golden hair fell in wisps around her face as she carried a laundry basket from the kettle toward the clothesline. Stopping mid-stride, she raised her head as if she sensed something. I rose in my stirrups and waved my hat broadly.

She dropped her burden and began to run toward me. I heard her shout to the children, "It's your daddy! Oh, God be praised! Jesse! My own Jesse!"

I kicked the horse, but he would not move faster. Leaping from the saddle I left him behind, covering the ground at a lope.

Alcie was weeping with joy when she reached me. The children galloped along behind her. We met beside the well, and I was surrounded by the sweet embrace of my dear family.

Alcie would not let go of me and cried, "Oh, Jesse, you've come home to us at last! How I've prayed for this moment!"

Loren, thumping me on the back in a manly way, said, "Will you stay awhile, Father?"

In a chorus the little ones chimed in, "How long will you stay?"

"Are you home forever now?"

"Is the war over?"

Such eager hopes filled me with sadness.

Alcie caught the answer in my eyes. She answered for me, "Your father cannot stay long." She searched my face and kissed me. "How long, Jesse? How long will you be with us?"

I swallowed hard. "Only today."

The young'uns fell silent at this terrible reply.

"Ah," Alcie managed. She took my hands and held her chin up bravely. "Look at you, Jesse Dodson. You're a sight! I'll heat some water. You'll not go back to fight the Rebs looking like a scarecrow."

And so she wasted no time in caring for me as she had in the old days. She shooed the young'uns out and set Loren to tend my poor mount. As I soaked in a steaming tub, she shaved me and soaped me and scrubbed me like I was one of the babies. But I had not seen her in so many months that the mere touch of her hands awakened a hunger in me deeper than any need I had for food and drink. We passed a sweet afternoon behind locked doors. It all made me wonder how I would ever say good-bye to her again.

Afterward, she lay against my chest and told me what it had been like without me.

"I know the Rebs were here," I said. "I watched you from the hill."

"I felt your eyes on me," she said in a soft voice. "Your thoughts comforted me. Did you feel the nights I lay abed dreaming of you, Jesse?"

"I have not forgotten my promise to you."

"What news of William?"

"No news."

"The Rebs have stripped the smokehouse clean."

"I heard as much."

"The livestock are gone. Trafalger went with them. Loren tried to hide him, but they found him out."

"I have eighty dollars in Union gold. Enough to feed you and the young'uns till I get back permanent."

"R. J. has been provisioning us. Beans and cornmeal and such like."

"A good man, R. J. is. I'll settle the account with him before I leave."

"Where will you go?"

"Chasing Forrest again, I reckon. South."

"I want you to stay, Jesse. I need you to . . ." She began to weep, and her tears nearly melted my resolve.

"Please, Alcie. I will break if you cry."

"I cannot help it. It is harder to think of you being gone again when I have you back for such a short time! It is a dream. Only a dream."

I stroked her back and spoke quietly to her. "Then we will dream together, Alcie! We have tonight! Let's not waste a moment of it!"

This was the only pleasant night I had as a soldier in Mister Lincoln's army.

Come morning, Alcie removed a box from beneath a floorboard. In it was a fresh, new uniform that she had stitched for me and a new pair of boots that she declared she had bought in case I came home for Christmas.

"I see you are not a private any longer. If there was time I would sew your stripes on."

But there was no time for that. I kissed her and the children farewell, not knowing if I would ever see them again in this hard world.

I could not dream what heartache lay ahead for us as I rode away from my home and rejoined my unit that day.

451

After the skirmish at Jasper's Ford, Company F was shot up enough that we were detached from our service to General Crittenden. Despite what I had told Alcie, we were sent back to the regiment at Camp Spear. Because of that decision, we missed the Union capture of Chattanooga, but we also missed being in the shellacking our boys would take at Chickamauga.

Forrest again, just as I might have predicted.

General Rosecrans, maneuvering the jaws of the Union nutcracker around Chattanooga, forced the Reb general Bragg to withdraw across into Georgia almost without bloodshed. The Rebs could not afford to be bottled up in a siege as had happened at Vicksburg. When the Twenty-first Corps came down the Tennessee from the north and Thomas's and McCook's outfits crossed Raccoon Mountain from the south, Bragg up and fell back along the line of the Western and Atlantic Railroad.

All well and good. Chattanooga was secured. Then Rosecrans

overplayed his hand. He set out in pursuit of the retreating secesh but with his forces divided and spread out over sixty miles of country.

It was Old Bedford's command that discovered the gaping holes in the Union line and Old Bedford again who led the skirmishing around Tunnel Hill and Ringgold.

Then, on September 19, it was Forrest's outfit once more that opened the fighting at Jay's Sawmill, and the Battle of Chickamauga was on. For two days of slaughter on the creek whose Indian name means "River of Death," Forrest's men pinned down the Union left flank and prevented reinforcements from arriving in time.

When a gap appeared in the Yankee front, Rebel General James Longstreet sent twelve thousand men pouring across and the Union lines rolled up like a carpet. Many of the bluecoats dropped their arms and fled, racing each other all the way back to Chattanooga.

The battle ended with the Union army still in possession of Chattanooga but surrounded there and besieged. Afterward, both Union General Rosecrans and Confederate General Bragg were sacked from high command.

All of which had little to do with me. Before returning to Nashville, we put our more seriously wounded men aboard the hospital ship *Morning Star*. Hamilton, Dobbs, and I were assisting with the loading of stretcher cases and amputees. No sign of Cochran.

Hamilton and I carried a twenty-year-old soldier whose thigh-bone had been hit by a minié ball. The shattered remains of his leg had been removed halfway between hip and knee. As we toted the soldier from the field hospital toward the gangplank, he was raving to an imaginary surgeon not to do what had already been done. "Don't take my leg," he moaned. "Don't want to live with only one leg. Don't cut it off!"

Hamilton shuddered and tried to look everywhere but at the wounded man. But turning away did no good; the broken remnants of humans were everywhere we looked. In fact, we passed a barrel overflowing with removed human limbs. One arm balanced upright, palm open, as if giving a friendly wave.

That was all Hamilton could take. Without warning he abruptly set down his end of the stretcher and puked over a rail fence.

"Here, now," urged a man in the uniform of a naval officer. "You'll have to do better than that, Soldier. If it was you on the stretcher, you'd want those taking care of you to be made of sterner stuff, right?"

Hamilton nodded weakly and apologized. "It came to me that it could have been me. If Jesse here had not led me away after I got blinded, it could have been me lying here . . . or worse."

The naval officer was almost six feet tall, and his hair was the color of buckwheat honey. There was a notch missing from one of his ears. He nodded his understanding and directed us where to carry the wounded man. When we reemerged on the upper deck of the side-wheel steamer, he introduced himself. "Rafer Maddox. Captain of *Morning Star.*"

As Hamilton was pasty-faced and wobbly on his feet, Captain Maddox invited us to sit down in his cabin for a spell. "Can't have you falling overboard," he said to Hamilton. "Turning you into a patient would be bad for the morale of the other stretcher bearers."

The captain's cabin was on the top deck, two rooms in back of the wheelhouse. When we entered the spartan room, a blue-and-gold bird screamed hello and bobbed his head by way of greeting. "I'm Scrimshaw," the bird announced in the voice of Captain Maddox. "How are you?"

"Scrimshaw there has been with me ever since I went round the Horn in the early days of the gold rush," Maddox commented as he handed the bird a bit of hardtack.

"Then he must be—" I did a little mental arithmetic—"he's at least twelve or fifteen years old. I didn't know any kind of bird, even a parrot, could live so long."

"Nobody really knows how long they can live," Maddox said. "Some of these jungle birds make it to fifty or sixty years . . . maybe more. Scrim here could outlive me." He thrust a dram of something into Hamilton's hand. "Drink that. It'll do you good. What outfit are you boys with?"

Hamilton drained the amber liquid, coughed, and got some color back in his cheeks.

I explained where we had come from and about the fighting we had seen.

Hamilton reached for the bottle and refilled his glass without waiting to be asked.

Maddox nodded his understanding. "Heard about Old Bedford even way out in California where I hail from. They say his troopers ride like cavalry and fight like infantry and that Forrest thinks the proper way to defend a position is to attack first."

I agreed. "That all squares with what we have seen of him. If it was up to me I'd just as soon not see any more of him—ever."

"Not see any more war ever," Hamilton muttered, tossing back the rest of the drink in one gulp.

"Here," Maddox protested. "You were just supposed to sip that."

"Thought I could whip all the Rebs myself," Hamilton mumbled. "Gonna show all the hayseed farmhands how to fight! Yessir! Was gonna show ever'body what real so'jers were."

Maddox glanced at me with a curious questioning look. "Had he been drinking already? He hasn't had that much here."

Shaking my head, I explained, "He hasn't slept since the battle at the ford. Got a bellyful of fighting and seeing men shot to rags. Had to leave a wounded comrade behind. Other men in the outfit tell me he hasn't slept a wink since that day."

"Oh, oh!" Scrimshaw announced, dropping his cracker.

Hamilton leaned sideways on the small sofa, and his eyelids drooped.

"Looks like he will now," Maddox observed. "What say I give you a hand with the stretchers, and we let your friend catch forty winks?"

An hour later I roused Hamilton, and the two of us rejoined our outfit on the docks.

"Thanks, Captain," Hamilton mumbled.

"Don't mention it," Maddox returned with a wave. "God go with you. Mayhap we'll meet again."

✳ CHAPTER 8 ✳

When we got back to Camp Spear, we found out that more than Cochran had left us. Melvin Long was also dead. His wound, which had not bled much and was thought to be healing fine, turned septic. Lockjaw set in; he was dead in days.

Throughout the autumn of 1863, the Third Regiment remained on guard duty at Nashville and patrolled the railroads in the vicinity. Old Unconditional Surrender, General Grant, was appointed the top commander of Union forces in the West.

Grant replaced Rosecrans with General Thomas, then went on to reinforce Chattanooga and break the siege. The Confederates were beaten at the battles of Lookout Mountain and Missionary Ridge. Then in December General Longstreet led his Rebel army away from Knoxville and back into Georgia for the winter.

By the end of the year, most of Tennessee west of the mountains was free of Confederate control for the first time since the war began. But not east. I reflected that the old woman Cochran and I had encountered was right to be canny. The Rebs still held much of my home county.

Our nemesis, General Forrest, was everywhere or nowhere, depending on which rumor one chose to believe. He was wounded at Chickamauga (which was true enough); he was dead (not true at all); he was in East Tennessee with Longstreet; he had argued with his superiors and gone home to his wife; he had rebelled against the rebellion and set up his own kingdom in Mississippi and made himself emperor.

All of these possibilities enlivened campfire conversations as the cold of winter closed in on Nashville. But on guard duty my solitary thoughts were still on home and on my son William.

I sometimes received permission to attend prisoner exchanges. I would stand for hours waiting in the relentless rain that came to Tennessee as two hundred wretched Confederates would shuffle across the lines and two hundred of our boys, thin and ragged, would shamble back toward our side. I went from gaunt face to meager frame, studying intently each form. Never did I find William nor encounter any who knew of him. Still I kept trying.

The only campaigning done by the Third Tennessee Cavalry Regiment was in late December, right before Christmas. Nathan Bedford Forrest, despite all hearsay to the contrary, was truly raiding into West Tennessee, blowing up bridges, tearing up track, mustering recruits, and rounding up Confederate deserters for enforced reenlistment. The response of our commanders was to send us southwest to intercept him. We were part of a five-pronged attack designed to surround Old Bedford and end his depredations once and for all. Since there were fifteen thousand of us opposed to Forrest's estimated three thousand, our prospects looked fair to finally waylay the Gray Ghost.

We received our orders to move out on December 18. For the first part of our journey we loaded our mounts into train cars (and ourselves as well—eight horses or forty men to a drafty, unheated carriage). Traveling down the line from Nashville, we unloaded across the Tennessee River into the west. Three days later we were in position.

Forrest had set himself up a command headquarters at Jackson. He was reported to be fleeing south toward Mississippi with his three thousand men, captured weapons, looted stores, and two hundred head of cattle. Surrounded as he was and with the rivers swollen and the bridges guarded, we thought we had him trapped for fair.

It was on Christmas Eve that our company went racing ahead of the foot soldiers to a crossing of the Hatchie River south of Jackson. The rain had stopped, and a cold blue moon hung over the bare branches of the oaks. Beyond the encircling trees stood a field of cornstalks, frozen stiff like a harvest of bayonets. Owing to the sudden freeze after so much rain, all the tree limbs were glazed with ice, and every puddle was a glassy slide to trap the unwary.

The men were huddled around fires, alternately squeezing close to the meager warmth and standing up to pound their fists on their shoulders and stamp their feet to get the blood going. Dobbs made an attempt at singing Christmas carols, but the response was half-hearted at best. It was too cold, and thoughts of home and Christmas made the lonely night worse somehow.

Along about midnight, our infantry regiment arrived, about six hundred of them, and encamped next to us.

As corporal of the guard, I walked the rounds of the picket posts. As I approached Blankenbeckler's position, an alarm sounded. Outside of camp in the darkness came a sharp snap like a single rifle shot. I snapped back the hammer on my carbine and was already racing forward as Blanket called, "Corporal of da guard, post nummer eins . . . I mean, one, one!"

The German was staring intently into the dark shadows cast by the moon and jumped when I touched his shoulder and drew him to a kneeling position. "Hunker down here," I whispered, "and listen for a minute. Frozen twigs will crack underfoot if anything much moves out there."

After some time passed without further noise, another sharp report alarmed the sentries. This time the sudden noise was succeeded by a dull thud.

"Tree branch breaking from the weight of the ice," I said. "I'll pass the word."

Two hours later I was off duty and huddled inside a miserable shebang made of two shelter halves buttoned together. Dobbs and I were curled up in the dog tent, with one gum poncho under us and another over us and still not enough warmth between us to melt a pat of butter.

In the extreme cold, I was in a half-waking, half-dreaming state.

I vaguely heard of a further change of the watch, then somehow imagined I was at another prisoner exchange. Peering into every face that
passed, I despaired of finding William. Each returning prisoner looked
me in the eye, seemingly as eager as I to find someone who would care
about him. Then to my vision was added a new distress: I believed
William had already come past me and I had not recognized him! I
frantically raced up the line, calling his name, then could not recall
where I had left off looking. I panicked and pleaded with the captain
not to load the men in the wagons just yet, that I had to find my son.

The officer in my dream opened his mouth to reply, but what he
said made no sense. "Brigade—charge!"

I woke with a start to find that the alarm was real, even if the
dream had not been.

"Regiment—charge! . . . Company—charge!" The order was
repeated down through the chain of command as out on the icy

plain bugles blew, and there came a crashing tramp like the boots of
ten thousand men. A rattle of musket fire crackled down the length
of a quarter-mile-long line of battle.

"Fall back," ordered the infantry colonel, a man named Prince.

"Wait," I heard Captain Briant argue. "We don't know what's out
there. Let my men scout before we up and skedaddle."

"Are you deaf?" demanded Prince. "There are just six hundred
of us here, and that's a full brigade out there . . . three thousand of
them."

Another clatter of gunfire swept down the line, and a few bullets
whizzed through camp.

"We've got to pull back!"

Rebel yells from half of the compass pierced the stillness of the
night.

"There, you see?" Prince wailed. "We are about to be surrounded.
. . . We are pulling back at once, and your troopers are to cover our
flank on the march. Do you hear me, Captain? At once!"

By five of the clock Christmas morning, we were ten miles away
at Somerville, where the presence of a bigger Union force stiffened
Prince's backbone. All morning we waited for the command to ride
out, to challenge Forrest, to deny him the road, but it was not until

near two in the afternoon that Company F rode off toward Lafayette on the Wolf River.

We reached a covered bridge at dusk, a bridge that was supposed to have been destroyed to keep the Rebs from crossing. Instead the planks had merely been stacked and left unguarded. Secesh infiltrators had tiptoed over the naked beams, relaid the flooring, and Forrest and his men had already crossed.

Company F was dispatched south at high speed to attempt to overtake the Reb column, though what we were supposed to do if we caught them was beyond me. We had not ridden above a mile when a shot rang out.

I thought immediately of the snipers on Calfkiller Creek and ordered my men to dismount and stay back of cover till we had located his whereabouts.

No more shots came.

When Dobbs, Blanket, Hamilton, and I advanced again with our carbines at the ready, a lone Rebel lieutenant stood upright from behind a dirt bank and raised his arms. "I give," he said. "Only had but one bullet anyway."

"Why'd you stay behind then?" I asked suspiciously, scanning the surrounding woods.

The Confederate soldier looked chagrined. "Busted my ankle when I slipped on some ice, so I dropped out so as not to hold up the others."

As it was dark, we took the solitary prisoner back to infantry headquarters. Colonel Prince had a nice, warm cabin in which to interrogate him. "Whose regiment are you with?" he demanded.

"Forrest's," was the proud reply.

"Yes, that's the brigade commander," Prince said irritably. "But what regiment?"

That Reb junior officer laughed right in his face. "Guess it don't hurt nothin' to tell you now. Last night . . . in the cornfield . . . there weren't no brigade. Gen'ral said if we couldn't sneak up, we'd get louder instead." He guffawed. "Weren't even a regiment. Old Bedford had all of us repeat every command like we was forty companies, 'stead of just one."

"One?" Prince asked with alarm. "One company? Clear this room at once," he demanded, forcing Captain Briant and me out of the cabin.

We left but not before we heard the prisoner say, "I declare, Colonel, there warn't but sixty of us! But the way those cornstalks snapped like gunshots, you must of thought we was thousands all firin' at once and comin' on like billy-o!"

✳ ✳ ✳

We did not get back to Nashville. Instead, after the failed attempt to corner Forrest in West Tennessee, it was decided to keep us there to guard against future raids. Hamilton remarked that such strategy was locking the barn door after the horse was out, and no one disagreed with him. First we were in Memphis, and then shortly after that were moved to Colliersville on the rail line, hard by the Mississippi border.

That winter was pretty much the coldest ever known or heard tell of in those parts. When we came back from riding patrol we could not dismount on account of our legs would not bend, nor our backs either. We had to sort of fall out of the saddles and hope that the hostlers catching us were not themselves too stiff to manage it.

At first we were still housed in dog tents, but when it appeared that we would be staying all the cold season, we cobbled together all manner of contrived shelters. We built shanties, log huts, brush arbors, and most everything else we could think of that would be some protection against the cold.

Dobbs, Hamilton, Sergeant Cate, Blanket, and me had a prime stockaded tent. It came about this way: We offered to build Captain Briant a sturdy log cabin out of the sparse material available if he would let us take over his tent in exchange. He agreed, and both parties felt like winners. (Especially since the cabin turned out so nice that some other officer would have demanded it from us poor enlisted men if we had not made the deal beforehand with Briant.)

Our tent likewise finished us proper, it being roofed with vulcanized rubber ponchos and half-walled with sticks. We even caulked between the sticks with mud, but it rained so much we had to replace the chinking about once a week.

Anyway, on February 10 we were snug in our tent and had a fire going on our stone hearth and fireplace. The stones had been liberated from a Rebel back fence. We had likewise foraged for some empty barrels as had lately contained salt beef (called "old horse" by us seasoned veterans). By knocking out the ends and stacking the barrels one atop the other, we made a passable chimney. Our flue drew all right so long as the wind was not above five miles an hour. With any more breeze than that the fumes reversed themselves and turned our lodging into a smokehouse.

We were taking turns doing mess duty, and it fell to Dobbs to prepare supper for all of us. The regiment had received a fresh beef allotment that day, much appreciated after the run of salt pork and army beans that had been our fare for weeks. Dobbs was very proud of his ingenuity. He had located a store of onions and traded some of them for pork fat in which to fry up the beefsteak and onions.

The fat was sizzling in the fry pan, and our mouths were beginning to water when all at once the bugle sounded. It was so unexpected that we all jumped up, including Dobbs, who had been squatting near the cook fire. His long-handled fork caught on the grip of the fry pan, upsetting the load of grease into the flames.

With a rush and a roar, the fat exploded up the chimney, which, being made of wooden barrels, likewise erupted into blaze! In moments our chimney was a conflagration.

Now chimney fires in winter camp were not uncommon. The usual practice was to push the flaming barrels over and away from the tent with long poles, then reconstruct the flue later.

On this occasion, however, there was no opportunity to extinguish the inferno. The bugle call that had roused us was assembly, and it was shortly followed by boots and saddles. We were going winter campaigning, leaving immediately, and not even a burning tent was permitted to disrupt the progress of the army.

Because of the ferocious blaze, we did not have any chance to gather more than a few belongings by grabbing our haversacks. All our other possessions went up in smoke, including our extra clothing and the gum ponchos that had been our roof.

"Where we going, Captain?" Blanket asked.

"Mississippi," was the compact reply.

461

"Iss any warmer dare?"

Captain Briant looked at the fiery remains of our tent, at Dobbs, and then back at the German. "We got Private Dobbs, don't we? Maybe it'll get some warmer after we get there." To the laughing and jeering that responded, Briant added, "And we want to make it real hot for the Rebs . . . we're gonna burn us down a Forrest!"

✳ ✳ ✳

It was not until we were on the move that we found out about our destination and the plan that called for such sudden action. General William Tecumseh Sherman, newly appointed commander of Union forces along the Mississippi, intended to strike a blow into the heart of Dixie.

Sherman would personally lead a twenty-thousand-man infantry force from Vicksburg overland toward Selma, Alabama. To defend his flank, seventy-five hundred cavalry troopers, of whom I was one, were to take off southwest from Colliersville toward Okolona, Mississippi, and then down the line of the Mobile and Ohio Railroad. The two converging columns of foot and horse soldiers would unite somewhere around Meridian.

Commanding the cavalry force was Brigadier General William Sooy Smith.

It was the common belief of Sherman and Smith that General Forrest could not successfully face two parallel threats into Mississippi. If the attacks were launched without preamble in the dead of winter and as Sherman put it "with celebrity," there would be no opportunity for the Rebs to set up a defense.

At least, that was the reasoning.

We soon found out that though our tent had burned, we were not much worse off than the other men. No one was allowed extra belongings on the march. General Smith had ordered speed, which meant five days' rations per man, another five days' rations to follow by mule, spare horseshoes for each trooper, and nothing else except what would fit in a haversack. There would be no wagon train to encumber the columns of horsemen. Even the twenty cannons accompanying us were hauled by double teams of draft animals to defeat the Mississippi mud.

The other reason for the haste was that we were late. Unbeknownst to us in the companies, General Smith had delayed our launch until another force of Union cavalry joined us from Memphis. By the time we actually heard "Column of twos. Compnee! Forward . . . ho!" Sherman was already in Meridian, wondering where his cavalry had got to.

We rode for six days through some of the meanest country on God's earth.

"Where are we?" Hamilton wondered aloud.

"Tippah County, Miss-sippi," I explained.

Hamilton looked around at the abrupt, treeless knolls and the clay-filled canyons and muttered, "What holds the cabins and the barns up on the hills? Looks like a light rain would wash them into the creeks."

"Often does," I agreed. "Folk hereabouts teach their cattle to swim before they turn them out to graze."

Hamilton looked at me to see if I was joking, then added, "I know you're joshing me, but tell me this: Why do we want this country? Seems to me we'd do more harm to the Rebs to make them keep it."

Everything about that land was mud colored. Houses seemed to have been whitewashed with brown clay, and the sheep and chickens were somewhere between gray and tan. Even the folks thereabouts were coffee colored, and it was the white folks we was looking at. A line of laundry hanging between a swaybacked shanty and a leaning outhouse may have been clean, but the ragged pieces of cloth were universally ochre hued. The onlookers we saw appeared to all be gray in their outlook on life too: None loosed a round and none waved to cheer us. Life was too hardscrabble to care much one way or the other who was passing by.

It was that same way clear to the crossing of the Tallahatchie River—no opposition at all. We were deep in Mississippi without firing a shot. It made me wonder where Old Bedford was, made me nervous. I only hoped it made our officers that way too.

By February 19 both the scenery and the attitudes had changed.

The muddy bottoms and steep defiles were replaced with rolling prairie, fertile and farmable and waiting for the kiss of spring to burst into exuberant green.

Exuberance among part of the population did not require the warmth of spring to bloom; the slave population, that is. South of New Albany we began to pick up contrabands, runaways from the plantations we passed. By the time we reached Pontotoc a full three thousand souls followed in our train.

General Smith fretted and fumed, appealed and decreed, but no amount of words, kind or otherwise, could make them leave off following us. Their presence pretty near doubled the size of our column, stretched us out, slowed us down. But how could we run them off or run off and leave them?

These were not freemen with homes of their own to which they could go. This was not Nashville, safe for runaways because of the protection of fifty thousand men in blue uniforms.

Until just days before, every man, woman, and child of the multitude now traipsing after us had been a slave, liable to be bought and sold, lost in a card game, beaten on a whim, or worked to death as the owner chose. No matter what genteel Southerners might protest about the Negroes being incapable of caring for themselves, no matter how much Rebels might argue that no right-minded slave owner abused valuable poverty, regardless of high-sounding words and pat arguments, slavery was a great evil—the great evil of America. If slavery was not put away once and for all, then the Union did not deserve to exist.

If freedom was not important even to folks who had never tasted it, why did they leave the only homes they had ever known and what little possessions they had to cast their lot with us? They had seen, lived with, and tasted the dire consequences of revolution against their masters. They knew there was no going back.

I thought about the runaways who had crossed my land. I remembered Cyrus and old Samuel. But I saw the war in a new light down here in Mississippi; it had a different face. Before the war I had believed slavery to be wrong, had known that the God of mercy and justice could not agree with it, but I had not gone to war to stop it. No, I had gone to war to find my son and to be able to live at home again in peace and safety.

Now three thousand souls danced for joy when we came. They shouted "Glory!" and "Hallelujah!" They cried out praises to the Lord God Almighty for "Massa Linkum's sojers." It made me frightened for them. They looked to us for protection and liberty, and we were taking them *south*!

There was a huge bonfire whereon a whole ox was being roasted. Hundreds of black men and women, who one day before had toiled on plantations under the watchful eye of their overseers and the threat of the lash, gathered and sang! They danced, clapped, and prayed, but most of all, they sang. Over frozen fields, filling the frosty skies, "Roll, Jordan, Roll" reverberated, and then we heard:

> *"Oh, freedom! Oh, freedom! Oh, freedom over me*
> *And before I'll be a slave, I'll be buried in my grave*
> *Go home to my Lord and be free!"*

Finally, to my amazement, they joined hands, and in a prayerful tone, with more feeling than I had ever heard applied to the words before, they sang:

> *"My country, 'tis of thee.*
> *Sweet land of liberty,*
> *Of thee, I sing!"*

This from folks who had never had a country to call their own before or at least not one that meant anything kindly to them and theirs. It made me both proud and humbled at the same time to be wearing the blue uniform—to represent *freedom* to those folks. I could not work it all out somehow. But I could feel God Himself smiling down at their joy.

✳ ✳ ✳

It was on the morning of February 21 that the whereabouts of Old Bedford again became clear. After ten days of no opposition to speak of, Rebel skirmishers falling back whenever more than one company of us appeared, suddenly everything changed. As Hamilton said, "We got him right where he wants us."

What he meant by that was this: The cavalry column was way south, near the town of West Point on the rail line. We were smack-spraddle between Sakatonchee Creek and the Tombigbee River. The country on both sides of the tracks was swampy bottomland—good for hogs and cane, bad for horsemen.

"We can't maneuver off the roads," Colonel Minnis fretted to Captain Briant in my hearing. "We have them outnumbered four to one, but it doesn't count for a thing if we can only approach in a force that is twelve men across!"

To his credit, General Smith figured out the same thing and swore he would not let his command march straight into a trap. We received orders to attack the Rebs holding the bank of the Sakatonchee at a place called Ellis Bridge. The purpose of the assault was not to force a crossing but rather to disguise a retreat back the way we came.

"No heroics, Jesse," Cate urged. "We don't even want this piece of land, so don't go getting yourself killed."

I assured him I had no such intention. "I learned my lesson long ago. You won't catch me doing nothing heroic."

In any event, the Rebs made it easy for us not to capture the bridge. Before we had come within twelve hundred yards, they opened up on us with a battery of six-pounders. Shells burst over-head, not doing any harm at such extreme range but putting us on notice.

"Dismount!" Captain Briant ordered. "Every fourth man to hold the horses. Advance on foot."

Leaving Blanket with a fistful of reins, we spread out in a skir-mish line a couple hundred yards across. From culvert to ditch we went, through a slough deep with slime, until musket volleys from the Rebs pattered in the branches like rain.

"If they can do that, then so can we. Give it to 'em, boys!" Cate ordered, and we opened fire.

There were some secesh pickets still on our side of the water, but when they saw our line of men approaching, some of them turned

and ran. That was how I got another glimpse of Old Bedford. One
Reb sentry threw away his rifle and sprinted across the bridge just
as I cautiously poked my head up among some brush. About thirty
yards on the other side of the river I saw a high-foreheaded officer
spur forward on his black horse and deliberately knock his own man
down. The officer jumped from his mount, yanked the deserter to
his feet, busted him backward again with his fist, pulled him upright
once more, spun him around, kicked him in the behind, and gave
him a shove back toward the battle line. I was so astonished I forgot
to raise my rifle till the scene had played out and the moment had
passed.

"Pass the word," Sergeant Cate called to me. "We've driven in
their pickets. Hold here now."

I relayed the command to the others, then in a lull in the shooting had time to tell Dobbs what I had witnessed. "Saw how Old
Bedford trains his recruits."

"Too bad you didn't give him a lead-ball salute," he replied. "Him
and his brother, too." General Forrest's younger brother, Colonel
Jeffrey Forrest, was reported to also be in the fighting that day. "Be
something to ground sluice a brace of Forrests, eh, Jesse?"

After about two hours of no further real fighting, our regiment
was told to withdraw. We had made enough of a show. I do not know
how General Forrest knew what was afoot, but no sooner had we
begun to fade back toward the main body than he launched a cavalry
charge across the bridge. The sporadic staccato popping of muskets
was replaced with a thundering rumble as the horsemen clattered
over the wooden planks.

"Fall back!" Briant ordered. "Back to the horses."

Sergeant Cate and I covered the withdrawal, shooting into the
oncoming riders and tangling up the front rank of what were now
the attackers. Then we also turned to go.

Cate fired a shot from his carbine before jumping atop a levee
to see if we had left anyone behind. That was when the Reb cannon
opened up again. A blast into a water oak close behind the sergeant
blew him head over heels into the river, and when he surfaced he was
floating facedown.

There was not even time for conscious thought, so I take no credit for doing anything courageous. Courage, I have heard it said, is when there is time to think about not doing something fearful and then doing it anyway.

At any rate, I tossed aside haversack and carbine without regard. My running flat dive into the stream would have impressed my own children, but that notion did not come till later either.

The icy water made me gasp. I surfaced and saw Cate floating downstream, away from me. Reb bullets tossed up splashes close to my head, so I ducked under again into the pea green liquid. When I came up next I grabbed Cate's leg and towed him over to the cover of some willows that overhung the water. Once under the trailing veil of limbs, I tossed him over a low branch.

Pounding him on the back brought no response at first, so I pounded harder. At last he gagged and coughed, so my treatment was working. I thumped some more, even though I could hear Reb snipers calling to each other, "Did y'all see where they went?"

Finally Cate groaned and said, "Jesse, is that you?"

I acknowledged as much.

"Would you leave off thrashing me then," he said. "I believe you've busted me ribs."

We stayed under cover for the space of two hours, half in the water and half on the muddy bank. I would have been hard-pressed to say which was the colder. Cate seemed to have taken no hurt from the concussion, and both of us had escaped being punctured by Reb bullets.

Finally, we snaked up and over the levee, drawing no more than a lazy parting shot. By following the stream northward, we rejoined our troop. Blanket had volunteered to be part of the rear guard, so as to be nearby with our horses.

"Corporal Dodson, I thought I made it clear there were to be no heroics done this day," Cate chided, his teeth chattering.

"So you did," I agreed, sniffling. "Shall I throw you back?"

✳ ✳ ✳

We retreated all that afternoon and into the evening, stopping to fight brief skirmishes on the road. We were slowed considerably

by the contraband men, women, and children who were scurry-
ing along behind us, but we did not abandon them. They were the
cause we were fighting for—freedom and equality for all, regardless
of race—and their presence among us was a good reminder. I was
humbled, too, by their thankfulness in the midst of such grim times.
It prompted me to my knees.

At one point, a few miles north of West Point, we halted to
regroup. It was not, at least not at first, General Smith's intention
to completely abandon the mission. So we formed again in line of
battle and waited for Forrest's brigade to come up. Soon enough they
launched an assault against the front of our position, even though
the place was heavily wooded and provided us with good cover.

The onslaught by the dismounted Rebs was so fierce that we
had no time to think about why they were pressing so hard against a
strong location, until we heard the fearful cries from the contrabands.

Old Bedford had sent a detachment of his men on a hard ride all
the way around our position to attack it from the rear. To come near
to us, the Rebs first cut and slashed their way through the former
slaves. Just seeing the way the Rebs treated defenseless men, women,
and children made me fighting mad. As we fended off the onslaught
at the front with cannon fire of our own, Colonel Strong ordered
a surging counterattack on the single regiment behind us. We batted them aside after a sharp fight and continued northward. But not
without damage to the Union men and a lot of casualties among the
black folk.

In front of me on my saddle rode a small black child who had
gotten separated from his mother in the fight. I hoped that when
we were able to stop, I could find her . . . that she was not one of the
many who had fallen. Behind me clung an old, white-haired man
with a saber cut over his ear. Again and again he kept repeating,
"Lawd, Lawd, deliver us from Ol' Bedford."

I could not agree with him more. From what I had seen, it
seemed as if Old Bedford were the devil himself, dispatching folks
to their death with a slash of his saber or the thundering hooves of
his mount.

It was near two o'clock in the morning when we finally halted again and made camp about four miles south of Okolona. We had retreated close on thirty miles, fighting much of the way.

Having seen no pursuit since midnight, we felt secure enough to throw out pickets and build fires. We were almost too tired to cook a meal, though we had not eaten in twenty hours.

I was chilled clean through and real grateful when Blanket left off reading his book to put a cup of coffee in my trembling hands. There had been no chance to dry out since my unplanned swim in the river, and now rain began to fall.

Drinking about half the thick brew, I then crumbled a hardtack biscuit in the rest. Since I had thrown away my haversack, I had no spoon, so I lifted the gruel to my lips and slurped.

Midslurp I saw the eyes of the child on me. I still had not located his mother, and I feared she was dead. "Here, son. Find a cup or a can, and I'll share some of this with you."

470

Wide-eyed, the child only stared, but I could hear his stomach rumble.

"Please, suh," offered the elderly black man, "if you don' mind, the chile and I can share that soup in dis y'ar cup."

"I don't mind," I said. "It's a mighty poor excuse for soup, though." Shortly after that I drifted into a fitful sleep.

I was feverish and chilled. As I had no blanket I was huddled next to the fire, but I awoke to find a scrap of faded cotton jacket over me. It belonged to the old man. "Where'd he go?" I asked Hamilton, who was bent over a fry pan of sizzling bacon.

"Said he knew there'd be more fightin' soon, and he wanted to take the child out of harm's way."

"But his coat," I protested.

"Said God bless you and you keep it" was the reply.

It was not even dawn when the cry "Here they come!" was raised, and it was so. Forrest's hard-riding troopers had rested for no more than two hours and had overtaken us again.

We did not even try to make a fight of it there but mounted up and rode through Okolona to a wooded hilltop. There we would make another stand and try to prevent our retreat from turning into another rout as had happened at Chickamauga.

Hamilton cursed once as we rode out ahead of the column, then apologized for the slip. "It's just that we had to leave so fast I didn't even get to eat."

"So?" I inquired crossly. "It's only a hunk of bacon."

"It isn't the meat that bothers me," he replied. "I just figure some Johnny Reb rode into our camp and is probably helping himself to it right now!"

✳ ✳ ✳

By dawn of February 22, General Smith knew that the upcoming battle would tell the tale of the Mississippi expedition. Either we would stand our ground and be able to reassert our presence in Dixie or we would be routed and go home in shame.

We troopers recognized the same fork in the road as well.

As for the contraband folk, they had already seen the future and expressed their opinion with their feet. Before a drizzling sky had grayed into morning, our camp followers up and left. They were putting more miles between themselves and the return to captivity that would surely follow a Yankee loss.

We were on a rise called Ivey's Hill that gave us a spot for our remaining guns and a vantage point to observe our pursuers. Directly back the way we had come was a small group of milling horsemen. They were easily seen across the open prairie and numbered no more than company strength.

Hamilton remarked, pointing, "Old Bedford's escort?"

I nodded, loading the replacement weapon I had taken from a dead trooper. "Figgers that way. He pushes all his men hard, and the ones nearest him he pushes hardest of all."

Off to our left was another mass of gray uniforms. The figures moved about in the brush that obscured the banks of the Tombigbee River, so we could not judge their numbers. But they looked to be at least brigade force. We also knew that there was another Reb column trying to approach on our right to keep us boxed, but they had yet to put in an appearance.

"So far we still got 'em outnumbered," Hamilton remarked. "You figure Forrest will attack anyway?"

Sergeant Cate nodded without hesitation. "You be looking to your cartridges and swab that barrel out again. And do it sooner rather than later, if you take my meaning." Because of the rain we could not keep anything dry, not ourselves and not our weapons.

"But, Sergeant," Dobbs protested, "how can you be so certain?"

"It's his nature, me boyo," Cate replied, inspecting Dobbs's carbine and handing it back. "I heard it said that when Bedford was a child he was thrown from a young horse into a pack of wild dogs that had been harrying the colt."

He had all our attention now. "Go on," I urged. "What then? And speak up; I'm having trouble with my ears."

Cate made us count cartridges before he would resume. "Forty rounds a man. You'll be wanting all of them before this morning's work is finished. Now as to Old Bedford—far from being torn to shreds, his body lit on top of two of the biggest mutts. He grabbed one in each hand and dashed their brains out. Scared the pack so bad they up and fled."

472

"So even when he's outnumbered . . ."

"Let me see those bayonets," Cate demanded. "Aye, that's his way—throw himself on the pack of his enemies and expect them to run. Forrest is black-hearted as they come, but never doubt his audacity."

At this point Hamilton chimed in. "The *New York Tribune* agrees with you, Sergeant. One of our boys, who was captured after the fight at Fort Donelson and later escaped, said he heard Forrest say to General Pillow, 'Wal, now, Gen'ral, we cain't hold 'em, but we can shore enuff run over 'em.'" Hamilton's mimicry of a broad backwoods accent applied to Old Bedford made everybody laugh.

"Well, now," Cate said, "it is a fine thing when the likes of a great man like Editor Horace Greeley sees eye to eye with the likes of me!"

At that moment the accuracy of Sergeant Cate's judgment was confirmed. The cry of "Here they come!" scattered us to the lee side of a three-rail fence, our carbines cocked and leveled.

"Don't be scared, men!" Captain Briant urged.

"I am not scared," replied Blankenbeckler, just as if Briant had spoken to him in particular. None of the rest of us paid any heed.

In full view over the prairie grass was a tall figure who trotted his black horse to the front of the Rebs. He stretched upright in his stirrups, removed his hat, and swung to face our lines while waving the hat in his right hand.

Our own six-pounder guns saluted their charge, throwing up gouts of mud and smoke. At each explosion we looked to see the attack waver and splinter. Instead each blast seemed only to propel the riders forward with greater urgency and in no fewer numbers, or so it appeared.

We gave one volley from our rifles as they passed the center of the field, and then the horsemen swept around to our right and out of sight. That Forrest was leading an assault on our flank was proven within moments as first our boys from the Second Tennessee ran into us shouting and scrambling. These were succeeded almost immediately by troopers from the Fourth Regiment who stumbled as they ran, throwing aside weapons and haversacks.

"Stand and fight, yellow curs!" Cate bellowed, standing and knocking one deserter down. He thrust a weapon into the man's hand and bodily flung him against a fence post. "May as well be killed fighting right here as go to running and be killed by me."

The wild-eyed private with the insignia of the Second Cavalry grabbed the split-oak upright and blubbered, "They're rolling us up! Let me go, Sergeant, please!"

"Form a line here!" demanded Captain Briant, storming along the fence. "Here! Right angles to the fence!" He grabbed two other fleeing men and forced them down, turned me sideways, and said, "Corporal, you are the anchor of this corner." Then off he went setting others in place so we formed a broad arrow shape with the point toward the sound of battle now sweeping toward us.

General Forrest's bodyguard was joined by the brigade under the command of his brother. The combined force of riders thrust along the fencerow, sweeping up Union soldiers like a farmer raking brush. Then the line they were following dipped into a small hollow before rising again to our knoll.

"Now!" Briant yelled. "Pour it into 'em!"

Four cannons in our battery unleashed loads of canister, and the

473

lead pellets coursed across the field like blasts from giant scatterguns. We fired volley after volley into the mass of horsemen and succeeded in breaking up the charge.

Opposite me and lower, but still in an exposed position on a cleared knob of earth, was the tall figure on a black horse that I knew to be General Forrest. I laid my rifle across the top rail of the fence. His back was to me, and I could not shoot him that way. The wait for him to turn seemed endless, until at last he faced around.

Heedless of the shouting, the smoke, and the cries, I drew down on the topmost button of Old Bedford's uniform. There was no wind, and the shot was just slightly downhill. I blew out my breath, wheezed, then drew a lungful and held it as I tightened my finger on the trigger.

My gaze was so locked on the brass fittings on his jacket that I did not see the other rider gallop into my sight picture until the very moment I squeezed off the round.

The new arrival was in the midst of saluting General Forrest. His hand went clear up over the top of his head instead, and he toppled from his saddle.

I reloaded quick as I could, but when I drew down again on Forrest he was off his horse and kneeling beside the fallen man. Then a new surge of riders coursed toward me, and I transferred my attention elsewhere.

When I next had time to look for General Forrest, he was galloping toward our position at the head of a small band of men. A Reb bugler was blowing charge like it was the last trump.

Forrest waved his saber over his head. Though I could not hear his voice, the contortions of his face told me that he was screaming at the top of his lungs.

"Get ready!" Cate urged unnecessarily, and then the Rebs were on us. Old Bedford put his horse at the rail not twenty feet from me. As he cleared the jump, Forrest slashed downward with his saber. This blade hit Blankenbeckler between the neck and shoulder. The German gave a sudden shout and fell halfway through the fence rails.

I swung my gun to follow the attackers, squeezed the trigger, and shot.

General Forrest's horse screamed, reared, and plunged forward before falling to its forelegs.

A cannon boomed close behind me, and a surge of smoke billowed over the scene, closing off everything more than an arm's length away. And . . . I was out of ammunition.

Briant and Cate were both shouting for us to fall back, but I crouched and ran toward Blanket. He was dead, of course. From the front of his blouse had fallen his slim, leather-bound volume. I grabbed it and then seeing myself about to be surrounded and cut off, I turned and ran.

Fortunately, the Rebs had not captured our horses, so those of us who were left mounted and made our escape from Ivey's Hill. We retreated another thirty miles that day. I was stone deaf in both ears and fevered, but I stayed in the saddle some way or other.

That was much the end of the Mississippi expedition. General Smith reported that we made a "fighting withdrawal." Unsympathetic papers called it a "stampede." What I know is this: We went back to Memphis in half the time it took going. We never did meet with General Sherman's infantry, so he gave it up and turned back too.

Two more things: The man killed on the knobby hill while reporting to General Forrest was his brother, Jeffrey. The book that fell from Blanket's tunic was in German. Its title read *Wie die Religion Taeglich zu Ueben Sey*. It was not until some time later that I located how it translated: *How to Practice Religion in Daily Life*.

Although Blanket and I had not talked man-to-man about our faith, him not being scared now made sense. Blanket had known where he was going, and I was glad I did too. Only I wished Blanket hadn't made it there quite so soon.

✦ CHAPTER 9 ✦

Fort Pillow
April 1864

The shattered pieces of the Third Regiment had been ordered back to Camp Spear in Nashville for the rest of the winter. Unlike our previous times in camp, there was little drill. Morale was low. As Dobbs said, "We had been whupped for fair." There was no arguing the point, and it seemed that no one was likely going to give us a chance to redeem ourselves anytime soon.

Along about the middle of March, Sergeant Cate had hunted me up and told me I had a visitor. When I came outside our tent I found a slim but broad-shouldered, young black man waiting for me. He was wearing the red-braided blue tunic of a private in the light artillery.

"Can I help you?" I said, thinking there was some mistake.

"Don't ya know me, Mistuh, I mean, Corp'ral Dodson?" he asked, grinning.

The familiarity in the voice made me look more closely at his face and then, "Cyrus! Is it really you?"

The smile got even broader till it lit up the overcast day. "It shore enuff is me. Can we set a spell and talk?"

I invited him in, asking only that he speak up. I had regained the hearing in my right ear but was still having trouble with my left. I was also still subject to a recurring fever, but of this I said nothing.

Cyrus explained that after our meeting in Nashville he had wandered north, enjoying his newfound freedom but not knowing what to do with it. "Then it come to me what you said about giving back to the Lawd as He has prospered me. Well, suh, the onliest thing I gots to give is this here hide. So I says, Cyrus, you go on down and jine up and learn to sojer like Mistuh Jesse. And here I is."

He could not stay long as his outfit was moving out that very day. "But if'n you gets a chance, come see me at my new post," he said proudly. "Fort Pillow on the Miss-sippi River!"

It chanced that only a couple of weeks later I learned of a prisoner exchange to be held in West Tennessee, and off I went to look again for William, hoping to find him alive. After all, prisoners were able to write letters sometimes or to send word out to the families by way of those being exchanged. If William was still breathing somewhere, I should by then have known it. I recognized all this, but still I never gave up, and no one tried to talk me out of it neither.

Anyway, that was how I came to be on the Mississippi on the night of April 11. The prisoner exchange had been one day earlier at Hernando, just below Memphis. There was no William among the ranks of the ragged but elated Union soldiers, and I was fixing to hop a train back toward Nashville when a voice hailed me. "Hey, Corporal, didn't we meet up back near Chattanooga?"

It was Captain Rafer Maddox of the hospital ship *Morning Star*. On his shoulder rode the blue-and-gold parrot, Scrimshaw. Maddox was in Memphis to transport some of the seriously wounded soldiers up the river to a hospital in Ohio.

We visited for a bit, and he offered me a ride on the steamer.

I declined. "Gotta get back to camp. I'll be catching a train in an hour or so."

"Haven't you heard?" he asked with some surprise. "Reb cavalry busted up the tracks in a raid between here and Brownsville. It'll be two days or better before your train will run."

I fell into a brown study, thinking how, if I was late returning to Nashville, not only would Captain Briant skin me, he would never let me go off to another prisoner exchange. I said as much to Rafer.

"Tell you what," he replied. "Go with me as far as Hickman, Kentucky. You can catch a train there for Nashville."

After the *Morning Star* got under way, I found out that she was putting in at Fort Pillow to drop off some medical supplies. So it appeared that if I had met Captain Maddox again by Providence, I was also fated to see Cyrus on this same trip.

Fort Pillow was forty miles overland north of Memphis and eighty by the loops and curls of Old Man River. Going against the current, it was midday on the twelfth before we drew abreast of the last bend below the fort.

There was smoke billowing over the headland, and when Rafer stopped the engine we could hear the sound of guns. Another captain would have put the helm over and run for cover or idled until he knew it was safe but not Captain Maddox. He rang the engine room for full speed, reasoning that his was a hospital ship, and where there was shooting, she would be needed.

Around the bend we came in sight of the outpost. Fort Pillow was a small place, perched on the brow of the Chickasaw Bluff. It had but six guns and was defended by about six hundred men. It was so far up the river that no one thought it would be attacked, seeing as the war had moved south.

Once again the Federal commanders had reckoned without General Forrest. His way of defending by attacking carried over whether it was one battle or a whole campaign. Not content with having kicked us out of Mississippi, he had struck into West Tennessee. It had been his troops who cut the rail lines, and now they were assaulting Fort Pillow. Its capture would threaten Union shipping on the river.

When the steamer arrived, a Union gunboat was blasting away at the ravines that lay on both sides of the fort. From our vantage point on the water, we could see that the shells were having little effect. Every time the floating-gun platform maneuvered to lob a canister at the Rebs, the graybacks moved around to the other canyon and continued the attack.

Upon the clay knoll the defenders were hard-pressed. The slope was so steep that they could not depress the guns in the fort low enough to sweep the ravines. Worse yet, Rebs had found high ground beyond the fort from which they could snipe at the men inside.

The fighting went on for three more hours or till about midafternoon. The Rebs gained the ground just outside the walls. Whenever the defenders leaned over to fire their rifles down, Reb sharpshooters would pick them off.

I saw a flag of truce go up to the fort from the attackers, and for a time the firing ceased. Whatever parley took place, Old Glory was not lowered from the staff over the fort's walls, and the assault resumed, but the stalemate was over.

The Rebs stormed the walls and boosted one another up. I counted near eight hundred Confederates achieve the top of the parapet. When they jumped inside, I groaned in the expectation of surrender.

What followed was worse than any capitulation. As the Rebs poured over the walls, the defenders, mostly black men, streamed out the gate and tumbled toward the river, just as the victorious Rebels tore down the U.S. flag.

But there was no surrender.

As Captain Maddox and I watched with horror, the Rebs surrounded men who had cast away their guns and shot them! Even those whose upraised arms could be plainly seen were bayoneted to death or sabered and their bodies pushed into the river. I saw black troops fling themselves into the stream attempting to escape the slaughter.

The Union gunboat stood in toward the bank to try and pick up some of the survivors. Immediately, the cannons in the fort, now manned by secesh gunners, fired at the gunboat and drove it off.

Onshore the massacre continued until a red stain floated with the current. For two hundred yards the Mississippi ran crimson with blood.

"Do something!" I pleaded with Captain Maddox.

The good captain needed no urging. *Morning Star* forged across the stream toward those floundering in the water. His second in command protested that using a hospital ship to rescue men in conflict was a violation of the rules of war.

Rafer backhanded his lieutenant and ordered him out of the

wheelhouse. "Do you see that!" Rafer shouted, his face fiery with anger. "Is that butchery according to the rules of war?"

Without further thought, Captain Maddox imposed the bulk of the steamer between the shore and the swimming survivors. Racing below, I helped pluck wounded and drowning men from the current.

I saw an arm wave, heard a gurgling cry for help, and saw a soldier go under. As at the fight at Ellis Bridge, I jumped without thinking into the water.

It was not Cyrus that I rescued that time, nor were any of the three other bodies that I plunged into the muddy water after. But Cyrus *was* plucked from the Mississippi that day, a bullet wound in his shoulder from where he had been shot in the back. He went into the hospital. Cyrus lived, but he would fight no more after his first battle.

The Rebs took the cannon from Fort Pillow; they held the fort for only about a day before retiring, and the raid was over.

General Forrest was reviled in the Northern papers for ordering the massacre. His printed reply was that he had not ordered it but was incapable of preventing it.

Forrest was not sorry. His statement in the Southern papers was "It is hoped that these facts will demonstrate to the Northern people that Negro soldiers are no match for Southerners."

Fort Pillow had two personal consequences for me: my repeated immersions into the water brought on a new bout of fever, and I lost what little remained of the hearing in my left ear. Also, I went no more to prisoner exchanges, because there were none. As a result of the atrocity, General Grant refused to exchange any more Reb soldiers.

Both the nation's conflict and my personal one had grown more bitter than ever.

✳ ✳ ✳

The regimental surgeon, Dr. Souers, waited for me to button my tunic and seat myself on a camp stool next to his desk. Despite his frequent recourse to the one medication for all complaints, Doc did not this time offer me the familiar cork-stoppered brown bottle of quinine.

"Corporal," he said in a low voice, "you are a very sick man."

"What?" I said. "You'll have to speak up. I've gone deaf in my left ear, you know."

"I know," he agreed, moving to my right side. "I did that on purpose to make a point. You are stone-deaf on one side, and you've lost about 25 percent of your hearing on the other."

"I'm better now," I protested. "Getting stronger every day."

"Corporal," Dr. Souers stressed again, "I may be an old country sawbones when it comes to modern medicine and such, but even I know the rheumatic when I see it. Besides the hearing loss, it's weakened your heart and lungs. Why you don't have consumption I'll never know. As it is, the first bout of camp fever may carry you off. At the very least any more sickness and you'll be deaf as a post for the rest of your life."

That brought me up short. I thought of not being able to hear Alcie's sweet voice, the laughter of my children, the songs in church, the muted whispers of mornings in Alcie's arms before the children waked. It was hard.

I hung my head. "What's the answer, then?" I asked without lifting my gaze, for I already knew the response.

"I'm sending you home," he said. "Given time, rest, and proper food and care, you may beat this thing. But not here, not under these conditions. Do you know how many men have been killed in battle since this regiment was formed?"

His question took me by surprise. "No. Blankenbeckler. That lieutenant ..."

"Eight," Dr. Souers said distinctly. "That's all. Do you know the number of good men who have died of illness or of wounds that should not have killed them?"

I made no reply.

He ran his fingers through his thinning gray hair and propped his sagging jowls on weary fingers. "We just don't know enough," he said softly, then repeated louder. "We don't know enough to save them."

481

"Can you make me leave?" I asked. "Isn't it my choice?"

Dr. Souers nodded slowly. "You don't have to accept a medical discharge unless you are endangering the lives of others. But why stay? Don't you have a family? Haven't you seen plenty of maiming and killing for one lifetime?"

"My boy William," I replied. "He may still be a prisoner . . . or he may already be dead. Either way, I owe him. He was stronger of his convictions than me, a better man than me. Other good men too: Long, Cochran. I owe it to them to see this thing through." My heart sank inside me even as I proclaimed the words. We had just heard that the Rebs had retreated from East Tennessee; I *could* have gone home again but could not.

There was a long silence as the doctor and I regarded each other.

When he spoke again it was in a matter-of-fact tone. "Don't get chilled. Treat the least sore throat or fever as life threatening, because it is. Stay warm and dry, or I won't answer for the consequences."

Nodding slowly, I thanked him and rose to leave.

He stopped me at the tent flap by mumbling something I could not hear. "What was that?"

"Four hundred thirteen," the doctor said. "Fever, bloody flux, little scratches that didn't bleed a teaspoonful . . . four hundred thirteen dead from this regiment alone."

* CHAPTER 10 *

Sulphur Branch Trestle, Alabama
September 1864

By late spring of 1864, the Union strategy for ending the war was at last being realized. General Sherman was moving to cut the Confederacy in two, from Tennessee to the ocean. In the East, Grant kept the pressure on Lee so that the Reb Army of Virginia could not go to the rescue of Atlanta.

Sherman's biggest worry was his five-hundred-mile-long supply line. Since it stretched from Louisville, Kentucky, clear through Nashville to Chattanooga and on into Georgia, a strong Reb force in Middle Tennessee could cut him off.

Everybody in blue—from the highest major general to the rankest private—knew that Forrest was the danger. Who else but Old Bedford could move fast enough and hit hard enough to endanger Sherman's march to the sea?

So it fell to the Tennessee Volunteer cavalry regiments to counter that threat. During this time, I and the rest of the Third Regiment were still guarding trains out of Nashville, but we eagerly followed the news.

To begin with, just the Union troopers stationed in Memphis were enough to hold Forrest back. Sherman rightly guessed that General Forrest would not leave Mississippi undefended against another Yankee invasion, and that strategy worked for a time.

Then came June and the fight at Brice's Crossroads, Mississippi.

Old Bedford whipped Union cavalry and then infantry, one after the other. The Union force went reeling back to Memphis, having lost six hundred men killed or wounded and nearly two thousand captured. Once more Negro soldiers were slaughtered, the number of dead from their brigade greater than those from the other five brigades combined.

If the fighting in Mississippi was again a disaster for the North, it at last accomplished its purpose. Forrest was unable to attack Sherman's railroad lifeline. Another Union invasion of Mississippi in July also resulted in defeat but again kept Forrest in check. It was God's own providence that the leadership of the Rebels preferred to keep Forrest back rather than unleashing him on Tennessee.

In mid-August Old Bedford shook up the Union commanders by launching an offensive of his own. He reasoned that if he could not cut off Sherman's supplies, the next best thing would be an attack northward that would force our generals to leave off attack in favor of defense.

So Forrest raided Memphis in the early morning hours. Despite the fact that the city had been solidly in Union hands for two years and was full of blue uniforms, Forrest's men achieved complete surprise and captured six hundred men.

At Camp Spear, on a muggy August night, those of us of Company F were discussing all these things.

"They say Forrest has fifty thousand men, and he's coming to attack Nashville." A new recruit named Friesen gulped.

Dobbs snorted, with the air of a seasoned campaigner who discounted 90 percent of any rumor he heard. "Old Bedford may be worth a lot, but to make up fifty thousand he'd have to count for forty-five thousand of them his own self."

"Won't Sherman have to turn back now?" Friesen persisted.

"Not a chance," Hamilton concluded. "But I do know this: Next time somebody gets up an expedition after Forrest, it'll be our turn again."

We thought that over with mixed emotions.

I knew that Hamilton was undoubtedly right. The Third

Regiment had been out of the line for six months. Our number was sure to come up again soon.

That night I wrote a letter home to Alcie. I proclaimed again my intention to keep my promises. I would still believe that William was alive, and I would live to come home to her. I made brief remark of my ailments; it was little enough to do to spare her fretting. I could not resist telling her how much I missed her and ached to hold her.

On September 2, Atlanta fell to Sherman's invasion, and the awakening at the end of the long nightmare of the rebellion was near. Too late the Rebel high command recognized the need to use Forrest on the offensive—too late to defeat Sherman but not too late to involve the Third Tennessee in another campaign against Old Bedford.

It was reported that Forrest had moved his command to Cherokee Station, Alabama. If such news was true, it could only mean that he was preparing an assault north toward Nashville. We were dispatched to deal with him.

One thing of note occurred before our departure: Our trusty, single-shot carbines were taken from us and replaced with Spencer seven-shooters. "Load 'em in the morning and fight all day," Hamilton quipped. Other units had already been using the repeaters with the tube magazine that fitted into the stock. They were supposed to make one man fight like a company and a company like a regiment. Friesen said he felt invincible. The rest of us just hoped we would finally be able to lick Old Bedford instead of coming back with our tails between our legs.

We loaded into railcars and over the line of Nashville and Decatur were moved to Athens . . . Alabama. Not my home near Athens, Tennessee, but one hundred twenty miles from there.

We rode out toward Decatur on September 23 and almost immediately had a skirmish with some Reb troopers. Sure enough, the Spencers worked like champs. The Rebs charged with their usual dash and clamor, but each time we were able to turn them back without loss to ourselves. After three tries, they drew off to reconsider, and we returned to the fort at a place called Sulphur Branch Trestle.

* * *

"Did you ever see anything like that?" Dobbs asked me. "Ain't that the biggest bridge you ever seen?"

I agreed with him that the wooden structure was enormous. Spanning a tributary of the Tennessee River, the trestle was over seventy feet high and more than three hundred feet long. It was of major importance to the line of the Nashville and Decatur Railroad. The platform was to be protected to allow our troops to move into Alabama or, failing that, to be destroyed to make it tougher for Forrest to move north.

As we were rubbing down our horses, I overheard a conversation between Colonel Minnis and the commander of the fort, Colonel Lathrop.

"Minnis," Lathrop said, "have your men stable their horses and draw ammunition. Then have them see Captain Pierce for their assigned positions."

"Assigned positions?" Minnis questioned. "Colonel, my men are ready to take the fight to the enemy. We can punch right through their line tomorrow or harry them until reinforcements come up."

Lathrop snorted. "How many men do you have, Colonel? Four hundred? Don't you know that Old Bedford is coming on with thousands?"

"Begging your pardon, then," said Minnis reasonably. "In that case, wouldn't it be prudent to torch the scaffold now and fall back on Pulaski?"

"From bravado to timidity so quickly, Colonel?"

I could see Minnis swell up and redden about the back of the neck. Our orders put him specially under Lathrop's command, so there was no arguing.

In any case, Lathrop continued, "Besides, Colonel, we can hold them off here! Look at the works of this fort. And what about your new Spencer repeaters? Let me show you around the walls, and we can discuss the defense."

"Did I hear the man?" Cate hissed in my ear. "Defense, he says!

Sure, and I'd rather have a fine animal beneath me and a field crawling with Johnny Rebs in front of me than be stuck in here!"

Straightening up from clenching horseshoe nails, I turned round and regarded the fort. The fortifications consisted of a pair of blockhouses made of railroad ties and a surrounding earthwork. "Them blockhouse walls are three feet thick. Maybe the web-footed colonel knows his stuff?"

"And I'm Saint Patrick," mumbled Cate. "All right, then, Corporal Dodson. After the good captain lets us in on our positions, you and me will see how we can make the best of it."

We shared the defense of Sulphur Branch Trestle with two hundred Indiana cavalrymen and four hundred colored infantry. Together with our regiment, we totaled about a thousand.

Our company was detailed as part of the defense of the south wall of the earthwork.

"Did you happen to notice something odd about this fort?" Hamilton asked; without pausing, he answered his own question. "No cannon. The platforms are in place, but there are no guns mounted."

"So?" I said cautiously, not wanting to broach my own concerns.

Hamilton looked me square in the eye. "Don't try that on me, Jesse Dodson, corporal or not. You see it as plainly as I do. If we have no cannons and Forrest does, we're in a quicksand bog up to our necks and no mistake."

* * *

Colonel Minnis suggested to Colonel Lathrop that we throw out a picket line outside the earthworks, even volunteered our company for the job. Our commander hinted that some advance warning of the arrival of the Rebs would be a good thing, said we might even disrupt their attack and make them draw back.

Lathrop refused. "Can't spare any of the defenders. Besides, if one of your boys got himself captured, he might shoot his mouth off about our defenses here. Can't have that now, can we?"

So as night fell, we took turns patrolling the six-foot-high berm around the compound. When we were not on guard, we sat beside small campfires on the sultry, warm, Alabama night.

"'Scuse me, Corporal," one of the Negro soldiers said to me. "Is you name of Dodson?"

"That's me," I admitted.

"Wal, my name is Private Fletcher, suh. My cousin be Cyrus, you know, him you save from the river?"

"I didn't exactly save him," I confessed. "But I was there. How is he?"

"He doin' much better, suh. He still in the hospital, but he gonna be fine, they says. He tole me to watch out for you if'n I met up with the Third Tennessee."

I shook Fletcher's hand warmly, told him I was glad of the news about Cyrus, and expected the private to return to his post. Instead he hung about expectantly, as if there was more he wanted to say.

At last he spoke again, "You at Fort Pillow. You seen what the Rebs done there?"

"I did," I replied. "I won't ever forget it, neither."

"And Ol' Bedford, he the same what comin' here?"

I allowed as how that was what we had heard. "Are you afraid?"

"No, suh!" Fletcher said promptly. "I been wantin' a chance to settle up with Gen'ral Forrest. Evuhbody in my outfit feel the same way too. Just wish . . ." His voice trailed off into the starry sky.

"Wish what?"

"Wish we outside, 'stead of waitin' in here. Don' know what kinda fightin' we gonna see."

I nodded. "Tell your outfit just to soldier like they know how. That's all any of us can do."

Fletcher nodded and left me.

Almost immediately Dobbs came over. "Jesse, you been my friend since I first joined up, and we fought a heap of battles together."

"That we have."

"Skull Camp Bridge, Jasper's Ford, Ivey's Hill," he called the roll of conflicts. "Anyways," he continued, then stopped. "Anyways, I want you to do somethin' for me."

"Shore," I said. "What?"

"Hold these for me." He handed me a scrap of paper folded twice over. It was heavy. "My watch and chain. It was my daddy's, and if tomorrow . . . if tomorrow . . ."

"Don't talk like that," I urged. "We've come through tough spots before. Tomorrow won't be any different. We even got reinforcements coming down from Pulaski. We'll be fine."

Dobbs was already shaking his head before I had finished speaking. "Promise me, Jesse. See that my family gets it if I don't make it."

What was left for me to say? "'Course. But you'll see. I'll be giving it back to you tomorrow night."

Later on, Hamilton asked me if I ever had any premonitions before a battle.

"Premonition?" I repeated. "You mean, foreboding? I guess everybody does some. Anytime you know there's gonna be a battle, you can't help but think on it."

"How do you handle it?"

The last thing I wanted was to give a hackneyed answer to a serious question. Even though I was not an officer, lots of those boys looked on me as a kind of father on account of my age. What would I say to my own son if he had been in the spot we were in?

Finally the answer came. "Can you promise me that you will wake up tomorrow when you go to sleep tonight?"

"No," Hamilton admitted.

"Or testify that your heart will keep beating or that you will keep breathing after the very next breath?"

"You're driving at something, Jesse," he said. "Say it."

"None of us has a bridle on our own life," I said. "Doctor says I could die from catching a cold . . . wouldn't even have to stop a bullet. Just a raindrop would do it. So . . . a man's gotta live as though he's ready to meet God any day or night. That way, it don't matter whether you think something's gonna happen or not. If I walk outta this skin tomorrow or not for seventy years, the main thing is I want to be ready to see Jesus right after."

I locked my eyes on Hamilton's. "I'm sure of it for myself. That I'll be seeing Jesus right after. Are you sure of it for you, Hamilton?"

He dropped his eyes and was silent a while. Finally he nodded slowly. "Thought that's what you'd say. Just wanted to hear it directly from you. Guess I have some thinking to do."

There was a lot of praying and quiet hymn singing in camp that night. We did not know what the next morning would bring. Would some of us be ushered into the presence of God Almighty?

✳ ✳ ✳

I do not think that anyone in the garrison at Sulphur Branch Trestle slept much, even though the night seemed to last a hundred years. When dawn finally winked a gray eye on the eastern horizon, every man was on the parapet, straining to see.

"There!" Hamilton exclaimed, pointing. "What's that row of dark shapes over there?"

Similar discoveries were made all around the fort. On every side of the compound, too far in the half-light to be clearly made out, were squat, black forms, like rows of obediently crouching dogs.

"Batteries," Sergeant Cate observed. "Moved 'em up all around us in the night."

Because of Colonel Lathrop's unwillingness to allow night patrols, our position was now ringed by guns, their open mouths gaping. We had no cannon of our own with which to reply to this peril. The Rebs must have known our predicament, too, because they had planted their batteries in plain sight.

"Too far for us to snipe at the gunners," Hamilton observed. "We'd best get up and charge 'em before they start throwing shots."

I agreed with that reasoning: Take a page from Old Bedford's book and defend by attacking.

But Colonel Lathrop would have none of it. "We'll shelter here or inside the blockhouses. They can't attack until they stop firing their cannons, and then our rifles can pick them off before they cross the open stretch all around."

What Lathrop failed to consider was that since we were surrounded by cannons on every side, the Rebs could lob shells into the compound without regard to the bulwarks.

A mass of milling figures on horseback surged into view in front of one battery. Presently a white cloth tied to the end of a saber floated aloft.

"Parley!" Lathrop yelled. "Hold your fire! Let's hear what they have to say."

"Lathrop likely thinks they'll be wantin' to surrender to us," Cate grunted.

Accompanied by an escort of four troopers, a tall man on a black horse cantered toward the gates. He reined up at a distance of some fifty yards and hollered for the commander.

"I command here," Lathrop responded, his tone prideful and haughty. "Colonel William H. Lathrop. And whom do I have the honor of addressing?"

He must have been the only man in the fort who did not already know the answer.

"Gen'ral Nathan Bedford Forrest" was the reply. "Suh, as you see, yore position is surrounded and untenable. I beg you to prevent unnecessary loss of life by surrendering now."

Whether pride, fear for the fate of his black soldiers, or genuine though ill-considered confidence caused Lathrop's decision, I cannot say. His reply was abrupt and offhand: "Never! If you think you can achieve my position, then, sir, come and take it!"

Before Forrest and his honor guard had returned to their ranks, the bombardment began. With a precise cadence, like a formal salute at a funeral, eight cannons boomed in turn. The very first shell landed on top of a blockhouse and blew a hole through the roof.

Crouching in the dirt of the embankment, I used my saber to scratch out a depression in the earth into which I could fold myself. All around me, everyone was doing the same.

After the first volley, there was no rhythm to the guns. The explosions of their charges rolled over and on top of one another, as if each gun crew was competing to see who could fire rounds the fastest. It was like thunder, only without a letup. It was like a barn being struck by lightning over and over and over.

A solid shot hit the earthwork just on the other side of me. Had the cannonball struck six inches higher, it would have taken my head off. Another round crashed into a blockhouse, punching completely through the wall like an auger. The batteries fired solid shot, exploding shot, canister, and grapeshot, using every shell that came to hand, it seemed.

Once when I was very young, I had wrestled with my brother for the possession of a fishing pole on the bank of the Tennessee River. Clutching the prize, we both fell into the current. He surfaced at once, and since we could both swim like fish, he made it easily back to shore. But I was swept by the current under a bank. My ankle caught in the forked root of a half-submerged willow. I could not free myself by going either up or down, and to move back against the current was impossible. Finally, just before I gave in and sucked water into my lungs, my struggles broke the root and freed my ankle. I floated downstream to a sandy shore. My brother helped haul me out, and I lay there, more drowned than alive. We never told of that experience for fear of getting whupped. Afterward I forced myself to overcome the fear and made myself be a strong swimmer in spite of it.

Being under that bombardment was like drowning. There was no way to fight back, and there was no escape. Breathing became labored. I gasped for breath and held each one, as if sucking in a single puff of air would draw a shell. The ground wavered under my feet and tossed me about like waves. The air was foul with the stench of gunpowder and smoke. The crash of the shells was so numbing that everyone was deafened, and I found an opportunity to be grateful for my own lessened hearing. I could still feel every concussion, and it was as though the rounds were bursting inside my head, inside my stomach, and inside my legs.

I saw Colonel Lathrop shouting orders from the blockhouses. An instant later a shell exploded above the center of the compound, and the colonel paid the price for his foolish arrogance. Shrapnel ripped him to pieces, and his body, though momentarily upright, appeared to have been savaged by wolves.

Another exploding shell bounded into the fort with its fuse still sputtering. It ricocheted off the top of the earthwork and spun to a stop no more than thirty feet from me.

Hamilton and I saw the bomb at the same instant. Before I could move or even think, Hamilton shouted, "Look out, Jesse!" He threw himself over my body, covering it with his own.

The shell detonated. Hamilton and I were tossed into the air and tumbled in a heap. By the time I collected my dazed wits, it was clear that he was dying. "Glad . . . I'm ready . . . to go," Hamilton gasped. "Because you . . . God bless . . ." And he was gone.

There was no time to grieve. Our commander tried to rally us for an attack. "Mount up!" Colonel Minnis urged. "Mount up, before we are all slaughtered in here!"

The horses were panicked and surged back and forth across the compound with every explosion. I laid my hand on the broken lead rope around the neck of one, only to have the horse struck by a shell fragment and die at the end of the tether.

Minnis then tried to organize an attack on foot. "Captain Briant! Have your men form up beside the gate. We'll rush the battery near the blackberry thicket. We must have something with which to fight back! We can turn captured guns on the Rebs!"

There was not a chance we would have ever survived such a rush. Before we crossed half the distance to the Reb position, they would have mowed us down with grape and canister.

As it was, the charge was never even launched. Another exploding shell detonated on the wall of the blockhouse right behind Minnis. The wooden wall absorbed much of the impact, but a chunk of metal rebounded from the blow and hit the colonel in the back of the head. He fell senseless to the ground.

For two hours—and, as I heard later, over eight hundred rounds of ammunition—the carnage continued.

Then the roar fell silent.

Again General Forrest approached under a flag of truce. "Will you surrender the fort now?"

"Colonel Lathrop is dead," Captain Briant replied, "and Colonel Minnis is badly wounded. But I accept your offer."

"Stack yore arms and come out," Forrest ordered, and so we did.

Old Bedford had captured Sulphur Branch Trestle intact. Besides four hundred dead and wounded and the rest of us taken prisoner, he also collected three hundred horses. Of his own command, nary a single man was hurt or killed.

Forrest allowed us to gather in burial details and give our dead proper treatment. Carrying bodies out of the fort, I walked near the Reb general several times. I wondered if he would recognize me as the deserter from his forced Nashville recruiting or if he connected me with the death of his brother, Jeffrey. Perhaps my gaunt, smoke-stained face was unrecognizable or perhaps he let it pass. Either way, he said nothing. Perhaps his mind was occupied with the hundreds of repeating rifles he had suddenly acquired: One-fourth of his men had begun the Middle Tennessee campaign without any firearms at all. Old Bedford had promised to see them fitted out, and he had delivered.

When the burying was done and the wounded made ready for travel, we formed marching columns to go into captivity. All the Negro soldiers were sent off separately from the rest. . . . I do not know what became of them. But I prayed that they would not share the fate of those at Fort Pillow.

CHAPTER 11

Cahaba Prison, Alabama
September 1864–April 1865

W
hen were herded away from the burned-out hulk of the fort, I had no idea where we were going. Our captors rode while we walked, and they were anxious for us to hurry. It seems that Forrest had requested Confederate provost guards to accompany his prisoners and been refused.

So there was nothing left to do but to divide his command and use some of his own troops as wardens. Since Forrest's raid was headed into Middle Tennessee, he could hardly spare any men. The result was that he was in a foul mood, and the men detailed to accompany us were in no great spirits either. They were in a lather to get us into somebody else's keeping and get back to the foray.

They hiked us overland to Cherokee Station, a distance of sixty weary miles. Covering the distance in forced marches took only three days. We carried our own wounded and had only hardtack to eat. Our escorts relieved us of all our other supplies and rations but were prevented by their officers from stealing our clothing, boots, or personal belongings.

On the second day of the march they allowed us to fall out for five minutes of rest beside a slough covered in green scum. While the guards filled their canteens from the only clear spring, we were forced to drink our fill from the swamp.

That night and all the next day, fully two-thirds of those captured

495

were deathly ill with the flux. It made no difference in the attitude of the guards. If a man had to fall out of the column because of an urgent sickness it was permitted, but thereafter he was made to stagger at bayonet point to catch up.

I was one of the afflicted. Dazed from the shelling, numbed because of the death of young Hamilton, wearied to the point of collapse by the march, and then sapped of any reserve through the action of the distemper, I was near the end of my string.

Captain Briant found me lying beside the road. I was facedown in a pool of mud not over two inches deep but likely to drown there just the same. "Come on, Jesse. Get up, man."

"I don't think I can, Cap."

"Sure you can. Dobbs, lend a hand here."

The remaining leagues of our trek are only a blur in my memory. I know that Dobbs and the captain supported me between them. As for the ground we crossed, I cannot recover any particle of my own recollection, except for one snatch of conversation. During another all too brief respite for stale water and weevily bread, Dobbs and the captain leaned me back against a fence post, and I slid downward. The captain went off to demand fresh drinking water for the men.

Dobbs knelt beside me. "Jesse, you gonna make it?"

I shook my head ponderously. Even that little movement seemed like too much effort. "I'm mighty used up. Don't know how you keep going and carry me at the same time."

"It ain't nothin'." He shrugged. Then, "Say, Jesse, do you still got that letter and watch I give you to keep for me?"

Reaching inside my tunic to search for the packet, I overbalanced sideways and would have sprawled on the ground had Dobbs not caught me. I drew out the parcel with trembling fingers. "Here it is."

"Thanks," he said, then added with embarrassment, "Guess I was wrong about it bein' my time."

My eyelids would barely remain open enough for me to focus on his face, but I gave my best effort. "It *was* for lots of others," I said, remembering Hamilton's sacrifice.

"Been thinkin' about that," Dobbs said. "I still don't know why I lived. Why me?"

When I answered, my words were slurred. "Maybe because God was gracious and knew you weren't ready to face Him . . . and maybe because He still has important things for you to do here."

Dobbs nodded slowly. "'Spose it could be both?"

Nodding was the best response I could manage, but he seemed satisfied. I could not speak more, but I shot a prayer skyward that the young Dobbs would live a long and worthy life before he went to meet his Maker.

Soon Captain Briant returned. We were rationed only one canteen of fresh water among every three men, but it was better than before.

Another fifty men died on the march.

At the rail yard at Cherokee Station we were crowded into a stockade like so many head of cattle, along with other prisoners gathered by Forrest's sweep through northern Alabama. Guards patrolled a narrow catwalk atop the board fence. On our part, we milled around ceaselessly because there were so many prisoners crammed into the space there was no room to sit or lie down.

On our third day in the corral we met a provost guard named Mills. He was an unshaven, snaggletoothed rascal with a head shaped like a cannonball and an intellect to match. His eye gleamed with a native shrewdness and gave him a crafty, furtive look.

"Psst," he hissed at Dobbs from the platform. "You got big feet, same as me. Give you a loaf of bread for them shoes o'yourn." He wiggled his toes to show where his own footgear had worn through.

"My boots?" Dobbs argued. "What'm I gonna march in then?"

But, like all of us, Dobbs was hungry. So at last he passed up the boots and got a lumpy, dark brown loaf of bread in return. It was coarse and the texture full of grit, but it was better than anything we had eaten for six days.

The exchange gave Captain Briant an idea.

The next night only Mills and one other guard were on watch. When the two sentries were the farthest apart, Briant hailed Mills. "Private," he called, "how'd you like to get a solid gold watch?"

Mills's eyes lit up with greed. "Whatcha want fer it?" he asked without hesitation.

497

"There's over a thousand of us in here," Briant said. "You know we haven't been registered yet, and nobody will know if a few go missing. If you look the other way while ten of us slip out the gate, the watch is yours."

"Not no officers," Mills protested. "They'll have my guts for garters if'n I lose an officer."

"All right," Briant said without hesitation. "Ten of my men, then."

"Three" was the sharp reply.

"Six," responded Briant. "And now, tonight, or the deal is off." Briant pointed out five other men and me. "You six will break out tonight. Due north will take you to the river. Follow it east and you'll find one of our patrols in a day or so."

I was already shaking my head. "God bless you, Captain, but I can't go. Send someone else in my place. I'd never make it as far as the river."

Captain Briant looked me in the eyes for a long moment, then nodded and named another to go in my stead.

Soon six shadows flitted out beyond the faint light of the torches and disappeared in the darkness.

Then Briant whispered, "Anybody else have a watch or valuable to barter? More of you can make the attempt."

Dobbs extracted his pocket watch and chain and passed it to the captain. "Use mine."

The negotiation with Mills was even briefer. The captain said to Dobbs, "It's your watch, Private. You name the others to accompany you."

"You pick 'em, Captain," Dobbs replied. "And go on and name six. If Jesse can't leave, reckon I'll stay with him."

Six more of our men slipped away in the night.

The next morning it was announced that officers were to be sent to a different prison from the enlisted men and that all of us were shipping out that very day.

"Good-bye, Corporal," Briant said to me. "I'll pray for you."

"And I for you, Captain," I said.

When they loaded us aboard cattle cars, a hundred to a car, the remaining members of Company F were all crammed in together:

me, Dobbs, Sergeant Cate, and fifteen more from other messes. Out of a hundred men plus replacements, the rest were gone.

✸ ✸ ✸

Before the rebellion, Cahaba Prison had not been a prison. It had not been a jail, a stockade, or a barracks . . . it had been a cotton warehouse. Located on the west bank of the Alabama River, Cahaba was a dilapidated high-roofed shed and a muddy slope open to the rain. Structures that had once been docks and loading platforms had been torn down, and a fence taller than a man could reach now reared from waist-deep, brown water. There were guards on the roof and on a walkway that surrounded the compound. We were only ten miles south of Selma, Alabama, but we might as well have been in darkest Africa, so far from anything like civilization did we feel.

When we arrived I could hardly walk, but after the cramped transport in the cattle cars, neither could anyone else. Dobbs and I leaned toward each other like a pair of drunks. It took two hours for our captors to move us from the rail siding into the prison.

Once we were all inside, a pair of iron-barred gates slammed shut behind us. A Reb officer yelled, "Line up fer rations! Move along lively now!"

We all shuffled forward as best we were able, approaching a long, narrow table heaped with cornmeal and dried peas. As each prisoner neared the counter, a double handful of each foodstuff was poured into his haversack, if he still had one, or into his cupped hand or shirttails if he did not. A chunk of green salt beef furnished the rest of our food allowance.

Sergeant Cate squinted a bloodshot eye at the dirty, yellow meal spilling from his grimy hands and asked, "Would this be dinner or supper you're issuing here?"

The greasy-faced corporal ladling out the grain laughed. "What are you thinkin', Billy Yank? That there is all you gonna get till tomorrow this time . . . if you're lucky."

"And what are we supposed to be cooking it in?" Cate continued.

"Well, now, that'd be yore problem, wouldn't it?"

Cate asked me, "Jesse, would you be having a pan to cook this in?"

I did not, nor was one easily located. When we finally did come across a soldier still carrying a skillet, there was yet another problem to be faced.

"Where's the firewood?" Dobbs asked a guard.

"Ask yore Gen'ral Sherman," replied the stony-faced sentry. "He's been burnin' houses and such clean across Georgia, so we don't let you Yanks play with no fire."

We were permitted to build campfires on the clay slope that ran down to the river, if firewood could be located. For a price—Yankee dollars, gold watches, or jewelry—our wardens would part with a few miserable pieces of wood that burned with very little heat.

The first night we followed the practice of most of the prisoners: We stirred the meal into a tin cup of water and drank it. When weevils floated up out of the meal, Cate's response was "Don't be complaining about that. It's better than the other meat in this rat hole."

There was something like two thousand prisoners in Cahaba, despite the fact that it had been planned to house only three hundred. Worse yet, for most of the war Cahaba had been only a transfer point for Yankees being shipped elsewhere. After the loss of Atlanta and the slicing in two of the Confederacy, Cahaba was now bursting its seams.

Cate, Dobbs, and I, as some of the later arrivals, could find no place under the roofed shed. We pitched our camp on an unoccupied stretch of clay hillside. That's all the decision there was to be made.

✳ ✳ ✳

By the winter of 1865, it was clear to everyone in Cahaba, prisoners and guards both, that the war was not going well for the Confederacy. Just before Christmas in '64, Sherman completed his march to the sea by swallowing up Savannah. His army destroyed hundreds of miles of railroad track, turning the rails into "Sherman hairpins," by bending heated steel around tree stumps. Hundreds of liberated slaves followed in Sherman's wake, even as he turned north trailing a swath of destruction toward Columbia, South Carolina.

Up north, Grant had Lee pinned behind his defense at Petersburg. While Grant's men kept warm and snug in their solid bombproof structures, the Rebs starved, suffered from the icy blasts, and deserted in droves.

Despite his capture of the Spencer rifles, Nathan Bedford Forrest was driven back. The high tide of the Confederate Army of Tennessee crested at Nashville, there to be thrown into confusion. They retreated, a disordered rabble.

The worse the news from the Rebel front, the harsher our treatment became. No longer were we given any opportunity to wash our clothes except in the filthy, muddy river. We pleaded to be allowed one pair of scissors so we could crop our hair, but this was denied us. Lice multiplied and spread throughout the camp. Our jailers no longer entered the compound with our supplies; they merely tossed the sacks over the wall to be pounced on by us like so many animals.

Our daily ration of dried peas was stopped; then our quarter pound of salt meat was limited to every other day, and finally it was halted altogether. We lived on a quart of cornmeal a day, baked if we had a pan, boiled in tin cans, or stirred into cold water and drank if no other means presented itself.

The short rations made us lose weight until our bones almost protruded through the skin. Cate, Dobbs, and I managed to keep warm enough and sheltered inside our poor tent. I had remained miraculously free of illness, despite the harsh treatment. I knew it had to be the Lord Himself looking out for me. I reminded myself of my promise to Alcie: I must get home to her again; I had given my word on it.

Then came the rains.

For the first two weeks of March it rained almost continuously. Sergeant Cate and Dobbs were careful of my health and demanded that I keep close and not expose myself unnecessarily to the damp and the harsh winds.

The river rose.

It encroached on two feet of the mud bank the first day, driving back those encamped on the verge. We were all squeezed into a smaller space.

The next day the climbing Alabama River reclaimed ten feet of its shoreline from the Yankee invaders, and we retreated still more— cold water, no dry place, no firewood.

For three more days the river continued to rise. Passing the highest flood crest ever remembered in those parts, the swell lapped inside the old warehouse building itself.

Those nearest the iron grate hammered and screamed to be let out. They were smashed against the locked portal by those displaced by the water. Six men were crushed to death by the press of the mob. The rest of us stood in water up to our knees, with no escape.

That was when our guards disappeared.

Perhaps they were fearful for their lives. Perhaps they thought that such a mass of men as we would overpower the bars and force our escape. Perhaps they had no authority to move us and preferred not to see what was happening.

502

Whatever the reason, all our wardens left us. If we had possessed the strength, we could have freed the entire prison, but of course we had not the means. Along with the guards went any hope of medical treatment and the last of the paltry rations.

Some prisoners went mad and drowned themselves. Some just died standing up, starved to death or sick. No one came to remove the bodies.

After a time, hunger retreated to become a gnawing ache and a hollow place inside. But to stand in two feet of muck with nothing to drink is torture beyond belief.

After three days with no food and no clean water, I drank from the river. That night my head pounded like it was the anvil underneath the hammers of all the blacksmiths in the world. My neck stiffened until I could not turn my head. Lights began flashing in front of my eyes, and I could no longer make out the features of my friends.

I knew that Cate and Dobbs took turns holding me on their shoulders to raise me above the flood for a time. It was only because I had shrunk to ninety-five pounds that they could do so at all. My legs were so swollen and my frame so shrunken that I resembled a man stuck together of mismatched halves.

Sleep was all I had left, but even it was a torment. William appeared before my eyes, only to be shot or drowned or stabbed before I could reach him. I saw my home in flames, Alcie and the little ones turned out on the road in the rain. My fever raged, and delirium played on me like the cascade of a waterfall striking rocks below, splintering me into a thousand unconnected fragments.

I thought I heard someone say, "Oh, God, don't let him die. Not now! Not now!"

Am I dying? I wondered. *It is news to me that I am still alive now. Is this only another dream?*

"Now that I've found him, don't let him die!" the voice implored the Almighty.

Summoning up my last reserve of strength, I opened one eye and croaked, "Not dead just yet."

Staring down at me was a thin, bearded stranger, a young man by the sparse, fine whiskers. He seemed to be someone I knew but could not place . . . someone from a long time before.

"Father!" he said. "Don't you know me? It's William."

✻ ✻ ✻

There is still a little more to tell.

William had been shifted from one Confederate prison to another, always being moved south. He was never allowed to be exchanged because a Tellico Junction neighbor fighting for the Rebs had denounced him for helping runaway slaves. Cahaba was the sixth confinement he had suffered since his capture.

Before William came to Cahaba, the water had receded, and I had been moved to a hospital bed. A new commander had been appointed by the Rebs, and he, knowing the end of the Confederacy was near, was fearful of Union reprisals if conditions were not improved.

I had been in a stupor for weeks, but after my son's arrival I knew I would live. God had answered my biggest prayer of all: William was alive! I was determined to live so I might walk back into my own hayfield, with William by my side. I could see, in my mind's eye, Alcie—tears of joy streaming down her face—and the other children running to meet us.

Lee surrendered in Virginia, and then Joe Johnston did the same with the remnant of the Reb Army of Tennessee. We heard that Forrest thought about fleeing to Mexico and continuing to fight, but in the end he, too, surrendered.

The war was over.

As soon as I was able, I sent a joyful message to Athens to be delivered in care of R. J. Ferguson, Tellico Junction, to Mrs. Jesse Dodson: *Found William. Am coming home. Kept both promises.*

I was still too weak to even stand, let alone walk, so I was transported by river to the army hospital in Vicksburg, Mississippi, where I was formally released from captivity.

William never left my side. The progress of my illness was not steady, with many ups and downs. For a while I thought I was completely deaf before I regained some hearing in my right ear. I also was fearful that I would never walk again, but in time the dropsy subsided, and the paralysis also passed.

William and I were slated to go north to Camp Chase in Ohio to be mustered out of the army. We had our passage arranged on a steamer and were excited about being that much nearer home. Then I took a turn for the worse, and we could not go.

Urging William, I said, "Get home to your mother. Tell her I'll be along as soon as I'm able."

Despite my insistence, he refused. He always was a headstrong boy.

That night, the *Sultana*, the steamer that was to have taken us north, blew up on the river. Her boiler exploded, and fifteen hundred men, all returning Yankee prisoners of war, were scalded to death or drowned.

The Almighty had plenty of opportunities to take my life, but instead He used Hamilton, Dobbs, Sergeant Cate, and finally my boy William to keep giving it back to me. It certainly gave me pause. Perhaps God had something particular in mind for my life, and I was not about to disappoint him.

A very different man crossed back over the Cumberland Mountains in the summer of 1865 than had journeyed there two years before. I resolved never to forget what I had learned . . . and to never forget what I had been given.

✶AUTHORS' NOTE✶

espite being wounded nine times and having forty horses shot out from under him, Nathan Bedford Forrest survived the war. One of the most enigmatic figures of the American Civil War, he truly can be described as alternately chivalrous, cruel, coarse, daring, hot-tempered, brilliant, and harsh. An unremarkable postwar businessman, Forrest went on to achieve notoriety in another way. Though it was never publicly acknowledged, Old Bedford was reputedly the first Grand Wizard of the Ku Klux Klan.

Jesse Dodson and his son returned home to Tellico Junction. Though completely deaf in one ear and partially so in the other and regardless of lifelong bouts with rheumatism, dysentery, and heart disease, Jesse lived to be ninety-three. In all he and Alcie had nine children. Three of these were born after the war, one of them being Brock's great-grandmother.

✴DEAR READER✴

We hope you've enjoyed these legends of the Wild West—tales of adventurous and courageous men and women who faced down danger, overcame impossible odds to triumph over their circumstances with God's help, and discovered the truth about what is most meaningful in life.

As you travel on your life's journey, you too will face numerous challenges that will impact your heart, mind, and soul. We'd love to hear from you! To write us, or for further information about the Legends of the West series (including behind-the-scenes stories and details you won't want to miss), visit:

WWW.THOENEBOOKS.COM

WWW.FAMILYAUDIOLIBRARY.COM

We pray that through these legends you will "discover the Truth through Fiction." For we are convinced that if you seek diligently, you will find the One who holds all the answers to the universe (1 Chronicles 28:9).

BROCK & BODIE THOENE

❋ABOUT THE AUTHORS❋

BROCK AND BODIE THOENE
(pronounced *Tay-nee)* have written over 45
works of historical fiction. That these best
sellers have sold more than 10 million copies
and won eight ECPA Gold Medallion Awards
affirms what millions of readers have already
discovered—the Thoenes are not only master
stylists but experts at capturing readers' minds
and hearts.

In their timeless classic series about Israel (The Zion Chronicles,
The Zion Covenant, and The Zion Legacy), the Thoenes' love for
both story and research shines.

With the Shiloh Legacy series and *Shiloh Autumn* (poignant por-
trayals of the American Depression), the Galway Chronicles series
(dramatic stories of the 1840s famine in Ireland), and their Legends
of the West series (gripping tales of adventure and danger in a land
without law), the Thoenes have made their mark in modern history.

In the A.D. Chronicles series they step seamlessly into the world
of Jerusalem and Rome, in the days when Yeshua walked the earth
and transformed lives with His touch.

Bodie began her writing career as a teen journalist for her local
newspaper. Eventually her byline appeared in prestigious periodi-
cals such as *U.S. News and World Report, The American West,* and
The Saturday Evening Post. She also worked for John Wayne's Batjac
Productions (she's best known as author of *The Fall Guy*) and ABC

Circle Films as a writer and researcher. John Wayne described her as "a writer with talent that captures the people and the times!" She has degrees in journalism and communications.

Brock has often been described by Bodie as "an essential half of this writing team." With degrees in both history and education, Brock has, in his role as researcher and story-line consultant, added the vital dimension of historical accuracy. Due to such careful research, the Zion Covenant and Zion Chronicles series are recognized by the American Library Association, as well as Zionist libraries around the world, as classic historical novels and are used to teach history in college classrooms.

Bodie and Brock have four grown children—Rachel, Jake, Luke, and Ellie—and seven grandchildren. Their children are carrying on the Thoene family talent as the next generation of writers, and Luke produces the Thoene audiobooks. Bodie and Brock divide their time between London and Nevada.

For more information visit:
WWW.THOENEBOOKS.COM
WWW.FAMILYAUDIOLIBRARY.COM

THOENE FAMILY CLASSICS™

✪ ✪ ✪

THOENE FAMILY CLASSIC HISTORICALS
by Bodie and Brock Thoene
*Gold Medallion Winners**

THE ZION COVENANT
*Vienna Prelude**
Prague Counterpoint
Munich Signature
Jerusalem Interlude
Danzig Passage
*Warsaw Requiem**
London Refrain
Paris Encore
Dunkirk Crescendo

THE ZION CHRONICLES
*The Gates of Zion**
A Daughter of Zion
The Return to Zion
A Light in Zion
*The Key to Zion**

THE SHILOH LEGACY
*In My Father's House**
A Thousand Shall Fall
Say to This Mountain

SHILOH AUTUMN

THE GALWAY CHRONICLES
*Only the River Runs Free**
Of Men and of Angels
*Ashes of Remembrance**
All Rivers to the Sea

THE ZION LEGACY
Jerusalem Vigil
Thunder from Jerusalem
Jerusalem's Heart
Jerusalem Scrolls
Stones of Jerusalem
Jerusalem's Hope

A.D. CHRONICLES
First Light
Second Touch
Third Watch
Fourth Dawn
Fifth Seal
Sixth Covenant
Seventh Day
and more to come!

THOENE FAMILY CLASSICS™

✪ ✪ ✪

THOENE FAMILY CLASSIC AMERICAN LEGENDS

LEGENDS OF THE WEST
by Bodie and Brock Thoene

Legends of the West, Volume One
Sequoia Scout
The Year of the Grizzly
Shooting Star
Legends of the West, Volume Two
Gold Rush Prodigal
Delta Passage
Hangtown Lawman
Legends of the West, Volume Three
Hope Valley War
The Legend of Storey County
Cumberland Crossing
Legends of the West, Volume Four
The Man from Shadow Ridge
Cannons of the Comstock
Riders of the Silver Rim

LEGENDS OF VALOR
by Luke Thoene

Sons of Valor
Brothers of Valor
Fathers of Valor

✪ ✪ ✪

THOENE CLASSIC NONFICTION
by Bodie and Brock Thoene

Writer-to-Writer

THOENE FAMILY CLASSIC SUSPENSE
by Jake Thoene

CHAPTER 16 SERIES
Shaiton's Fire
Firefly Blue
Fuel the Fire

✪ ✪ ✪

THOENE FAMILY CLASSICS FOR KIDS

BAKER STREET DETECTIVES
by Jake and Luke Thoene

The Mystery of the Yellow Hands
The Giant Rat of Sumatra
The Jeweled Peacock of Persia
The Thundering Underground

LAST CHANCE DETECTIVES
by Jake and Luke Thoene
Mystery Lights of Navajo Mesa
Legend of the Desert Bigfoot

THE VASE OF MANY COLORS
by Rachel Thoene (Illustrations by Christian Cinder)

✪ ✪ ✪

THOENE FAMILY CLASSIC AUDIOBOOKS

Available from
www.thoenebooks.com or
www.familyaudiolibrary.com

CP0064